THE BARONET'S BARTERED BRIDE

MISTY URBAN

CHAPTER ONE

LONDON, MAY 1777

Joseph Illingworth had been sacked enough times to know how to handle himself when he was tossed out on his ear.

He'd learned, through plenty of practice, how to retain a gallant smile when a lady trod all over his heart.

But now that he was a man of the world and some connections, who had paid his dues and acquired the necessary polish, it was time he made something of himself. It was essential that he stand on his own two feet and prove his worth. He refused to ride the coattails of his relations or collect unearned awards and preferments, fattening himself at another's table.

He would earn his own keep, advance by the sweat of his own brow, carve his own way through the ruthless and uncaring world. He wanted to fatten himself at his *own* table.

And he couldn't even obtain a position to be sacked *from*.

"Your sister is the Duchess of Hunsdon?" At this point in the interview, which inevitably came, the agent or steward or whoever was reviewing his references would let the paper fall to the desk and peer at Joseph with curiosity, affecting a squint, a fatuous smile, or sometimes pulling a monocle from a fob to magnify him in all his fortune and flaws.

"Your brother is the Duke of Hunsdon," his interviewer would then hasten to clarify.

"Brother by marriage," Joseph would say, resigning himself to what came next. Sometimes it was fulsome admiration that Joseph should stand so close to the halo of ducal glory. Sometimes his interlocutor's attitude turned to suspicion, if the interviewer knew the duke's political views and suspected Joseph was as radical.

Once or twice, someone mentioned Amaranthe's antiquarian bookshop, of which she was inordinately proud and also rather infamous in London, being a duchess engaged in trade.

But such interviews always ended in the same manner: with Joseph being shown the door.

"I'm afraid we don't have a position for someone of your qualifications."

"St. John's College, Oxford," Joseph would argue at this point. "I was tutor to the Duke of Hunsdon's siblings before they went off to school." This was where his interviewer would rise, signaling the discussion was at an end.

"I'm freshly returned from my Grand Tour," he'd hasten to add as the interviewer conducted him to the doorway of the parlor or office or study from which he was about to be ejected. "Fencing in Paris. Carnival in Vienna. Put my shovel into the excavations at the Roman Forum. Dined with Hamilton in Naples and watched Vesuvius spilling over."

He wouldn't clarify that, while most young blades on their Grand Tour devoted years to the effort, Joseph had discharged his in mere months, being observant of his lack of funds. There was only so far a man could stand to be under the thumb of a younger sister who had made herself over from an orphaned vicar's daughter and slightly disreputable tradeswoman into a young, admired, and, some would say, a rather dashing duchess.

A man had pride, for God's sake, and Joseph wanted to

blaze his own path through society, not always be dragging in a ducal train. Even if, all things considered, Malden Grey was more tolerable than the usual run of paunchy, self-satisfied, condescending peers.

"Over-qualified, I mean to say," was the current response to Joseph's protest. "This post couldn't possibly suit someone of your knowledge and talents. You would find your vast gifts sadly underutilized educating three young boys." The solicitor hesitated. "Particularly these boys."

"I daresay it would be more of a challenge than you'd expect," Joseph argued. He saw one more plum position slipping through his grasp as the solicitor, wearing an antique bag wig and coats with many-buttoned sleeves, handed him his hat. "My Greek is rather weak, all things considered, and my sister, the duchess, is the one who drills me on my Latin declensions."

He'd staked everything on this last gamble paying off. The Earl of Aldthorpe's two younger sons were rumored to be devils, but surely it would behoove the family to have a duke's brother by marriage looking after boys who were the grandsons of a marquess.

To his surprise, his objection didn't work in Joseph's favor. The reminder that Joseph had a duke's strings to pull, and a duchess's sisterly affections, raised a visible degree of alarm in the Bales family solicitor. The discreet advert had raised all his hopes, promising the opportunity he needed. And now this milk-pale, bug-eyed man, who already had a secure position and income and place in the world, was going to deny Joseph his.

"I have Hunsdon's ear," Joseph said desperately as the solicitor herded him toward the door of the London office. "I dine at the ducal table quite often. Surely the Earl has some special cause—a relative looking for advancement?"

The Marquess of Langford, Aldthorpe's father, was a staunch Tory, mingling much in the upper echelons of government and lending his weight to the matters of war and conquest. Quite likely Mal, the Duke, who was publicly in favor of granting the American colonies their independence, was *persona non grata* to the current cabinet.

"It's because Hunsdon is a relatively new creation, isn't it?" Joseph clutched his cocked hat to his chest, unwilling to concede that the interview was over. "Or is it his politics? Because I can assure you—"

"Good day, Mr. Illingworth. I will be in touch if a post becomes available for which I can sincerely recommend you." And the door to the solicitor's office slammed shut in his face.

Joseph jammed his hat on his head, took up his brass walking stick, and huffed down the Strand, for once not being conciliatory and moving out of the way of the steady flow of other male pedestrians. For a lady, of course, he stepped out of his way and touched the brim on his hat. He wasn't an entire heathen.

But he had spent his life being conciliatory, and perhaps that was the problem. He was too pliable. He was ever the one who bent, who accommodated, who placated. His father had taught him this was how a good man, a man of Christian morals and good sense, made his way in the world.

But Jonas Illingworth had been nothing more than the second son of a gentleman and led the humble life of a vicar in an obscure if lovely parish in Cornwall. He had been well on his way to making absolutely no mark on the world before typhus carried him off in his prime and made certain he left no legacy whatsoever.

Joseph was traveling the same path. If he fell off the edge of the earth tomorrow, what would he leave behind?

A string of positions he had failed at or found unsuitable. A string of women who had played marbles with his heart. A sister who was moving in the highest circles, rising on a tide of acclaim and admiration and accomplishment while he continued sinking into the waters of obscurity.

At this rate he would leave nothing of worth behind, nothing proclaiming "Joseph Illingworth was here," and suggesting the world was a better place for it.

He rounded the King's Mews, where George kept his royal stables, and advanced up Princes Street with a grim stride. It was time for a change in his life. It was time for a change in *him*. The old ways had failed him, and a new man must be born. A man of vigor. A man of purpose. A man of unbendable steel.

He wheeled into the narrow channel of George Court that connected Princes and Rupert Street and nearly collided with the carter bearing a load of casks from the Blue Posts. Even horses found him of so little consequence that they would run him down in the street. All the more reason Joseph needed to become, somehow, a man of substance.

The snug little house he stopped at wasn't even his, though he'd lived there for several years. In a further taunt, his own lodgings had latched the door against him, and as Joseph sorted through his fobs and various pockets, he realized with growing outrage that he had neglected to carry the key.

He was a man with nothing. No wife and family, which he thought he'd have by now. No position in the world where his work mattered and gained him comfortable remuneration. He didn't even have a home he could call his own.

Amaranthe had located and arranged for the premises when they first moved to London seven years ago, after Joseph took his degree from Oxford. With no means to live on but the tiny income from the inheritance left them by their parents, Joseph had agreed that sharing accommodations was the most financially sound decision. He had done his part as the man of the household and gone out to earn an income, leaving Anth to oversee the household and make all the little decisions about furnishings and food, assuming she would apply to him when she had need.

He'd not noticed she never applied to him. He'd not noticed she'd been supporting their household—and him—on her work as a copyist, letting Joseph build his savings for the home and family he dreamed of supporting one day.

The year before, after a thorough and humiliating jilting by one Miss Susannah Pettigrew, Joseph had collected his savings and taken himself on that overdue Grand Tour, desperate to have *somewhere* to go while his sister vaunted up the social ladder and tucked herself into a duke's bed and a palatial house in Hanover Square. After the customary rounds of carousing and culture absorbing, with a few interactions with women that could be called highly informative if not character building, Joseph had returned to London determined to establish himself.

And found every door shut in his face.

Including his own.

His ire fed itself to a towering wall as he pounded on the portal. He stood with a fist raised in the air, about to deliver another blow, when the door burst inward and a young woman appeared there like a thunderbolt dropped from Heaven.

His ire collapsed, as did his arm. A strange heat crawled up his insides, as it always did when she was near. She disrupted his internal organs the same way she up-tilted his life, making all the stable, known, and reliable surfaces slide away in new and alarming directions. While she stood in the center of the destruction like a deadly, beautiful pillar of fire, always burning, throwing a heat it would scald him to touch.

Inez had come back to him.

Again.

CHAPTER TWO

"Why the devil would you lock a man out of his own home?" Joseph barked, taking refuge in spleen. Better that than stand on his own stoop gaping at her, pole-axed.

Inez wasn't her usual tidy self. A riot of dark curls spilled from beneath the white linen cap with its ribbon of red silk. Flour spattered her linen apron, and while it made sense for her to loop up her skirts to keep them from brushing the floor or the dirt of the ground when she went outside, the effect was to make her look like a lopsided pudding.

Thinking of her as a lopsided pudding allowed Joseph to pretend that her dark beauty wasn't a punch to his belly every single time they met.

Being impatient and surly with her also made certain she would never guess that the mere sight of her left him reeling like a pig brought out for slaughter and knocked over the head with a stick.

"*Desculpe, Senhor* Illingworth," Inez snapped, yanking the door wide with not the least apology in her manner. She glanced behind him, then leaned forward to check the narrow street on either side. She smelled of yeast and barley, and Joseph manfully resisted the urge to lean forward and bite her slender neck. Her voice was a low, husky purr, and every time he heard it, *every* time, he had to shove aside a sudden desire to hear that voice purring in his ear in the dark of his bed.

"Are you in some sort of trouble, Inez? Again?"

Trouble always seemed to loom at his door; Amaranthe had made a habit of inviting it in. Joseph didn't know Inez's complete circumstances, only that her father was a sailor and her mother, she never spoke of. She seemed to have difficulty keeping positions, for she never stayed in George Court for any great length of time. But after trying her luck elsewhere, she always turned up again in his hall, her dark hair bound beneath a scrap of lace, a plain gown outlining her extraordinary figure, her beauty a haunting accusation.

Most other gents establishing their standing as tutors of young gentlemen in history and languages, Joseph was aware, didn't permit their maids to leave and then turn up again whenever they pleased. No one, not even his own employees, thought him worthy of respect.

"Trouble? Why would you presume I am in some sort of trouble?" She smoothed a hand over her cap, discovered the locks of escaping hair, and made to put them in order. Her fingers trembled. "Or are you suggesting *I* am the cause of the trouble?"

"You behave as if you are hiding from something. Why bar my own door against me?" He stalked into the small parlor, filled with light from the tall, many-paned windows, and threw himself into the upholstered chair. He scowled at Inez.

"Why do you not have your key?" She scowled back.

"I have my misplaced my key." He leaned his head on the back of the wooden chair and stared at the plastered ceiling. "I have misplaced the key to everything, it would seem."

Inez stood a moment as if debating whether this was an English idiom she had not yet learned. She left the room with a quiet rustle of her skirts.

Another man might not have heard her. But Joseph, regrettably, was attuned to every movement she made. Every flutter of a dark curl against her silken check. Every whisper of breath that filled and lifted her deliciously curved bosom. Her scent, sweet and earthy, pervaded his house. The maddening fragrance compounded every time she arrived without explanation or notice, and lingered each time she disappeared.

"Eat." She returned with a tray, interrupting his speculations. "You left without breaking your fast. And you could not have stopped at a shop along the way, because you left your purse here too."

He had, drat it. Joseph sat up as she deposited the tray on a small occasional table at his side. A golden-brown cake of bread exuded a delicious yeasty smell through its cracked crust, and small dishes held fresh butter and honey. The coffee was dark and hot and black, with a small dish of warmed milk to go with.

Inez didn't drink tea; apparently, in Portugal, it was a habit reserved for the elite, and that Inez's mother had not been. Amaranthe had rarely served tea, given the tax, but Inez liked coffee. So did Joseph. He often visited the nearby coffee houses, but Inez knew where to find some rich, delicious blend that showed up in the house when she did.

She'd been showing up for two years, on and off, with no account of where she came from—at least to him—and no account of where she went when she left. When Amaranthe married the duke and went off to live in his many houses, Joseph had kept the premises in George Court. And when Joseph left for his Grand Tour, Inez watched over the house.

He didn't know how she had become acquainted with his sister, and had never asked. Women's friendships were their business, and he was well aware that women inhabited a secret world of their own making, one men were rarely permitted to glimpse, much less enter.

Inez's place in the world seemed even less secure than Joseph's. She wasn't his housekeeper, nor was she his guest. She appeared when she needed a roof over her head and worked in whatever capacity his housekeeper required, and she departed as easily as she came. Without leaving information about where to contact her.

She didn't come to rob him; the housekeeper reported nothing missing following one of Inez's vanishing acts, not food, not trinkets, not moveable goods. The last time she'd left, he'd inquired after her whereabouts and was surprised that no one knew where she'd gone.

Yet here she was again.

"Join me." It wasn't a request.

She curled her fingers into her apron. Her brown skin was a warm contrast against the bleached linen, her coal-black hair a more vivid contrast still. With her full red lips and the deep brown eyes heavy with dark lashes, she was a splash of vibrant color, an unforgettable tumult of a woman.

"Sit." He pointed to one of the delicate Queen Anne chairs, Amaranthe's selection, as was most everything in the house. He tipped a mouthful of milk into a cup, then filled it with coffee and passed the dish to her. "Where have you been?"

She sat where he indicated, her face growing guarded. Some veil dropped behind her eyes—not that he could read her under any conditions. She was the most eye-catching and yet inscrutable woman he had ever met—an irritating combination.

"I've been taking care of my father."

That gentleman seemed to be ill often; he was the excuse Inez used often to account for her disappearances. When she bothered to make an account at all.

"And he is well now?"

Her lashes swept over her cheeks. "He will not need me again."

"Good Lord. I'm very sorry." Joseph clacked his cup of coffee on the tray, taken aback.

She'd given no sign that she was suffering, no indications of mourning in her attire.

"I had no idea you were bereaved. Shouldn't you be—are there arrangements that need to be made?"

The lashes flew up, and as always, the attention of her dark eyes, with glints the color of well-aged whiskey, hit him like a smack to the face.

"He is not dead," she said. "But he left on a sailing ship bound for Macau. I will not see him for over two years, if he ever returns."

She said this in such a flat tone, Joseph was bewildered. Granted, having been deprived of his parents nearly ten years ago, he was not an expert on filial relations. But if his father had suddenly announced he meant to part from the family for a span of months if not years, some distress would have accompanied this pronouncement, at least on Joseph's part.

"You will miss him?" he asked cautiously.

She pressed her lips together, a move that did little to tame their fullness. "I will not miss having to provide for him. Surrendering what coin I earn for his keep, or to pay his debts. I will not miss the search to hunt down whatever slum or sty he had taken cover in."

Her lips turned down at the corners, and a line furrowed her smooth brow. "But he is ill. This is likely to be his last voyage. And I will not be there to bury or to mourn him." She let her gaze fall to the floor. "He said he has been away from his people so long, he can have no claim to have his passing honored with his customs." Tears glimmered on her dark lashes. "Would you not think, after more than two score years, *I* could be considered his people?"

The pain in her expression had Joseph reaching out a hand to her. He caught himself before his bare fingers touched her cheek and snatched the offending limb back to his side.

He had no right to try to soothe. He had no place in her life that gave him the right to touch her, not even as a fellow being who knew how it felt to be left.

Fortunately she did not see his trespass. Joseph cleared his throat and strove for a placating tone.

"Perhaps his illness makes it difficult for him to perceive how you would feel about his departure. Surely, if he knew, he would not abandon you to fend for yourself."

She clasped her fingers to the sides of her apron. When she lifted her face, her expression was fierce. "I am not abandoned."

"I only meant—well, of course not."

"I have been fending for myself for over ten years. Ever since my mother died."

"No doubt you have." He wanted to say he had been doing the same, along with supporting a sister, but he had a glimmer of apprehension that Inez would not appreciate this confidence. Also, he had not exactly supported Amaranthe; she, like Inez, had a way of fending for herself, and taking pride in doing so.

Inez rose, the swish of her skirts delivering that subtle, delicious scent of hers into the air. "I did not intend to become maudlin. I should be happy that he has finally found work. It did not suit him, life on shore, and his actions did not make it likely any other crew would want to hire him. He is doing what he loves, what meant more than the world to him, and if he should d-d—"

She couldn't force out the word, instead took a deep breath. "If he ends his life in the work he prefers, that is no small thing."

"It always hurts," Joseph said. "When they leave us. Even if they die. It is the way of the world, and even so, it feels like an abandonment."

She sat suddenly and blinked at him, her eyes wide. "I had forgotten," she said quietly. "That you have lost your parents, too."

His circumstances were quite different, Joseph would admit. His father had been born the second son of a baronet and had lived like a gentleman, though his means were small; the parish of St. Cleer was not wealthy in a country known to be poor. His mother's father had attained the rank of gentleman by virtue of success at his trade. Joseph's parents had been much liked and respected in their community, and their connections to the baronet had elevated them to the top of St. Cleer's social world, or what passed for such. He had never known the insecurity of which Inez spoke.

Yet, given the demand for sailors on merchant ships and the Royal Navy's resorting to press gangs to find sailors, Inez's father should have had as steady of employment as he liked. Even being a lascar, which meant he'd be paid less and treated worse in a line of service legendary for its inhospitality, an able-bodied seaman wouldn't have been turned away. Britain's sea trade, and its burgeoning Navy, ran on men.

They stared at one another, and the air in the room changed. Waves of sound flowed and ebbed from the streets surrounding them: the clop of shod hooves, the halloos of chairmen, the creak of wheels and the calls of children searching out their playmates. The light slanted in, casting a golden burnish across her cheek and the slender arch of her collarbone. Tiny motes of dust twirled and floated in dazzling combinations.

She was so lovely it hurt his throat to look upon her, yet he wouldn't, for the life of him, tear his eyes away. That he should be confiding in Inez, of all people! The girl he'd been pulling caps with, like street cats fighting over territory, from the moment they met.

Her face softened, her guardedness giving way to a look almost tender.

"And now you have lost your sister as well," she said.

"I didn't misplace her. I know where she is." The words came out more sharply than she deserved. Joseph took a bracing gulp of coffee to clear his head and shake his brain box out of his fanciful reverie.

He must not think of touching Inez. Kissing Inez. Good heavens, the woman was employed under his roof. Or, if not employed, seeking shelter. He might not have much to recommend him, but he possessed some small scraps of honor.

"Anth is running tame in Hunsdon House and across the other ducal properties," he added. "Well, running as fast as she might with that belly, considering she's about to drop the ducal heir at any moment."

Inez pressed her lips again. "She is not a mare producing a foal."

He would admit he sounded like a jackanapes. Simply because Amaranthe, who had always claimed she was perfectly happy with her inks and her colors and her stodgy old manuscripts, had quite unexpectedly stumbled across a man who adored her, found three siblings in want of mothering whom she directly took in, then somehow unearthed proof that Malden Grey wasn't the bastard everyone had supposed.

His sister, who had said more than once she expected to live her life in pleasant spinsterhood—and whom Joseph had assumed he would kindly provide for, giving her a room in his house and the privilege of looking after his offspring—had gone and secured herself a home and family, not to mention a title that increased her stature in the world considerably.

And what did Joseph have?

The dregs of his coffee were bitter even with the sugar dissolved at the bottom. "I wasn't offered the Aldthorpe position," he said. "Got turned out of the office as soon as they caught a whiff of the Duke."

"Oh, that cannot be the reason," Inez said at once, commiserating. "They could not be so foolish."

He didn't have to explain himself to her. She understood immediately what had happened, and what it meant. Few women were as discerning.

His sister was one of them, but Joseph frequently had the sense, even when he did the right thing, that Amaranthe vaguely disapproved of him. But there was no trace of scorn or condescension in Inez's voice or expression. He was so accustomed to detecting it, he was surprised she should meet his eyes so steadily.

He already knew Inez was easy to converse with, and on serious subjects, when most girls her age had feathers in their head. When he had no other sounding board, she listened to him expound on length on what he was reading, the latest discoveries in natural philosophy, the latest historical theories.

But he'd never really paid close attention to *her* before. Not beyond what common courtesy demanded.

That shift in the room again, as if the earth had tilted.

He'd never permitted himself to *look*, frankly. Too concerned to hide the disconcerting physical effect she had on him with the liquid beauty of her eyes and hair and all that glowing brown skin.

He stared into the bottom of his cup as if it showed him his dark future. "The solicitor couldn't push me out the door fast enough. Said I was overqualified, if you can conscience the irony."

"They do not wish to risk angering a duke if they treat you poorly." Inez buttered a thick slice of bread and handed it to him. "You do not know what it is like to live at the whim of the great."

"I very well do," Joseph said, indignant.

Her gaze swept him from head to toe, and despite himself he straightened his shoulders, broadening his chest. She was a servant in his home. He should not feel the need to prove his worth to her.

"You are a man," she said, and bitterness laced her tone. "You are young and hale and handsome. You are the son of a gentleman, you were raised as a gentleman, and now you are brother to a duke." She set her chin at a stubborn angle. "You have no notion what it is like to live knowing a single stroke of fortune—or the whim of another man—could take everything from you."

"That's not true." Joseph sank his teeth into the bread, warm and surprisingly sweet. He'd been robbed of his parents, of half his family, in one cruel night. In some ways he still hadn't recovered from the shock. And he lived at the whim of an employer, so he expected he understood what it felt like to live at the caprice of others, thank you very much.

For God's sake, he had a Duke as a brother now. Everything Hunsdon did would reflect on Joseph. His very *being* cast a shadow over Joseph. How on earth was a man supposed to establish his own place in the world when he had to fight out from under the feet of a monument?

His mind clutched at, then skittered away from the observation that Inez had called him *handsome*.

She was his dependent. It was really not the done thing for him to confide in her, or for her to counsel him. He stuffed the last bite of bread in his mouth and chewed mightily.

He grew conscious that he was glowering at her, or rather, studying her intently. Inez drew herself up under his scrutiny.

"I don't suppose you need be concerned at not being offered this post. You will find better, and in short order."

Her English was proficient, nearly fluent, but an accent lingered. He wondered how long she had lived in London, and where she'd lived before then. He wondered where she lived in London when she wasn't in his house.

He wondered if she knew she'd accidentally brushed flour into her hair, so one dusty white streak stood out against the silky black mass stuffed under her cap.

He wondered what man's whims Inez was living under.

"What are you doing here?" he blurted.

Her look turned wary in an instant, from high summer to wintry frost. "What do you mean?"

He meant many things. What she was doing in this town, in his house, and what she was doing *here*, in the parlor, conversing with him as if they were intimate acquaintances. As if he were at liberty to confide in her, and she was at liberty to provide support.

He'd always wanted a companion he could think out loud with. A sensible woman of reason and intellect who could give him a proper perspective, as a man would, but without giving him instructions on what to do, as a man would. Amaranthe had served that role, but Amaranthe had other roles now.

And the women Joseph had previously attached himself to —well, one might say there wasn't a strong record of good sense and intellect there. Those qualities tended not to rouse passion or the instinct to provide and protect.

"Here." He cleared his throat and pointed to the Brussels carpet that covered the wooden floor. "What are you doing in this parlor?"

Because she *wasn't* a servant, at least not one who had applied and interviewed for a position. He supposed she received a salary—one hoped he paid her *something* for her labors—but what exactly did she do? He had a housekeeper, a dour and efficient woman Amaranthe had installed to look after Joseph when she abandoned him to become a duchess. Mrs. Frost had some tragic history Joseph had never inquired about because Amaranthe tended to take in people who had suffered some tragedy.

His mind stalled. Had Inez? Was there more preying on her than concern for her father and his fate abroad?

Her posture went taut and alert. She was a slim woman beneath the cascade of skirts and apron. She could easily be coerced. Manipulated.

Or, come to that, physically moved about by some man who considered himself superior. The thought made Joseph's blood thicken to a boil.

"I am bringing you coffee," she said, her voice quiet, her accent emerging. "I am bringing you bread."

"But why me? That is to say, you appear without forewarning. There is apparently some arrangement with my housekeeper that I don't know about. I presume I am paying you a salary since you clearly perform some household duties. But what are they? Why are you allowed to come and go as you wish, with no questions and no accounting? Are all my servants contracted thusly?"

"Allowed?" Her shoulders went tense. "*Allowed* to come and go as I please? Isn't every free person given that right?"

He brushed away her quibble; she was evading the point. "But why *here*? Why don't you have a home of your own?"

She rose and moved to a shelf of small items, oddments on display. Amaranthe's trinkets, of course; so little in this place was Joseph's. Inez pulled a scrap of cloth from her apron pocket and began dusting the case with short, jerky movements.

"Why do I not have a home of my own?" Her tone was low and wounded, yet her movements careful and precise. "Because my father has left for a voyage that will last two years if not longer. Because my mother is dead. Because I have no other family, which may be a blessing, as there would be no home for them either.

"My *place* in the world—" here her movements grew jerky, angry— "is wherever I can find employment, usually no better than the scullery or the laundry, and that is if a respectable home will take me. More often I am told to take me to the bagnio or brothel, where they want girls with my color skin. To be sure, if I did work in such places, I would at least receive coin for my services. If I cannot keep a place in a respectable home, it is because there must come along a son or a husband or a friend of the house who believes my *services* are his for free."

Whatever bitterness consumed him, hers had a sharper bite. Joseph sat chained to his chair, horrified by the picture she painted. Visions assaulted him of Inez being backed into dark corners, whether in the public baths or below stairs in great house, or even approached in the street, as it was a given that women in certain parts of town were displaying their wares for a purpose.

"I-I am...that should not be," he said finally. Joseph thought himself a man of the world, but the world she hinted at was one he hadn't known existed. "I— You should be allowed to work and move about without molestation."

"What a lovely world it would be if all men believed as you do." She slapped her dusting cloth at a small, enameled music box, one that had belonged to Joseph's mother, and he feared in her vehemence she would damage the delicate cylinder inside.

He longed, suddenly, for the simple world he had grown up in, one governed by clear manners and morals. Gentlemen were kind to ladies. Ladies were gracious and demure. The lower and the very upper classes might turn things about into any muddle they liked, but for a gentleman's family, courtesy ruled. Respect, dignity, and fair play.

If the world were fair, he would be head of his own bloody household already, with a beautiful wife and three lisping children he was teaching their letters, and a plum position that made him the envy of tutors throughout London and beyond.

Inez whirled to face him and crossed her arms over her chest. Joseph struggled not to let his eyes fall to the press of her bosom against her bodice and the linen neckerchief that swathed her, tied crosswise and tucked at her waist. He would not fall into that class of men who measured women by their potential to yield sexual satisfaction. He was a gentleman, for God's sake.

"So that is why," she said firmly, her lips once again making that movement where she seemed to press them together, yet their full shape made him able to think of nothing but ripe fruit, of licking and biting and sweetness.

"Why what?" he said, striving in vain not to think of other places on Inez where he would like to put his mouth.

"Why I am *here*." She pointed at the carpet with its complex floral design.

Because his house was a refuge. Because Amaranthe would have taken her in with no questions, giving her a place to be free of persecution, supposing Joseph, who tended to get caught up in his own mind very frequently, might not even notice she was there.

He had noticed. It was impossible to overlook Inez.

"Very well, then," he said gruffly.

She threw him a glare that would have shredded him, could glares cut. "Well *what*?"

"I understand now why you are here. And...you may stay."

"I may stay." Her eyes narrowed into slits, a golden-red fire deep within. "I might *stay*."

"Well, yes. You will be safe here. I will see that you are sheltered. And you might go about as you wish—" He swirled a hand in the air, aware even as he did so that it was an awkward gesture— "without fear of interference, I hope."

"You will suffer me to stay," she said again.

"Indeed I shall." Had he not been clear? Baffled by her sudden guard, and the fulminating fire in her eyes, he searched back through his words for the insult. What had he done?

She planted her hands on her hips, and the belligerent gesture was so at odds with her natural grace that Joseph smothered a smile.

She saw the smile and her eyes snapped into slits. He might have detected a flare of hurt first, but it was gone so quickly, the feeling mastered in a flash, that he might have imagined it.

"Thank you ever so much for your kindness, Master Illingworth. I don't know how I shall ever repay you for condescending to notice me, poor creature that I am. But be assured I will not linger to trouble your household." She wiped her hands on her apron and then swept up the tray with its bread and butter and half-drunk coffee.

Joseph leapt to secure the pot before she could remove it and only then, when he stepped back and saw the real hurt in her eyes, did he realize what he'd done. She'd more or less given him notice, and he'd made sure to collect the coffee before she left.

"You won't be going anywhere," he snapped. It was his regrettable habit to become defensive when he knew he'd done something wrong. "You shall stay here, where you are safe and I can look after you."

Her snort, too, was a complete contrast to the delicate lines of her face, her beauty that somehow became more intense, and more aggravating, the longer one stood in a room with her. A man could only take so much beating about the head, for God's sake.

"Look after me. As if you ever have." She whirled, her skirts flaring to reveal white stockings with cunning little clocks, an absurd point of luxury on a woman dressed like a servant. "Fare thee well, Master Illingworth."

Master, as if he were a small arrogant boy and not a *Mister*, lord and head of his own household. Such as it was. He looked about for a place to set the coffee pot.

"He's in the parlor." Outside the room, Inez's impatient voice drifted down the short hall that led to the servants' stair and below to the kitchen. "Mind your manners, he's in a temper today. World not bowing to his wishes, per the usual."

Temper? Joseph barely restrained himself from bellowing a response. He would *not* let the minx rile him, though she was the most provoking creature alive. So many of their interactions ended like this: she flew up in the boughs over some imagined slight when he hadn't committed the least offense against her. Then she threatened to leave, Mrs. Frost soothed, and Inez sulked and flounced for a while, throwing him dark looks to ensure he knew she was out of charity with him. And one day he'd look about and she'd be absent.

She never cared enough to say goodbye. She set him aside like an old hat. Then, when she wanted a roof and a bed and a place to bake her Portuguese bread, she scratched at the kitchen door and Mrs. Frost let her in and the whole merry round began again.

"Not this time," Joseph said aloud. "D'ye hear me?" He had no idea who he was speaking to, but a solemn vow must be witnessed, even if only by empty air. "By Gad, things are going to change around here."

He set the coffee pot on a side table with great emphasis, and gritted his teeth when hot liquid splashed onto his hand.

Dash it, that had held the temperature. One sturdy serving pot, that.

"Mr. Joseph?"

He looked up, assembling a reproof. Inez never returned so quickly, and never to apologize, but there was a first time for everything, wasn't there?

"I did not hear the front door," he said sternly, as if he might blame the girl who stood there for giving him a turn.

"I doesn't use th' front door, does I?"

It wasn't Inez in the door frame but Tamara, the young costermonger whom his sister had befriended and occasionally hired to run errands. Amaranthe was always finding people in distress and plucking them off the streets. All of the servants she'd hired into this house had come from some doleful and difficult circumstance. Who knew how many dozens she'd saved from want or debtor's prison or abject poverty, how many burdened women she'd offered sanctuary from whatever tragedy dogged their heels.

Like Inez. For whom he was supposed to be providing refuge, and who now meant to turn herself back into the street because she was in a pet with him, and he already knew she had no one to provide for her, shelter her, ensure she was not accosted as a young woman alone—

The girl cleared her throat impatiently, and Joseph scowled at her. "What do you require?"

"The Duchess said you mun see this." The girl held out a scrawny hand. In it was a vellum envelope, the seal broken, the edges inked black.

A black edge meant mourning. Someone had died.

Joseph's throat closed with panic. Anth—one of the children —not that robust, arrogant, aggravating Duke— "Who?" he croaked.

"A cousin, she said?" The girl waited.

A cousin...but they had no family. It had been him and Amaranthe, on their own, the last ten years. No one but...

Dash it all. "Reuben."

Joseph took the vellum and fumbled it open. Indignation surged first. The letter, while its news might concern both the remaining Illingworth relations, involved mainly Joseph, and yet the Illingworth solicitor had sent it first to Hunsdon House, because Amaranthe was a Duchess and Joseph was a nobody.

Or, had been a nobody up until this moment.

Now he was the 5th Baronet Illingworth, apparently.

He sat and read again, the vellum trembling slightly as shock set in.

After a brief and unpleasant illness, Reuben Illingworth, the 4th Baronet Illingworth of Penwellen, had died, leaving no issue. By terms of the entail, the estate and title should pass to the nearest heirs male. And Joseph, the grandson of the 2d Baronet and nephew to the 3rd, was the legitimate successor.

Assuming his birth would be validated as legitimate by the baptismal registry in the parish of St. Cleer, there would be the small matter of confirming the line through the pedigree chart and family tree held by the Herald's College, but since all of these documents were in order following Reuben's recent request to elaborate on the family's coat of arms, the solicitor felt confident to inform Joseph that he might take possession of the title, the estate, the house, and all other assets appertaining at his earliest convenience.

Joseph could hardly sort out the roil of emotions. How like Reuben to squander good money on attempting to register an Illingworth coat of arms, which no one used or cared about anyway. An obscure, fairly young baronetcy in the corner of Cornwall was nothing to brag about in London, though perhaps in his corner of Cornwall Reuben enjoyed playing lord of the manor.

The next roiling emotion to surface was a wish that Joseph could vindicate himself regarding the Aldthorpe situation. That he might write the solicitor who'd shoved him out the door and say regretfully he must turn down the offer for a position as tutor to the Earl of Aldthorpe's sons as he had inherited an estate and must take up his title and duties. It would serve as a tart reminder that Joseph was overqualified in truth.

Reuben's death, on its own, stirred no sense of loss. Joseph wondered at his own hardness. A man's life had ended, and not well, from the sounds of things. But Reuben had been an unpleasant man, unlikeable, unliked.

How horrifying to think one could leave this life and not be mourned. Joseph resolved at that moment that he must leave *someone* to mourn him when he shook off this mortal coil.

He set his hand with the letter in his lap and stared across the room at the small shelf with its music box that Inez had just dusted.

His grandmother had doted on music boxes, had a collection of them at Penwellen. He remembered a house with dark walls, heavy-browed ancestors glowering from backdrops of shadow. Under his aunt's reign, the parlors and sitting rooms had been in a constant state of renovation, and he might not sit on the upholstery or touch anything because he was a boy and likely had dirty hands.

He had not lived at Penwellen under Reuben's tenure. He'd hied himself off to Oxford as soon as the tuition could be paid. He'd never much cared for Reuben's fretful, fussy wife, who behaved as if every element and person of the outside world had been specifically placed there as a trial to her nerves.

Penwellen was his now, a stately house with good grounds and extensive lands. Amaranthe had reported that the place was growing rather shabby when she visited there last summer, but a shabby manor was quite a step up from rented premises in

George Court, and ever being run down by carters from the Blue Posts.

He would have a house of his own. Properties. Tenants. Servants in his own employ, not another's.

And he was no longer a mere Mister Illingworth. He would be styled Sir Joseph Illingworth of Penwellen, Bart.

He recalled his earlier vow of change and winced. Everything in his life had changed already, whether Joseph was ready or not.

CHAPTER THREE

A sixteen-year-old Reuben stood above the dog at the edge of the coppice of beech and buckthorn. The hound lay prone at his feet as Joseph, panting slightly from exertion, caught up to them. At first he thought red currants from the bush must have dropped along the dog's head and body; winded from the run, and not ever having been witness to violence in the course of his quiet life, Joseph didn't at first understand what he saw.

"You lazy beast! You cost me that hare!"

Reuben snarled at the animal and raised the butt of the shotgun. Joseph comprehended, his mind ticking along with irritating slowness, that Reuben had struck the animal down, and meant to strike again.

"Reuben! Desist," Joseph said sharply.

"He let the jack get away!" Reuben looked as if he might turn the blow on Joseph. "He's a cursed slow mongrel, and why m'father saddled me with him, I'll never know." The older boy sneered. "Much like yourself."

Joseph shook off the barb. His grandfather the baronet had

made it out to be an insult when his second son fell in love with and married the daughter of a tradesman, and his uncle, the current baronet, had inherited this sense of superiority. Joseph was more concerned about the hurt dog.

The Southern Hound lay on its side, panting after his run, its brown eyes wide and frightened. Though blood seeped from the wound on its skull, the animal tried to rise, paws scrabbling through the layer of fallen nuts and yellow leaves cloaking the ground. The hound had been bred to hunt and work, and even injured, instinct called it.

"The hare is fast, and the chase is the point." Joseph looked around and spotted where the brown hare had gone to ground, finding a form to huddle in at the edge of the barley field. The hare's bright brown eyes watched Reuben with an alert sense of danger that Joseph was beginning to understand. Something feral and *wrong* seemed to have taken possession of his cousin, who was prone to temper on his best days.

"You're such a sally. We're not here for the chase but for the kill." Reuben's lip curled back. He kicked the fallen hound. "Up, you cur! Let the jack escape, and I'll never hear the end of it."

The baronet's booming shout startled both boys. "What is the meaning of this?"

Swiftly Reuben pointed at Joseph. "He attacked my dog! The hare escaped, and Joseph said Wolfe was too slow, and struck him."

Joseph's eyes strained wide with surprise. His uncle's glare sent him a step backward, clutching his gun and stammering. "I-I never. I didn't hurt your dog, sir."

The baronet scowled, his spleen sharpened by Joseph's whimper, but he wasn't misled by his son's false claim. The glare he swung back to Reuben suggested he was as familiar with his son's lies as with his hot-headedness. Moreover, a betraying streak of crimson smeared the stock of Reuben's gun.

"You've cost me my favorite hound, you arrogant jackanapes. Alive or dead, his hide is worth more than yours."

Reuben flushed brick red, his look turning sullen. "He lost the scent! The hare sprang, and the doltish mutt brought us here rather than after it."

"So you struck the dog? In anger?" Joseph's father joined them. The quiet question in his voice lacked accusation; he was seasoned at resolving disputes. But his mild voice stirred both his brother and his nephew to greater ire.

"Stay out this, Jonas," the baronet snapped. "I won't have you rating my son when your own is a puling, lily-livered rabbit. Where's my keeper?"

"Sir?" The gamekeeper came up, another hound at his heels, the as-yet-empty game bag slung over his shoulder. His eyes widened as he took in the scene, but Joseph noticed he did not seem surprised.

The baronet gestured toward the animal on the ground. "Take care of this."

"Sir?" Joseph didn't miss the look of contempt that the keeper sent Reuben, nor the look of tender sorrow on the man's face as he regarded the injured animal. The man had tended this dog, raised and trained and fed it, and now would see it destroyed because of a temperamental and spiteful boy.

"I will do it," Joseph's father said.

Joseph held back a cry. He had never seen his father kill an animal. His mother couldn't even wring the neck of a chicken; she asked her housekeeper to do it. His father, the gentle vicar of St. Cleer, patted the heads of lambs in the meadow and called Joseph and Amaranthe from the house when he discovered a den of fox kits.

The baronet had already walked on but turned to call back

to Joseph. "Are you coming with, or will you stay here to puke up your guts?"

"Give him a moment, Josiah," his father said, and his tone was harder than Joseph was accustomed to hearing from his mild-mannered sire. "This is his first hunt."

"You've raised a mewling whelp," the baronet sneered. "You need to toughen that boy, Jonas. You'll turn him into a molly with your coddling."

"I'd rather a boy with a soft heart than a bully," Jonas answered swiftly.

Reuben watched with a greedy, nearly sickening expression as Jonas raised and sighted his flintlock.

"Look away, lad," Jonas said sharply. "Go with your father."

"Why does *he* get to watch?" Reuben groused, throwing a glare at Joseph.

"Because I am teaching him a lesson. Now go."

Reluctantly Reuben left with the baronet, who had walked away from the scene, leaving others to clean up the destruction made by his son. With a whistle Reuben set the second hound after the hare, which shot from its scrape and set off with its lolloping gait, hopping sideways now and again attempting to throw off the dog.

The shot echoed off the trees. Dirt flew as his father fired into the ground. Joseph nearly choked on his relief.

His father gave his spent gun to the keeper in return for another that was loaded and primed. "We will take the dog with us, Cobb," Jonas said. "If you can keep him at your cottage until we leave."

"Aye, I'll tend'un an keep'un from sight." Cobb rose soberly with the dog in his arms, the game sack wrapped around the animal. The hound stared mournfully at Joseph with its large, dark eyes, dull with incomprehension.

"That'un is a heller," Cobb said, his face dark with anger.

"And the baronet coaches it inee. Mark me, some day that lad will turn and bite the hand that feeds 'im." He cradled Wolfe. "This'un hound is worth ten of that boy."

"We'll take care of him. I am sorry to benefit from your loss." Jonas laid a hand on the other man's shoulder, squeezing slightly. The baronet hadn't addressed the keeper, his own trusted servant, but Joseph's father knew the man's name, and took the time to console him.

His father put an arm around Joseph's shoulder as they both watched the keeper walk back toward the house. "Don't ever become that, son," Jonas said quietly. "Don't you ever strike at a weaker creature."

"No, Papa."

"Use your strength to do good, Joseph. Not harm."

"Yes, Papa. But why will no one punish Reuben?" If Joseph had done such a thing, struck at another, man or beast, he would have gotten a sound thrashing, and a moralizing lecture to boot.

"We must trust in the Lord to work his will in his own way, and turn our sorrow to his good," his father said.

Joseph knew from that moment that whatever career he pursued, it would not be with the Church, because he would never be able to counsel people to accept the world as it was. He could not accept a world where the strong preyed on the weak, and some men were given power who did not deserve it.

Reuben had bagged a hare that day, but Joseph had killed nothing, not then nor any day after. Wolfe became a steady companion in the years that followed, accompanying Joseph on his treks, but adoring his father above all. Shortly after Jonas died, days after his wife, Wolfe laid down in the chicken pen with his heads on his paws and quietly finished the task Reuben had begun years before.

Perhaps this was the justice his father had meant, Joseph thought as he surfaced from that long-ago memory into his own parlor—well, Amaranthe's parlor—the vellum stiff in his fingers. Reuben had indeed become the baronet, but he had not managed to produce an heir of his own. And so it all went to the lily-livered cousin—whatever was left that Reuben hadn't managed to poison or destroy.

"Oh, it's herself, then!" The cheerful voice of the little costermonger sounded from the hallway. "Gave him a turn, I think I did. He's just been sitting there an age, staring into the air as if he seen a specter."

"No doubt Mr. Joseph has as many fond recollections of our cousin as I do." That was Amaranthe's voice. "You might stop by the kitchens, Tamara, and have Mrs. Frost pack a basket for you. How are your sisters faring today?"

"Fair blooming, on all counts," Tamara said proudly. "I'll be by with your violets tomorrow morning, mum."

"I shall look for them." A rustle of fabric announced Amaranthe's approach. Her dark hair was fashionably powdered and she wore a simple open robe, the stomacher laced lightly over her swelling middle.

"Well, Sir Joseph? I would have brought the letter myself, but I had to arrange to close the shop for the afternoon, and Tamara wanted an errand."

Joseph set the letter on the table. It had no more to tell him. "Shall we go into mourning? I suppose there ought to be some notice of the niceties."

"It seems a bit of a sham, since we won't actually miss him nor lament his loss, but it is the proper thing to do."

Joseph rose from his seat and prowled about the small chamber, which was tidy and sparsely furnished, and held almost nothing to indicate his possession of it. He tried to bend his imagination around the news that he would have a home to call his own.

A grand home. An estate. A title to append to his name.

Nothing approaching the honors of a dukedom, and baronets were not considered peers, but they, and knights, were in a class of their own above the common run of gentlemen esquires.

"All my life—my adult life—I have worked and studied, studied and worked my tail off to get precisely nowhere. And now, dropped in my lap—all this. When I haven't done a thing to earn it."

His sister nodded and lowered herself into an upholstered chair across the room, then tucked a cushion behind her back. Most women went into confinement when they were Amaranthe's size, and she could have easily taken to one of her many decorated parlors at Hunsdon House and summoned people to her. But she still went about her days, making calls and looking in on her bookshop, and the Duke had reported Amaranthe as saying that she wanted to stay on her feet until the babe was ready to drop out of her, as if she were a hardy peasant woman in the field.

Their breeding would show and continue to show, Joseph thought, even if they both had titles to decorate their names.

The Duchess indicated her person with a sweep of her hand: the expensive gown, the velvet cloak, the wedding ring sparkling on her finger. "I haven't deserved my place, either. But Father would say some things in this world cannot be earned, only granted by the grace of God."

"I thought it was Mother who said that."

"How pleased they would be to see you settled, Joseph. Though not at Reuben's expense. And, if Father were alive, he would be accepting the estate and title of course," she reflected. "But nevertheless I am sure they are happy in heaven to see you come into some security."

"If such it is." Joseph made another turn about the room, glancing out the window at the gathering clouds casting a pall on the day. "You said when you visited, Reuben had let the place go to rack and ruin. I wonder what I shall find."

"Shall you go soon to take possession and put things in order? I would go with you, save that Parliament is still sitting and not likely to adjourn until June, and then I am expecting a happy event." She patted her round belly.

"I wouldn't expect you to accompany me unless you wished it. I'm sure Hunsdon would have something to say about my pulling you away for rough travels when you are so near your time."

She frowned slightly. "He is Mal to you, Joseph. You are brothers."

"We are not related, and he is the Duke." The Duke to blame for all of Joseph's rejections, including the episode from that morning. Joseph couldn't seem to set his resentment aside even in light of the more recent news; he harbored other, deeper veins of bitterness he would not let even Amaranthe see.

"I hope at some point you two might become friends," she said in a quiet tone.

"Not likely, when his friend stole my intended bride away."

The Duchess shook her head, lightly shifting the dyed ostrich feathers atop the extravagant hat pinned to her curls. It took a great deal of powder to make her dark locks come close to the fashionable white; both she and Joseph had inherited their mother's coloring, with dark hair and eyes and a faint sepia tint to their skin. It continued to surprise him that Amaranthe, who had always chosen to keep herself plain but tidy, should have become so dashing with the application of wealth and her new status in the fashionable world.

Joseph might be expected to become dashing now. Callington, Cornwall, lay far from London's tonnish circles, but a new suit or three would be a welcome enlargement to his wardrobe. Perhaps solicitors and other such men who ought to consider themselves his peers would grant him a sight more respect if he had silk suits with rows and rows of buttons and loads of embroidery.

Amaranthe made a small moue of disapproval. "Viktor Vierling did not *steal* Susannah Pettigrew away from you. It rather appears she played you false, allowing you both to court her when she had bestowed her heart elsewhere. And I am still put out that you intended to wed her without inviting your own sister to the ceremony."

Joseph flung himself back into his seat with a sigh. "Better you weren't there to see me made a fool."

He'd been so besotted with Susannah Pettigrew he'd acted irrationally, and Joseph valued rational action above all else. Whatever Amaranthe might believe, his head wasn't typically turned by a cloud of golden hair and cornflower blue eyes set in porcelain skin. Or, at least, not those attributes alone.

He had met Susannah when she was dispensing leaflets at the Speaker's Corner in Hyde Park and she had fired him up with her animation over the cause of poor relief, abolition of the slave trade, and education. He'd considered converting to Quakerism for her. He'd proposed to marry her. He'd laid his heart at her feet and, moreover, offered to conduct her to visit her parents in Gloucestershire to seek their blessing on a marriage.

Instead, Susannah had run away with Mal's friend, Viktor Vierling, a Hessian employed in the King's Household Calvary. She had gone on to run away from Vierling also, leaving him holding his hat same as Joseph, so perhaps her inconstancy said more about Miss Susannah Pettigrew than it did any of her suitors.

Still, he'd been a fool, and it rankled. He'd never be a fool over a woman again.

"You must stop following the lures of the likes of Susannah Pettigrew and find a woman who is a good match for you,

Joseph. And your prospects will be considerably improved now. You'll be able to offer a woman a lovely home and make her your lady. You'll have the family you always wanted."

Offer hand and heart to another woman, only to have her quash him like Susannah Pettigrew and all the others before her? Or, worse yet, accept him because now he came with a title and an estate?

Joseph poured another cup of coffee from the pot Inez had left behind. He offered it to Amaranthe, but she shook her head.

"I don't suppose I shall rush into wooing anyone," he said. "I expect there will be a great deal to do setting the estate in order. Our uncle was not the most intelligent businessman, and I don't imagine our cousin was a generous landlord."

"When do you suppose you'll return to London?"

"I will have a house and an estate to oversee, Anth, and no doubt many other duties as the chief landowner in the area. What is there in London for me?"

"Well, putting aside me and the rest of your family," she said, "you're more likely to find a wife here than in Cornwall."

Joseph was not contrary by nature; only Inez brought stubbornness out in him. But the recent flare-up had lingered, it seemed, for he found himself suddenly deciding he would not consider any well-bred society miss for a wife.

"If you are so eager for me to wed, you might as well do my wooing for me."

She leaned back in her chair, eyes widening at his snappish tone. "How are you getting on with Inez?"

He frowned at the non sequitur. "My household affairs—or rather, your household affairs are currently all in order, to my understanding. As I am sure your little Cornish spy already told you."

"I have not set Tamara to spy on you. Really, Joseph, why so peevish? You've just been elevated to a title and a secure income. I came to applaud you and imagined I would find you rejoicing, not sunk in gloom." She looked about. "Where *is* Inez?"

"Sulking in the scullery, I don't doubt, because I had the temerity to ask her about her comings and goings. Imagining, if you can conscience the audacity, that as her employer I might have some interest in how she discharges her duties."

"She is not a *servant*, Joseph!"

"If she earns a wage from me—all right, from you—what else am I to call her?" he argued. "You might call for her if you wish a chat. I'm sure she's somewhere about."

The little costermonger, Tamara, thrust her head around the doorframe, eyeing them both. "Her as cut sticks, if yer talkin' of the lascar girl. Saw er high-steppin' out the door with er bag, I did."

"Joseph! What have you done?" Amaranthe braced her hands on the arms of her chair and attempted to lever herself out of it. "Why are you always pulling caps with her?"

"I asked a simple question, and she took a bee in her bonnet!" Joseph strode forward to hoist his swollen sister to her feet. "Why'd you have to saddle me with such a termagant?"

Amaranthe frowned. "You must go after her."

"What the devil?" Joseph stared. "I never have before."

Amaranthe chewed on her lip, something she did when she didn't have a quill or the handle of her penknife to nibble on. "It's not safe for her out there."

A heat of irritation, and of shame, touched the back of Joseph's neck. Hadn't Inez said that she was prone to being accosted, that everywhere she went, men were begging her for sexual favors? The consequence, and the cost, of great beauty.

Or of simply being an unprotected female in the world.

That contrary streak seemed to be taking over his good sense entirely; he was as graceful as a sack of doorknobs today, all his customary aplomb vanished. He could not bear the look of accusation in his sister's eyes.

"She'll return. She always does," he said mulishly.

Were a boy saying such a thing, Joseph would have cuffed him to bring him to a sense of his duty. He guessed Amaranthe was considering the same thing. She wrung her hands around the drawstring closure of her reticule for a moment, then blurted, "Derwa is his daughter."

"What's that?" Joseph stopped short in the circle of furious pacing he only now realized he'd taken up again.

"Derwa, who is the daughter of—"

"Your dresser, Eyde. Yes, I know. She was pregnant when you both came to me in Oxford—I'm not such a dolt I don't remember. And I was witness when she wed Davy a year later, if you'll recall."

Davy was the Welshman whom Amaranthe had hired as their manservant once they'd gotten settled in George Court, a few months after Joseph took his degree from St. John's College and began his first post in London as tutor to an admiral's sons. Eyde was the maidservant Amaranthe had towed along with her when she suddenly appeared in Joseph's university lodgings seven years ago, having fled Penwellen and Reuben's wardship and refusing to say a word to Joseph about what had happened.

Refusing to explain why she was showing up with a maid with a belly as her only chaperone, and why she begged Joseph not to send her back.

Derwa, born a few months later, had the deep-set eyes and nocked chin of an Illingworth, an eerie resemblance to Joseph's own.

He sagged into a chair. "Explain."

Amaranthe resumed pacing the circuit Joseph had trod into the Brussels carpet. The carpet he'd called Inez out on just half an hour earlier.

"Eyde was a maid at Penwellen while I lived there."

"Yes, you said."

After their parents' deaths, their cousin had taken them in, housing and clothing them and offering nominal status as gentlemen's offspring. It later emerged that Reuben was squandering the meager funds their parents had left for Amaranthe's support on Reuben's comfort, instead of Amaranthe's. Joseph at least had been able to escape to university. It was only when Amaranthe showed up three years later, vowing she'd never return, that Joseph had the faintest hint all was not rolling quietly along at Penwellen as he'd assumed.

"Favella, as you know, was...delicate."

Favella, Reuben's wife, had died the year before. Amaranthe had gone south with Mal as her escort thinking to attend her cousin's wife in childbirth and had instead found a black wreath on the door. Reuben had, at the time, proposed Amaranthe marry him so he might occupy himself with begetting an heir as early as possible. Amaranthe, being already inconveniently in love with Mal at the time, had declined.

That, at least, was the story Joseph had been told.

"Reuben..."

A chill cruised down his arms and shoulders. Men in dark corners, coming into the pantry, the scullery. Men believing the maid in their service was their property. That a young woman without family, of the servant class, was another good they could use at their convenience... Hadn't Inez warned him some men like thought like that? The world was suddenly crueler, and more soiled, than Joseph in his naivete had ever imagined.

"Derwa is Reuben's daughter," Joseph said, his voice hoarse as the full weight of it hit him. Eyde, a maid in the employ of a married man, would know she could lose her position and her salary if she displeased the master.

A man who hurt a dog wouldn't shrink from hurting a woman.

"Does she know?"

"Derwa? I don't believe Eyde has told her yet. She's known Davy as her father all her life, and they are the happier for it. But Eyde has always said she would tell her someday, when Reuben could no longer hurt them."

Reuben, already in the ground by the time the letter had reached them, couldn't reach from the grave and harm anyone now. At least, not like that.

"But the estate can't go to her when she is illegitimate," Joseph pointed out.

"Of course not. It's entailed to you. Reuben acknowledged his crime when I confronted him, but he never offered to support her."

"But you are asking me to," Joseph realized.

His sister inclined her head. "You are, of course, under no obligation, any more than was Reuben. But it is the right thing to do, Joseph. She is his child. Eyde has a good salary as my dresser, Davy just as good as our first footman. They have a home with us as long as they wish. But Derwa...if she had some small funds held in trust, some remembrance, it would help her establish herself in the world, later. Though she'll have Mal and I, of course."

Derwa had been like an adopted daughter to Amaranthe well before she married and took in the duke's three half-siblings. "But if you arranged for the estate to provide her with something, after her natural father turned her out of the house... it would go a way toward making things right."

And repairing the injustice Reuben had committed.

How many other men, Joseph wondered, had looked away from Reuben's crimes? How many other men had been left to dispose of the bodies he left in his wake?

"Of course I will. Only let me get down there and see what the estate will bear."

"Thank you. I knew I could trust you to do what is right." Amaranthe gathered her reticule and tugged on her gloves.

"Is that why?" Joseph asked, standing again as he was, after all, a gentleman, and his sister considerably outranked him now.

"Why I came by? Partly, yes."

"Why you left Cornwall all those years ago. To get Eyde away from Reuben?"

She stilled, and he didn't like what lay in that stillness. The alertness. The sense of warning.

Inez had that same taut alertness sometimes, when she was alone in a room with Joseph. As if he were the larger predator, and she all too aware she was soft prey.

Nonsense. He wasn't a predator. He'd never hurt Inez; he'd never made the slightest move to intimidate her. He'd never intimidated his sister, either; quite the opposite.

He stilled, too, with a sudden realization. Inez didn't need prior evidence from him. He was a man; that was enough. He was of the breed she knew to be a danger to her, and even he in his own self offered no threat, that might mean little.

That wasn't why she'd *run*, was it? Because she was afraid of him? A sour taste rose in his throat, and that cold chill on his back turned clammy.

"Let me guess," Joseph said, acid in his mouth as he faced his sister. Seeing the delicate girl she was seven years ago, no more than eighteen, weary from a journey over several counties and hundreds of miles to find safety with him. "You needed to get both of you away from Reuben."

She concentrated on precisely squaring each finger of her glove over the digit it enclosed. "Yes."

"*Anth.*" His voice came out anguished. "Did he—?" He couldn't frame the words. God above, he wasn't a fool, but he'd never considered, then or now, that she would be in danger from their cousin.

And why hadn't he, when he knew better? When he knew full well what Reuben was?

A cold drop of sweat slithered down his spine.

"Not me. He threatened, but I brought Eyde away before he could make good on his threats."

"If he weren't already dead," Joseph said stonily, "I would kill him. As it is, I think I will spit on his grave."

"He can't hurt us now. And I think you can do much good as the baronet, Joseph. You might repair some of the damage he has done."

She paused to regard him with a soft, fond smile. "It isn't fair to you, I know. You deserve to inherit an estate in good heart, unburdened by debts or foul memories. But we get the world we have, don't we? And it is our part to build the world we want."

"Mother always said that, too," Joseph remembered. He rubbed at the back of his neck. "I'll start preparing to leave at once."

"I shall ask Mrs. Frost if she wishes to look after the house, or if she wishes to close it up. Normally I would ask Inez, but it seems she is out of charity with you again? Really, Joseph, she is the sweetest of women. I don't know how you manage to bring out her temper—"

"My God, she's out there alone." Joseph took his sister's arm to steer her toward the door. "I have to find her."

"She's very capable of looking after herself, come to that," Amaranthe soothed. "I only meant, if you had insulted her, it is your part—"

"Someday, Anth, you will recognize that I am the elder sibling, and perfectly capable of conducting my own affairs," Joseph snapped. His body felt as if he stood on a waking fire, showered with sparks. He recalled Inez's nervous look up and down the street, as if she were watching for something.

Something outside of his house posed a threat to her, and he had just sent her running from the one place she was safe.

"Along with you, Duchess, if I can trust your man to see you home." He practically pushed his sister toward the front door of the little hall. "Something terrible is about to happen to Inez. I have to find her *now*."

CHAPTER FOUR

———————————

Her Portuguese *mamãe* had warned Inez that the devil always came to collect his due.

She had the prickling, uneasy sensation today was that day.

She knew, before she was a block from George Court with her cloth bag in hand and a spring sun smiling down on the day, that she would regret leaving without bargaining with Mrs. Frost for her wages earned so far this quarter. Inez had given what remained of last quarter's salary to her father, who had promptly exchanged it for a celebratory drink, which meant she had no small coins in her pocket to pay for decent lodgings or a meal.

Only the larger things lay wrapped in their concealing layers at the bottom of her bag, and those, she could not disclose to anyone. It meant her life if she did.

Furtively she glanced around, fearing that even here, in the more posh part of town, she could be found and recognized. Hanged for a criminal. She was going to do it, then? Storm away from her place of refuge just because Joseph Illingworth was a thick-headed oaf?

Yes. Inez pushed back a falling lock of hair and lifted her

chin. She could pawn her clean linen apron, her pretty lace cap, or her extra petticoat, if it came to that. She'd bought these things to be tidy and fresh for Joseph Illingworth, and the great staggering sod hadn't once looked on her as a man looks on a woman. She might as well be rubbed in the stinking mud of the river, the way he turned up his nose.

She scrubbed her eyes to rub away the threat of frustrated tears as she pushed down Princes Street. She'd been in this position before. Turned out without a character, with no family to succor her and no shelter to take her in. Later, storming away from George Court in a temper because Joseph Illingworth was the most irritating male ever shaped to walk the planet.

How he got under her skin so instantly, Inez couldn't say. Every glare from his dark brown eyes dismissed her, his gaze shearing away as if he couldn't bear the sight of her. Many another man liked the sight of her, and begged for a touch to see if that pleased him as well. Yet Joseph Illingworth turned away as if she were something unseemly.

He was impossible to please. She never won a single compliment from him, no matter how prettily she dressed her hair or how much bosom she let show above her neckcloth when she brought him his bread and butter. How many times had she kept that man alive, feeding him when he was so caught up in a book that he forgot the outside world was passing him by? How many times had she kept him from falling into a brown study over his prospects with a cheerful, bracing word or the promise of better things to come? And still he regarded her with that scowl as if she were a beetle that crawled out of the coal scuttle.

But where to next? Where could she go that would be safe?

She could ask for help at Hunsdon House, she knew. It was the duchess's dresser, the Cornishwoman, Eyde, who had first found Inez at the mop fair huddled around a threadbare broom, trying desperately to win the attention of the respectable matrons and housekeepers who walked by, their eyes sliding over and past Inez as smoothly as if she were a butter dish. Eyde had given Inez refuge in Miss Amaranthe's house when her post as a chambermaid turned out to involve being pawed by the randy son of the house, and again when her next post as a kitchen maid came with an uncle who had a habit of backing Inez into corners and demanding caresses.

If she went to Hunsdon House now, the housekeeper, Mrs. Blackthorn, would take her in directly, of that Inez had no doubt. She'd proven herself honest and discreet, setting aside the matter of her occasional vanishing acts. But if she went to Hunsdon House, Joseph Illingworth would know where she was.

And knowing he *knew* where to find her, but would never come for her—that was one more humiliation she wasn't prepared to bear.

She paused for moment on the edge of Leicester Square, considering. Was her pride worth her life?

But if there were no one to miss or lament her if she disappeared—then pride was all she had. Inez turned her face to the east and began the long trek to the City.

Joseph Illingworth would never find her there, and hopefully, the devil wouldn't, either.

In Covent Garden piazza, Inez wove her way past the market stalls, enjoying the rowdy riot of color and noise and keeping her bag hugged to her chest. The colorful cart of a flower seller caught her eye, a handbarrow blooming with geraniums and azaleas, tulips and peonies. She ought to take a posy to Mother if she meant to come as a supplicant.

As she watched, a man in a dark velvet suit and a cocked hat stepped near and whispered in the flower seller's ear. The young woman colored but nodded and, with a word to the young girl with her, took the gentleman's arm and stepped away.

His lips curved in a greedy smile, and he nearly put his foot in a pile of horse dung in his eagerness to pull his prize under the nearest arcade.

Inez halted at the look on the younger girl's face as she watched the departing pair: bitter resentment, resignation, and a touch of wrath. Inez could surmise the reason the comely elder had been summoned, and it was easy to see how the younger felt about it.

"Your mum?" Inez asked, lifting a spray of purplish bell-flowers.

The girl bit her lip. "M'sister." Swiftly she wrapped the spray in her silvered paper and ferns, her dexterity suggesting years of practice.

"She's a handsome suitor."

The girl gave a bitter laugh that said, despite her age, innocence had long departed. "'E's a john. They's only ever johns. But they pays better than the flowers, and so she goes and turns up 'er 'eels, don't she."

Inez tucked the stems into the band of her apron, a dainty stretch of crisp linen in contrast to the girl's, which was much-mended and turned to hide stains. This was the fate that awaited a woman when she didn't have means or when the family that could succor her fell away, one by one.

Many a woman went into the business of selling herself if a regular wage wasn't available. All too often, a seamstress or milliner or mantua-maker struggling to pay for her bread, or longing for a new length of silk she couldn't buy with the coin she had, would step for a moment into a different kind of trade. In Covent Garden, lists circulated, compiled by a helpful and experienced gentleman named Harris, who identified the professional ladies of trade, described where to find them, and shared his thoughts on the quality of their service.

And it wasn't Covent Garden alone; the business of buying

and selling pleasure thrived all through this town busily building itself day by day. Walking along The Strand, one in the know could follow a discreet set of stairs above a regular shop or business to find an upscale bordello furnished with tasteful luxury and beautiful, expensive women. Inez had been invited to join one or two of them, as they liked having a dark-skinned girl in the inventory.

A gentleman might happen into a lucky encounter if he solicited a woman on Fleet Street, for there was as much as a chance she would be an available companion as she might be a respectable tradeswoman who would reprimand him for his impertinence. Of course, there were other streets where a gentleman couldn't walk along without a cluster of women tugging at his coattails, an effort to gain his custom and take the opportunity to rob him.

More than one cell in any given watch house was occupied by a working girl who'd walked away with her john's watch or jewelry or purse and made the mistake of not walking far or fast enough, or of being distinct enough in her appearance that the john, constable in his wake, could identify her later.

Around St. Paul's Churchyard there were all manner of services for sale, including women, men, and sometimes boys. Inez took care not to meet the eye of any passing gentleman lest he take her look for an invitation. Her chest felt heavy and tight, like a brick was pressing down on her lungs. Along Cheapside, several medieval alleys offered a convenient locale for a short interlude away from the bustle of other businesses. Some of the women strolling the street regarded her with the interest they would give the competition. Inez clutched her cloak closer about her as she ducked her head and hurried along.

Here she was, steering herself toward the status of the demi-mondaine when she had tried so hard to escape that fate. She didn't decry anything a woman did to keep herself alive; God knew Inez herself had real sins to repent of. But while some women could find their way back to a trade that wouldn't get them fined or imprisoned, for too many, their first foray into the demimonde was the step across a precarious threshold onto a path that led to misery and ruin.

Inez couldn't follow. She'd made a promise long ago, to another and to herself, and that promise had been sealed by death. It wasn't just her honor but her soul she risked if she angered the restless spirits.

She cursed Joseph Illingworth for being the instrument of her ruin, for pushing her out of the safe, warm nest she'd found in his house. Were it not his stubborn thick-headedness, she'd not be toeing the ledge of self-preservation, clinging with bared nails to that last slender thread of self-respect. He'd offered her refuge in his home; was it too much to hope he could also offer her kindness?

It is not kindness you wish he would show you, menininha, said her mother's voice in her head.

Ah, *mamãe.* That voice never let her deceive herself too long.

No, it wasn't fraternal care she wanted from Joseph Illingworth.

Inez flounced away from his house in high dudgeon every time—*every* time—because her pride couldn't tolerate that he did not see her as a woman.

And why not? Other men found her alluring. They praised her large, dark eyes, her graceful bearing, the generous curves of hips and bosom that filled out the fashions of the day. She'd been longed for. Desired. Many a man offered a quick tumble, if not an enduring devotion. So what was wrong in the head with Joseph Illingworth that he had not once gazed at her with open appreciation, if not outright lust in his eyes?

Inez held her head high as she wove up Threadneedle

Street, past the imposing temple that served as the Bank of England, and along Bishopgate Street, where the medieval gate had been demolished, the city having long outgrown its ancient footprint. She passed the fields surrounding Devonshire Square and turned from Petticoat Lane, the clothing market, into the smaller Smock Alley, sure of herself now and stepping confidently among the flow of traffic, carters and porters and chairmen and so very many women like her, women in search of employment to keep body and soul together.

There were so many beggars, children lacking eyes or limbs, soldiers and sailors too worn and broken for service, old women who had lost the families who ought to have given them shelter. Inez put a hand over her apron, guarding against pickpockets, and slid her eyes away. She'd help if she were able, but right now, she was a beggar herself. And Joseph Illingworth had made her so.

She, Inez da Costa Shirodkar, reduced to begging.

Better that than stealing, of course. Less dangerous.

She turned down the small outlet known to locals and denizens as Dark Lane, a narrow tunnel of tall houses that gradually opened into a sort of courtyard, not quite square. This gathering space had many names. The Abbey. The School. Gropecunt Alley, given the services that drew most of the visiting men.

Inez had made a solemn vow to her mother on her deathbed that she would never trade her body for coin, and here she was, seeking lodging from whores.

A fountain stood in one corner of the dirt-packed square, the source of clean water for the inhabitants of Dark Lane and a holdover from when this area had been part of the ancient St. Mary Hospital, or Spital, as it was called, because the British were too lazy to pronounce all of their words. The area had become prosperous from the clothing trade, especially when the

Huguenot weavers took up residence nearby and, free of the guild restrictions that prevailed in the confines of the city, added silk to the English costume of cotton, worsted, and wool.

Inez sat on the lip of the fountain and touched her finger to the water, piped from a cistern some distance away and kept a closely guarded secret. She would take up weaving if she had any talent at it, or the slightest skill. But she found her mind wandered too easily at the repetitive tasks, and then she dropped stitches or lost the thread of warp and weft, and her results were crooked and uneven.

Her one skill was looking after people, and she had a bit of her mother's talent at baking, when she was allowed to work in peace. She was a social creature, liked being around people, and wasn't suited to employment that left her for long stretches alone. One reason she kept returning to the little house in George Court. There was always someone coming in and out of the Illingworth premises, if not pupils or friends of Joseph's then the servants' friends, the neighbors, and the neighbors' friends. Miss Amaranthe, when she lived there, had been known never to turn away someone in distress. One day, three children of a duke showed up at her door, and thus was her fortune made.

But the house in George Court held Joseph Illingworth, and Inez was done hanging her hopes, and her heart, on foolish men.

So she came here, the one other place that had never turned her away, a place where women leaned on one another as they all did their best to survive in the world.

Across the square towered a black mulberry tree, said to have been planted at the time of King James. A brace of girls sat in the shade, with aprons and tuckers over their wrapping gowns, one reading from a book as another wrote on a slate. A kitchen maid walked through with a bucket of kitchen slops to feed the chickens kept in the mews, which sat behind the building they called the Temple.

Most of the girls inside this old, medieval-looking building would still be abed, resting after the business of the night. A chambermaid with mop and bucket emerged from the side door and walked across the square to knock at the kitchen entrance of the building they called the Factory, where the seamstresses, who slept at night, would be toiling by the light of day. Inez wondered who might remain who knew her here. Many residents of Dark Lane came and went, taking shelter in this secret courtyard as circumstances demanded, then moving on and upward as chance allowed.

One woman could be depended on, and that was Mother. While her girls slept, Mother would observe her usual ritual: a Spartan breakfast, a careful accounting of the previous day's income concluding with an update to the household ledgers, then the task of dressing and preparing for her morning calls.

Soon enough a woman in a sober silk robe stepped from the front door of the Temple. With her tasseled shawl, a sheer apron pinned to her bodice, her jaunty hat, and pattens on her shoes, she could be anyone from a tradesman's wife to the Queen. Indeed she was a queen, at least in this domain, and Inez scrambled to her feet to join her much like the little maid jogging at the woman's heels.

"Mother Vesta," Inez said, using her title. Very few in Dark Lane used their names. The madame who oversaw the girls nicknamed the Vestals was referred to by the name of the Roman goddess of hearth and family, and most of the others who came to live in Dark Lane set aside their old identities for new.

"Inanna," Mother said, regarding Inez with surprise. Inanna was the name of some powerful and ancient goddess of love, war, and fertility. Not an apt name, since Inez had none of those things in her life. She had spinsterhood, solitude, and deceit.

"What brings you back to us, m'dear? A visit to show off your good fortune? Someone is keeping you quite fine."

"I am looking for work, Mother," Inez said meekly. "Again."

Mother looked her up and down, taking in the changes Inez had seen in her own small hand mirror. A new fullness to her cheeks and a sparkle in her eye when she was well-fed and happy. She'd lost the ragged, hunted look she'd been wearing the last time she returned to George Court, and in the weeks since Joseph's return from his Grand Tour, she'd become as sleek and contented as a well-fed lap cat.

Mother's darkened eyebrows rose in interest. "As a Vestal?"

Inez pleated the sides of her apron with her fingers. "I'd hoped as a housekeeper. Or a nurse to the youngers. I would work in the Factory. Or teach in the school?"

"Sure and you'd earn more coin in the Temple," Mother said.

Inez shook her head. Dark Lane was more than just the service referred to by its patrons and workers as the Vestal Temple. The Dorter, the old house where the medieval nuns had lived, now sheltered women who hailed from all strata of society and needed a place of safety before they could brave the wide world. Orphans, mostly girls, were taught at the school, if teachers could be found, then apprenticed to trades. No one hungry was turned away, and most all of it was paid for by the work of the Vestals and the canny management of Mother Vesta.

Not for the first time, Inez wondered what had brought a woman of clear breeding and likely a gentlewoman's status to be the madame of a brothel tucked into a corner of Spitalfields and kept a secret from the world, as much as could be. Inez didn't know all the dialects of England, not like she could listen to Portuguese and know exactly where a speaker was from, but she thought Mother Vesta might have come from the north.

Mother nodded toward the building behind her, once part of the old medieval hospital, then redone as a rich merchant's house, now home to the kind of activities that would have had the poor nuns crossing themselves and saying prayers for their souls. "I've a tom who likes the ones he thinks is exotic. We can tell him you're Spanish. Or Chinese."

"Portuguese," Inez said, slightly offended. Her father was from Goa, a place many English had heard of but couldn't locate on a map. Inez knew where it was, and her father's island home was still a turn of the world away from the reaches of the Far Eastern Orient.

Mother waved a hand to invite Inez to walk her survey of the square with her. "He won't know. Whisper to him in whatever language he likes, swat him on the arse with a stick, and he'll give you an armload of guineas. He's one of those," she said with a knowing nod.

Inez was aware that the Vestals catered to all manner of tastes, and the stranger the request, the more the man paid. She had seen the same with her mother.

Bile rose in the back of her throat and she pushed back the memory of her mother's men. So many men, knocking on the frame of their small house tucked into the alley, barely more than a lean-to, a shanty crouched in the shade of a larger house, a house where there were servants and rooms with rugs and where real people lived. Such a far cry was the life in that house from the miserable existence Inez had known, scrounging for scraps of firewood before daybreak, picking from the refuse that rich folk left outside for their animals to find food that might make part of a meal.

The men her mother took behind the worn curtain that served to divide her parents' bed from the rest of the room that comprised their house. The way Inez would sit outside until it was over. She would have taken herself away at those times, but she'd learned that she was needed to help clean up after, some-times the linen and sometimes her mother.

It wasn't always that her mother entertained, and it wasn't her regular trade. Only when her father had been gone too long on a sail, or when he had been home too long and not bringing home wages from other work. Inez's mother had her baked goods to sell, but sometimes it wasn't enough. But if the women at market knew of the men who came sometimes to the alley where they lived and stepped behind the curtain, then they wouldn't buy anything. They'd sneer at her mother—Inez's beautiful, dignified mother, who said her prayers to Santa Maria every morning, who made the most delicious *broa,* who had the softest hands and a low, musical voice and a smile like the sun setting over the sea.

If her mother had been a courtesan to the rich, she would have been fed the best sweetmeats, showered with jewels, shown off in a fancy carriage in silks and velvets and furs. She would have commanded respect, adoration. But because she was married to a poor sailor, not even a Portuguese sailor but a man from afar, and because what she sometimes sold was her embrace to men who paid for the chance to take their ease with her, she was dirt on the street to the merchants' wives and daughters. It wasn't a life either of them would have wished for.

Inez had hoped things would be better when they came to England to find her father. England was a rich land, wasn't it? London was the biggest city in the world, so they said, bigger than Paris, if not as grand. There would be work. There would be a better home than the shanty and better life for her mother at a different market.

But it wasn't a better life. For her mother, it was more of the same life, hard and wearing and hungry, only with different men who came to the door when her father was absent, and different women who turned up their noses when they passed their stall at market.

On her deathbed, when her beautiful mother had been worn to a shadow and then the shadow had worn down to nothing, Inez had promised her mother she'd only ever take respectable work. She'd never let herself be used. She would do better; she would *have* better.

If only her mother had made her promise never to hang her heart after an unsuitable man, Inez thought now. And what did it gain her to cling to virtue and respectability anyway? They mattered to the women who hired her but not the men of the house trying to pull Inez into dark halls and doorways. And no one would believe her claims of innocence if they knew she frequented Dark Lane.

"Go see Ceres," Mother said. "I'm certain she will welcome you. We've missed your *broa*."

Mother Ceres was the name given the cook, and Inez was relieved to see the Ceres presiding over the kitchens now was the one she'd known from before, a woman with skin darker than Inez and a round face that broke into a ready smile when Inez entered.

"Mother of mercy, it's been an age since we've seen you hereabouts, Inanna. Come to stay with us again?"

"Come to work with you, Mother Ceres, if you'll have me."

"You know you'll make more coin as a Vestal."

"*Certo*, but I like to work in the daylight hours and sleep in my nights," Inez said.

The cook chuckled. "You'll find late hours when Mother wants to throw a banquet or the ladies are up late entertaining. But I could use a set of clever hands." She nodded toward a battered brass pot perched on the huge black cookstove. "You can make the gravy for the fowl, then dress the turnips."

Inez fetched a stew pot down from the shelf, then collected

a scoop of butter from the ceramic dish kept cool in the scullery. She put the kettle to boil, then hunted up a knife to hack up bits of lean beef and mutton for a proper gravy. The kitchens of Dark Lane were a low set of rooms with thick oak beams bracing the ceiling and an ancient brick hearth, not like the sunny and high-ceilinged room at George Court. But the ladies of Dark Lane welcomed her back, and Joseph Illingworth never did.

Inez carved off a slice of bacon with more force than was strictly called for. Why had she been such a fool for that man, again and again and again?

"So did the lord ever find ye?" Mother Ceres inquired as she withdrew a pan of bread from the brick oven. "The one as was looking for ye a while afore."

Inez's heart stopped beating for a too-long moment, then did a slow flip in her chest.

"A man? Dark brown hair, deep set eyes, too handsome for his own good or anyone's?" Her heart tripped trying to resume its beat, blast that worthless organ. Had he come looking for her before? Had he finally *wanted* her, and she'd been too dim to see it? "He's not a lord," she added.

The cook's eyebrows rose to the lace border of her cap. "Well, he makes Bess call him his lordship, don't he? One o' the high and mighty ones, for certain." Ceres sniggered. "Bess told us once as how his wig fell off during a lively moment, and he stopped and made her look away until he could get adjusted."

Inez didn't laugh along with Ceres's hearty chuckle. "Large hooked nose, very thin lips? Wears a toupée with a pigtail in the back?"

"Aye, that's the wig." Ceres chortled. "How d'ye know him? He was particular keen to find ye."

Of course he was, because Inez was in possession of something very, very valuable that rightly belonged to the lord. And she'd done him a greater wrong than mere thievery.

"I worked in his house for a time," Inez answered. "When did he ask about me?"

"Oh, several times, well nigh pestered me and Mother for a month, swore he'd seen ye here and said we were hidin' ye. But you'd kicked off long before and we'd no notion where ye'd gone, and so Mother Vesta told him. Vowed he'd bring the constable down on us, which ye know Mother Vesta won't like, as she pays the man well to look aside from us and would have to pay him even more if a lord kicks up a fuss. Now he just looks about all keen-like, hunting through the halls where he oughtn't be, but he pays well and he's a regular customer, so Mother don't want to lose a fat cull."

Inez fumbled with a carrot she was slicing, sending a chunk skittering to the floor. Mother Vesta's dog, a small greyhound, shot out from under the table to snap it up, then retreated before Ceres would reach for her broom.

"When do you think he'll be back?"

Ceres shrugged and took up a cloth to turn the roast sizzling on its spit over the hearth. "Usually every few days, when he's in town. Haven't seen him in a bit, so maybe he's done for the season and is headed off to his estate for the summer. Shame he didn't bring Bess along this time, but I suppose he's got his bits hidden all over, and it's too much extra luggage to cart along."

Inez sliced an onion to arrange over her ingredients in the gravy pan and let that excuse the tears starting to her eyes. If his lordship was gone from town, she was safe.

He couldn't know enough to accuse her, could he? She'd fled that accursed house as fast as she could. But why else would he be looking for her, unless he knew?

A bell rang along the board hung high on the wall, and Ceres glanced up at it. "That'll be Queen Bess wanting laced up, I'll wager. She'll have had an easy night so I don't doubt she wants to spend her day in the shops. That means she'll want her chocolate and a bit of honey on her toast. Will you take it, Inanna? Certain she'll be pleased to see you."

The cook grinned as she popped two slices of bread onto the toasting stick and handed it to Inez. "She might invite you to go along with her, but be prepared to look aside if you must. I'd wager our Bessie'll find another john and take him in the alley outside the milliner's so she can have a new length of silk ribbon for her hat."

Inez grazed the bread over the flames of the low fire hearth, lightly toasting both sides. "D'you think Bessie would? She's such a fear of the pox."

The pox was a fear rightly held by many in the trade, along with the clap and the itch. More than one former Vestal endured regular treatments of mercury because a john had cheerfully passed on his coin along with a disease he had acquired from previous adventures.

Not everyone died in the festering agony that Inez's mother had experienced. But that memory alone, separate from her promise, was enough to make Inez shrink from the thought of sharing her body with a stranger.

She turned the toast onto a plate and scooped a dollop of honey into a dish, then poured a cup of chocolate from the pot perched on the hob. "The pan is ready for you to shake some flour in, Mother Ceres, then add the hot water for the gravy. I'll be back to check on you in a moment."

"Na, child, take your time for a gossip. The Vestals will be happy to see you again. You're a favorite here and you ought to know that." The cook bestowed a fond smile upon her, and it arrowed into Inez's heart.

It was good to be a favorite somewhere. She'd been accepted in the household at George Court, warmly, at least by the other small servants and staff. But things hadn't been the same since Miss Amaranthe became a duchess. The servants Inez knew went with her, and a new housekeeper and maid arrived. Joseph, after he had his heart broken by the faithless Miss Pettigrew, grew irritated and distracted. Then he was gone for months, and Inez drifted through the house, dusting and airing, keeping the mice away, hiding like a coward and longing for his return.

Fool of a man. Anyone could have seen at a moment that Miss Pettigrew wasn't a girl willing to be won. Her face might be soft as fresh dough, but her heart was adamant. She let men woo her because she thought it would be cruel to squash their hopes when doing so was in fact a kindness. She was a girl whose heart ran in train with her convictions, and only a man as devoted to the same morals would be able to soften that heart.

Inez was the opposite, she supposed as she lifted the wooden tray and set out. She had no convictions to guide her, and a soft heart that spilled everywhere, nothing to contain it. She felt like a great pulsing vein exposed to the world, and every little cut made her bleed.

Certainly she was soft in the head to fall as she had for Joseph Illingworth. What did the man have to recommend him? The son of a vicar in one of the poorest corners of Britain. A man whose head was filled with old languages and book lore and not enough common sense to keep him out of the cold when he had a new thought to occupy him.

The first time she took shelter there, over two years ago now, Inez had been at George Court a week before she saw the man of the house. She'd been told on her arrival that he was traveling with the family he tutored but wouldn't be much bother when he returned. Miss Amaranthe promised that Joseph was easy to please but must be looked after as he would forget to eat or trim his candle, and then he would come to the kitchens in a huff looking for hot soup and a new candlestick, and at such times he could be a bother to everyone, so it was best to anticipate his needs.

And so Inez had been sent to his study when he first returned, this brother Miss Amaranthe spoke of with equal parts admiration for his intelligence and exasperated affection for his absent-mindedness. Inez had the duty of bringing tea to both the Illingworths, each of them absorbed in their separate tasks, Miss Amaranthe in the parlor making a copy of some unreadable ancient manuscript, Mr. Illingworth in the smaller study mewed up with his books.

The study lay at the back of the small house, catching the light from the open yard beyond. The wind that day was blowing all the smoke from the coal fires away to the west, and the sun was golden and clear as it fell through the panes of windows. Inez crept softly, not sure yet what sort of creature this brother of Miss Amaranthe's would turn out to be, and far too accustomed to the predations of men to expect he would be much different.

Sunlight, sprinkled with sparkles of dust, fell on the dark brown curls of a man bent over a desk. At ease in his home, he wore his hair pulled back in a queue and had hung his morning coat over the ladder back of his chair. His waistcoat, plain linen in the back, hugged a strong chest and broad shoulders. He'd rolled up the billowing sleeves of his white shirt to keep them free of ink as he jotted notes on papers spread over the desk.

He was left-handed, thus the need to keep his sleeves rolled and out of the fresh ink. That he would use his preferred hand in his own home told Inez he was the kind of man who might conform to outward convention to keep the peace, but in privacy, he could easily set convention aside.

His right hand he held splayed over the pages of the book he was reading, and Inez stared, struck by how a man's hand could seem so strong and forceful at the end of a bared forearm, where the cord of a tendon stood in outline. He had the same faint tint to his skin as Miss Amaranthe, not as brown as Inez, but not the pale milk of the other English.

He lifted his head to look out the window, a muttered word on his lips, and Inez paused with tray in the air at the sight of his profile. Then he turned his head to look at her, as if he had sensed her silent approach, and Inez couldn't breathe.

She'd never been struck breathless by the sight of a man, not even when her father appeared after months or years abroad. What she'd felt, she assumed later, must be fear and the nervous need to please. He had a wide mouth that didn't belong on a man and lips with a steep curve on top and bottom, a mesmerizing mouth. A bold nose arrowed between jutting cheekbones, and his dark eyes were deep set beneath a prominent brow from which the dark curls fell away as if he'd been tugging his hands through them.

His direct gaze held hers, then shuttered with a slow blink, and Inez wondered—hoped, for a brief, wild moment—that he felt the same bedazzled sensation she did, as if she'd stepped from shadow into full sunlight.

"He's done it," the man said to Inez as if picking up a conversation they'd left off. "He's made Hartley's observations intelligible. Captured them quite brilliantly, in fact. Better than I could have done myself."

"Who?" Inez stepped forward cautiously, testing that the floor beneath her feet wouldn't tip or sway. She wasn't certain she had recovered her balance.

"Joseph Priestley. Quite a grasp on natural philosophy, that one. I read his essay on different types of air a year or so ago. But this one is discussing Hartley's theories of mind, and he describes the principle of association better than anyone else has."

"Oh." Inez didn't understand a word of his speech, though

she'd lived in Britain for ten years at that point and her English was fluent. She slid her tray onto a corner of his wide, sturdy desk. "Miss Amaranthe thought you'd like tea."

She hovered, self-conscious as he studied her with that dark, unreadable gaze. She resisted touching her linen cap to see if her hair was misbehaving again, or trying to rearrange the kerchief crossed over her bodice. She didn't want him to think she was trying to draw his attention to her breasts, though she was all of a sudden very aware of them. Her entire body prickled, as if held to a fire, yet there was no coal in the small grate.

"Shall I pour for you?"

"Yes, please." He watched as she tipped a bit of milk into the porcelain cup, then poured out the tea. "Just a bit of sugar, no bigger than your thumbnail. Thank you."

His fingers touched hers as she handed him the cup, and Inez nearly jumped out of her skin. He wasn't leering. He wasn't aggressive. He looked like he'd been far away and she'd surprised him, and he was trying to orient himself to the physical world and her place in it.

"Are you new?" he asked suddenly.

"Yes, sir." This time she couldn't resist tugging at her linen apron, nervous she wouldn't pass muster. "I've been here a week, sir."

"That accent." His eyes narrowed slightly in thought. "Spanish?"

"Portuguese."

"Ah." His sharply defined lips stretched into a smile, at least on one side of his mouth. Inez told herself to stop staring at his mouth.

"My mother's family was from Portugal, long ago," he remarked. His voice hummed in the air around her, rich, resonating.

Inez twisted a hand in her apron. This man made her feel

her insides had been tied into knots. "Miss Amaranthe said as much."

He turned back to his desk, the delicate cup dwarfed in his hands. Once again Inez found herself entranced by his long, strong fingers, the turn of his wrist and the lean muscle of his forearms, lightly dusted with hair. "What is your name?"

She swallowed hard. "Inez."

"Well. *Bem-vinda à minha casa*, Inez."

"Thank you, sir," she said, and suddenly wanted to cry at his words of welcome. When had she ever been welcomed anywhere?

He said no more to her, caught up again in his book. Inez already knew that Miss Amaranthe paid the rent on the house, though of course it was in her brother's name, she being a woman. She knew that Miss Amaranthe ordered her whole life around providing comfort and ease for her brother, and Inez understood. She too felt the same inexplicable wish to ease the way for this man, to keep the space around him soft and quiet while his mind worked, for she sensed that his was extraordinary.

And because he never once looked at her with lust—was never other than scrupulously polite to her, when he noted her presence—Inez was nearly mad with the wish to make him *see* her.

She, who for years had worked and wished to make herself invisible to men. She, who had gratefully decided after she buried her husband that she need never notice a man again, had been hooked like a fish at her first sight of Joseph Illingworth and would never be able to forget him.

She'd never again meet a man whose mind worked like his, a swift and efficient machine, so stimulated by the world of ideas. She'd never meet a man whose character was so deeply sweet and untroubled, though he was stubborn and astonishingly dense in his understanding of people.

She'd never meet a man she so ached to touch, and be touched by. So much so that sometimes at night she lay on her narrow cot in the room that was once a dressing room, kept awake by the empty ache in her body, the longing that arrowed down to the bone.

So focused was Inez on the things she wouldn't have that she forgot what she *did* have: the warning from Ceres that the lord she'd wronged was looking for her. And so it was no fault but her own that she plunged without thinking through the servant's door into the long hallway where the Vestals entertained and came face to face with a man emerging from one of the rooms.

She recognized him instantly: the Roman nose with the indent at the top as if he'd taken a blow there when the flesh was being formed. The thin, leering lips and watery eyes. The pigtail of his wig lying over the shoulder of his coat, a lustrous and heavily embroidered silk lined with rows of heavy buttons.

"*You!*" The word leapt from him like an accusation, a feral snarl.

Inez, fingers frozen, dropped the tray. All she could think in that terrified moment was how Bessie's chocolate would stain the carpet, but her body would barely leave an imprint once he'd strangled and left her for dead.

CHAPTER FIVE

"I've been searching for you for months, you thieving wench." Lord Wigsby stalked toward her, step by heavy step.

"I-I'm not. I didn't."

A lie. If he searched her things, he'd find the jewels in her bag. The reason Inez had run the first time.

Her shoe squelched as she stepped in a puddle of the spilled liquid. Honey formed a sticky crust on her fingertips.

"Hanging's not good enough for you. I'll have you drawn and quartered."

His sweat smelled foul. Dimly, her mind working only on the edges while her brain was preoccupied with fear, Inez wondered how Bessie could stand the smell of him. Did she burn pastilles while she pleasured him? Did she hold her breath?

"I didn't do anything. I didn't mean any of it." Without thinking, she switched into Portuguese, the language of her birth.

"Speak English, you filthy foreigner. You're all the same, and I'm sick of it. Lying beggars who come here to steal from your betters, from honest Englishmen. But only the stupidest of whores would steal from an English lord and think she could get away with it."

As if English lords were a superior being because they'd been born to the accident of a title, or she any less human because she had been born with dark skin. Inez flushed hot with anger and humiliation.

"You have mistaken me for someone else." She pressed out the English words, straining to free them of her soft accent, still present after all these years on the isle.

"Oh, I know you. I remember how you tried to tempt me, twitching your tight little arse as you went about your business."

He stalked her as she retreated. Inez wondered how far until she hit the wall and was trapped. If she bolted for the servant's stair, would he pursue, or would he find such egress beneath him? He was a man much attached to the privileges of his station, if not the obligations.

She'd never tried to lure this man. She'd been terrified of him.

So had his daughter.

"You're the reason Priscilla left." His red-veined eyes narrowed to slits. "You helped her, I know you did. You whores always stick together. You let her be carried away by that jackanapes, and then you stole all her jewels—all *my* jewels. Cleared out the house, like the filthy, foreign rat you are. My butler told me everything."

The butler in that house would lie at will if it gained him anything; he was more craven than his employer, and just as greedy and cruel. Inez wondered how much moveable property the butler had absconded with and blamed the servants who fled the house that awful night.

"Which is it you regret more, your lordship? The loss of your daughter, or the jewels?"

Oh, foolish to taunt him, but the words leapt to her lips before Inez could stop herself. Balanced on the edge of death, she was finally bold enough to speak the truth.

"Your daughter left because you were cruel. She escaped you to find love, true love. Priscilla asked your blessing, don't you remember? She would have listened if you were reasonable. But you were not."

"You dare speak to me of my daughter! You aren't fit to pronounce her name. Helping her elope, and *stealing* from me to boot? I'll see your hands chopped off." Spittle spewed from his mouth, so frothed was he with rage. His face mottled red, and veins bulged above the white stock at this throat. If he had apoplexy and expired here on the stained rug, would Inez be held accountable?

She turned to bolt, but Wigsby snaked out a fleshy hand and closed his fingers around her wrist. A low cry escaped her.

"Run, and I'll have the watch down on you all. I'll flush the filth from every corner of this wretched place, and your little whoring friends will have nowhere to go."

Inez fought to tug her arm from his grip. She moaned as the pressure on his wrist threatened to snap the bones.

"Where are the jewels? I want back what you stole from me, you bitch!"

"Priscilla took them. So she could run away and be free of you."

"I sent a man to hunt down her and her doltish husband. They weren't smart enough to cover their tracks." At last, he had her cornered against the small occasional table standing at the end of the hall. The edge pressed into her back. His sneer turned feral. "They have nothing. They'll always have nothing —I'll make sure of that for crossing me. But you."

He wrapped his other hand around her throat. His fingers

were thick and fleshy, dirt caked around the nail beds and knuckles.

"I don't trust the law to deal rightly with you. Think I'll have to do it myself."

The scream had no time to rise. Inez grappled at the manacle around her neck, but she was so much smaller. She writhed and kicked out her feet, trying to connect with his swollen belly, his thighs, his groin, any soft part she could injure. He wrapped his hands all the more tightly and squeezed. She gagged, and he smiled. A gleam of lust and madness entered his eyes.

A shattering crack pierced the growing fog in her mind, and the hold on her neck slackened. Inez staggered back, hands to her injured throat, sucking in air. She blinked. A cloud of white bloomed around his lordship's head, like a halo. He made a stuttered, cut-off sound and swayed on his feet, shaking his head.

"Damn it. That should have dropped him." An angelic voice spoke at her ear.

Inez blinked again. She must be seeing things in the throes of death. "Joseph?"

She moaned and tilted toward him, as if the world had shifted. He was warm, solid, and real. He smelled like horse.

"Would have dropped him, if it were earthenware instead of porcelain." Joseph shoved the broken top of a decorated jug into her hand, the handle still attached. "If he gets past me, use the edges. Go for his eyes or under the throat, here." He tapped the side of his arrogant jaw, the soft skin beneath. He was smooth-shaven, as usual, and the lean column of his throat, part and parcel of his splendid *maleness*, had her staring, stupefied, for a frozen second.

"You attacked a lord!" Wigsby bellowed. "I'll have you hanged right along with her, you cur."

"Oh, I'm not done. You attacked a defenseless woman." Joseph turned and drove his fist into his lordship's fleshy cheek.

She wasn't defenseless, Inez thought hazily, clutching the broken top of the porcelain jar to her middle as she pressed against the small side table and watched. She had *him*. She had never been one to watch bare knuckle boxing, thinking it a brutal sport, but there was something beautiful in the way Joseph moved with controlled, lethal grace.

His opponent was a brawler, a bully who relied on his size and weight to carry him in a match, but Joseph had technique. His lordship, who outweighed Joseph by at least two stone, most of it fat, swung wildly, throwing his bulk around. Joseph ducked his broad swings and landed his punches with precision. Belly. Ribs. A flurry of jabs to the face, then another deep blow in the gut.

The strength and fury of him was magnificent. A hot flush moved from her throat to her breasts and down to her belly.

His lordship snorted out air and stumbled backward. "I... will...kill...you," he huffed.

"In my sleep, I don't doubt. Coward." As his opponent lunged forward, trying to catch him in a bear hug, Joseph ducked and delivered two blows to Wigsby's stomach, where his coat gapped open over an embroidered waistcoat. Each fist summoned a grunt of pain, and the other man halted, hanging in the air, panting.

"Mercy?" Joseph said, though the cold set to his face told Inez he'd rather not.

"Mercy," Wigsby wheezed, swaying on his feet.

"You don't deserve it." Joseph turned to regard Inez, and the granite line of his jaw softened. "Are you—"

"*Cuidado!*" The malicious smile alerted her first, before the meaty arm rose in the air. Inez threw her porcelain weapon over Joseph's shoulder, aiming for Wigsby's face.

Her missile bounced off him, but it slowed him a beat from delivering a rabbit punch to the back of Joseph's neck, the blow that even Inez knew could fell or kill a man. Joseph feinted to the side instinctively, his reflexes faster than hers, and his lordship's fist grazed his temple. A spurt of blood arced in the air, and Inez swallowed a scream.

Joseph, his face pure vengeance, turned and chopped the side of his palm into his lordship's windpipe. Wigsby clutched his throat, gagging, his face purpling as he sagged to his knees. He swung one arm convulsively, trying even then to grab Joseph's ankles and bring him down. With a contemptuous lift of his lip, Joseph curled his fingers, drew back his arm, and drove his fist against the side of Wigsby's head. The hairpiece tilted and fell along with its master, and his lordship keeled face-first onto the floor.

"'E ain't gettin' up nowise soon," remarked Titus. He was one of the bully backs Mother Vesta kept to look after her girls and occasionally usher out a gentleman patron who became rowdy or demanded services he hadn't paid for.

Straightening from his position leaning against the wall, some distance down the hallway, the large man came forward and observed his lordship's prone form with interest, then gave Joseph an admiring look. "Ye got in some good cracks, that ye did. Regular Jack Slack."

"Nowhere near champion level." Joseph winced as he flexed his hands. Both of his knuckles bled freely, skin scraped raw. "Damn his fancy buttons. I think I cracked a bone."

"Ice them fives for a time, onest or twice, then wrap 'em." Nero, the second heavy and a match for Titus in sheer bulk, came forward from the stairs. "And a raw steak for the glimms, so ye don't show up black and fright off the ladybirds," he advised, tapping the side of his head near one eye.

Inez realized both men could have intervened but didn't;

they believed Joseph had the fight well in hand. Her chest swelled as she sucked in air. She'd been holding her breath all this time.

"What will happen to him?" Inez croaked.

"We'll let the molls roll 'im, then dump the cull in Smock Alley. Let 'im think 'e got taken by the anglers and swig men," Titus suggested.

"I say lump 'im in the Spital Market an let the tradesmen have their way," Nero offered.

"Dump him in the Thames," Inez said shakily. "Perhaps then Priscilla's husband can inherit the estate, and do better with it."

"A bloodthirsty wench, are you? I never knew."

Joseph put a finger to her chin to inspect her face. Rage and the fight had given his face a cast she barely recognized. His shoulders seemed enormous, his hands were weapons, and the lines of his face seemed sharper, bolder. He looked like a warrior. A king.

"You're the bloody one." A trickle of crimson streamed from his temple where his lordship's signet ring had cut the skin. Without thinking Inez yanked out the neckerchief tucked at her bodice and pressed it to his head, cupping his other cheek with her palm. His skin was warm and firm and soft, so soft.

She'd thought men were only ever rough and dark and hairy, but Joseph was a pillow of silk drawn over sturdy muscle and bone. The jut of his cheekbone against her palm felt vulnerable. He could have been hurt. He *had* been hurt, for her.

His gaze moved over every line of her countenance, then down her neck. Stuttered and stopped at the sight of her breasts, the tops exposed in the tight bodice. She couldn't slow the rise and fall of her breath, still sharp and panicked as blood beat through her.

He stared, and she wondered if the hot flush she felt everywhere showed on her skin. Joseph Illingworth had noticed her breasts.

He dragged his gaze back up to meet her eyes, and there it was, what she'd longed to see: desire. At long last, he looked at her as a man looks at a woman he covets.

His voice was hoarse and strangled. "Are you—"

She rose up on her toes, pulled his face toward her with both hands, and kissed him.

His lips were as soft as the skin beneath her palms and the curls of hair falling over her fingertips. He tasted delicious. She couldn't go one more instant of her life without kissing Joseph Illingworth, and if she had to pay for her trespass, so be it.

For a tortured moment he stood completely still, as if she'd delivered the kind of blow he'd given to Wigsby, who even now was being carried down the hall and, Inez hoped, out of her life forever. Joseph didn't want to kiss her. He'd appeared out of nowhere, he'd fought for her, he'd looked stunned at the sight of her bosoms pushed up by the tight bodice, but he didn't want —

All of a sudden her feet lifted off the ground and Inez tumbled backwards, as if the carpet had been yanked from her feet. Joseph's arms closed around her like the swoop of a hawk's wings. She felt giddy. His mouth was hot and devouring and pressed to hers as if he meant to swallow her whole.

Her heart jumped into her throat and pulsed there with wild joy. His entire body was pressed to hers and she couldn't breathe with the shock of it, the heat and firmness of his body when his tongue in her mouth was a silken thrust.

She was going to expire from happiness. Joseph Illingworth, kissing her, *finally*, and kissing her with a desperation that made her head whirl, as if he didn't consume all of her, this instant, he would die or disappear. There was something almost clumsy in the press of his tongue inside her mouth, in the clutch of his fingers close to painful in her hair, in the bruising press of his lips. She moaned and shifted, wishing she could press herself closer.

She didn't care if he was all demand and no skill. She felt the hardness of his arousal pressing between her legs, and need whooshed through her like a catching fire, sucking all the strength from her knees. She wanted to wrap her legs around him and pull him inside of her. She wanted him to take her, right here in the hallway against the painted paper wall, as heedless as any whore, so at last, at last she could be fully his.

But she couldn't breathe with all of him upon her, so much of him all at once, the great gush of need that threatened to engulf her. Inez tore her mouth away and gulped for air. He was panting too, his eyes dark with passion, as glassy and dazed as she felt. For an endless moment they stared into one another's eyes, breathing in unison, and Inez felt locked into something she didn't understand, so large she didn't know how she was to hold it.

Then he stepped back. "Good God."

"No," she murmured, reaching for him. He couldn't pull away now. "Come back."

But he dropped his arms, stepping away, and cold air rushed all around her. Her feet on the floor had to hold her up on their own, and she didn't think they could. She didn't want them to.

"Inez. I'm so sorry."

"No," she cried hoarsely. He must not regret this. There must be a promise of more of this later. There could be no *sorry*.

He turned away. Titus and Nero had carried out Wigsby's body, but girls stood at their doors all along the hallway, some of them in stages of dressing for the day, one or two still in wrappers and nightcaps. They hooted, applauded, clamored for information. Inez hadn't heard a thing.

Another maid came through the servant's door with a mop

and bucket. Her cheeks blazing with heat, Inez reached for a cloth. "Let me help."

Joseph ignored all the Vestals calling to him, demanding to know his name, some inviting him into their room to make a closer acquaintance. The light in his eye was embarrassment.

"We must get you away from here," he said to Inez. "That man will come back, or send a constable. You can't stay."

"Wigsby." Inez twisted her hands in her apron as the consequences of what he'd done fell into her mind. "His estate is in Monmouthshire, I think."

"Then he is a lord." Joseph flexed his battered fingers. "The Bloody Code will call for an execution, I don't doubt."

There were any number of crimes that were capital offences on the English law books, Inez had learned. And she had thought Portugal, where the favored capital punishment had long been the garrote or burning at the stake, a savage country.

"More like the judge'll try to transport you," Bess reasoned. She stepped into the hallway holding her stays to her bosom, unconcerned about her state of dishabille. "Sentence you off to fight in the American Colonies, fine strapping 'un as yerself."

She surveyed Joseph's frame with frank appreciation, and Inez battled the urge to claw out the eyes of this woman who had been nothing but friendly to her. "How bad did ye hurt 'im?" Bess asked. "'Cause he's one as pays us well, though he be a bit dirty, come down to it."

"I wants to know what our Inanna did." Another young woman came forward, a pretty redhead they called Freya. She wore a loose nightgown of nearly sheer linen, but Joseph, to his credit, kept his eyes in the area of the enormous cap protecting her wig.

The sudden rush of gratitude for him made Inez bolder than she ever had been with these girls. She might also still be dizzy because Joseph Illingworth had kissed her. "I worked in Wigsby's London house as a lady's maid for a time, and I helped his daughter elope. His only child, and he objected to the marriage. He was understandably upset."

She wouldn't mention her other crimes, not before Joseph. He'd *kissed* her. Inez's entire being was comprised of two urges: escaping the wrath of Wigsby, and finding a way to coax Joseph Illingworth into kissing her again.

"Oy, well done. An 'ere I thought you the veriest mouse." Bess gave Inez a frank smile, bestowing her appreciation, and again Inez wanted to snap at her. She wasn't a violent person! Seeing Wigsby, being nearly choked to death at his hands, then watching Joseph so valiantly defend her had set up a roil of emotions she didn't know how to tame.

"How did you find me?" she finally thought to ask.

The blood had turned to a slow seep at his temple, and Inez dabbed the wound one more time, not caring if the blood never washed out of her linen. She'd carry the scrap as a kerchief beneath her dress if it held a part of Joseph Illingworth, she was that much a fool.

Her knees were as liquid as a chocolate cream. Her belly sloshed with dread and desire. And that place deep within, that place Joseph Illingworth had awakened—after his kiss it burned bright as the morning star, shining through the fog of everything else, a brilliant, true beacon to guide her.

"The costermonger." His steady gaze was a snare, and she would never be free. He studied each line of her face as if she were a priceless painting on exhibit by the Royal Academy. As if he had never seen her before, in all the days and months she had moved in his orbit. Her heart slowed and swelled to one enormous throb of longing. She wished his body were pressed against his once more.

"Tamara," he added, as if Inez wouldn't recall the little costermonger who regularly visited George Court, bringing news from the Big House—what she called Hunsdon House, the ducal townhome—or from other parts around town. "She heard you say something once, apparently, that made her guess you knew this...area. It seems she knows it as well, for her directions were quite accurate."

Inez still held her hand to his temple. She didn't want to stop touching him. The gesture lifted her breasts to his awareness, and his gaze swept there again, but then back to her throat, where the imprint of Wigsby's fingers burned into her skin.

"Gather your things, Inez. We are leaving."

The command did something strange to her insides, turned them to melting wax. She didn't even care that he had used her real name, in this place where all went veiled.

"With you?" Instead of activating her stubbornness, as would a command from everyone else, she found herself cravenly eager to comply. If he'd held out a leash, she might very well slip it around her wrist. Anything if it meant she might follow him. Be tethered to him.

When had she lost her mind for this man?

"Yes. We're going home."

His home. With her in it. As if they belonged in the same place.

"You'll come see us again, won't ye?" Bess called. "Wee Inanna. And bring yer great gorger along, if ye wish."

The ruddy glow in Joseph's cheeks as they descended to the kitchens told Inez he wasn't accustomed to invitations or flattery from women. He blushed as if he'd never been valued, appreciated, sought after by a girl. But how could he not, a man who looked as he did? Whole, unscarred, with his well-cut visage and well-knit frame. He had to have had maids throwing their caps at him from the days he exchanged his boy's gown for breeches. Inez could hardly be blamed for falling victim.

"Leaving so soon, are ye? A right shame, that is." Ceres

winked from her place turning the roast on its spit. "But yer gravy is doing up fine, and we'll drink to your health tonight, dearie. Not every day a girl gains herself a fine protector."

Now it was Inez flushing with embarrassment, but she only mumbled a quick thanks as Joseph, with a courteous salute to the cook, drew her out the door. If only he wanted to be her protector. If only.

Mother Vesta waited in the courtyard, the afternoon breeze stirring the heavy arrangement of feathers and flowers on her hat. She held the cloth stocking bag, and for a moment Inez's heart forgot to beat. Did Mother know?

"You certainly didn't stay long."

Mother's shrewd stare evaluated Joseph, but not as the other Vestals had. Mother was placing his age, his station, his means, and his temperament in a glance, deciding what kind of john he would make. "And I'm to trust him with you, Inanna, when you came here fleeing him?"

"It wasn't him, Mother," Inez admitted. "He would never hurt me."

At least not deliberately. Joseph Illingworth caught mice and spiders and transferred them out of doors when he found them. He couldn't take the life of an insect, much less a person.

Though he had defended her rather splendidly against Wigsby, and Inez wanted to ask where he learned how to fight.

"And what am I to say when his lordship comes back with the watch?" Mother spoke to Joseph, still taking his measure.

"You will tell the watch he laid hands on a woman in your employ. That he accused her of crimes without due process, and attempted murder by his own hand." With a finger he lifted Inez's chin, showing her bruised throat. Inez sucked in her breath at the silken touch. The contact was a small coal, branding her.

"And you have witnesses. Your bully backs. Several of your

girls. Your chambermaid, if they'll take her testimony." Likely they wouldn't, nor that of the Vestals, for the word of women and servants counted less in a court of law than the word of a man, especially a lord or a gentleman, even in this enlightened age.

But Mother was not without her own resources. She simply nodded and held out the bag. "I'll find a way to soothe Wigsby. A free night or two with his favorites, or one of my special banquets. I've never allowed him one before."

Her gaze snared Inez's as their fingers touched. "But you'll come again if you've need, child. You are safe here."

Her breath caught on her reply, so Inez simply nodded. Wax melted about her insides again. She'd known she would find refuge here, but to have it stated so frankly, as if she were welcome—the words meant more than she could say.

Joseph slid an arm around her waist. *Her waist.* Inez went entirely still, as if the gesture were accidental and, were she to remind him, he might withdraw the caress.

"She is safe with me also," he said firmly.

Inez felt the bottom of her bag, seeking the familiar weight and bulk with her fingers. Mother might have searched it—*would* have searched it—but the jewels were there.

Mother knew what she'd done, if Joseph didn't. Yet she handed the spoils back as if the bag and its contents belonged to Inez.

"Your horse is in the mews." Mother pointed. "That way."

And Joseph pulled her away as if Inez belonged with him. As if she were his in truth, and his home was hers also.

It was possible Wigsby had killed her, and this was all a dream. If so, Inez didn't want to wake up.

CHAPTER SIX

"Where did you find a horse?"

She had never known Joseph to ride, and this was the first question that seemed safe as Inez guided them across the square to the stables that lodged the neighborhood horses and occasional carriage of a patron. Visitors to Dark Lane ranged from every social class and background, and no one with solid coin and good manners was turned away.

"The Blue Posts," Joseph answered, naming the pub that stood at the end of George Court, on the busier Rupert Street. The pub took its name from the ubiquitous blue posts where a traveler could hire a sedan chair, but the place also kept a horse or two for hire. "Myers let me borrow one of his Norfolk Trotters, but I must be back with it quickly lest I lose him custom."

Inez regarded the tall horse with its deep chest and short legs, made for covering distance. "I did not know you rode."

"Up with you." He set his hands to her waist and swung her into the air as easily as she lifted her bag. He was strong for a man whose typical labor was hefting nothing heavier than a book.

His was not a practiced move, and there was some fumbling

as he helped her find her seat in the flat saddle. She was all the more pleased with this bit of clumsiness; his was not a rehearsed charm. He did not sweep ladies away upon horseback with regularity.

She let her legs dangle on either side, the way she as a child had ridden the Garrano pony their neighbor in Portugal used to take to market. Only when Joseph fit his foot into the stirrup and swung up behind her did she recall that ladies rose with both legs to one side.

"Every English gentleman's son can ride, and every baronet's grandson," he said.

Joseph reached on either side of her to take the reins, and Inez sucked in her breath as his body fitted around hers. Her bottom was cradled against his groin, the front of his thighs snugging the backs of hers. His shoulder brushed her back as he shook out the ribbons. He was so large and warm and *solid*.

Her head felt light, as if the air were not moving properly upward, though no fingers were obstructing her windpipe this time.

"But where was I to stable a horse in Oxford, and on my income?" he said as he nudged the animal out of doors. "Or in London, for that matter, when it would cost more to house an animal than it would to keep a roof over my head."

There was no rancor in his tone, no scolding. No impatience that he'd had to come fetch her, nor anger that she'd left him. No cutting inflection noting her ignorance about him and his life.

"My thanks," he said to the boy who had tended the horse, and tossed the lad a silver coin as they stepped out onto the square.

She, Inez da Costa Shirodkar, being led out on a horse as if she were a fine lady, and worth the rescue.

"You came for me. Did you know I was in trouble?"

"Amaranthe did. She came to the house soon after you left."

All the melting going on about inside Inez seized to a stop as if she were a candle snuffed out. He hadn't come for her of his own volition. He'd obeyed the directive of his sister.

"And where are you taking me now?" She forced out the words.

"As I said. Home."

He turned the horse onto Bishopgate Street, heading away from Dark Lane, and she wondered if she would ever see this place again. If she dared come back.

Her throat still felt as if she were choking. Could she return to George Court with him and go about their business as if nothing had changed?

She'd kissed him. She could not pretend everything was as it had been.

"Are you going to tell me?"

His voice was low, falling into her ear and raising a shiver. The press of his chest was there against her back, through the thick leather and twill padding of her stays. Joseph didn't wear padding in his coats the way some men did to give themselves a proper silhouette. His coats and waistcoats were wool tabby or broadcloth, inexpensive fabrics but cut well. And they smelled of him, of cassia and rosewood oil, as she knew from the stolen moments she rubbed his garments across her cheek when they came downstairs for cleaning.

"Tell you what?" she breathed. His scent filled her head, along with base notes of musk, his own scent beneath the cologne. He steered them deftly through the traffic on the street, carts and carriages and chairs and pedestrians, as if riding came naturally to him. The horse had a smooth gait, brisk and even, yet each rolling stride tucked her more closely to him. But not close enough.

"Why you left."

She tried casting her mind back to the substance of their argument, the high-handedness, that particular steely tone as he demanded she explain her comings and goings. He deserved that, didn't he, as her employer?

But she couldn't go back to bringing him trays when he never lifted his head from his studies, just cleared a corner of his desk and muttered a thanks, then didn't notice when she came later to take away the crumbs. She couldn't bear bringing dishes to set on the small folding table where he took the dinner Mrs. Frost had made for him, alone with his book and his candle, and no companion.

She hated seeing him dine alone almost as much as she hated the many nights he was away dining at Hunsdon House or at some entertainment where he was invited by the duke and duchess. The house lay empty and hollow on those nights until he returned, the fixed smile on his mouth relaxing as soon as he was in his own domain, among his books and studies.

It hurt too much to have only scraps of him. A few remarks when she brought him a cup of warm milk or cider on those late nights, to calm him before sleep, sharing a brief exchange of words as he told her about his evening and she soaked up every bit of knowledge she could about the life he led outside those walls. It would tear her heart to brush his coats free of the scent of smoke and chicory after he went to the coffeehouse to meet and argue with his friends. She would disappear, dusting rooms that felt soulless without him when he was away working with his pupils, or looking for work.

She could not go back to being a servant. To being furniture in his life.

"I would have thought you more interested in why Lord Wigsby was trying to kill me."

"My next question."

He closed his arm around her as a sudden stop from a

wagon in front of them made their horse draw up, and the temperamental Shire horse in the heavy harness turned and snapped at their Trotter, who sidestepped quickly. Joseph had the reflexes of an active man, though she had only ever known him to live in his head.

What else did she not know about him, after living with him all this time?

"It is as I said."

She gripped his forearm, holding his leather glove to her middle, not entirely for fear that she might fall from the horse. A deep, steady heat spread through her from the press of his arm.

"I helped his daughter elope, and he was angry."

"Angry enough to kill? If she shamed him so much, I should think he'd try throttling her. Though I don't approve of the measure," he added as she twisted her head to look up at him.

A mistake. His head was close, the angle of his jaw in line with her lips, close enough to press in a kiss.

"He—the groom—was a penniless rogue, with more debts than prospects, but enough charm to beguile my lady and every other lass he met." Including Inez, who would have caved to Priscilla's pleading even without the honeyed promises of her elegant beau. It had seemed the truest of love.

"And he can't have hoped for financial support from Wigsby, for the man disowned his daughter on the spot, once he discovered her theft."

"So the source of his ire?"

Inez swallowed. "Several priceless items—family jewels— disappeared along with his daughter."

She couldn't say that Priscilla had carried them away, because that was not true. Inez had secured the jewels to deliver to Priscilla, to give her and her lover a new life together. But when Priscilla was not at the designated meeting area, and word came that she and her new husband had made a hasty passage to France, Inez was left holding the bag of spoils.

She hadn't dared return to Wigsby's house to replace them, not with the theft already discovered. And she couldn't very well take ship to France and track down the newlyweds.

So she decided to disappear. And the quiet little house in George Court, home to a vicar's daughter and tradeswoman who rarely entertained and a vicar's son who came and went at odd hours around the demands of his noble employer, had been safe.

Until the moment she first brought Joseph Illingworth his tea, and realized her heart, which she had thought scarred to firmness, had become soft again.

Her head must have gone soft too. All this time, while the jewels lay hidden in Priscilla's old work bag, she'd hoped in a childish part of her mind that the whole affair would be forgotten. When she ought to have been aware every moment that Lord Wigsby would be on the hunt. Not for his daughter, whom he surrendered easily, but for that which had more value to him: his pride, and his riches.

"He believes you abetted her escape, and the theft?"

"So it would seem." Inez swallowed hard and felt the iron ring around her throat, the bruising taking effect. It would be hard to eat and drink for a day or three.

But she had gone without food before, when she was younger. And she had survived other bangs and bruises.

"You will be safe in my house," Joseph said firmly.

Inez pushed down a near-hysterical laugh. Safe from what? Not from her own foolishness, certainly. She had tried to pull herself out of that cook fire, and here she was, jumping with both legs back into it.

"His lordship won't find you there," Joseph said, as if he sensed she didn't believe him.

For a moment, as they rode along, Inez tried to imagine it. Tried to imagine living in harmony with him as his maid, passing him in the hall, bleaching his linens, consoling him when he got turned down for a position, congratulating him when he was accepted. Night after night, to watch him absorbed in his book and feel that strange ache that he should be so far away, though there beneath her nose.

Worse, to watch him woo and win another woman, as he had wooed that vapid Susannah Pettigrew. Inez had guessed from the first that the Quaker girl, for all her passionate moral principles, wasn't a girl who knew her own heart. Inez had suspected—as had Joseph's sister—that Miss Pettigrew would cause Joseph heartbreak, and she had.

Could Inez stand by and watch him lose his heart to another, when it would break her own heart to lose him all over again?

He took a different route out of Cheapside, up Snow Hill to Holborn, and Inez distracted herself by observing this part of London that was unknown to her. Her family had taken up lodgings by the docks when they first followed her father to England, after receiving his note that he'd been discharged from his crew and was stranded. She'd hoped, as had her mother, that London would be a new world for them. Such a thriving city, the largest in all of Europe, had to offer opportunities for all three of them.

Instead, London had brought more penury, disappointment, and struggle. What did it matter to live in Europe's grandest city, when one was poor? Inez was never likely to see a theater production on Drury Lane, though she peered down the street as they passed. She could look at these houses but she couldn't imagine what life was like for the grand or rich, those who had no worries about where to find the next day's food, or repair their clothing, or find medicine when their mother was ill.

She had tried, once, to be more than a maid, and that had come to a horrible end. She didn't have the skill to be a tradeswoman, and she had promised her mother she would not become a woman of the street. She would be trapped in other people's houses for the rest of her life, in service to other people's dreams and not her own.

Joseph didn't speak, and at first, his chest against her back was as unyielding as a brick wall. Then, in time, he relaxed and let her relax against him. She grew lulled and drowsy by the heat and the pleasant scent of him, a counterpoint to the foul and varied odors of the streets they passed through.

He rode well, his body in fluid motion with the gait of the horse, and his arm around her, his hand with the ribbons resting on the pommel of the saddle before her, promised he would not let her fall. His body cradled hers, the way hers had cradled his when he pressed her against the wall and kissed her.

She oughtn't dwell on this kiss, particularly with the way the memory and the awareness of him flushed her blood and heated her skin. She was acutely aware of the tops of her breasts, exposed without her neckerchief, freely available to his view.

Was he looking? Did he want her still? What would have happened in Dark Lane if she had pulled him into a room, a room with a soft and available bed, and there had been nothing to stop their desperate seeking?

She had not thought he desired her, and he did. The knowledge lit her like a spill. Anything she touched would take flame.

At the same time, she felt encased by him. Protected. Sheltered, and utterly safe. He had fought for her, freed her from the monster, pried her from the clutches of the man she had feared for more than two years, and now he was taking her to his home, *their* home, and then—

The drowsy, contented feeling evaporated like mist shaken from a cloak. And then what?

He went first to the Blue Posts to return the horse, and her legs wobbled beneath her as Joseph lifted her down in the cobbled courtyard, his hands gripping her waist. His hands with the knuckles bruised and covered with dried blood, as was the side of his head where Wigsby had struck him. She had thought Joseph the mildest of men, a scholar with soft hands and a magnificent mind. And he brawled like a sailor home on shore leave.

There might be so much more she'd never seen in him, never sensed.

She held herself tensely as they walked the short distance down George Court to the house, his lean fingers wrapped around her palm. As if he were holding her so she couldn't bolt. He, too, seemed tense, and he swore to find the latch stood free and the front door opened easily. Anyone could have come in and rifled the place while he was absent, though they would have had a time dealing with Mrs. Frost, and with her sturdy hall boy, were he about.

By the time he tugged her up the stairs, hauling at her arm like a sack of potatoes, Inez realized Joseph wasn't protecting her any longer. He was angry.

Well, so was she.

He half dragged, half shoved her into the narrow room that held her bed and a small washstand. It had once been a dressing room but converted, since Amaranthe, when she had lived here, paid little attention to dressing. Inez stumbled, her shoe catching on the hand-woven rug when he suddenly released her.

His beautiful face was a mask of fury. Much like when he had faced Lord Wigsby, only this time, Inez was the focus of his disdain.

"So that is where you go when you leave me?" His voice was a snarl, but not a shout, as if he had some awareness there were always eyes, and ears, in that house. "You go there to hire out as a whore?"

Inez rubbed her wrist, not because he'd hurt her, but because without his warmth and solid nearness, she felt off balance and cold. His about-face in temper was more disorienting than anything else.

"I was taking work as a maid. Not a Vestal."

"That is a place for whoring. Tamara told me what happens in Dark Lane."

That he didn't know already left an odd spot of tenderness in her heart that made her all the angrier with him. Why couldn't she turn hard, like he did? He had no right to become judgmental when he didn't know anything about her. When he didn't know the promise she'd made and clung to, even when it would have been easier to submit.

He was suddenly quite close, his face dark as he glared down at her. "Is that what Wigsby wanted from you? Is that why he was so angry—because you denied him? Or because you did not?"

"I told you. I stole—he thinks I stole from him."

All of a sudden, facing him, Inez was aware what a sight she must look. Her cap wrinkled and her hair in all directions. Her apron and gown stained with the contents of the spilled tray. She tore free her apron by its strings and threw it on the floor. Who knew how many washings it would take to remove the chocolate stains.

She threw her hands to her hips, heaving for breath. "I am not a whore."

His gaze fell to her breasts, and he stared, riveted as a starving man led before a feast. "But you keep leaving. I never know where you've gone. I never know when you'll be back. And you told me...all those men..."

"Just because they ask doesn't mean I say yes! I made a vow. I haven't been with a man since...since..."

His eyes flew to her face. "Since?"

"Since my husband died," she whispered. The bruise on her throat had turned into a boulder, pressing on her windpipe.

His expression turned pole-axed. "You were married?"

She couldn't stay in her soiled gown any longer. It felt like a heavy net over her skin, a trap. She turned away from him and struggled with the hooks at the front of her gown.

"I was young. Very young. We had not been in England long. My mother was sick, and—and I couldn't bear the trade she had taken up to support us. My father could not find work. There was a rich man, a merchant, who...offered for me. My mother didn't condone it. But my father convinced me to take him."

"Inez. What happened?" Joseph spoke softly as she stepped forward. He laid hands on her shoulders and turned her toward him. His hands were so warm, his touch so gentle as he undid the pins at the front of her gown. She'd never known tenderness from a man.

She pressed her hands over her eyes, unable to look at him while he provided this small, kind service. Unable to think, or feel, anything but the graze of his ungloved hands at her breasts.

"He...died." Best not to say how. She was already like to be hanged as a thief, so why add suspicion of murder to the stew?

"Do you miss him?" He gave her a handful of the straight steel pins, then let his hands fall to his sides. All the anger had soared out of him, leaving him almost wounded. The red bruise on his face was beginning to purple.

Heated from the memory, Inez pulled off her bodice and threw it over the washstand, then untied her petticoat and gave it the same fate. She whirled to face him in only her shift and stays. She kicked off her shoes and curled her stockinged toes into the rug.

She wanted a bath. She wanted to crawl into her bed and hide under the covers and hold her breath until she passed out and she could forget everything.

She wanted Joseph Illingworth to kiss her, and now that he knew she was soiled, he would never kiss her again.

"Miss him?" Her laugh was a strangled bark, like a kicked dog. "It was a blessing when he died." She pointed to her bruised throat. "He was not kind. He never went so far as this, but his passing was a relief to most who knew him."

All of a sudden he stood close before her, not an inch between their bodies, the tips of her breasts grazing his coat. He cradled her face in his hands, his expression haggard, haunted. "Inez. Shh. It's all right now."

She was weeping. When had she begun weeping? She wasn't a watering pot. She *never* cried. Not when she'd buried her mother, not when her father packed and left her without looking back. Not when she'd realized what her husband was, and not when she realized she was free. Yet she stood here, pouring tears before Joseph Illingworth, and he wiped her cheeks with his hands.

"You're safe," he whispered. "No one will hurt you. You will stay here and be safe."

It was her doing, again. She wondered, fleetingly, if it would always be her doing, drawing him into an embrace. But she pulled his head down to hers and he kissed her, and she thought of nothing else.

"Stay here with you?"

He groaned and surrounded her, and she was swept away. He kissed her as if their ride and the press of their bodies and the constant, hot contact had been as much a torment to him as to her. He kissed her as if he had stopped breathing when their mouths parted and only took in air once they connected.

She kissed him back as if she belonged in his arms and knew it.

He wasn't an experienced kisser, but she would teach him. They had time. She cupped her hands around his cheeks, careful not to touch where Wigsby had struck him. He was such a strange and delightful contrast, the soft textures of him and his firm, hot skin. And his raw need fired her own want as nothing else could.

He dragged his hands into her hair, pushing against the pins that held the heavy coils, and she moaned at the press of his fingers against her scalp. His mouth followed hers as she tipped her head back, and she slanted her lips to fit more precisely against his.

Then he broke away, and she gave a little mewling cry. But he didn't pull away, still stood with her arms wrapped around him. His hands cupped her head, thumbs stroking her throat. His eyes were hazy but wide with astonishment, and she stared at the dark ring around his iris, purple-black against the deep shades of brown.

"Inez. You're so beautiful." He sounded astonished, as if he had never realized this before. It was about time he did.

"Touch me," she whispered, pressing herself against him. She looped her fingers around his wrist—so *soft*, his skin—and pulled his hand over her collarbone, down to her breast. She whimpered as his palm immediately closed around her flesh, sensitive and aching.

"Inez. You're—I'm—"

"I want you to kiss me there. *Please.*"

She'd never begged in her life, not for anything. Yet this man reduced her to groveling with no more than a hand on her breast

—a hot, heavy hand delivering a pressure that made her mad and yet soothed at the same time.

He surged against her, as if her request had released something in him, and slid his other arm around her waist to pull her as close as skin. His arousal bloomed against her belly, and she gave a little moan of satisfaction. Oh, yes, he wanted her. He stared at her bosom as if he'd never seen a woman's bare breasts before, and Inez felt warm between her legs at his look of amazement and desire. She wanted to stand here forever in this breath of anticipation, tilted on the brink of a fall into the moment that Joseph Illingworth finally made love to her.

And then she couldn't stand to wait an instant longer.

"Come here." She slid her hands to his jaw and kissed him again, unable to resist the look of wonder and delight and boyish greed on his face. His weight against her made her stagger, and she let herself fall onto her narrow cot, pulling him down atop her.

Yes. This was what she wanted. Had wanted for so long. Joseph Illingworth in her arms, pressed against her body, his weight a shield against the world, promising that nothing could hurt her.

"Inez." He kissed down her face and neck to her breastbone, then dragged his lips across the tops of her breasts. The groan from him was raw need. She lifted her hips, pressing shamelessly into him, greedy for the evidence of his desire. His need for her.

"Yes." She tugged down the drawstring bodice of her shift and at last his mouth moved where she wanted it, that hot, delicious mouth on her breast. Kissing the curve of her cautiously, reverently, as if he couldn't believe the delights he'd been offered. As if he worshipped at a holy shrine.

Then he cupped a hand around one globe and pulled her nipple into his mouth, and Inez nearly screamed with pleasure.

"Yes. *Yes.*"

She dragged her hands along every inch of him that she could reach. Plunged her fingers into his soft hair, coating her fingers with the powder he'd applied for his interview that morning. It seemed an eon away; the world had shifted in the meantime. A new epoch of her life had begun, one where she was with Joseph Illingworth and he kissed and licked and nipped at her breasts, feasting like a man at a banquet, and she lay there panting and simmering with pleasure, need heating like an iron rod at her core.

She scraped her fingers over the hard curve of his back, the coat too thick to give her a proper sense of him. She slid her hands down his sides to his waist, plucking his shirt free from the waistband of his breeches. She needed her hands on him. She needed him to never stop what he was doing to her breasts, nibbling and sucking and swirling his tongue around her nipples, which pulled a thread at her center into a taut, burning ache.

But she needed to touch him. Her hand brushed his arousal as she fumbled with the buttons, and his entire body froze like a hound pointing. She cupped his cock within her hand, cradling him through the fabric, and he gave a small, strangled gasp.

His response emboldened her. She freed a button and slipped her hand inside his breeches. He was wearing drawers of soft, worn linen, but warm bare flesh had pushed through the opening. His cock lengthened in her hand as she slid her fingers around the silken skin, and she laughed, a rich, throaty chuckle, at the look of profound astonishment on his face.

"My God," he rasped. "Inez..."

She wriggled. She would get to have him inside of her. She would be joined to him, completely and entirely his. She wasn't afraid. She didn't dread him as she had the times with her husband. Her body felt warm and open and ready for him, drenched with longing. A little mewl of pleasure escaped her as she stroked her hand along him, eager to have him inside of her.

"*Inez.*" His body trembled as he held himself frozen above her, every muscle taut and straining, as if the entire focus of his attention had moved to her hand. *Men.* He was so strong and arrogant, and had been so fierce when he fought Wigsby—even now the memory of his swift, brutal blows made her lower parts quiver and ache for him. But take his cock in her hand, and he was completely at her mercy, hers to command. She could lead him as on a string.

She kissed him, overcome with tenderness all of a sudden, touched by his complete surrender. But he panted, almost as if in distress, and dropped his forehead to her shoulder. His back arched, tensing.

"Inez...I..." His breath blew over one nipple, already sensitized from his kisses, and she squeezed in reflex, urging him toward her.

His body spasmed from head to toe, one great tremor, and then he was spilling over her hand, his seed warm and soft as the rest of him.

"Oh, God." He gave an embarrassed moan.

Inez smiled and kissed his hair as she withdrew her hand from his breeches. He'd wanted her so much he couldn't hold. She considered it a compliment, and a sign that it had been a while since he had sought relief with a woman. He didn't go about swiving just any maid; she was special.

And while her husband had always withdrawn to his own bed when he was finished, she knew from overhearing her mother's guests that some men could be ready again quite quickly. They had plenty of time.

Suddenly he pulled away, leaping off the bed like he'd been shot, then backing across the room. His eyes were wide with anguish.

"I'm sorry. I'm very sorry."

"It's all right." She wiped her hand on her shift, leaning up on one elbow. "Come back."

"I can't. I should never have touched you."

"What?"

He fumbled with his breeches, rebuttoning them swiftly and shoving in his shirt, then tugging down his coat. Fully dressed in an instant, as if their embrace had never happened.

A wave of cold horror fell over her. Inez yanked up her shift to cover her breasts and climbed to her feet, her stockinged feet sliding against the rug.

"What do you mean?"

She'd begged him to touch her. She'd welcomed him. She was his, his completely. Didn't he understand that?"

"I'm leaving," he blurted.

"No," she whispered. "Don't leave now. Stay with me."

"I meant—I am leaving this house. Leaving London."

She felt Wigsby choking her all over again. "Because—because of me?"

"No. No. I...my cousin...there's an estate...I have to go." He drew in a steadying breath, and his eyes shifted away, as if he couldn't look at her.

"There's a family estate in Cornwall. Which is mine now. I am going to look after things. You can stay here. As long as you want. It will be safe for you."

"When will you be back?" she whispered. He would kiss and her leave. He could do that. Their embrace had meant nothing to him.

His gaze met hers briefly and pulled away again, like he'd touched his hand to a fire. "I don't know."

"Take me with." She stepped toward him, buoyed on a tide of something fierce and angry. He couldn't leave her. He'd finally come for her. He'd finally *seen* her. "I want to go with you."

"You cannot."

"I can. You can bring me."

"I cannot. Inez. You cannot travel with me alone, and I can't afford to pay for a chaperone. Besides, what would you do there?"

Be his. Be with him. She couldn't think through the whole of it; her mind felt like a wet blanket had been tossed over her head, suffocating.

"I wouldn't be any trouble," she whispered, and the humiliation of begging made her eyes burn. Why could she never keep her dignity around him?

"Inez." His face softened, the austere lines smoothed with an expression of gentleness. Pity? She abhorred pity. She refused to be pitied.

"I cannot..."

"Cannot what?"

She was always the one being left. What was it about her that made people leave? Her mother had wasted away, if not by her choice. Her father had gone East without a glance behind. The home Inez had found here with Amaranthe and Eyde and the others had vanished when they all picked up and merrily moved to Hunsdon House, leaving her behind.

She'd been turned out, or forced out, of every position of service. Even her marriage had been an abandonment, as if she didn't deserve tender cherishing like another woman would. And now Joseph was simply going to leave her here, like she was a wardrobe or part of the furniture, as if he'd never kissed her like a desperate man, as if he hadn't desired her so much he couldn't contain himself. Why did she always mean *nothing*?

He spread his hands wide and raked them through his hair.

Powder shook free, and the tousling made him more adorable, not less. She hated his beauty. Hated him.

"You are making this very difficult for me."

"I'm difficult? I am?" The rage filled and lifted her like the cooler current that would well up around Sagres in the warmest months of summer, the cold water always a shock against the heat. She was the easiest of women. She never asked anything. She never demanded. She never forced her own way. Perhaps that was why she was so easy to leave.

She curled her hands into fists and stalked towards him, her feet shuffling across the carpet. "I am not making this difficult. You are. You are the one who is difficult."

She was appalled to realize she had raised her fists and was hitting him on the chest. The blows had almost no effect on him, her blows not strong enough to force their way through cloth and muscle, but she swung at him nevertheless, wild with hurt.

"You have been an *idiot*—a dull, unthinking—" What was the worst insult she could deal a man like him? "*Clodpate*," she cried. "Rocks in your head. You—are—so—*infuriating*. And so dim, you never *see*—"

He captured her fists in his hands and she realized her blows were like grasshoppers landing, the merest brush, and so easily brushed away. "Inez. I am indeed sorry if I have hurt you. In any fashion."

As if he had *done* something. It was what he *hadn't* done that was making her mad. She wanted to shake him. She wanted to push him down. She wanted to slap him out of his self-absorption, his complete assurance that the world ran one way, his complete obliviousness to everything else around him.

She wanted to be impossible to leave.

"Just go." She pushed him toward the door, and he went. He was fully dressed after all. Still wearing his boots.

That put her over the edge into a raw, keening fury. He'd

fallen into bed with her, kissed her breasts as if he'd never seen breasts before, spent in her hand as if he were a green lad pushed past his limits of endurance, and the whole time, he'd been wearing his boots.

"I don't need you." She shouted in his face and was gratified to see his eyes flare with brief surprise, then hurt. Good. One of her blows had finally landed.

It brought no satisfaction. "I don't want you," she lied. "Go." She pushed him over the threshold into the short, narrow hallway at the top of the stairs. "Go, and don't come back."

She gave into the impulse to slam the door in his face. It crashed shut with a smack, but there was no satisfaction.

He was going, and he wouldn't come back. Not for her. Inez put her hands to her face and for the first time in years—for the first time in memory—she sank to the floor in her shift and stockings and cried till the tears ran dry.

CHAPTER SEVEN

Joseph was thirteen, and his sister was a pest.

He'd been at his Latin homework for hours, and he wanted to be outside. The bitter cold that had clutched the countryside from Christmas to the end of January had at last broken, and it would be pleasant to go out of doors. They'd had a day of snow that hadn't completely melted, and Joseph was far more interested in what Prudence Lovedy might be doing than he was interested in his lessons. Prudence's parents worked at Rosecraddoc Manor, and Prudence had long hair the color of ripe wheat and, as of a few months ago, breasts swelling the front of her prim wool gown.

"Stell*am* is the declension for the accusative case, if it's singular."

Amaranthe, as usual, was looking at Joseph's work while she copied over pages of the manuscript their father was working on. At ten years of age she already had a neat, steady hand, transforming their father's crossed and crumpled pages into tidy script, and she'd been correcting Joseph's work since she was six. She was entirely exasperating.

"And stell*arum* for the plural gentitive," she added. "Since it is an *a*-stem declension."

"I know that." In trying to hide his paper from her scrutiny, he smeared the fresh ink. Joseph clenched his teeth. "Don't you have your own work to concern you?"

"Papa's book on folklore and ancient monuments." She nodded. "It's coming along nicely. He has such exciting ideas, Joseph. He's at the chapter speculating that the Lady of the Lake of the Arthurian stories lived by Dozmary Pool, up by—"

"I know where it is. Thanks to Papa, I know every stone circle, carn, and fougou within fifty kilometers of St. Cleer. There's not a thing you can tell me about The Hurlers, the Cheesewring, or Trethevy Quoit."

With a yank, Joseph pulled a sheet of paper toward him and began a fresh list of declensions. Amaranthe scowled at him but shut her mouth on the protest. Paper being expensive, Joseph was supposed to use his sheets to the very margins, then turn them sidewise and write across the existing text when he could. Amaranthe got the fresh paper because she was making a neat copy of his work that Papa could share with other folklore enthusiasts and from them gain stories to add to his compendium of Cornish history, which he meant to be comprehensive.

Amaranthe always got the better things because she was the baby, because she was the girl, and Joseph, older and more experienced, was expected to concede her everything. The older she grew, the nosier she became, until he had nothing of his own any longer.

He sharpened his pen with too much force and growled when he broke the nib of the quill.

He pushed away from the table, the legs of his ladderback chair screeching along the wooden floor of the parlor. "I'm going outside."

Immediately Amaranthe set down her pen, though he knew she loved writing more than anything else except saffron cakes. "Me too."

"God's hooks, Anth, do you have to do everything I do?"

Her eyes widened and she pressed her mouth into a solemn line. "You're not supposed to swear."

"God's wounds, you're a numpty. God's teeth, I wish you wouldn't clack at me all of the time."

"I'm telling Mam." She hurried after him as he strode into the narrow hallway and grabbed the greatcoat and a wool cap hanging on their pegs. There was a jacket that his father wore when working around the yard, but Joseph couldn't take the chance that Prudence Lovedy might see him in the attire of a sailor or common laborer.

Amaranthe struggled to tie the strings of her cloak and find a cap to cover her thick pile of curls. She wouldn't tattle on him, or at least, not at this moment. Mam was in the kitchen helping Cook, and if Amaranthe pulled her aside for stories, she might delay the hot dinner that would be waiting when they returned. Also, Mam would insist Joseph explain himself, and that might ruin the outing for both of them.

"Joseph! Wait. Where are we going?"

"*I* am going to the Well. You can go to Hades."

"Joseph!"

He knew he was being unkind, but he couldn't seem to tame the irritation that soared up within him so quickly of late. He felt hot and itchy under his skin, and his limbs ached in the bones. He'd outgrown all his clothes in a month's time and had to wait while his mother replaced them piece by piece, weaving and knitting and making what she could, buying what she could not.

Walter Robings of Rosecraddoc Manor had a new suit every time he came to service at St. Clarus, with rows of shiny buttons at his hems and cuffs, the like which Joseph would never possess. Prudence Lovedy thought Walter cut a marvelous figure, and she didn't know Joseph existed.

He set up off Well Lane, skirting the cemetery, the quiet peace of which always accused him for being too quick to anger, unlike his father, who rarely riled at anything. His father was the son of a baronet, for heaven's sake, and there was no one so high hereabouts; not even the Robings of Rosecraddoc could claim titles among their relations. But instead of making something of himself, his scholarly father was content to be vicar of the rural and quiet St. Clarus, which could boast less than a thousand souls within the parish.

Callington, where his uncle the baronet lived on his estate of Penwellen, was not all that much larger, but was situated on a road that went somewhere. The village of St. Cleer perched on the edge of the vast rough outcropping that was Bodwin Moor, inhabited by nothing but rocks and sheep.

If his uncle cared, Joseph could be living in the grand house of Penwellen with Reuben and taking lessons with a real tutor rather than a down-at-heels friend of his father's who had made even less of himself since Oxford than Joseph's father had. Joseph could be wearing velvet coats like his cousin, Reuben, and sitting down to dinners in fine parlors decorated with hand-painted paper and furniture bought from London warehouses. He could be learning the manners of a gentleman and losing the bits of Cornish dialect that crept into his speech.

He would be free of his pestilent sister, whose quick mind and quiet studiousness was applauded by their father and whose tidy, demure manner was lauded by all the women of the parish as being a credit to her mother, which made Amaranthe glow with smug pride.

"Why'd you want to see the old Well anyway?" Amaranthe panted, catching up as Joseph paused before the granite enclosure housing the spring that flowed with its sacred bounty year round. A fine sheen of ice covered the contents of the basin where visitors were known to dip hands, heads, or ailing parts of their body for which they sought a cure. In medieval times, it was said, the well had been used as a ducking pool to try to shock sense back into the witless, or douse the evil in a witch.

In a carved niche at the back of the porch with its medieval arched columns and vaulted roof stood the stubby statue of St. Clarus, who had come to preach the true religion and built the ancient church over which Joseph's father presided. Legend ran that a local chieftainess had been so ardently enflamed by Clarus's cause that she attempted to compel him to break his vow of celibacy to marry her, and when he refused and fled her advances, she had him hunted down and murdered.

Joseph could not imagine Prudence Lovedy becoming so impassioned she hunted down anyone. However, he could, and frequently did, imagine her giving Joseph license to touch her breasts and perhaps even kiss her.

"I'm at the well to make a wish, you ninny," Joseph said with irritation. "A wish that you'd go away and give me a moment of peace."

Amaranthe took off her mitten and dipped her fingers into the cold, clear water of the well. "I hope Miss Rebecca's cough goes away," she said, naming one of the spinster sisters who lived on a farm nearby and who, after their brother's death, subsisted mostly on the kindness of strangers who helped them reap the wheat that could pay their tithe, dropped gifts of food at their doorstep, and, in the case of Joseph's mother, brewed her special remedies whenever one or another of the sisters took ill, which it seemed they were always doing.

Amaranthe had been allowed that summer to help their mother collect honey from the beehives in their small garden, and it was just like Amaranthe to use her wish for the benefit of the coughing elder for whom she'd been making honey drops all winter and not for the benefit of herself. Joseph felt he would burst from the aggravation.

"We can't cross Diggory's Field!" Amaranthe called as he cut east with angry strides. "You'll anger the rams."

"I'm not crossing Diggory's Field," Joseph tossed over his shoulder. He knew that Mrs. Lovedy frequently visited Rowan Cottage in Tremar Coombe, and he could take the much-used Well Lane to circle about, or he could take a shortcut through the Penhale farm and possibly discourage Amaranthe enough that she would go home. The shorn fields and hedges lay tucked under a white brim of frost, and his boots left satisfying prints as he strode along, as if he were finally leaving a mark on something. It felt overdue.

He forgot, and so did Amaranthe, that the Penhales had recently found china clay on their land and had constructed a clay pit nearby, which was used to separate the richer deposits from the mud by suspending them in water. Jocko Penhale thought it would be great fun to keep the pond and stock it with ruffe and loach, and provide the family with stargazy pie the year round.

With the hard freeze and the gentle snow that followed, the landscape looked like any other piece of land bitten off the edge of rocky Bodwin Moor and tortured into something arable. For all he knew, Joseph weakened the sheet of ice over the new-made pond when he stormed across it.

So when Amaranthe crossed in his wake, stepping where he had stepped so as not to soil her new boots, a thunderous crack rang out.

There wasn't much of a rise for it to echo from; the church and cemetery and consequently the vicarage lay on slightly higher ground, and the land sloped gently down from the Holy Well to Tremar Coombe, which meant the frozen top of the Penhale's pond had begun to soften with the warming days.

And with Amaranthe standing upon it, the thin crust of ice gave way. Joseph turned to face one frozen moment where his sister stared at him, her eyes round as guineas, and then she simply slid from view as if the trapdoor to the hanging scaffold had swung open beneath her.

"Joseph!"

Her cry would echo in his ears for days. The shriek of his name, reproaching him for putting her in harm's way.

A mittened hand emerged from the dark hole that had swallowed her, and then her head broke the surface. He'd be haunted ever after by the expression on her face, white and terrified and, he was sure, accusatory. He felt the crush of ice giving way, an odd softening beneath his feet as he crossed the smooth stretch that he now realized must be frozen water, hidden under a dusting of snow.

But frozen no longer. A musical cascade of cracks sang in tune, and spider webs appeared in the snow.

Joseph reacted out of instinct and threw himself onto his belly. Snow tipped down the collar of his waistcoat and the tops of his boots. Anth's damp wool mitten slid across his leather gloves as he reached for her. He clamped onto her wrists with both hands.

"Climb out."

"I can't." She wriggled, her feet fruitlessly kicking through the cold water. She began to sink. "It's too deep. Pull me out."

He wasn't strong enough. He didn't have the leverage. There was no way to brace his feet for purchase, and nothing to hold against so he could take her weight.

He stared into his sister's face, her pale red lips edged with blue, her eyes dark pools ringed with violet. He could not lose her.

He could not be the reason she was hurt.

God, give me strength, he prayed, and said, calmly, "Three. Two. *One*."

She lunged, and he heaved. It must be that angels helped him, given the weight of her sodden wool coat and dress. But there was Amaranthe, gasping, on the ice beside him, rolled in snow that clung to her like a glaze of powdered sugar.

"The ice is c-c-cracking," she observed through chattering teeth.

They crawled toward shore like spider crabs on the summer sand, hauling themselves forward by their elbows until tufts of grass poked through the snow, the stiff blades ticking Joseph's wrists. His mind was blank with stupefaction, his body a mechanical toy as he tugged her home. He didn't know how he was to explain himself to his parents. He was supposed to look out for his sister, and he'd been too busy brooding and fretting and biting himself over all the things he didn't have, he nearly lost one of the most important things that he did.

"*Aree fah*, what is gone with the cheldern?" Cook cried when Joseph gave a soggy knock on the kitchen door. His damp gloves had frozen in the shape of hands and he couldn't feel his feet. He'd pulled Amaranthe under his arm and wrapped his great coat about them both, and beneath it he could feel the shudders that racked her body.

Pulling her from the water had only been the first step, he realized. Now the goal was to keep the icy water from freezing her blood and bones.

"P-p-penhale," he managed.

"I knowed it! I knowed they'd let the pullan frizz over and not put a quoit up to mark ee." Cook pulled the kettle over the fire and sent the maid running to fetch water from the scullery. "Get those sloshy things off ee both, then, dreckly."

His mother's face had resembled Amaranthe's, stiff and

bloodless, until she managed to unwind the sodden cloak and saw her daughter was intact. She whisked off Amaranthe's mittens and rubbed her pale fingertips between her hands, then pressed Amaranthe's fingers to the back of her neck as she knelt to unlace her boots. Joseph kicked at his own boots, heavy stones clumped around his feet, feeling the heat of the kitchen like a bite on his skin.

"What happened?" Bracha Illingworth was not a demonstrative woman, not prone to frights or frenzies. She was as steady and sure as the flow of water in the St. Cleer Well, a fit companion to their father, who was a solid and dependable as King Doniert's Stone. But when she lifted her gaze to meet Joseph's eyes, he saw the depth of her fear.

"She f-fell in the clay pit. The ice broke. I pulled her out."

"Bells of St. Mary. You could have both fallen in."

Joseph was afraid, as his mother's eyes searched his, that she saw what had happened in his face, as if she were a bird that had watched from above. Surely she could see his guilt. How he had been responsible. He had marched across the frozen pond, not thinking about the terrain because he was thinking of Prudence Lovedy's bosom and whether it would show beneath her winter cloak, or if she'd set her cloak aside to visit at Rowan Cottage. His mother would see that Joseph had tried to outrun Amaranthe—had wanted to lose her—and had almost lost her entirely.

She would see what a weak, selfish creature he was, no better than Reuben after all.

"Cheel *vean.*" His mother rose and pulled both her children to her, her arms wrapping him in a cloud of warmth. She smelled like cooking spice and mead, every warm and delicious thing. Amaranthe burrowed into her, pressing her nose into the crook of her mother's arm.

Their mother didn't use the Cornish dialect often, as her

own family had worked hard to appear English when they emigrated from Portugal years earlier. But she spent more time with Cook and the working women of her parish than she did calling on the fancy ladies with their English ways, and the Kernow slipped out every now and again.

"Ah, cheel *vean*." She rocked them both against her, murmuring in a language her ancestors had left in a long ago place, in a long ago time, and Joseph knew it was a prayer of gratitude.

Amaranthe regarded him with wide, solemn eyes. "I s-s-spose I'd be b-blessed for life if I'd only f-fallen in the h-holy w-w-well," she managed to say around chattering teeth.

Their mother laughed, and so did Cook, and Joseph heard the relief and the fierce determination behind it. He didn't deserve to be held or forgiven.

He learned his lesson that day. He had set his own selfish desires above someone who needed him, and it had almost cost all of their lives.

And here he was, doing the same all over again, Joseph thought as he watched his trunk be strapped to the basket behind the stagecoach. There was a fine, misty drizzle in the morning air—a mizzle, they'd call it in Cornwall—and already he missed the cheerful fire in the common room of the Coach and Horses.

Inez would be safe in her bed in George Court, and Mrs. Frost would be cooking her a warm porridge, more of the same breakfast she'd made for Joseph in the wee hours that morning.

It was callous and craven of him to sneak away from his house like a thief in the night, all because he couldn't bear for a set of large, deep brown eyes to reproach him from their bed of ridiculously thick lashes and dewy skin. All because he knew that if those luscious lips of hers turned down in a pout, he'd be tempted to kiss her hurt away, and if he began to kiss her, he'd never leave.

For a moment his muddled brain circled that thought. What if he stayed? What if he stayed in his house with Inez, to ensure she was safe from Wigsby and anyone else who wanted to hurt her. What if he simply sent word to his Callington solicitor to make the necessary arrangements regarding Penwellen and forward the quarterly incomes to Joseph's bank?

Because, he reminded himself, taking a bracing breath of damp air, Inez wasn't his to keep. She was a beautiful, wounded distraction, but she wasn't his. She'd made that clear all the times she'd run away. She used him for shelter when she needed, and she was done with him the moment something else took her fancy. This was better: she could take refuge at his house, and he wouldn't have to endure the rejection when some-thing—or someone—else lured her away.

And there was the small matter of his needing to attend in person to whatever mess Reuben had left behind. If what Amaranthe had seen on her previous visit was any indication, Penwellen, and Reuben, had been falling into a derelict state. There would be repairs. There would, no doubt, be apologies to render. It was highly likely that Eyde, and Amaranthe, were not the only people Reuben had wounded in his tenure as the baronet.

The passengers on the top of the stagecoach had already loaded by the time the interior passengers began to seat them-selves. One woman held a chicken in a cage. Joseph didn't doubt they would be subject to its squawking for hours, if not the day. The roof was packed with people who had chosen to pay the lesser fare, and Joseph could have sworn that one young man, sitting next to the woman with the chicken, shrank from his gaze as he scanned the group. None of his business why a youth might not wish to be noticed.

None of his business what Inez would find to occupy herself while he was gone. No one here in London needed him. Mrs. Frost would look after the house, and Amaranthe was ensconced in Hunsdon House with a duke and the best medical care London could offer to watch over her lying-in. She'd send Joseph word when the babe was born, and he'd send a gift for his new niece or nephew.

There was no one else waiting for him, there or here. He firmed his grip on his valise and stepped inside the coach, climbing over boots, knees, and the voluminous skirts and coats of passengers to claim the narrow slot on the hard wooden seat that he had paid for.

Once again, he was leaving.

He'd left his parents at every opportunity in his youth, staying with Walter Robings at Rosecraddoc for weeks on end, though Joseph had a perfectly good home of his own. But Walter lived in a manor house and had a footman to wait at table, and when Walter wanted a bun and a drink before bed, after dinner had been cleared away, he wasn't told he must wait until morning. Instead, a maidservant brought a tray and there was hot cider or warmed milk or even a cup of small ale, along with a bun and, very often, butter and preserves to spread upon it.

Joseph had left Amaranthe at Penwellen after their parents died, taking his position at Oxford and leaving his sister to their domineering, temperamental cousin and his nervous wife. He'd told himself Amaranthe simply had to buck up and accept the change in circumstances, as they all did.

But the hole in his heart was guilt as the coachman cracked the whip and the horses jerked the coach into motion. The hardest leaving was this one—departing from Inez with only that last kiss goodbye.

CHAPTER EIGHT

Three hours later, when they descended at the Nag's Head in Hounslow, Joseph's back was stiff, his legs were sore, and his arse ached from jouncing along the road. And this was the well-traveled Great Western Road, one of the busiest routes in England, with coaches flying past them at regular intervals and a steady flow of wheeled traffic keeping the road smooth. He remembered what the roads were like in Cornwall and shuddered to think of his fate two days hence.

Hounslow, the first coaching stop out of London for those heading to any points west, was where the Bath Road and the Exeter Road parted ways, and so the inn was crowded. Joseph stretched his aching shoulders and stomped his feet to get the blood flowing through his legs as he stepped inside the common room. There wasn't enough time to visit a real pub and have a decent meal; the coach would pause only long enough to change horses, and then it would be another rocky three hours to Staines. And a full day of this, and then another, and then another.

His mind wandered, as it did every unguarded moment, to

Inez. He wondered what she had felt when she woke in the morning to find him gone. Satisfaction? Freedom? Relief?

Would she miss him at all as she returned to her life? She was a young and beautiful woman. She would be safe in his house. If the incomes from Penwellen allowed, he would send money to support her so that she didn't have to work. She could be a lady of leisure, like Amaranthe was now, making calls and taking on causes and letting herself be seen in all the fashionable places.

Perhaps she would be courted. Perhaps she would find a husband—another husband—who would take her to his bed and worship her as she deserved.

He must not think of Inez's mouth when she'd kissed him, the way she tasted of black currants. He must not think about the softness of her breasts in his mouth, the ripe full curves and the way she gasped when he sucked and nibbled on her nipples. He *must not* think of her hand on his cock, the way she'd grasped him with a touch delicate and firm at the same time, and stroked him to a pleasure that made his eyes roll back in his head and made his bones feel hollow.

No, he must not think of Inez's hands on him, because he'd have a cockstand all the way to Basingstoke, and such things were difficult to overlook when eight adults were crammed into an interior designed for six. At least he was indoors and protected from the rain, unlike the second-class passengers traveling in the basket with the luggage, or the poor souls on the roof. He wondered how the chicken was faring when he saw its owner deposit the animal on a table, where it gave a bedraggled squawk.

His neck prickled. Someone was watching him. Perhaps one of the infamous highwaymen who haunted Hounslow Heath, taking his next mark. Though Joseph wasn't the most well-heeled man in the room, nor the ripest plum for picking. That designation went to the large gentleman in the expensive suit who was inserting himself among the passengers from the roof who were huddled near the fire.

One in particular had caught the large gentleman's eye—the same lad that Joseph had spotted sitting next to the chicken. The one who'd seemed to shrink from his gaze when Joseph scanned the passengers. No doubt a boy running away from his tutor, or an apprentice running away from his master, or perhaps a boy with ambitions to travel all the way to Falmouth and take a ship for points west and find his fortune on the high seas.

Another prickle passed over Joseph's neck. The runaway wore a leather working man's jacket that looked familiar. A wool cap caught up his dark hair, but beneath the floppy brim showed glimpses of warm brown skin. He had a delicate neck and smooth jaw, in the way of some boys who never did become rough-hewed men, and a furtive manner, in the way of boys hiding a secret.

He also trembled, as if afraid, or cold, or wary of the large gentleman, who insisted on buying the lad a pint of the horse piss the innkeeper was distributing for ale. The large gentleman, sporting shiny rows of buttons on his velvet coat and stark white lace at his sleeves, said something in a deep growl to the boy, who shook his head and moved away.

He wouldn't be able to do anything even if he did intervene, Joseph told himself. Any more than he'd been able to stop Reuben striking his hound all those years ago, or Reuben menacing his own housemaid and then his niece, or Amaranthe falling through the ice.

But he'd stopped Wigsby from tormenting Inez, he remembered with the twist in his gut that came with every thought of Inez. The woman he'd rescued and then betrayed. It wasn't like he could rescue her again if he protected this boy. It wasn't like he, Joseph Illingworth, could stand alone against all the injustice in the world.

But as he worked his way down the bar he saw the large gentleman sidling his bulk toward the boy, who sidled away as far as he could go without tipping over the blacksmith on the stool beside him. Saw the gentleman reach toward the boy's waist and, when the boy moved his hand between them, saw the fat fingers in their expensive gloves wrap around the boy's slender wrist.

The boy's ineffectual push said everything, as did the large man's leer.

"Is this yours?" Joseph tapped the larger man on the shoulder.

"Ey?" The other had an overfed, jowly look to him, narrow eyes blinking as he swung his gaze around. "Wot's that?"

"This yours." Joseph pointed his thumb in the direction of the boy.

"No," the boy said quickly, his voice a high yelp. He quickly adjusted his tone to a lower register. "No."

"Then he'd best let you go," Joseph advised.

Like most bullies, the gentleman looked frankly surprised to be challenged. Then, after a slow interval, annoyance registered. He shook the boy— who wasn't a boy—with his meaty hand. "I'll do what I like."

"Oh, for the love of St. Agnes." Joseph drew back his fist, giving the man plenty of time to correct his error. The other only blinked, slow rage suffusing his face. He'd barely begun the snarl when Joseph's fist crashed into it.

"Hell in a hand basket," Joseph swore, shaking out his hand. His knuckles were still bruised from Wigsby's face.

The giant crashed into the bar and flailed like a beached whale, sending tankards and glasses crashing and ale spilling every which way. Joseph turned to the freed captive.

"This is getting tiresome," he said. "Having to rescue you."

Her eyes flared wide with surprise, and she clapped both hands to the brim of her hat. "How did you know?"

He put a hand on her upper arm and drew her away from where the giant was slowly lumbering to his feet.

"Because that is a terrible disguise," he said. "How long did you think you could keep it up?"

His voice was harsher than he intended, temper getting the best of him as it always seemed to do around her. He wasn't about to tell her he knew when she was in a room because the very air changed. He knew her tread on the wooden floor of his house and could tell if her tray held a full pot of coffee or bread and butter for tea.

He knew her scent because it had been branded on his senses. He'd known her by her intake of breath when the brute grabbed her, that little gasp she made when she was surprised.

By now the gentleman had recovered command of himself and arranged his bulk on his feet. His piggy face screwed into the rage of vengeance. "I'll have you arrested," he shouted. Spittle flew from his mouth. "I'll have you hung! Who do you think you are?"

A silence prevailed, since every gaze in the room was fixed on the altercation, including that of the innkeep, who clutched a wad of wet cloth against his apron. A new voice carried across the room.

"Sir Joseph Illingworth," the voice said with command. "I'm looking for the baronet."

"Yes." Joseph turned with a sigh. "Can it wait?" He swung a hand in the air between him and the man who had assailed Inez, who was seemingly choking for air. "We're just finishing up here."

"Don't think a title can protect you," his opponent whined. "I'll call the constable. I'll have the watch—"

"You're the baronet?" said the man at the door. "The one as is brother to the Duchess of Hunsdon?"

The piggy face of his opponent paled to pink. He held out his hands.

"I didn't touch 'im. I didn't say nuthin' to 'im. It was an accident. A misunderstanding."

"Her," Joseph snapped. "Did you even know you were propositioning a woman?"

The florid face of his opponent paled further. "I—what? Your woman, see? Swear to me mother's rib I didn't touch 'er. Now, no 'arm done, is there?"

"If you pay for the broken glassware, there won't be," Joseph said pleasantly, flexing his bruised hand. The man complied, all too aware that if Joseph made accusations that he had propositioned a boy, the tone of the quarrel would go in a far different direction.

Joseph recognized the man at the door. He was small in stature, the wiry stretch of his upper body out of proportion to the crooked legs propped between two wooden crutches. He wore the saffron breeches and brick-red coat of the Hunsdon livery with, incongruously, a pair of well-worn leather gloves.

"I thought you were in the service of the Earl of Renwick," Joseph said as he neared the newcomer.

He'd seen this groom many times accompanying the Earl's wife, who was the duchess of some obscure Continental duchy and also a school chum of Amaranthe's. Apparently the two duchesses had wed and birthed babies around the same time, and this, along with the sudden social elevation experienced by both, had cemented their reliance on one another.

"'Ad to leave Renwick House of a sudden. Took a job for yer sister. Name's Jock." The groom flicked the brim of his cocked hat. "Duchess sent me t'tell you she's arranged a post chaise and horses. Knew you'd be too cheap to stand the expense yerself."

"Henry Jock." Inez stared at the man as if he were a map to buried treasure. "My father bet on you every time."

The man's face twisted. "Not th' last time, I hope."

Inez spotted Joseph's puzzled expression. "They called him the King of Newmarket, he won the prize plate so many times. My father wept when he read of your accident."

"What happened?" asked Joseph, who was only vaguely aware that Newmarket was a place to do with horses and racing, activities he couldn't afford and had no interest in.

"Lost," Jock said briefly. "The rig's in the stableyard, horses fresh. We can leave when you wish. Change at the usual posting stops, but she said I'm to take you the whole way through."

Amaranthe again, ruling his life as if he were part of her duchessing duties. Trying to manage him as she had from the age of six. Joseph looked from Jock to Inez to the door to the stableyard, a blur of movement and noise.

He focused his gaze on the woman. The disguise wouldn't have held for an instant if he'd seen her face earlier. No other woman had that gracious slope to her nose, that luscious lilt of cheekbone, those pillowy lips. No other woman—well, very few —would be so daft and determined to plague him.

"When?" he asked. "Were you there before me?"

"Followed you." She pulled her hat brim closer around her face, aware of the many curious stares upon them. "I didn't know quite where you were going."

"And where is your luggage?"

With a sullen hunch to her shoulders, she pulled her ragged work bag across her body. He ached to see how little she had in the world to call her own.

Nevertheless she met his gaze with a defiant lilt to her chin. He couldn't meet her eyes and the longing laid bare as she searched his face for signs of softening. He steeled himself against any. He had to do what was best for her, whether she agreed with him or not.

"How far did you pay your fare?"

"To Basingstoke."

Likely she didn't have coin to go further. She would have been hoping to throw herself on his mercy and hope he could provide for her.

And he couldn't. He barely had coin enough for his own fare and lodging. Taking coins from his very slender purse would mean a missed lunch or three, relying on the hope there were kitchens in Penwellen and servants to staff them. Nevertheless, he was responsible for her, and besides, a man had his pride. Joseph dug out his purse and tipped out two crowns.

"Here."

Cautiously, she took the money and slipped it inside her jacket, which was his jacket, an old piece of rubbish he'd kept from boyhood. The leather held memories of rare afternoons hunting with his father and days dispersed about the parish at various labors that parishioners were supposed to furnish for their tithes and which his father always oversaw, nay, participated in. His clothes on her lissome frame—for he recognized the scraps from the bottom of his wardrobe, though where she found those awful boots, he wasn't about to ask. His coin was in her pocket, and Amaranthe's groom was here to take her wherever she wished. Joseph stepped back.

Why couldn't he keep her? Remembered sensation fogged his brain. The silken slide of her skin, warm and soft. The heated curve of her body shaping to his, like the twine of honeysuckle. Pleasure keeling him over like a hammer to the gut, an ecstasy he'd never known but suspected he would feel every time, with her.

Because her friends and her life were all in London, and he

couldn't uproot her to the rocky moors of Cornwall for his pleasure alone.

Because he was Joseph Illingworth, born the son of a poor vicar and a foreign-born woman, and he wasn't granted what other men were granted, the most banal and ordinary of dreams.

Because he had no sure place in the world to offer her, not yet.

Joseph swung his gaze to the groom, who was far less disturbing to his steadiness of mind than her dark, bottomless, seeking eyes.

"My trunk is on the stagecoach, and I'll be going with it," he said gruffly. "Take her back to George Court, if she wants, and to Hunsdon House, if she doesn't." He risked a glance at Inez. "Amaranthe can help you."

"And you won't." She held herself carefully still, her voice flat, but the knuckles of her fingers suggested she had a death grip on her bag.

"This is the best way. Go."

She lifted her chin. "Not even a goodbye. Sneaking off without a word. Like a thief who has stolen something."

"Doing my duty, as I must." He scowled. The urge to reach for her was nearly unbearable. The urge to pull her to his side and hold her there. Keep her, as if she belonged to him.

As if she might ever see anything in him that would make her want to stay.

"Fare thee well," he said, then nodded to Jock and strode toward the stagecoach, hauling himself inside it before he had a chance to waver and break.

From the window he watched as Jock crutched beside her to the waiting chaise and helped her up the step as if she were a fine lady and not a servant girl dressed as a street urchin. Then he watched as Jock tucked his crutches beneath the front fender of the vehicle and pulled himself on the back of the leader of the pair. On the ground the man might look broken, but atop the horse, he was a centaur.

Joseph would never have such a commanding presence or such an impressive skill. He had...skill at languages. A college degree. Tales from his Grand Tour.

A sister as a duchess, parents whose memories were starting to dim in his mind, and an estate in Cornwall waiting for him, in what shape God alone knew.

One too many times in his past he had been foolish over a woman, and he'd resolved never to be so again. Inez was better off in London. She would be safe from Wigsby, she would be fed and housed, and Amaranthe would look after her, as she had before.

Nevertheless the image of her crestfallen shoulders, slumping in defeat as she climbed inside the chaise, stayed burned into his mind as his coach rolled into motion down the road toward Staines. It was all he could think about.

Right up until the attack.

CHAPTER NINE

He was just going to send her home again.

And she would just keep coming back.

For one thing, she had nowhere else to go. That was the reason she would give him, Inez decided. If she didn't belong anywhere, then why not go with him?

She peered anxiously out the window of the chaise, trying to see through the rain that had become a full-blown downpour shortly after the coach departed Hounslow. Surely the rain would keep away gentlemen of the road, who infamously haunted this well-traveled five-mile stretch of Hounslow Heath. And not all of them were as courteous as the legendary Claude Duval. Lord North, the prime minister, had been attacked here a few years ago, and more recently, Lord Berkley had shot his assailant, or so went the reports of the broadsheets and street hawkers.

She didn't want to imagine what Joseph might do if a robber stopped his coach, given the current state of his temper.

She would have, until quite recently, thought Joseph Illingworth the most mild-tempered of men. She would never have put money on him in a fight, unless it were with words. He was a man who lived almost entirely in his head and had to be reminded to eat on occasion.

Something had happened on his Grand Tour to change and age him. Like a Madeira wine, he'd matured, deepened, grown complex. More polished on the outside, and stronger on the inside. When he'd turned at the call of "baronet," his back straight, his jaw thrust at that arrogant angle, she'd have believed him a man bred from the cradle to believe he was superior to other people, and thus deserved more.

Perhaps that was why he'd refused to bring her with him, even after their embrace. Perhaps that was the reason he sent her away when she followed, too stubborn to heed his directive. He was a baronet now.

She apprehended British titles somewhat, and while baronet was not the greatest—not a peer, not a position that merited a seat in the House of Lords—it meant he was called Sir Joseph Illingworth. He would bear a family emblem and motto and a coat of arms and have a genealogy he could roll out to impress the lesser, as had all the great and ancient houses of Portugal. He would command an estate of his own in the pocket of the island where he hailed from, Cornwall, which both he and Amaranthe spoke of as if it might be the last remnant of the Garden of Eden.

There was no place in his life for a servant girl, a widow, a penniless orphan who was one misfortune away from selling herself for coin.

So why couldn't she simply walk away from him? How many times would she allow him to reject her? This was a terrible idea, she saw that now. The chaise, though well-sprung and far more comfortable to travel in than the stagecoach, dipped and tilted as its wheel went through a widening puddle. The road was becoming treacherous, and she was being a fool.

She struggled to lower the pane of the window without

letting the rain lash her face. "Jock," she called as they passed a stand of tall shrubs, ideal for sheltering thieves. The words stung her tongue, but she would concede that the groom had been right and they were better off returning to London than, as Jock had put it, raking after her swell in a mud not fit for hogs. "I think—"

"Aye, the rattler's spilt, that's what," Jock called back. "I see it too."

"Spilt?" Inez pressed her face to the opening in the window. "Do you mean the coach has tipped over?"

"Their knight o' the whip's no fly one, iffen he let a rig like that off its wheels," Jock scoffed. "Well, let's go see what the lay is, then, and hope we can keep the mumpers and buffers away."

Mumpers, Inez knew, where those who robbed coaches, and buffers killed horses to sell their skins. One did not spend time in Dark Lane without acquiring some knowledge of street cant or developing an awareness of the lively and inventive trade of theft, as well as meager ways to guard oneself from it.

She did not fear highwaymen; she had nothing of value to lose, except him. Inez yanked at the window, attempting to wrestle the recalcitrant pane into submission. If Joseph were injured—if Joseph were *dead*—and her last image was of him staring at her as if she were a feast and he a man determined to deny himself... She had to know *why* she wasn't good enough for him. She needed to know that, and then, perhaps, she could let go.

She jumped from the chaise before Jock had fully halted the horses. "Hey now, mind yerself!" the groom called. "Them nags'll be gummy after a spill."

She wasn't concerned about the horses. The coachman had the team of four corralled at the verge of the road, his whip out as he kept them from bolting. Rain glistened on the harness and their coats of bay and gray and black. Jock checked his own mounts, then, while Inez approached the fallen coach, he swung to the ground, pulled his crutches from the fender of the chaise, and went to the heads of the coach horses. In a moment he had all four of the blinkered heads pulled together, the animals quieting as he rubbed noses and fed them grass from his hand. The man wasn't simply a skilled groom and jockey; he was a sorcerer.

The coach lay on its side along the muddy road, one axle cracked where the wheel had caught and wrenched in a rut. Belongings lay strewn along the verge, and some lumps turned out to be passengers, huddling under their coats and complaining. Moans and curses filled the air, along with the whimpers of women and the wailing of a small child.

A mother sat with her mud-splattered knees drawn to her chest, hugging her infant to her with one arm and a basket of goods with the other, desperately trying to shush the shrieking child. A young boy with a red welt marking the side of his face helped an elderly gent to his feet, searching for and finding the round hat of black wool that the lad punched back into shape before handing to his elder.

Another young man who had been thrown from the roof staggered to his feet, looked groggily about him, and then took off at a run over the tall grass of the heath, rain splattering his leather coat and workman's cap. Inez hadn't time to wonder what crime he was escaping.

Joseph was nowhere in sight.

"I won't!" From inside the vehicle came the screech of a woman's voice in the accents of one aspiring to the middling class. "The indignity of it! Right the coach this instant and I will descend in the proper fashion."

"The coach isn't going to be righted any time soon, madame."

That was Joseph's voice, clipped and frustrated, but full of that new command. An odd current weakened Inez's knees, and she leaned a hand on the battered body of the coach to hold herself upright. One wheel still spun slowly through the air, as if it recalled its function even though it had been parted from the ground.

"Your only recourse is to climb out," Joseph insisted. "Call for someone above to help you."

"As if I would allow just anyone to touch me!" the woman exclaimed. "You, sir, have no notion how to treat a lady."

"A lady would have the proper sense to get herself out of this coach," came Joseph's sharp response. "If you wish to remain, then move aside and let me depart."

A muttering filled the ensuing pause, and then a grudging, "Oh, all right then. Since you must be so *uncivil* about it."

A woman's head emerged from the open door of the stage-coach, now slanted incongruously on its side. Her powdered wig was enveloped in a calash, one of those enormous collapsible bonnets, this one decorated with ribbons and bows of a bilious green.

"I require assistance," she announced as if she were a duchess commanding help from a footman. Inez almost giggled. Amaranthe, an actual duchess, would never take such a super-cilious tone with someone in her employ.

Inez started forward. "I can help you."

She *heard* the stillness, the alertness that traveled through Joseph's body at the sound of her voice. She felt the same prickle of awareness traveling down her spine. She felt the same height-ened nervousness, knowing he was near.

"You might call for Jock," Joseph said after a moment, and she sensed the effort he made to keep his voice even and cordial. "He'll have the upper body strength required to—er, be of aid."

"He's with the horses," Inez answered. She pointed to the

young man with the developing bruise. "You. Take one arm, and I'll take the other."

"Ruffians," the woman moaned. "Urchins. Putting their hands upon my person."

As if subjecting herself to the rack, she held out her arms. She would not be easy to lever out of the turned vehicle, as Joseph had warned. Her layers and layers of wool sheathed the form of a woman who enjoyed the luxury of abundant food as well as abundant clothing, along with the luxury of having a laundress to get her linens that glowing white.

"You pull, I'll push," Joseph said from inside.

Inez glimpsed a sliver of his face. He was crouched on the opposite door, which had been bent out of its frame by the impact. His cocked hat held a dent she hoped had shielded the precious head within. A gleam of red-gold in his eyes held an emotion she couldn't decipher.

He was unhurt. He was here. Her insides turned to a mash resembling the cornmeal porridge she had eaten so many times as a child, an inexpensive dish that the cook in the neighboring house often seemed to make too much of for the family breakfast.

"Your hands, sirrah!" the woman shrieked as Joseph disappeared behind her massive skirts.

"It's a rump pad anyway," came Joseph's muffled voice. "Heave, ho!"

The woman sprang free of the aperture with a scuff of damp wool and the fumes of a toilet water heavily scented with attar of roses. "I shall never recover!" she wailed. "My husband the brewer shall have something to say to all of you. The coachman. The innkeep. The owner of this shabby, unfit vehicle—"

"Anyone else in there?" Inez called down once it was clear to peer inside.

His strange expression was acquiring more definition. It

wasn't annoyance. It wasn't resentment or long-suffering forbearance. He looked a man who had been served his favorite pudding and could not bring himself to believe it was all for him.

Inez sat back as he levered himself out of the door, the last of the occupants to clear. He did not need her assistance; the flex of his shoulders and arms in the greatcoat said he possessed the required upper body strength.

The cries and calls and imprecations around her fell away. The low moans of the wounded and indignant were the murmur of insects in her ear. Joseph slid to his feet on the road, then turned and held out his arms for her. Without a word, Inez tilted into them.

And *this*, finally, was what she'd been waiting for. What she'd wanted all along. His arms around her.

"What will happen next?" she asked to keep her mouth occupied, because it wouldn't do to kiss him here in the middle of the muddy road with all these people about them.

"The coachman sent a boy to run for help. He'll ask for a wagon at the gunpowder mill, I expect, or go on to Feltham to see if they can spare a conveyance. Come to the worst, Bedfont is only a mile or two ahead, I think. Most will be able to walk it."

He was tall, his shoulder at the level of her ear, and she felt safe in the circle of his arms. He eyed the brewer's wife, who was busily dressing down the coachman for his inefficiency and threatening all the ways the brewer was destined to demonstrate his disapproval of how his fair lady had been treated.

"Lud, what a clutter yer makin'!" the coachman griped at her. "Want you bring out the gemmun of the road? They'd be happy to relieve ye of yer baubles, and mayhap that nugging dress. Sure and go on to draw their attention, won't ye? Whyn't ye flash the King's picture and set all the Tyburn blossoms upon us while yer about it."

CHAPTER TEN

"So you grew up in Sagres." They would have hours together on the road, Joseph reasoned, so he might as well make conversation.

"Yes. It's a beautiful town, surrounded by water. Prince Henry the Infante had holdings there. King Sebastian liked to walk the cliffs, they say, and listen to the music of the winds. My grandmother worked for the Convent of São Vicente do Cabo, and my mother, too, before she met my father. My grandfather was a fisherman, in the manner of his family. I think my mother's ancestors lived in that area since before the Christians came."

They'd never spoken like this, Joseph reflected, not with such honesty, and as equals. He knew nothing of Inez's history. He'd confided in her now and again, or rather updated her on his activities. But he'd never asked her about her past; he'd never been sure she would talk to him. Yet she spoke with him freely as their chaise rolled on the road from Basingstoke, where'd they'd paused for a midday nuncheon of cold meats, local cheese, and bread baked fresh that morning with the same yeast the innkeep's wife used in her ale.

The food tasted surprisingly good to Joseph, who normally paid no attention to what he put in his mouth. He wondered if it were the exercise of the morning, the apprehension of what awaited him in Cornwall, or the stimulation of his companion that had sharpened his appetite and his general awareness of his circumstances.

They traveled in easy stages, pausing often to rest or change the horses and give themselves a stretch. Jock seemed tireless, unconcerned that the day continued to mizzle, but Joseph appreciated the chance to warm himself now and again before a fire and take a moment to clear his head from the intoxicating effect of sitting near Inez for long stretches.

At the Swan in Staines, Jock spent a great deal of time interrogating the groom who would escort the Hunsdon horses back to London, taking such care with the negotiations that Joseph offered to vouch, with his life, that the matched set would turn up in the Hunsdon mews without a scratch or a single hair from a mane missing. Jock had sent him a look suggesting Joseph didn't understand the gravity of the matter, but Joseph was too busy dealing with the sight of Inez in petticoat and bodice to mull much over Jock's feelings.

The disguise of boyhood had allowed him mental distance enough to deal with her as a fellow human, his charge and responsibility. In a skirt, she was again the temptress, the woman who charged his senses past bearing. Though she wore a cloak over her bosom, he *knew* her breasts were there, beneath the layers of linen and wool, and so was the delicious rest of her, all the complicated curves and silken shadows.

He dragged his mind back to Sagres. "And your father was from—somewhere else?"

"Goa," she said quietly. "In India." She said no more, as if she didn't want to talk about her father—or, he guessed, about her foreign birth and darker skin, which made her stand out among pale English women like a hollyhock among wood anemones.

"Goa," Joseph said. "That's been a Portuguese colony for, what, a hundred years now?"

"Over two hundred," she said. "My grandfather's family served in the court of the viceroy, or so I'm told. My grandmother's family were traders." She ran her fingers along the fringe of her shawl, woven in a bright pattern.

"Shirodkar," he said, remembering her father's name and finding it rolled easily from his tongue. "Does it have a meaning?"

"Someone from the village of Shirod." She smiled. "To hear my father tell it, his family ruled the village for centuries. But the family name or traditions meant little to him. He found, once he left, they meant little elsewhere also."

Joseph nodded. He remembered how grand his uncle, and then Reuben, had behaved once they wore the mantle of baronet. And how little such a paltry title meant outside their own sense of self-importance. He had never held the title in reverence, and didn't suppose anyone else should.

"My father left Goa before the king made the decree that would have made him a Portuguese citizen, but I doubt even that would have made him stay," Inez reflected. "He was always restless, full of ambition, my *pai*. He fought against the Maratha armies for a while, but he always said he was not born for land. Though my grandfather thought it a demotion that he would serve on a ship and not command it, my father went to sea."

She fell silent for a moment. "He was right about himself in the end. He was never happy on land. Nor for long."

"He met your mother in Sagres?"

Traffic was steady on what was still called the London Road, though they were nearly a day from London now. They'd stopped on the road twice, once near Oakley to let a flock of sheep draggle across their path, the shepherd boy shooing and the sheepdog snapping at hooves to keep the animals moving. At Laverstoke he asked Jock to pause the horses to show Inez the mill that produced the paper for England's banknotes. She wasn't terribly impressed, which led him to wonder if she'd ever held a banknote in her life.

The road edged the southern side of the North Wessex Downs, the green-clad slopes and valleys of chalk for which Joseph suspected the term "rolling hills" had been invented. The sight agreed with him, and Joseph felt his breath deepening, growing steady in the clearer air, now they were away from the constant industry of London.

Inez, too, seemed to settle, growing quiet and contemplative at his side as they rocked along. They'd stop in Whitchurch, then again in Andover to rest the horses after a hilly stretch before pressing on to Amesbury for the night. Jock spoke well of The George inn there, and Joseph had a notion of driving by the great stone circle to see what Inez thought of it before setting out for another long day of travel.

Yet the days need only be as long as they wished. They had Jock and the chaise, and the purse that Amaranthe had sent with Jock, which he kept possession of. So far, the combination of Jock's expertise and reputation, the Hunsdon livery, and the ducal purse had contrived to ensure that at every inn, fresh and well-tempered horses were available for their chaise, and there was mutton or ham on offer along with small beer and sometimes coffee. At the Maidenhead in Basingstoke, a commodious inn with stabling for one hundred horses and common rooms where the local magistrate held court, Inez had been served a French claret that made her eyes widen with appreciation and that she sipped as slowly as she could, as if she never wanted the experience to end.

He wasn't bound to the schedule of the coach and coachman, trying to shovel cold meats and bread into his mouth, down a cup of ale, and visit the necessary all in the few minutes required to change the team of horses. He wasn't subject to the common room at all unless he wanted; Sir Joseph Illingworth of Penwellen, whom Jock made certain to announce at every stop, was offered a private parlor if there was one.

His graceful companion was only eyed with some askance rather than outright disdain, and when Joseph explained that she was a ward of his sister's, practically a sister of his own, she was served as graciously as he.

Never mind that a man oughtn't look at his ward, his sister, or his sister's ward the way Joseph stared at Inez. His eyes caught continually on the curves and shadows of her face, the features delicate on their own yet coming together in an aspect that promised strength of character and determination of spirit. He couldn't look away from the swells of bosom and hip beneath her plain but tidy attire.

And he couldn't forget the taste of her. The heat of her skin. The lushness of her breasts in his hands, in his mouth.

"My mother and father met in Sagres, yes." She hadn't let her thoughts wander, as he had. He watched her face as she looked out at the countryside, catching the sorrow that hitched her brows, pulled at the corners of her generous lips. "She dreamed of more than her tiny village, and he carried stories and the scent of the sea."

She sighed. "Do you think, if we fall in love with the dream of a person, there is any way it cannot be a disappointment when we find our idol is real flesh and blood? Flawed and human?"

Was she talking about her parents still? "Who was the idol in their relationship?" he asked cautiously.

"Both of them, I think, fell in love with the dream. He saw a lovely young woman with the sun of a distant land in her eyes and who wanted to be more than a fisherman's daughter. She found a man who had been weathered by the sun of the Arabian Sea, who had tasted the food of the Far Orient, who had rounded the Cape of Good Hope. But he wasn't prepared to put down roots, and she wasn't allowed to sail with him."

"But they were in love once."

"And remained so, I think. But love does not always demand you are kind to your beloved. He was gone so much, and she—" She pulled her full lip between her teeth. "He did not like what she did to keep us during his time away. But we had to eat somehow, and with no family to offer aid because they did not approve of her marriage to an Indian, what else could she do?"

Joseph wondered mightily what compromises her mother had made, but feared to press her and lose this fragile connection. "Were you their only child?"

Her mouth twisted. "The only one who lived."

Ah, that pierced his heart. Her mother had walked a hard road, it seemed. "What brought you to England?"

"My father's ship was sold and he couldn't sign on with another crew, so he was stranded here. My mother arranged for us to join him."

"And how long have you been here?"

"Ten years."

"Do you miss Portugal?"

"Every day," she said softly. "Not the life we had there, but the people. The sea. The warm winds, and the sun always shining, and the way it seemed you could see for miles in any direction. The food, and our neighbors, and the sight of the Infante Henry's fortress jutting over the water..." She fell silent for another long moment. "There is nothing like it."

Joseph felt touched by a similar longing, not for the place she envisioned in her memories, but to bring that expression of softness, of wistful joy, to her face. He cleared his throat.

"Cornwall is surrounded by sea. Land's End, they call the tip of it."

"Oh, I am sure I will find it much the same." Her eyes flashed, and it took him a moment to understand the glint was a merry one. She was becoming playful.

"Little but rocks and sheep," he cautioned. "Heather and gorse, at least on the moors. Near Penzance there are palm trees, I'm told, but I've never seen them."

"You might take me there, in that case."

"I might." He stared straight ahead, curling his hands into fists on his thighs. The rocking motion of the coach as it moved meant he couldn't avoid the press of her hip against his.

How would he take her anywhere? What was she to him? A woman who served now again in his employ but who was also a friend to his sister. A whore, or friend of whores—he knew the business of Dark Lane—who hobnobbed with a duchess.

He was going to arrive at Penwellen with her in tow, and then what was he to do with her?

"When did you lose your parents?" she asked quietly.

The question took him by surprise, and Joseph blinked quickly, gathering himself. "Ah. I was seventeen and left for Oxford shortly thereafter, so, ten years."

Ten years since he had seen Penwellen and realized he couldn't live with his cousin and his new bride, seeing their happiness and their comfortable life when he had lost everything. Ten years since he and Amaranthe had assembled their meager belongings—it was barely enough to fill a coach—and left the quiet vicarage of St. Cleer empty for the next tenant.

Ten years since he had stood at the graves of his parents in the St. Cleer cemetery, the patch of earth he had looked at every day of his conscious years of life as meaningless scenery and now did not think he could bear to see again.

He wished now he had thought to ask Reuben that his

parents be laid to rest in the small family graveyard at Penwellen. Joseph's father had been the son of a baronet, even if in life that status had never accorded him much in the name of wealth or esteem. He had lived and died on the edges of dignity, earning just enough from his vicar's stipend and the parish tithes to support his family.

Jonas Illingworth had never demanded special accord for being the son of a gentleman or the town's cleric. He had asked for little in his life and expected less, but he had always taken joy in his family.

And that was what Joseph had been searching for in the past ten years: family. Amaranthe was, or had been, a pleasant enough companion, someone to talk to in the evenings and stroll with through a garden or museum or exhibit. He had never taken for granted—well, not *much*—her quiet, steady good sense and the way she had anticipated his needs.

But he longed for the kind of affection he had witnessed daily between his mother and father. A partner in life's trials. A helpmeet. Someone with whom to share the joys and sorrows.

He'd been so eager to find that, he'd thrown his heart again and again after women who turned out not to want it. Susannah Pettigrew, for instance. He'd been certain he'd found a kindred soul who believed in justice and right and God's love for all creatures, but who also cared particularly for Joseph.

Instead, it turned out she cared particularly for what Joseph could give her, but only in the sense that these gifts increased her stature and influence among her friends. His heart wasn't the prize she'd wanted, which is why he'd been left standing in a Gloucestershire church a year ago with a marriage license and his best suit, broken hopes and no bride.

"What did they die of?" Inez asked softly.

Joseph hauled his mind back to the present. "My parents? Ah, typhus fever. Very sudden."

And brutal. Typhus was not an easy way to pass on to one's Maker. For some reason, no one else in the household had caught it. Joseph had been on a holiday with his tutor, Amaranthe visiting a friend when the visiting soldier came through the vicarage, on home for leave and bringing with him, unknowingly, the contagion of his barracks. Both children had returned home to witness the fevers, the rash, the wasting away. The helplessness and the weariness and then the sudden, awful quiet when it was over.

"My mother caught the smallpox," Inez said quietly.

"Ah. I'm very sorry."

"It was a mercy. The smallpox killed her body. The Spanish disease was taking her mind."

"The Spanish—oh."

The Spanish disease was the great pox, syphilis.

Inez's mother had supported herself the same way as the ladies of Dark Lane.

Inez was the daughter of a whore.

He probed his reaction to this. An upright, moral man who cleaved to chastity and cleanliness of body and mind ought to be horrified.

Instead he felt a great sympathy for what Inez had endured. He understood now her distaste at the idea of trading her body for coin. She'd seen, up close, the most punishing of consequences.

They were both of them orphans in the world, although he had the advantage of a duchess for a sister who still thought it her duty to smooth Joseph's way. Just as he felt it his duty to smooth the way for Inez. She was safe with him, for the time being, but what came next for them, he couldn't imagine.

He had learned his lesson, with a lash that still smarted when he thought of the fool he'd been. He would not be such a sapskull again, throwing his heart after the Susannah Pettigrews of the world. He would be careful and thoughtful in his selection of a companion. He would take the time to see a woman truly and know she was his match in temperament, in beliefs, in what she wanted from a shared life.

But first he had to put Penwellen in order.

And he had to decide what to do with the woman beside him, who baffled him, challenged him, was unlike any woman he'd ever met. And who lived in such a world apart from his, he didn't know how—or to what—he was meant to return her.

CHAPTER ELEVEN

He didn't know what to do with her; that was easy to see.

"My ward will require a separate room," Joseph told the innkeep at The George in Amesbury. This was a stately timber-framed edifice crowning Amesbury's High Street, showing its centuries of age in the wainscoting on the inside, the heavy chamfered beams of the ceiling, and the woodwork on the staircase leading to the rooms on the first floor. Outside, ivy crawled around the many-paned windows, and the dormers under the eaves stood open, suggesting the rooms were getting an airing now that the dripping clouds had moved away.

"Your ward. Aye," the innkeeper murmured, her glance at Inez suggesting she was frequently asked to arrange rooms for traveling men and their "wards." "You'll be wanting a room close by, I be thinking?"

"Of course, so I might keep an eye out. As she is a young, unmarried woman under my protection."

Inez closed her eyes briefly and thought about kicking him in the shin to silence him. Her dear Joseph babbled when he was nervous.

Her Joseph. But he wasn't hers, wasn't he? He wasn't her anything.

"She'll like water sent up for a bath, when you can arrange it," Joseph went on. "And a private parlor for dining."

"No private parlor available, I'm afraid. Sir," the innkeep said. "The Historical and Philosophical Society is usin' it this evening for their meetin.'"

Joseph perked up at this. "A Philosophical Society? In a town this size? Splendid that there should be an interest in such subjects."

"That's as what they call themselves, sir, but it's an excuse for the men to gather and smoke, and that's a fact," the innkeep said. "The wives drive them and they clay pipes out o' the house, so they comes here."

"Yes, I had read that Amesbury is famous for making clay pipes," Joseph said. "Something about the white clay at Chitterne St. Mary Down being the best in the country, they say."

Inez saw how it would be. He would look for a way to insert himself into this meeting, he would be welcomed, and he would spend the evening smoking and drinking and exercising his astonishing mind for the benefit of utter strangers, and she would be left to sit in her room and stare out the window at the street.

"We could dine in my room," she said quickly. "If a supper might be sent up."

"Yes, yes, that will be fine," Joseph said, preoccupied by the thought of a scholarly convention. Inez saw she would have to strip down naked if she wanted to catch his attention.

And if she did? He'd offered her his hand, and she'd taken it. Her stomach curled around the memory of his large, warm hand holding hers. She could follow him to Cornwall, but what then?

She had to make him see that he needed her. She had to *make* him need her.

She had to find a way to ensure that she would not be turned out and left homeless again.

The room given Inez was a small, spare chamber on the second floor, tucked beneath the eaves. It was plain but tidy, the mattress on the cot stuffed with tick and her pillow with goose feathers. Inez was attempting to knock the dust of the road off the hem of her skirt when the innkeep entered with a servant girl bearing a large wooden basin and a boy behind lugging a yoke with two buckets sloshing water.

"You needn't have brought it up all this way," Inez said at once. "I could have come down."

"His ward, ye say." The innkeep gave a sidewise glance as she directed her staff where to set the things, and Inez realized she had betrayed herself.

"After a fashion," she said, conscious she stood in shift and stays, apron and cap discarded on the bed. Her stays were leather, her petticoat much mended, and her battered half boots broadcast that she was no man's ward, certainly not to a man of stature.

Her worsted socks said she was no one's courtesan, either.

So what did that make her?

"I serve in his house," she said. "Have served. His sister, not him. That is to say—"

"I can brush that gown," the innkeep said in a brisk tone, reaching for Inez's outer robe, "and Polly can launder yer shift, if ye've got a spare. I've lavender for your water, and they's no bugs in the tick."

She directed the boy to set down the buckets, then shooed him out the door and turned to Inez with a stern face. "But mind he's not seen a-comin' or goin', aye? There'll be many a fellow below tonight has the ear of a magistrate and will take note of a woman entertainin'."

"I'm not—we won't—" Inez bit her lip as the innkeep sent

her a sharp look, and wisely fell silent. Polly, gathering up Inez's apron, held out her hand for the linens with a small smirk.

"I don't think the gent will be calling on me." Inez handed over her petticoat first. "He doesn't want an arrangement."

The innkeeper's eyebrows raised with surprise, and her gaze swept Inez from toe to top. "With you? But you're comely enough."

"A proper party," Polly agreed, eyes wide.

"Thank you. But he tried to leave me behind in London. I don't think he wants me with him in his new home. We're going to Cornwall," Inez said, surprised by this sudden urge to confess. It was unlike her.

"Kernow!" Polly cried. "Where to? Never say Callington."

"Actually, yes. I believe his estate lies nearby."

Polly blinked and snapped her fingers, summoning Inez to strip out of her stays. "The only estate thereabout is Penwellen."

"That is where we—he is going, I believe."

Polly's eyes kindled with rage. "Is the old baronet dead, then? Good riddance. A very slawterpooch, ee was. All us maids knew not to work there, couldn't keep his snib in his breeches."

"The new baronet is quite the opposite," Inez hurried to say, wondering whether she might press for more information about the man Joseph was succeeding, and the place he had inherited. Polly looked to be a handful of years younger than she was, perhaps no more than six or seven and ten years, though a hard world put a woman's face on a girl early, Inez knew.

"And that Treen." Polly snapped her fingers again, indicating that Inez was to surrender her shift. The innkeep handed her a towel to shield her nakedness. "Tell that'un ee's a polrumptious, pluffy, pussivanting *piggy-whidden*." The girl's eyes flared with righteous anger. "And don't trust a word that comes out o' ee's clunker, neither."

Inez nodded obediently. "I won't."

Polly sniffed, still bristling. "A pair o' grammersows, those two. If Sir Reuben is gone, it's a blessing for every cheel in that town, it is."

"He sounds horrible," Inez said.

"Granfer to half the town, ee'd be, all the maids he kindid-dled." Polly curled up her lip as if she meant to spit on the past baronet's memory, until a sharp look from her employer halted her mid-insult.

"Giss on, and be about your work," said the innkeep, shooing Polly toward the door. She turned back to Inez with a businesslike air. "Speaking of which. If you've any need of making certain...all comes regular-like with the woman's curse. She circled a hand before her midsection. "I've a tea I can make you."

"The woman's—oh." Inez felt her face draw taut with heat. So much for convincing the landlady she was not a whore.

She oughtn't be ashamed. Conversations on the preventions for catching a babe were common in Dark Lane; they had to be, for the health and protection of the Vestals. Inez suddenly recalled the redolent herbs her mother stewed now and again over their small fire, and the bitter concoctions she made herself drink though Inez could tell she hated the taste of them.

"Actually," Inez said. "I might be interested in such a tea." She glanced toward the door, lowering her voice as if she feared to be overheard. And yet these were precautions she ought to consider did she wish to pursue certain thoughts she was developing in relation to Joseph Illingworth.

The innkeep tilted her head to the side and regarded Inez with a speculative look. "If ye catch, thas one way t'spring the shackle."

"I don't intend to trick him into marriage."

Her mother had extracted her deathbed promise mainly to keep Inez from disease, because no one should have to die in slow stages or poison themselves with mercury merely to prolong their pain. But a babe was the other consequence, and one that put a hamper on the commerce of Dark Lane.

Inez couldn't think about marriage, not again. Marriage was a shackle for the woman, as good as a rope tying her the hearth and kitchen. Marriage meant her husband could say where she went when she left the house, and with whom she associated. Marriage meant every coin laid in the wife's hand ended up in the husband's pocket.

Marriage meant a woman could not say no when her spouse came to her bed demanding the exercise of his marital rights, no matter how cruel or callous he was in his usage of her, no matter whether he stank of vile dealings and sometimes other women.

Marriage meant that, when a husband died, the wife watched their home dismantled into the hands of those who held his debts, and the little left over seized by those who claimed with however slender a right to be his heirs. Marriage was to be bound to the stake with a noose around one's neck and a trap door that could fall open at any time. She wouldn't put her head in that harness again.

And yet, as the innkeep sprinkled lavender in her bath water and the sharp, clean scent rose to her nostrils, Inez allowed herself to wonder, for the briefest moment, what marriage to Joseph Illingworth would be like.

His warm smile when she brought his tray of bread and butter and steaming coffee, which he liked hot enough to scald.

Chatting with him in the parlor at the end of a day, hearing of his projects and the ideas that engaged his mind, glimpsing that beautiful and orderly and thoughtful world he dwelled in.

Having his big body at her side to protect her from want, from harm, from the Wigsbys of the world.

"I've a tincture I'll bring you," the innkeep said as Inez took up a cloth and settled her feet in the basin. "And an oil for yer hair, such lovely locks as ye have. Also a virgin's milk for yer skin, if you wish to—be a bit paler here." She made another motion, this one encompassing her face. "Unless, of course, yer gent likes ye dark. Some do."

And just like that, Inez was reminded why Joseph Illingworth would never marry her.

It took her a moment to speak past the obstruction in her throat. She bent her head toward the wash basin, focused on bathing her feet. "The lavender water will do for my face, thank you. But I would be grateful for the hair oil and the tincture you mention. In the event that...well."

She couldn't say what she intended by seducing him. She'd never entertained the thought of seducing a man before; she spent too much time trying to elude them.

What did she want from him?

Right now, simply his *attention*.

That look of hunger in his eyes. The dazed delight when he reached his pleasure, as if her touch brought him to heaven. That need set free in him, when he was so buttoned-down, so correct otherwise.

She wanted to see it again. His desire for her, unleashed. She simply wanted to know it was there, no matter how hard he tried to hide or fight it.

And she wanted him to give in. She wanted to be, for once, with him, the woman who could not be left.

The innkeep sent up the same bill of fare amusing the patrons of the Philosophical Society: a haunch of beef, roasted rabbit, buttered greens and carrots, and a gravy soup, with what Polly called the Duke of Cumberland's pudding.

This last, a thick red-brown cake, smelled of nutmeg and looked to be studded with currants and apples, and Inez suspected it would be the richest thing she had ever tasted. And she accustomed to scraps from the kitchen of Mrs. Blackthorn, now the chief cook at Hunsdon House.

"Which Duke of Cumberland?" Inez had wondered aloud as Polly unloaded her platter and the serving boy nudged the legs of the folding table into place. Inez laid out the dining plates, a set of glazed earthenware with a pretty floral design. It seemed the innkeep wanted Sir Joseph Illingworth, Bart., to leave Amesbury with a good report of The George.

"The Duke as killed all the Jacobites?" suggested the boy, speaking for the first time and in an accent Inez guessed was local to this part of the country.

"Or the one now, Prince Henry." Polly sighed.

The widely distributed prints of Prince Henry, the Duke of Cumberland and Strathearn and younger brother to the King, stirred many a female heart with their depiction of a tall, well-made man with the Hanoverian nose and probing blue eyes. Female hearts had lifted further when Prince Henry's romance with a lovely widow led to their marriage, and many a romantic imagination had been inspired by the idea that a royal prince might marry a widow and a commoner, set up a merry and luxurious home in London with her, and carry on with gladness, no matter how strenuously the King disapproved.

The King had disapproved so strenuously that he had passed a law about it, which just showed how careful men in power were about how they bestowed the honor of their hand. There were the Dark Lane ladies, actresses and dancers at the theaters, well-groomed courtesans to see to a man's need for companionship, and then there were the ladies with birth and breeding and the fairest of skin to oversee his home and the rearing of children.

The same was true in Portugal; the same was true the world over. The divides between classes were wide and well-established, and one risked one's life to cross them. A prince marrying a commoner had outraged a king to the point that he made up laws to prohibit the practice. A baronet and a gentleman's son would never marry the daughter of a whore.

It wasn't the thought of losing him that pinched her heart like a hawk stooping to its kill; it was the knowledge that she'd never *had* him. And when they reached Callington, all her chances to be with him would be lost. He would be Sir Joseph of Penwellen, and she would be left to find her own way back to London and her few friends in Dark Lane, to take up what livelihood she could find, and hope Wigsby did not run her to ground and kill her.

Some wild impulse had made her tell Jock not to set the chaise on course for London but follow Joseph instead. Some sure conviction that he needed her.

But what *she* needed, Inez thought as she dressed with care in the one change of clothes she owned, was him. She'd run after him with the mad wish to have his arms about her just one more time. Fully and completely, cleaving together like husband and wife.

She had little other pleasure in her life. Was it wrong that she wanted this before they must part?

"Enter," she called when she heard his knock.

<h1 style="text-align:center">CHAPTER TWELVE</h1>

<hr>

Inez was glad she was sitting and could not betray the weakness in her knees at the sight of Joseph when he stepped into her room. He'd tidied himself, leaving traces of damp in the hair that tumbled across his forehead and the sideburns that framed his lean, carved cheeks. He'd brushed his coat and changed his neckcloth. He traveled with no less than three so he always had fresh while one was being laundered and one lay ready and waiting in his valise.

The man would forget to polish the buttons on his coats—someone else must have done it for him, she thought, seeing the gleam—but he was meticulous about his neckcloths. The knowledge was yet another tender shoot curling about her heart, to be yanked free in a day or three when they parted.

He gave her a small bow. "You look lovely. Refreshed."

"The bath was just what I needed. Thank you."

She smelled lavender on her skin and the blend of jasmine and sweet oil she had combed through her hair. The innkeep had also delivered a tooth powder, which smelled of alum and myrrh. The woman was her own version of Mother Vesta, beautifying Inez for her night and sending up their meal accompanied by elderflower wine, her own, she had sworn, which tasted very like Frontiniac.

Inez didn't know the least thing about French wines, but she could affirm that Mrs. Truckle's wine was delicious. The warmth curled her toes and sent exploratory fingers of giddiness around her sides and into her belly.

Or perhaps that was due to Joseph.

He tugged at the back of one of the carved oak folding chairs that the boots boy had delivered, shortly after the table. Inez supposed such pieces of furniture were reliably handy for inns regularly used as meeting places.

"I could have dined with the Philosophical Club and saved you the trouble." He flared the tails of his coat over the sides of the chair as he sat, his posture as erect as if he were at a military drill. His knees lightly tugged at the cloth laid over the table. He picked up and examined his fork, tapping the ends of each of the three tines with his finger.

For some reason, that gesture, his noting the old fashioned style of the silver, when more modern forks had four tines, made Inez acutely conscious that they sat in a pub nearly two centuries old in a town that was said to have been founded by the Romans, but which boasted, not far away, the silent soaring henge of a much earlier people. They sat together, sharing a meal, inside a tradition that stretched back to the dawn of Creation, man and woman together, she made for him as companion and lifemate.

Bedmates.

Joseph was nervous. She could tell by the way he lifted and examined his knife, then put that down too. She pushed the platter of beef his way with a gentle nudge.

"Will you carve?"

"Of course," he said, clearly grateful for the task. Inez watched his hands. He had left off his gloves for dining, as had she, and the intimacy of his bare fingers made her think of how those hands might feel sliding across her skin.

"When do we reach Callington?" she asked, to give him something more to occupy his mind.

"Two more days on the road, I'm afraid. Tomorrow night, unless we wish to stop somewhere else, we'll stay in Honiton. There's a coaching inn there Jock likes, run by a friend of his, apparently. He says everyone in Exeter is a shark or a snaffler, which I believe means he is apprehensive they will steal his purse."

Inez smiled and accepted the plate with its slab of beef. It was more than she was accustomed to eating, a man's portion, and the small gesture—that he would give her as much as he would take for himself—fed those small tendrils sprouting about her middle. She'd be choked by them before the meal ended if she weren't careful.

She poured wine for him into one of the goblets, glass, not pewter. This was the finest table she'd been at in some time, and that spoke to her unworthiness of him, didn't it? What was stooping to traveler's lodgings for him, making do with earthen-ware plates and homemade wine, was to her as fine as a feast.

Aye, she couldn't keep him, not one as she was. But she could have him for a night or some, couldn't she? Did she not deserve a bit of comfort and tenderness, and didn't he as well? Mrs. Truckle had as much as assumed that they were intimates. She saw no reason Joseph wouldn't want Inez, even with her past, even with her dark skin.

"The wine is well enough?" Her smile widened as he drank from his cup, then looked into the goblet with surprise.

"As good as any that I had in France, though I admit I could not afford the very best wines. Rabbit?"

"Yes, and some greens as well, please."

Her heart softened like a bruised fruit as he arranged her

plate, though all was well enough within her reach that she could select her own fare. He didn't serve himself first and expect her to fend for herself; he fixed her plate first, then his. She slid her fingers against his palm as he handed her the heavy earthenware, and he startled slightly.

Revulsion, or something else?

"Isn't it your purse?" Inez asked, cutting her meat. "That Jock is carrying, I mean."

Joseph scowled at his plate. "It's Amaranthe's bit. She sent a purse with Jock. I'm fortunate she didn't send the Hunsdon traveling carriage. That would call down the snafflers for certain."

"Your own coach would ease your travel considerably, I should think." And most men would want that. Joseph Illingworth was indeed very much unlike other men.

He shuddered. "And make us a spectacle. People turning into the street to watch a ducal carriage go by. Children running ahead of us into the inn, hoping to get a glimpse of a duke or duchess. And then to find it is only my plain self. And you, of course."

She lifted one eyebrow. She had learned this early on, how to raise only one brow, and she enjoyed the intimidating effect it generally had on men making her offers she did not wish to accept. "I am a disappointment too, you are saying?"

"Well, they would want to see a beautiful woman done up quite fine, all the silks and velvets and the extravagant hats, don't you think?" His cheeks grew ruddy. "I did not mean to suggest—"

"I am funning you, Joseph."

His name slipped out, easy on her lips, familiar as a whistle or a song. She tensed, fearing a gentle setdown, but he didn't seem to mark the intimacy. He poked a spoon into his soup and scowled.

This would not do. He must be easy with her. Relaxed. Warm. She wanted *that* Joseph. "Why do you not wish the Duchess smoothing the way for you?"

His gaze flew up to meet hers. The spoon halted halfway to his mouth. This was not a question to make him easy. "What do you mean?"

"Only that many brothers, if their sister has married a duke, would make free in the ducal household, and make ready use of his carriage and every other advantage on offer. They would drop the title with every other sentence, especially when traveling abroad. You seem abashed when Jock announces you as the baronet, and that title, you have earned."

He put down his spoon. "I haven't earned any of it."

She continued eating. The fare was delicious, and she would need strength for what lay ahead. "But it *is* yours. The title. The status. The brother who is a duke."

He took up his knife and stabbed at the roasted rabbit. "I didn't marry a duke. Amaranthe did. And she thinks she must provide for me, as if she were the elder sibling or the parent, when I am older by two years, devil take it. She is still looking after me as if I were yet some young pup in university, as green as unripe cheese. I took my Grand Tour, I survived six months on my own legs, I came back a changed man, and she still has that little costermonger dropping in on me daily, along with any other number of spies, I don't doubt."

Inez chewed her greens, which were fresh and delicious. "How did your Grand Tour change you?"

She knew what she saw—more polish, more assurance. He was quieter since his return, and at the same time sharper. He hadn't affected any new fashions; his fobs held no more than his watch with its key and a small enameled miniature of his parents—she'd sneaked a peek on more than one occasion, curious about the pair who had given birth to and shaped this man.

He was still temperate, even abstemious in his ways; he never drank to excess, he rarely used tobacco, and he didn't keep a mistress. He didn't even visit prostitutes, that she knew of. Not that he was likely to boast of such activities, as some men did.

"My tour? It cured me of Susannah Pettigrew, to begin with."

Inez turned her attention to her own soup so she could avoid probing the stab that name delivered to her heart. Susannah Pettigrew, the woman he had resolved to marry, the woman he had escorted to Gloucestershire. With whom he had spent hours and days in the post chaise, just like this, taken meals at inns, just like this, and planned a future, which she and Joseph did not have.

She spooned the soup into her mouth and found it thick and bitter.

"Cured, you say?"

"Indeed. I won't be foolish in love again. I will be wise next time."

The dear, darling man. Inez snorted around her spoonful of soup. "Whoever is wise in love?"

"Do you wish to be married again?" he demanded. "To another man like your husband was."

He had his eyes on his meat, not on her, and Inez was glad he could not see how the words landed like a blow. In an instant she was there again, in the dark room because he wanted the curtains drawn and the candle out. One hand at her throat as he held her down, the other hand holding himself as he poked and prodded and then found his way in, grunting his way to release. She burned on the inside, as if she might physically erase the memory.

If only she could.

"No," she said, the words harsh and low. "I don't want that ever again."

"Then you see my point."

"But you wished to marry *her*." Her throat ached around the words. "So you do wish to marry."

"I wish to have a family of my own. More than anything, I confess." An expression chased across his face, a pained shadow. Longing. And guilt, as if he weren't allowed to ask for the basic comforts that even the poorest peasant in his hovel could ask of life.

"But I will be more careful of my choices, hereafter," he said, and tore a piece of rabbit from the bone with his teeth.

Something about that gesture, the primitive look to him at that moment, made Inez catch fire with a sudden, deep need she could no longer ignore. A craving like she'd never known sank its fangs into her. She wanted his teeth on her, biting, consuming. She wanted his body, his weight holding her down. She wanted him to kiss her until she couldn't breathe and all her memories vanished.

She wanted him like a blaze of fire that could tear through and empty her, and leave nothing but a shell behind, ready to be reformed.

"And what of pleasure?" she asked, her voice husky with need.

He halted, fork halfway to his mouth, and if he'd been checked by a halter. His eyes darkened.

"What pleasure?"

"The pleasure of man and woman, together." Or men and men, or men with several women, or women with any combination of partners; the pleasures offered in Dark Lane were varied, and many illicit to the light of day. But she wanted Joseph to think of pleasure and *her,* and she could tell by the sudden arrest of motion that he was.

She hoped.

"Until you marry. Where will you find your pleasure?"

She imagined him pleasuring himself, alone in his study with his books spread out before him and the physical need emptying his mind, his hand around his cock the way she had held him. Or alone in his bed, thinking of sinking into a woman as he worked himself, or imagining a woman's mouth around him.

Perhaps her mouth. A bright hot bead formed between her legs, that ache she felt so often around him, but which was so much stronger now that he'd kissed her.

"I—" He scowled. "This is not an appropriate topic of discussion."

"The innkeep thinks I am your mistress. She thinks you want me so much that you are bringing me from London to your new home in Cornwall because you cannot bear to be parted from me for long."

"I..." He flailed again. His scowl darkened. He set his jaw, a muscle flexing in those cheeks, the skin drawn tight over the bones in his anger. "That is none of her business."

"Don't you want it? Don't you want me?"

It was like she didn't know herself, or was watching herself from a distance. Who was this wanton woman? She fled from men. She didn't beg for them to swive her.

Her throat pulled tight with longing, with desperation. She had to have him in her arms, she had to be certain he wanted her, or she would die. She was as sure of this as her need for air. She could not let him leave this room without touching her, or she would die.

She rose. He put down his utensils. He watched her like she was a wild animal he thought might spring and tear out his throat. His gaze skimmed her hips as she walked slowly around the table toward him, then he stared at her breasts as she came to stand before him.

He licked his lips, and she knew she was right. He wanted her. She wanted him. She would bring him to her, finally. He would hold and love and care for her, and for a few moments in her life, an hour, an entire night, she would be beloved and cherished and held and safe.

He would erase the memories of the sterile scraping that had been her marriage, and she would know what it was meant to be like between a man and woman, at last. He would give her memories that were warm and new and beautiful, and she could hold them to her through all the long, lonely days that would follow once he sent her away.

She pressed at his shoulder and he turned in his chair, but before he could rise, she pushed his shoulder again, keeping him in his seat. She lifted her leg and straddled his lap and was gratified at the way he sucked in air between his teeth.

He was hard for her already; she felt the bulge against her inner thigh. She shifted so the head of his cock in his breeches was against that aching part of her, and she didn't bother to stop the low, begging cry that came out of her mouth. Instead she bent her head and let her whimper fall against his lips.

He kissed her as if he were a man released from prison and she were air and light and food altogether. He kissed her as if she were the first woman he'd ever kissed.

He kissed her as if this were his last meal and she was the memory he would take to the executioner's block, and he wanted every bit of life and passion he could consume before the axe fell.

She planted her hands on either side of his face, palms brushing his soft sideburns, his softer skin. Such soft skin for a man. So gentle, he was. Yet when she kissed him harder he met her, something ferocious in his need, and waves of greedy heat rolled over her.

As a child she'd loved to wade out from the beach into the water until the waves broke over her head, thrilled by that moment when the power caught her and she was lifted off her feet. When she might be knocked down and drowned, or rolled into shore like flotsam, or carried like wreckage out to sea. Not knowing her fate for that brief instant, if she would be carried or crash: it was the same when Joseph Illingworth kissed her.

He brushed his hands over her hips, then slid them up the sides of her body, and she swayed like a reed caught in the wind. She was lost, and she did not care.

"Kiss me," she demanded hoarsely.

He slid his tongue into her mouth and it was better this time, a sureness to his actions. He didn't plunder like he had before. He nibbled. He probed. He sipped. He tasted of butter and parsley, and she was starved for him.

"More," she whispered. "More."

He dragged his mouth across her cheek to her ear, biting at her earlobe and sending shivers of delight down her arms. Her nipples shrank into hard buttons. His breath was hot and sweet with wine and he moved his mouth down her jaw, nipping, nuzzling, and she shuddered. She pressed her hips against him, rubbing herself against his length, as wanton as a cat pushing into the hand that pet her. He groaned, and the wave lifted her. She was well and truly at sea.

His mouth moved to the tops of her breasts, his tongue tasting her skin and laying down trails of fire. She arched her back in surrender. She'd left off a zone or indeed any covering for precisely this reason, so he might look as much as he liked. She had also pinned her bodice loosely, to provide him ease of access.

Nevertheless as he parted the fabric, pins went flying, and she didn't care. Pins were dear, and she would hunt them all up later as she couldn't afford to buy more of them, but for now it was more important that her bodice was open and Joseph's clever, soft hands were scooping her breasts free from her shift and then yes, yes, his mouth was on her, his tongue swirled around a nipple, then his lips as he pulled her into his mouth and sucked. A bright hot arc of light soared through her, from breast to belly to that place between her legs that was hungry and aching for him.

"Joseph," she moaned. "Harder. *Harder.*"

He obeyed, and she gave a soft cry as the pleasure mounted, quickly, so quickly. She canted her hips and rolled against the hard length of him, growing harder still, and let the wave lift and lift her. Joseph, kissing her, so greedy with the clutch of his hands and mouth. Straining with desire for her.

Joseph, with his scent and his sweetness and his heady heat, wrapped around her, holding her at last. She had wanted this so desperately. She loved him so *much.* A throbbing began down below, where their bodies met, fed by the exquisite ache of his mouth on her breasts, and she didn't know if it were a climax or something else because she still craved him with an intensity close to pain.

He went perfectly still.

She opened her eyes. His were dark and wide, with slivers of molten gold.

"Inez," he whispered. "You're so beautiful."

"Touch me," she murmured. "*Please.*"

She was a wanton and she was not ashamed. She would beg on her knees if she had to. She would crawl after him, if she must, because there was *this* between them, and now that she knew it she could not turn away. She was trapped like an ant in honey.

"Inez," he whispered again. "Did you—?"

"Did I what?" She slid her hand to the back of his neck, tugging him back to her breasts, wanting his hands to move instead of resting so carefully at her sides, holding her like fragile china.

His brows knit, as if the concept were foreign. "Find... pleasure."

"Yes. And there can be more. Let me touch you." She shifted her hips and reached between them toward the flaps of his breeches, but he caught her wrist and held her firmly.

His words were a sharp rasp between them. "No."

She blinked. The wave still carried her, tilted her end over end. She could not find the ceiling, or her feet. "No?"

"We cannot do this." With both hands, carefully, he slid her to the floor, set her on her feet. Her knees threatened not to hold her.

"We can," she said stubbornly. She reached for his coat, for the band of his breeches. "There is nothing to stop us."

He shied away from her touch, rising from the chair. The distance between them was cold and terrible. There was something like despair in his eyes.

"I cannot," he said.

"Will not," she cried. "But why? Do you not desire me?"

Reason had left her long ago, with the first touch of his lips to her breasts. She didn't think about what she was doing, the wisdom of it, the danger. She only knew she wanted that control to snap. She wanted him in her arms, in her hands, convulsing, helpless. Surrendered to his want. To her.

"Do you not desire me?" Her bodice was already open; she flung it off and threw it to the floor. A yank of the string freed her petticoat, and she kicked it aside. Her stays took a moment longer, and she fumbled with the laces.

"Inez." He sounded like a man who was dying of thirst,

throat dry as a bone. He held out his hand, palm up in denial. "Do not."

"Do not what? Do not want you? It is too late for that."

With a fierce yank she shed her stays. It took only a moment to lift her shift from her head. She wanted to goad him. She wanted him to break. She stood before him in all her naked glory, shivering with rage and cool air and a frustration that made her want to howl to the heavens.

"I am yours," she said, tears welling in her throat with her anger. "Take me."

He stepped backward. The brute. The callous, unfeeling cad. She stood trembling before him, stripped to her essence, and any other man would have been on her in an instant, falling over himself to thrust his member inside her and find release. There could be no more blatant invitation.

And Joseph looked at her as if she had sunk a knife into his bowels.

"We...I..." He fumbled, squeezed his eyes shut like a man upon the rack. Then he did her the kindness of looking her straight in the eye as he sank in the knife. "I cannot."

Her mind went back to another embrace, when she had held his cock in his hand and he had shuddered and spent at her touch. She had thought it a victory. She had thought it a sign of want.

"Have you never been with a woman?" she demanded. "Do you not know what to do?"

That was cruel, and she knew it, and yet there was still satisfaction as the accusing words flew from her mouth and landed. Suddenly, everything made sense.

Joseph did not visit places like Dark Lane. He did not boast of his conquests. He did not approach women on the streets, nor bring them to his house. When he had come to her in her bed and spilled in her hand, his look of astonishment had not simply been because *she* was so potent. It might have been the first time a woman touched him and he understood the pleasure it could bring.

He drew himself up with dignity. His neckcloth was crumpled where she had pressed against him. There was a crease in his coat where she had clutched at him while he kissed her breasts and made her shudder with ecstasy. He still had a cockstand; she could see it. But he merely gave her a formal little bow, as if he were in the ducal drawing room and she was one of the duchess's friends.

"I will be going now," he said. "Thank you for dinner."

And then he was gone.

Inez let her knees give out and sank to the side of the bed. She shivered and reached for her shift.

She could weep, but she had wept already. Now was the time for something else.

Not rage. That had disappeared. She didn't hate him. She could never hate him. She had lived with this man for nearly two years, and she knew him to his soul. He fed the stray cats that came to his door, and there was one particular tabby she had found, more than once, making a bed on a cushion in his study while he read and wrote.

He had never once scolded Amaranthe for the food and clothing she gave away, even if it was his money he had contributed to the household funds. He grumbled about the little costermonger spying on him, but he always made sure she went through the kitchens when she left. He paid the street sweeps a ha'penny instead of a farthing, and he regularly invited to dinner his scholarly friends who were looking for posts and going hungry.

How many of his old students called at the house to tell him of their doings, report on their progress, take pride in his pride in them? Joseph Illingworth was a rare, good man and she was utterly, utterly in love with him.

If it were not *her* he objected to, but merely inexperience, then she required a different approach to seduce him. Inez brewed another cup of Mrs. Truckle's tea and stood regarding the leavings of dinner.

Then she dressed once more, went to the table, and finished her meal. She was a woman with a mission, and it would be wise to fortify herself for the task ahead.

She was a woman searching for a home, and unless she was very much mistaken, it was *him*.

All was not lost.

Not yet.

CHAPTER THIRTEEN

Henry Jock sat on a stool in the public room of The George, surrounded by a knot of men listening with fascination to his every word. The heavy exposed beams of the ceiling hung low over the room. The peat in the hearth puffed smoke and the scent of rich loam, which overpowered the odor of unwashed male bodies. Joseph caught the end of the tale as he made his way to the bar.

"—and by the time his lordship makes his way up on Blue Diamond, there he sees me, sittin' in the stands with his lady, just as I said I would be. Thought he would try to strangle me with his bare hands afore the judges could hand out the plate." The groom grinned.

His audience roared with appreciative laughter at this. Someone slapped Jock on the shoulder and ordered him another pint.

"King o' Newmarket," said another, shaking his head. "Shame about the stumps." He looked morosely at Jock's legs, dangling crookedly from the stool. "Damned shame."

"Hasn't hurt me with the ladies none," Jock said, accepting the fresh glass of ale.

His audience roared and hooted exclamations of encouragement, accompanied by more back-slapping.

"I thought owners rode their horses in the big races." Joseph inserted himself into the group without preamble, and with a dose of ill humor he instantly regretted. No sense bringing his blue devils on anyone else.

"Some do." Jock nodded. "But my Marquess never had a good seat, as like to fall off as cast up his accounts, no matter how smooth the goer. So he promises me a share of the purse, and I takes it."

Given the size of the prizes for a well-attended race, Jock would be a wealthy man, if he hadn't gambled all his coin. Or spent it on doctoring.

"Surprised they let you keep your sticks," Joseph said. "Would have thought the surgeon would have had 'em off you."

Jock shrugged. "Sawbones thought I was for the earth bath so didn't choose to squander his time. Turns out I pulled through." He took a long draught of ale.

The other men moved off to form their own group, uninterested in the conversation now that it had taken a darker turn. Or unwilling to rub elbows with a man introduced as a baronet, part of the overclass they would mock and complain about amongst themselves. Joseph's vault up the social ladder had shut him out of the company of those below.

He took one of the vacated stools next to the groom and stared glumly at the pint the barkeep shoved over the scarred and nocked countertop toward him.

"And I have to ask you to pay for that," he remarked to Jock. "As you're currently holding my purse."

"Whyn't ye upstairs tuppin' your lady?"

Joseph scowled into his cup. "She's not a lightskirt."

"Doesn't mean ye can't have a good tumble. All the better if she likes ye some."

Joseph tipped a long swallow into his mouth. He couldn't recall the advice from his university days. Was ale not to be consumed after wine, or was the concern over stronger spirits? He didn't care if he was sick as a dog tomorrow. He likely deserved it.

He supposed he was to chide Jock for talking about Inez as if she were a loose woman. He dragged a hand across the back of his mouth. "You think she fancies me?"

If he'd seen Inez, standing in that room gloriously nude with only her stockings and garters. A goddess come to earth to strike mortals blind with her beauty.

Or drive them blind with lust. And despair, once they knew they were unworthy.

Jock snorted. "Are ye blind, man? The lures that un's been casting at you? She wouldn't hear of going back to London without you. Me, I'd've stopped along the way to find a room in broad daylight for the two of us. Or a nice fresh hayloft would do as well."

Joseph glowered at him. "She's not—she's..." Not a lady. She was a servant. She was the daughter of a whore, and he'd found her at a brothel. A rather infamous brothel, truth be known.

So why wouldn't he simply take what she freely offered? Any red-blooded man would. The memory of her body gave him a cockstand again. The dark nipples tipping her generous breasts. The tuck of her waist and the flare of her hips. The pocket of dark curls in the glorious V between her legs. Just the thought of being inside her blotted every other scrap of sense from his mind.

He was going to spend in his breeches from the *idea* of her. How green could he be?

You've never been with a woman, have you? You don't know what to do.

That wasn't entirely accurate. He knew how it worked, the

mechanics of the act. Of a certain there was pleasure. He could guess that from how much effort his friends and acquaintances expended in getting a female to lift her skirts and permit them that paradise.

It was just he was shite at it, and that was his curse.

"She is a woman under my protection." He settled on that. One shred of gentlemanly dignity left to him. He was not a Reuben, not that, at least.

Jock laughed again, full-throated. "Coves like thee have been swiving women under their protection since Adam in the garden. Afeared she's going to spring the shackle on ye?"

"I'm not— I can't marry her," Joseph exclaimed. She had made it emphatically clear she did not wish another husband. The scorn on her face was more biting than the teeth of vermin. He wanted nothing but to marry, and she wanted nothing less.

Jock's face hardened around the nose and mouth. "Aye, marry her ye cannot. Because yer sound Saxon stock and she's born of a lascar, if I'm not mistaken."

Joseph glared at him. "That is the least of my concerns. My mother's family was Portuguese. And converted Jews. I'm no stickler for purity of blood."

Jock's expression turned curious. "Jews, you say?"

"*Conversos.* So, to put a fine point upon it, not practicing Jews for around two hundred years."

That was not to say his grandmother had not held her secrets. Joseph recalled nights she lit candles when it was not a holy day he knew of, no Christian saint's fast. He heard the prayers she would sometimes mutter that were not in Portuguese, and he'd seen the silver amulet engraved with a five-sided star that she kept tucked in a wooden box in her wardrobe.

But his mother had stood in full view of the Anglican church swearing her vows to love and obey and honor Jonas Illingworth her whole life long, and if she ever regretted departing from her family's heritage to follow the man who held her heart, Joseph had never seen sign of it.

Jock tilted his head to the side. His eyes were an uncanny blue. "Then it's as yer a swell and she's a blowen, and there's no mixing of kind."

"It's not because she's a servant," Joseph snapped. "Well, in part it is, because she works in my house and I can't—I won't be that man."

The kind of man who thought a woman was prey, or the lower classes were his to command. Joseph had grown up elbow to elbow with the sons of miners and carters and butchers and grooms, and he knew those boys were built of the same matter as he or Walter Robings of Rosecraddoc Manor, all of them made of blood and guts and bone.

It wasn't the common opinion of his class—he'd learned that at Oxford—but it was ingrained into him. One more reason Susannah Pettigrew and her Quaker beliefs had held such appeal for him.

Susannah Pettigrew, his last failure and warning.

"She fancies ye, and ye fancy 'er," Jock mused. "So the only reason to keep from making the beast w' two backs is ye can't provide for her after."

A thread of bitterness in the man's tone made Joseph look closely at him. They sat undisturbed in their corner of the bar as guests came and went, travelers from the passing coaches stepping in for a moment of warmth and ease, locals gathering for rest and gossip. The two sat slightly apart, and suddenly the well of quiet around them became a kind of confession.

"I can provide for her," Joseph said, prickling. "I'm a bloody baronet now, didn't you know? I don't intend to saddle her with a babe, but I can look after her well enough."

"Then have yer fun without leaving her a babe." Jock said this with the confidence of a man who knew well the pathways of pleasure, and indulged in them regularly. But there was that edge of bitterness again.

"That's why you're not shackled yourself," Joseph guessed. "You couldn't provide for her."

Jock winced. His pain was raw, and recent. "She swore she could live on the little I could offer. But I knew she wouldn't be happy, not once all her fine friends'd cut 'er. And her family'ud feel the strain too. 'Twas asking too much."

Perhaps he ought to have let the woman decide that, Joseph thought, but didn't say.

Amaranthe had been prepared to take Malden Grey when she thought he was the bastard son of a duke, doubted he would ever be called to the bar, and might very well have to support him on her work as a copyist, the way she'd supported Joseph. Only the stupendous surprise of discovering the marriage lines Mal's dead mother had always sworn existed had turned Amaranthe's straw to spun gold, making the bastard the Duke of Hunsdon. Not quite the same leap as lowly tutor Joseph Illingworth becoming Sir Joseph of Penwellen, but in the same vein.

"I thought you had a position with the Earl of Renwick," Joseph said.

"It's the Countess of Calenberg pays my salary. But I've spent a deal of time at Renwick House after her ladyship's niece wed the earl."

Joseph tried to remember. All the titles he'd encountered since Amaranthe skipped her way to the highest echelons of British society had frankly gotten muddled in his head. Renwick was an odd one—seemed a very deliberate, reserved man. Joseph had thought him an arrogant ass until Amaranthe whispered, at a breakfast she'd hosted one afternoon, that the man's stiff demeanor was compensation for a clubfoot and he didn't speak much because of his stammer.

The Countess of Calenberg was odder still. Her husband

had been the count of some tiny Germanic principality that no longer existed, given the near-constant wars on the Continent. She lived like an eccentric in a big house in London, merry as the day was long, sharing her house with outcast women who had artistic sensibilities and collecting servants who wouldn't be hired anywhere else. Witness Henry Jock, who without the patronage of an eccentric countess would be on the street with his beggar's bowl like so many other poor souls of London who had lost their legs or their eyes or their wits.

"The girl was a maid in Renwick's household," Joseph guessed.

Jock's mouth twisted. "The earl's sister."

Joseph blinked. "The devil you say. So his lordship threatened to kill you?"

"He doesn't know of it. No one does, saving her and I. And she won't speak of it."

"Cut you off when she was finished? That's a cold end."

"She'd have run away with me if I'd let her. Demanded it, actually. But what have I to give 'er? Told her so, broke her heart, and took m'self away instead."

Joseph contemplated the tangle of emotion on the other man's face. "And here you are, counseling me to have my way with Inez."

The other shrugged. "There's hell to pay after, to be sure, but to have her? Why'd you deny yourself that? If you want her, that is."

Oh, Joseph wanted Inez. He wanted her with an intensity that had taken him off guard.

He wasn't built like other men; he'd learned that in university. They could drop their breeches for any pretty face and not see the girl again after. Joseph required some sense of attachment to his partner before the blood could rise. He needed to feel she was a woman he could admire, possibly share a future with, and then the little head followed the lead of the larger.

Until it came to the actual act. There, he was rubbish. And he didn't want Inez to know that.

He hadn't known how much she riled his senses until he'd seen that eel Wigsby advancing on her. She was Inez. Bearer of trays. Baker of delicious bread. A proud, beautiful, prickly woman he could seem to offend just by looking at her.

He held her in esteem. He cared about her welfare. She stirred his heart and his senses together. That was why, when she tore off her gown and stood before him as perfect as God made her, he'd wanted to dive at her, bear her back to bed, and bury himself in her softness.

But. There were so many *buts*. So many risks that joining with her—or attempting such—would create a rend he couldn't repair.

You've never been with a woman. You don't know what to do.

"Tell me how not to leave her with a babe," Joseph said.

Before this night, Joseph had only known one way to find pleasure with a woman. By the time he'd bought and finished another round of ales with Henry Jock, he knew at least five.

CHAPTER FOURTEEN

A stir came from the direction of the private parlor, and the door opened to emit a cloud of fragrant tobacco smoke. Two gentlemen dressed in the style of the country, with old-fashioned coats and powdered wigs, tumbled out of the door, arguing. A third strolled behind them, holding a pipe to his mouth and puffing on it.

"—rests his entire system of classification on chives," one was saying. His speech, and the red knobs of his cheeks, hinted that he had already imbibed a great deal. "He ought to have based his classes on the number of pointals." He grasped a lapel of his coat with a decisive gesture, as if that closed the debate, and pointed a finger at his compatriot.

"But that too is highly debatable." The other shook his bagwig, tied up with a large black ribbon. The hair of the wig was yellowed and the whole in desperate need of refurbishment. "He ought've considered empalement as the organizing structure of his system."

The third puffed his pipe with a thoughtful air. "I still say he's confusing his orders and genera. One would take the construction of the florets into account before the arrangement of the chives."

"And—oh, I say." The first stopped short and fumbled with the chain over his waistcoat, producing a quizzing glass, which he held to his eye. "Suffice to observe that the production of perfect seed is the obvious use of the flower!"

"Lord in his heaven," breathed the second, staring with reverence. "How is such a vision of loveliness descended on the George?"

The third, feeling no need to join the competition, merely mouthed his pipe and stared in obvious appreciation. Joseph followed the direction of the man's gaze and found he was looking at Inez.

She had pinned her bodice back in place and tied a fresh apron over her petticoat, but she had left off her neckerchief, and the ruffled border of her shift left the full tops of her glossy brown breasts on display. Her cap was perched far back on her head, accenting rather than concealing the cascade of soft black curls and bringing attention to the proud, elegant slope of her neck. She walked with a saucy cant to her hips, and when the men of the philosophical meeting paused to gape at her, she fluttered her lashes at them.

Then, noting their rapt attention, she gave all three a sweet, small smile.

The little *trollop*. She had come downstairs looking so fresh and coy just to bait him, and Joseph rose to the lure with a snap.

"And why haven't *you* been serving us?" one of the men said with a smack of his lips. "We came to request more claret. I hope you will be the one who brings it."

Inez offered a low, throaty chuckle. "I don't work here, sir. I am a traveler passing through, much like yourself."

"Oh, we aren't travelers." The second man was eager to put

himself forward. "We are philosophers here for the meeting. I am Robert Smith—"

"And I am his brother, John Smith. Elder brother." The first asserted his claim with firmness.

The third blew on his pipe and surveyed Inez with the air of a connoisseur, his gaze lingering on breast and hip. "And you may call me Squire Heath. Where's such a pretty pet from, might I ask?"

"London," Inez said primly, smoothing her hair. The gesture drew attention to her lovely profile and also her lovely breasts. "Just this morn."

"Oh, I know a bit of London," the first man said. "I was just recently there, put down at the Swan with Two Necks—"

"I travel to London all the time," the second interrupted. "For my business. I am a dyer of cloth. Quite well off, it may be said—"

"And what brings a Londoner here?" The third man, without appearing to move, placed himself so that he was closest to Inez. In the perfect position to look down her bodice, or take her arm and steer her away from the others. He seemed older than the other two, more seasoned and more perceptive, and he had the hawkish stare of a practiced rake.

"Me." Joseph rose and shouldered his way into the group. "I brought her. She is my ward."

"Ward!" one Smith spluttered.

"Ward," the second muttered, with the clear connotation of *mistress*.

Inez narrowed her eyes at Joseph and pressed together her lips. This gesture only served to emphasize their fullness, and likely she knew that. He could have kissed those lips not half an hour before this. He could have had his mouth on any part of her body, if he hadn't been an incompetent arse.

"We shall see how much longer I continue as your ward, shan't we? For I have the sense you weary of me, Mr. Illingworth."

"Sir Joseph," he corrected, because he did not want her dressing him down in front of these local men. The curve of her lips said he'd fallen into the first of her traps.

Smith elder cleared his throat. "I say, miss, if you should require assistance—if this man has abused your gentle nature in any way—"

"I can offer you lodging," Smith the second fell over himself to say. "And unlike my brother, I do not have a wife."

Inez looked him over, and the man colored profusely at the lewd implication of his generosity.

"You are not going anywhere but back up to your room," Joseph told her. "Whatever you need, I shall have it sent up to you."

She faced him down, her chin at a cool angle, her eyes blazing. "Perhaps what I desire is company. It is very lonely up there in the attics."

"Oh, we can't have that!" Smith One rushed to say. "Do join us in our parlor. We are the Amesbury Philosophical Society, and we are currently discussing the recent publication by Dr. William Withering. *A Botanical Arrangement of all the Vegetables Naturally Growing in Great Britain.*"

"Vegetables." Inez blinked. "The kind you eat? What's to say about them?"

"Withering has undertaken a survey of all the vegetative matter that grows in Britain," Smith Two elucidated. "Or I believe that is his aim. We have been discussing the first volume. Marestail to toadflax, with helpful directions in identifying species, and preserving them."

Joseph's attention swerved suddenly. "His is the catalogue

based on the system developed by Linneus? And he discusses the plants by their common English names?"

"Being an attempt to render them familiar to those who are unacquainted with the learned languages," Smith the Second quoted. He seemed as eager to impress Joseph as he had Inez, and he furthermore seemed the type to lack a grasp of the learned languages.

"I've consulted the first volume," Joseph said, diverted. "Withering's. I noted he discusses the medical properties of plants, including poisons."

"Useful knowledge," Inez remarked, but the group's attention had moved to Joseph.

"Then you must indeed join our discussion," said the Squire, puffing around his pipe. "You would be the same Joseph Illingworth who wrote on the optative mood for Greek verbs, and gave an explanation of the aorist tense? The essay that appeared in the *Philosophical Transactions of the Royal Society*."

"That was I," Joseph said, embarrassed and pleased. "Would you agree with my distinctions about the future optative?"

"Don't recall a bit of my grammar, for how hard my tutor tried beating it into me." The Squire pulled an unused clay pipe from a pocket of his coat and held it out. "Should be tobacco enough left in there for a scholar such as yourself to edify us." He nodded toward Inez. "Bring your gel. We don't mind the ladies listening in. Gives us something to occupy our eyes while we exercise our minds."

Inez's eyes blazed with anger, but her voice was honey sweet. "Oh, how I would adore to listen to the men talk." She swayed closer to Smith the Second, seeming to have fixed on him as her most gullible object. Her victory was assured by the look of his face when she fluttered her eyelashes at him again. "Perhaps I might sit next to you?"

She tipped forward slightly, her smile one of supplication. The gesture brought her breasts into full frame in the tight bodice. The edges of her dark aureoles showed in a sliver behind the ruffle of her shift.

Joseph's mouth went searingly dry, and blood rushed to his groin, leaving his head. In a second he was at her side, hand on her arm. She was warm and firm and her glare ought to have sizzled him like an egg in a pan. He was burning for her already.

"You and I have something to discuss."

"But the *Botanical Arrangement*," a Smith cried, seeing his prize escaping.

"Forgive me, gentlemen, for stealing this one away," Joseph said without the slightest trace of contrition. "But my ward and I must settle a small matter between us."

She kept pace with him as he marched up the stairs like a general leading the attack. Her flesh was so warm, and she smelled of some intoxicating blend of spice and florals. At the first landing, a swath of shadow falling between the lamps below and above, he turned to her. "You little, conniving—"

She charged him. More correctly, she kissed him, her lips crashing against his. She pulled his lower lip into her mouth and bit down.

With a groan he pushed her against the wall with his body and held her. She fisted her hands in his hair and pulled as if she could not get his face close enough. His tongue in her mouth tasted of herbs and savory and so, so much sweetness.

She lifted a leg and wrapped it around his hip, fitting his cock neatly between her legs. He thought his head might burst with the jolt of sheer pleasure, his brains spilling out before his seed could.

"Upstairs," she panted against his mouth. "My room. Not *here*."

She didn't unwrap herself from around him, so he simply

carried her, a luscious armful of woman. No one passed them in the hall or stair, and if inhabitants of other rooms heard their passage, they wisely remained inside.

At the door to her room Inez reached behind her and pushed at the wooden portal, banging it against the jamb.

"You ought to leave it locked," he growled, crowding them inside.

"What's to steal?"

The table stood where they had left it, two plates still atop it, with the bottle of wine and the untouched pudding. The room swelled of nutmeg and currants. A candle in its lamp had been carefully trimmed, batting back the evening shadows. She hadn't meant to leave the room for long; likely she knew he would fall upon her.

Yes, he'd tumbled securely into her trap, and he didn't care to fight his way out. He wanted to be here, alone in a room, her in his arms, a bed before them. He was done pretending he wanted anything else.

He tipped her onto the bed, and she pulled him down atop her. The rope springs creaked, and the tick rustled. She deserved feathers of down beneath her and satin bedsheets against her skin. She deserved a full-scale seduction that would include red rose petals and expensive French wine and, oh, what all he didn't know, because he had never waged a full-scale seduction on a woman. He had always been awkward and unsure of himself and fumbling at the crucial moment.

She cradled him against her body and he propped himself on his elbows so he didn't suffocate her. Her body shaped to his so perfectly, full breasts pressing against his chest, her hips his anchor. He stared into her face, taking in her beauty. Her eyes held a deep red-brown flame, and her lips were plush and pouting at him.

"You can't kiss me when you're staring."

"By God, you're exquisite." He brushed his fingers along her brow, pushing aside the lock of dark hair. Soft as corn silk. "I couldn't bear to hurt you, Inez."

She tightened her arms around him, clasping the backs of his shoulders, urging him closer.

"What hurts is when you ignore me," she whispered. "Or walk away. Don't walk away this time, Joseph." She pressed her lips to his neck, lighting a fire there. "Be with me. Hold me."

Love me, he thought she said, the barest murmur against his skin. He could pretend he'd imagined the words as she rubbed her face in the crook of his shoulder, nipping his throat with her pillowy lips, pulling at his neckcloth with her teeth.

But he heard them, and he answered with a kiss. A kiss that broke the last of his restraint and surrendered all, reserving nothing. He would give her all of himself, and then she would know the sorry truth, but until then there was *this*.

"Oh, Joseph," she whispered as he moved his mouth down her throat, over her collarbone, to her breasts. "Oh, please."

She mewled and grappled with his coat as he browsed her breasts, her breath coming in ever shorter, shallower pants. Kissing her breasts pleasured her as much as it did him. She yanked at buttons and he helped her peel off his coat. With a yank she freed the neckcloth and tossed it aside.

"That will—"

She bit his earlobe, and he ceased caring about creases in his coat or a crumpled neckcloth. With a growl he pulled at her bodice to free her breasts. He meant to be careful with the pins —he'd scattered them earlier—but she yanked there too, pins hitting the floor with a small patter, and he smiled against the fresh, warm skin exposed to his mouth.

She was greedy for him, and her passion inflamed him. When he pulled a dark crest into his mouth and sucked, she arched and cried out, rubbing the opening of her legs against the bulge in his breeches.

He was so hard for her, hard to bursting. The self-doubt and consciousness and sheer awkwardness of the situation that usually seized him in this moment had the grace not to penetrate his mind. He had Inez's nipples in his mouth and her little cries of pleasure, the seeking way she rubbed her body against his, sent the blood pounding through him in great waves.

"Too much clothing," she panted, grasping the buttons of his waistcoat, and he helped her peel that off him, too. Then it was the heat of their bodies pressed together, her warm beneath her shift, he only in his shirt. Her hands slid everywhere, over his sides and back, shoulders and arms, and a dreamy smile curved her lips as he suckled and she surged against him.

Then she went still, and her eyes flew open. "Take off your *boots*."

He laughed. "They're not as easy to remove."

"You are not," she said, "going to have me with your *boots* on," and she rolled and pushed until he was sitting, letting go of her breasts with great regret. She climbed across his lap, backside toward him, seating herself directly on his cock, and Joseph fought the urge to nip at the back of her neck where her hair was falling over the back of her shift. Then he gave into the urge and grazed his teeth along her nape.

She gave a throaty chuckle and a shiver. Looking over her shoulder, he could see she'd left her shift pulled down and her breasts swinging free, and just watching them sway while she struggled with his jockey boots was going to make him spill in his breeches.

She sent him a laughing look. "At least this time—"

He didn't let her finish. With a growl he bore her onto the bed, face first, and she squealed and wriggled as his weight came down atop her. He yanked up her shift and started kissing her bare skin, down the sleek brown slope of her back, dipping his lips into the dimples above her bottom, then biting the round globes, not hard, but enough to make her squeal again. He kissed down her sleek, long legs, to her stockings, then flipped her over started kissing his way back up.

"Joseph." She lay with her eyes screwed shut, breasts rising with her pants of breath, her small hands fluttering through his hair, over his shoulders, squeezing the muscle in his arms. His name was a chant, a song. "Joseph. *Joseph.*"

"I haven't done this before," he said when he reached the crown of dark curls. "So you must tell me what you like."

Her eyes were dark pools, trusting, bewildered. "I've never —not like this," she whispered. "So I don't—I'm not—*oh.*"

He thrilled at her caught breath, then the long sigh when he licked his way into her woman's entry. Her entire body shuddered, held taut and still. Jock had been right: this was the key to her pleasure.

Joseph delved and explored, reading her gasps and sighs, grinning despite himself when she dove her hands into his hair to steer him. "There," she whispered once, and then, "oh, there," and after a moment, a moan, and a little buck of her hips, she pressed herself against his mouth, matching his rhythm. "*There.*" Then her entire body shuddered, her legs convulsing around him, and the little bud he was nursing pulsed madly, and Joseph felt such a primal surge of satisfaction that he almost roared with it.

He had pleasured a woman, *his* woman, and he'd done it right, Jove be praised. When he reached for her she burrowed into his arms, still shuddering in her ecstasy. Then she lifted her lashes to look at him with dazed eyes, and he was the most brilliant man in the world. Her look was hazy, astonished, as she met his gaze.

And then she burst into tears.

"Darling. Darling." He kissed her cheekbones, her nose, her chin, smoothing his hands through her hair, over her shaking shoulders. "What's wrong? What did I do?"

She put her hands over her face but did not pull away, instead burrowing closer, hiding her face in his shirt. "I've never —I couldn't—" She sniffled, then tried again. "I thought it would be...with you. But I've never—*that.*"

He smiled at her. He would admit to a trace of smugness. So her husband had never cared to pleasure her thoroughly, or consult men of great expertise, which Henry Jock clearly was.

He traced a finger at the corner of her lip. "I am glad I could share that with you."

She cried harder, and he didn't know what else to do, so he kissed her. She pressed herself against him fully, throwing a leg over his hip, and placing herself over his cock again. Joseph groaned.

"I want more," she whispered, nipping at his lip. Her tears made her face sticky, and his. "I want all of you."

He leaned his forehead to hers. "I want the same. But I fear leaving you with a babe."

That was what men like Reuben did. They planted a babe in a woman, then left her with a belly, and then because she could not find a position after that, she must find a rotten husband, or go into the streets to earn her keep.

He did not know what awaited him at Penwellen and could promise her nothing yet. He did not know if he would be able to support himself, much less a woman and child.

To say nothing of a wife.

"There are ways." She spoke hesitantly, glancing at the table behind them.

"There are...other concerns. Of mine," he said, when her face darkened instantly, and he feared he had tread on that sensitive nerve that he always seemed to tread on with her.

She drew back, her dark brows rushing together. Her gaze probed every inch of his face, looking too closely. He was too vulnerable with her, so bare.

"What concerns?"

"Hunger, at the moment," he lied, freeing himself from her arms and sliding out of the bed. "I want that pudding."

She let him go and watched from the bed, hair tousled, eyes dark and deep, her manner languid as a cat's. He cut a piece of pudding and put it on a plate. The scent of nutmeg filled his head, hot, smoky, every delicious thing. He would associate it forevermore with Inez, and likely get a cockstand every time he smelled it, remembering her like this, long legs tucked to her side, the tops of her breasts showing above her shift, a slope of brown skin gleaming above her stockings. Cotton stockings. She deserved silk.

He hopped back to bed, conscious of his own wool stockings, balancing the plate as he joined her once more.

"I've never done this either." His throat rasped around the confession. He was revealing too much. "The post-coital loll."

"You depart instantly?" She pulled the bedcovers over both of their feet, and the small gesture, so tender, went straight to his gut.

"I've never had the coitus part. So, no lolling after." Usually slinking away in shame, those few times until he grew wise to his own weakness.

"You've never—?"

He cut off the question by scooping up pudding and holding the spoon toward her. She leaned forward, allowing him a brilliant view of her breasts, and closed her mouth over the spoon. He watched her lips pull closed and his groin tightened.

"I think I'm impotent. Sorry to say."

She struggled not to—he watched the conflict on her face— then her eyes fell to the obvious bulge in his breeches. He was still hard as a bolt for her. He could hold the copper plating to the hull of a ship with this rod.

She swallowed. "I've heard that happens to some men. So you..." She lifted her gaze to his face. "Think you cannot? At all?"

There was no scorn in her face, no judgment. Not like he'd seen in others. She was the daughter of a town woman; she likely had heard reports. There were others like him. He'd done the reading, found what medical information he could. None of it told him why he was so difficult to arouse. It was likely why he pursued with such determination, when he finally found a woman who could stir him.

But every time, when it came to the act, and he realized the attachment was not what he had thought, he failed. Wilted like a wildflower plucked from its root.

"I told Susannah Pettigrew this," he admitted. "The night before we were to be married. Thought it fair to warn her. And the next day, there I stood at the church with the vicar, looking an utter fool, while she ran away with Viktor Vierling." Who likely swived her in the carriage front, back, and sideways before they reached the next posting stop.

She'd jilted Viktor, too, so he'd done something wrong also, but Joseph didn't doubt the Hessian could rise to the occasion and didn't need to like the girl to use his spear. Joseph was malformed, not like other men, and there was no remedy.

"Susannah Pettigrew was not for you."

Between them, they devoured the pudding, and Inez set the plate on the floor beside the bed. Then she crawled toward Joseph, and he couldn't decide if he wanted to stare at her eyes, her lips, her breasts, or the dark shadow of hair beneath the thin linen of her shift as she placed her knees of either side of his.

"Susannah Pettigrew was a mewling, milk-livered girl with no spine in her."

"You never met Susannah," he murmured, ridiculously pleased by the streak of jealousy in her tone.

"I saw her when you left for Gloucestershire with her, and I knew on sight there was no steel in her backbone."

"A little steel in her backbone," Joseph protested, leaning back on his elbows to hold her weight as she settled against his chest. "All those beliefs and such."

"She mouthed what other people told her and didn't know what she wanted for herself." That shadow between her legs hovered directly above his groin now. His cock brushed the inside of her thigh, and he tightened.

"You need a woman with fire," Inez said.

"Do I," he murmured, and met her mouth hungrily when she kissed him. He loved how direct she was. How knowledgeable about what pleased her, and how determined to procure it. He was so hard he ached.

She kissed him leisurely, exploring with her hands, squeezing his arms and shoulders, running her hands down his chest. She skated her palms over his ridges and made little murmurs of appreciation that kept his blood high. Lord in heaven, he was going to be stiff for days. Her admiration went straight into his vessels and plumped him up.

It had never been like this. He wasn't afraid he would fail or disappoint her. He wasn't afraid he would mean nothing. Inez showed him at every turn that she wanted and craved him. She'd chased him down in a hired carriage, point of fact, after he told her to go home and forget him.

"Will you let me pleasure you?" She whispered against his neck, and her hand drifted to his breeches. "The way you pleasured me?"

"Do you mean—" His throat strangled shut at the very thought.

He knew of the act. It was something his mates at university had paid women to perform at every opportunity. Young Reuben had bragged how the dairymaid at Penwellen loved to blow his pipe. Joseph suspected Reuben had paid or coerced the girl for the pleasure.

Joseph had never begged for it, himself. Another way he was squeamish, he supposed. He could imagine the distaste a complete stranger would feel at becoming acquainted with this intimate part of himself, and it made it easy to keep his coin in his pocket.

"You can't *want* to," he tried saying, desperately hoping she did.

"I do." She confirmed this by pushing him down on the bed, hand splayed to his chest, fingers a caress. She added a coy smile. "Tell me if I'm doing it wrong. Or to stop, if you don't like it."

He leaned on his elbows and watched with fascination as she pushed her hair over one shoulder. She unfastened his breeches with deft fingers, and his throat closed again, his mind snagging on a fear. "Have you..." *How many others*, he wanted to ask? And was it something she enjoyed or simply submitted to?

Her gaze rose to meet his. "None," she said softly. "Never. But I want this. With you."

And those were the magic words. When she released the flap of his leather breeches, his member sprang easily to her hand, as hard and armed as the Spartoi that sprang from the soil of Thebes when Cadmus sowed the dragon teeth.

She opened her mouth and licked up the length of him, and Joseph couldn't watch any longer. His eyes rolled back into his head in ecstasy. She closed her lips around him as she had done with the pudding and he surrendered to the caress.

She was tentative at first, then grew bolder as the noises bursting from him conveyed his obvious appreciation. He was caught in a tide of lava. A hot geyser gathering to erupt. This was nothing like when he dealt with himself in the furtive quiet of his bedchamber or study. His balls in her hand grew hot and tight and the pressure built and built in an endless cascade and the sweet heat of her mouth was a delight he wanted never to end and yet knew the end was coming, all too quickly.

He squeezed her arm, the words a hoarse mutter. "Inez...I'm going to..."

He wanted to warn her. The peak had already caught him and he was rushing at its headlong, every fiber in his body pulsing toward one goal.

She planted her hands on either side of his hips and sucked harder, as if she meant to consume him, and her murmurs of encouragement flung him over the precipice as if he'd been tossed by a giant hand. He pulsed and she held him and for a moment he thought his heart might stop beating. His breath tore in ragged bursts from his chest.

He was changed. Alchemized. And she had transformed him.

Awareness returned, slowly. Inez stretched out beside him, all soft heat and woman, a satisfied smile on her glistening lips.

"You liked that," she said, as smug as he'd felt when she shook apart beneath his mouth. So it was the same. It could be the same for both of them, a shared paradise.

"God. Yes. You." He drifted hand over her hair, the silken skin of her shoulder. "You," he said again. "Are so beautiful."

"You are mine now." She turned her face into his neck and a note of fierceness accompanied the words.

Yes. He thought he answered. He was drifting out of consciousness, the pleasure so complete it had blotted out his mind. This bed. The scent of spice and woman. Inez lush and warm beside him. The most fulfilling peace he had ever known.

Something was coming—something at the end of the road,

something dark he didn't completely comprehend and didn't entirely want. Penwellen. But he had this now, and Inez would be with him. All would be well.

He was hers now.

And she was his.

He had to find a way to deserve her.

CHAPTER FIFTEEN

Penwellen wasn't what Inez had expected.

She feared it wasn't what Joseph had expected, either.

The manor itself was lovely, a symmetrical box of dressed gray stone rising three stories under a slate roof. Four bays of windows stood on either side of a small porch with Doric columns twined with climbing ivy. It faced a southerly direction, warming like a nesting bird in the sun, and the aspect took in swelling green hills, a coppice that Joseph had called Birton Wood, and a small pond fed by the river they'd crossed on the dirt lane leading westward from Callington.

The cottages and outbuildings behind were fashioned of the same dressed stone, all laid out in pleasing proportions, and a larger cottage she guessed was the carriage house stood attached to a stables. A paddock held a bay gelding that watched their approach with pricked ears, and sheep browsed the pastures beside a few small cows that suggested the manor housed its own dairy. As long as she wasn't required to get closer to any hooved beast than she was from the horse right this moment, Inez thought she would go on fine on a country estate.

But the gravel approaching the drive had not been raked in

some time, and weeds poked through. A basin for a fountain stood empty of water, brown algae streaking the sides. Black wreaths hung from paned windows dull with dust, and as Jock pulled the carriage to a halt, Inez saw that the steps had not been whitewashed, nor the door repainted, in some time.

She glanced at Joseph in the chaise beside her. He looked as apprehensive as she felt.

"It's still standing, so that's a beginning." He climbed down from the carriage and held out his arms to help her descend.

"Did you think it would not be?"

His fingers brushed her ribs as he set her on her feet, and heat lanced through her innards like a charge set alight. She hungered every moment for his hands on her. Their time in Amesbury had formed an appetite that only seemed to grow when it was fed.

He'd spent the night in her bed at The George, only sneaking out in the morning after the boots boy had returned his footwear—so much for leaving no sign of himself, Inez thought. At the Lamb and Flag in Honiton he'd arranged adjoining rooms, which happened to comprise the entire upper story and thus secured them privacy. She'd thought it outrageous to pay for two unused rooms, but Jock and his purse seemed well able to stand the expense.

And so Inez had succumbed to the dangerous luxury of a spacious room, a hot dinner accompanied by more wine, and the body of the man she loved in bed beside her, hers to explore and touch and kiss at her leisure.

He still hadn't taken her properly, too cautious about planting a babe, and the ache for him was growing. What a harlot she was becoming, Inez thought, pushing back her cap to squint up at the house.

The late afternoon sun had lit their way from Honiton that morning, through Exeter and the great moor Joseph called Dartmoor, through a medieval-looking town he called Tavistock and then along a fresh turnpike to Callington. Penwellen was well-situated, enjoying the air of the country but within a stone's throw from a market town. It wasn't as lovely as Portugal, but this was Joseph's home now.

And she wanted to be where Joseph was.

The windows seemed to suck in rather than beam back the sunlight, giving the place a sullen aspect, and Inez heard no movement from humans behind or around or within. No calls of scullery maids sent out to fetch water, no boys shouting to the animals as they moved them along.

No one moved through the fields that ran in strips and hedged squares across the low hills, no one plowing or planting or walking a survey of boundary stones, though there had been plenty of other such activity everywhere else they'd passed, saving the moors. It was the season for it, after all.

No servants pouring out of the house to greet the new master.

Jock swung down from the horse they'd procured at the Queen's Head in Tavistock and retrieved his crutches. While she felt bruised and weary from the road, Jock looked as fresh as the morning they'd met.

"Not a terrible pile," he remarked, nodding toward the house.

Joseph straightened his coat and stepped toward the porch. The front door opened.

"And ye be?"

The woman standing in the frame was not much older than Inez. A pert cap held back hair the color of straw, and freckles covered her pink face. She had bright blue eyes and while her appearance was neat, her expression was wary and tired. Her apron was well worn, and so were her shoes.

Joseph paused at the bold address from what was clearly a servant.

"Illingworth," he said. "Joseph Illingworth. Er—Sir Joseph now, I suppose."

The girl rolled her eyes. "Another 'un coming to claim ee's the baronet!" She glared at all three of them in turn, her mouth pinched into a disapproving line. "Third this week."

"This week?" Joseph blinked. It was only Thursday.

"Aye, and they all do just the same. Stroll into th'ouse saying as they own it, poke and quiddle about a bit, and by the time the solicitor arrives, they's gone, and so's some of the silver."

"Pretendin' to be the gentry cove, and comin' to crack the crib?" Jock nodded, impressed. "Clean job, that."

"I am not here to steal the silver," Joseph said with great indignation. "It would be my silver, wouldn't it? That is to say, Illingworth silver, and so mine, for the moment."

"You've a letter or such identifying yourself, don't you?" Inez asked, trying to calm the waters. Joseph usually kept a level head, but he'd been twitching like a cat on hot bricks since Exeter. Being barred entry to this inheritance he wasn't yet certain he wanted was going to light the fuse on his temper.

"And what's that to me?" The young woman crossed her arms over her chest, not to be cozened. "Couldn't read it if ye did."

"Oh, for the love of Creation."

Joseph strode toward the door. The young woman grasped her broom stick with both hands and banged the butt of it on the stone steps, where the sound vibrated. Three bold strokes, like a summons. Her expression was fierce, and Inez marveled at her courage. She would have given in and bolted, herself.

What was the woman defending?

"Close my own door to me?" Joseph's mouth fell open. "I

hope you don't work here, you harpy. I'll turn you off without a character."

The other lifted her chin as a man came around the side of the house. Inez's chest squeezed. Jock stood next to the horses, but Jock couldn't stop a man bent on physical force.

And this one was big. Broad shoulders filled out his fustian jacket, and he wore the trousers and boots of a laborer. Dirty blond hair showed beneath his round hat. As he neared, his glower broke into a puzzled expression as he glanced over Jock, then studied Joseph from head to toe.

He looked back at the woman in the doorway. "Says he's the baronet," she told him, moving her hands as she spoke.

The man grunted, pointed to Joseph, then the house. He made another gesture, ending by tapping his chest.

The woman's face fell as she turned to regard Joseph. "Is ee un? Oh, dear. I hope he will'nt be the perjinkety type."

Joseph gaped at the new man, then shook his head as if to clear it. "Thaker?" He lifted his hands, moving them as he spoke much as the woman hand. "Is that you? You've—grown." He lifted one palm in the air, indicating the man's height.

The laborer grinned, showing stained teeth between a blond beard, and made more gestures in the direction of the doorway.

"Your wife?" Joseph said. "Well, that's—" He nodded stiffly to the woman, who had set the broomstick aside but close to hand, as if it might yet prove a method of defense. "I suppose I won't turn you off, then. Amaranthe said Thaker had married."

"Did the Duchess tell you of usun?" The other still employed her hands as she spoke. "I suppose so, if you're een."

"Her brother." Joseph nodded. "The new Baronet, if the solicitor's letter is to be believed."

"Ah, well. I hope you can see we weren't to let just anyone in, no matter if he called hisself the King of Rome." She surveyed Inez with interest. "And who's this party? Your wife? Sweetheart?"

"No." Joseph fumbled for words. "This is my—er—this is Inez."

Inez nodded, her throat pinching on the polite words of greeting. Her head ached, and her chest felt like one of the horses had sat on it. If he couldn't introduce her to his staff, how would he introduce her to his equals?

What *was* she to him?

The men busied themselves about the chaise, unloading luggage, and the woman in the doorway beckoned to Inez. "Come along then, and I'll give ee the tour. The others can follow about as they may."

Inez joined her on the porch. At least she was arriving at Penwellen through the front door. She hadn't been bid to go 'round back to the servant's entrance.

But she hadn't been introduced with a status, either. She had no proper place here.

Once again, she was all on her own.

"You cannot be all the staff," Inez said as she followed the other woman into the house.

The entrance hall was small but well-proportioned, light struggling through the smudged window set above the door. A carved wooden staircase lifted to the upper floor, with a wooden door behind closing off, Inez guessed, the servant's hallways. Doorways on either side opened into broad parlors. The woman led her into one. Everything within lay under a hazy film of dust.

"Me luv and I are the only uns as stayed. I'm Wenna. Ee's Thaker. We've two young'uns, a boy and a cheel, so if the sir don't like ee's people with cheldern, best we know now. An me Thaker don't hear, so if you speech at'un, ee'll only nod and give thee a grin." Wenna smiled fondly. "Ee sees t' the stables and the animals, now, though ee can't do for all'en. I cook."

Inez surveyed the parlor. The style was not old, but the dark, dull colors seemed inharmonious somehow, and the furniture ought to have been under covers. "Housekeeper? Maids?"

Wenna shook her head. "Himself, the old Baronet, we couldn't keep a maid about, ee'd 'ave at 'er if ee could. Mrs. Wadge was fusty as they come, but when the Baronet took ill and stopped paying wages, she skuppered off to another post. Took the footman an hall boy with her."

"You can't be looking after all this yourself." Inez peered into a smaller parlor set off the larger, this one lined with windows. It overlooked a lovely stone patio and the green swales beyond.

If she were the lady of Penwellen, she wouldn't use the dark, drab parlors but would sit on this sunny porch, taking her tea and catching up on correspondence, chatting with callers and planning with the housekeeper for dinners and holidays and small parties now and again for her and the baronet, to provide amusement and keep good relations with their neighbors.

But Penwellen did not have a lady. Nor a proper staff, from the looks of things, and had not in some time, if this lovely room had been given over to storage.

Four bedrooms occupied the upper floor, one suite with a large powder room useful for dressing, and a nursery with a small cupboard off the side with a bed for a nurse. Inez denied the pang that shot from her heart to her belly at the sight.

She had never longed for a child, never imagined herself with one. But the thought of Joseph's children asleep in this room, their brown curly hair spilling over these pillows, coals in the grate as their mother rocked in the chair and read to them—

She turned away. "The kitchens?"

The kitchens sat empty, the tables bare and waiting. The great hearth smoked quietly with a smothered fire, banked and ready to be stirred to life. Wenna set the broomstick in the scullery and wiped her hands in her apron as she looked around.

"I suppose the new sir will want his supper," she said, "and it's I and Old Jupe to make it. Just as well, as the stores'll be going pindy soon if we don't use 'em."

"I'll help." The words popped out before Inez could consider their wisdom.

Wenna raised an eyebrow. "You being—?"

She'd done it before, hadn't she? Worked her way onto his staff to be under his nose and look after him. Watched and longed for him from afar while he went about his Joseph-like ways, not seeing more than an inch of the way before him.

There was something, too, about the dignity of the woman beside her, confiding in Inez as if she were the overseer of the house already. Inez wanted to be her confidante. Her equal.

This was the way to fix her position here.

"I am his housekeeper," Inez said.

"YOU ARE NOT MY HOUSEKEEPER." Joseph faced the dressing mirror with a frown and flipped his neckcloth a different way.

"Then what am I?" She focused on folding the stack of white linen she'd unpacked from his valise.

Inez and Wenna had spent an hour earlier preparing the master's chambers for Joseph. Together they'd aired the drawers of the cupboard, tugged the embroidered coverlet off the bed, turned the goose down tick and beat it to a light airiness. Wenna knocked the dust from the rich brocade canopy that hung atop the four posters, catching what fell in her apron. Inez swept the rug and did her best to polish the windows. The dressing room was broad and airy with a window of its own and a writing desk, the flap tipped up and locked.

"Gad, I can't even do this right!" Joseph tugged at the band of linen and threw it on the desk.

"Let me."

She stepped close with a fresh length of linen in hand. Hiring a valet would be a necessity if he wanted to live the life of a country gentleman, but there was a whole host of things the house needed first. His meeting with the solicitor tonight would better reveal the state of things, for good or for ill, and Joseph was nervous as a cat on hot bricks about it.

He didn't answer her question, only studied her face as she twined the cloth gently about his neck, arranging the folds as he liked them. "You cannot pretend you are my housekeeper," he said at last, his voice low.

He was close enough that she could rise on her toes and press her lips to his. She wanted to. His mouth was pressed in the firm, worried expression he had worn since his first survey of the house and grounds with Thaker, and the report on the animals from Jock.

She wanted back the delighted, rumpled Joseph she'd found in her bed the last two nights, the one who grinned at her with brown curls tumbling across his brow, his eyes dancing with mischief, his mouth moist from kissing her. An ache traveled through her breasts and belly, a pain she feared would be her constant companion now.

The former Baronet had been a vain man, and mirrors stood all over the dressing room. Inez saw herself reflected back, so close to being in Joseph's arms, yet not held. Not bound by oaths or duty, only mutual desire.

She'd found the only way she could to hold him to her, to keep from being sent back to London with Jock. Would he allow her to stay?

"You've need of a housekeeper," she reminded him. "Mrs. Wadge didn't keep the place up as she ought have done, Wenna says."

"I am not going to behave as if you are a servant."

Then what was she to him? Why could he not say?

She twisted the ends of the neckcloth and tucked them among the ruffles of his shirt, then smoothed the deep lapels of his waistcoat. The heat of his skin, his neck, his strong chin, curled around her fingertips. She'd shaved him that morning, an office she'd performed for her husband and knew how to do well. Hours later, the stubble shadowed his splendid jaw, accenting rather than hiding the arrogant shape. She wanted to follow the line of that jaw with her lips.

"You mean to advertise me as your mistress, then?"

His thick eyebrows drew together. Had he not given this any thought? They'd had days on the road together. Had he truly brought her all the way to Cornwall with no notion of what to do with her when they arrived?

Her heart stumbled in her chest. Perhaps he'd had the same notion from the beginning. Send her back.

She wouldn't go. There was nothing for her in London without Joseph there. There was nothing for her anywhere, without him.

And *damn* him for becoming so absolutely necessary to her happiness. Making her stoop to being his servant again, which she swore she would not do, simply so she might be near him.

"I don't suppose it's the done thing, even in the country, to lodge one's mistress under one's own roof. Still, you are the Baronet now, and by all accounts your cousin Reuben kept his light o' loves within doors as well." A quick intake of breath said she'd hit a mark with that barb. She shook out the velvet of his best dinner coat and held it up, giving him a false, forced smile.

"I could put my things in the room opposite yours," she prattled as he slid his arms into the sleeves. How far could she goad him before he broke? "Fancy me then, setting myself up as the lady of the house. What shall I say to your callers, though? Am I to receive the gentry of the neighborhood and say I am your ward? They'll see through that in an instant, as fast as Mrs. Truckle from the George. I'm of an age to sign my own contracts." Briskly she buttoned his coat, wondering what lay in his heart beneath all these layers, such a mystery to her.

"Such an arrangement won't put you in good standing with the vicar, that's certain. He'll fear you'll begin a new fashion for the neighborhood, keeping one's ladybird under one's roof. But more expensive still to house me elsewhere, unless you choose one of the cottages."

"I am not going to put you in one of the cottages." His scowl darkened, and he fairly spit out the words. He seemed stumbling to find speech.

The cottages were comfortable, not fancy by any means, but warm and snug. Inez had gone with Wenna to fetch the one she called Old Jupe, a stretched-thin stick of a woman, a widow of ancient years, who minded the babes while Wenna worked. And such sweet babes they were, a young boy of about three and a girl half that age, toddling about on unsteady legs after her brother, who explained everything to her with the authority of the elder sibling.

With nothing else to do with them for the nonce they'd brought the babes to the kitchen and put them to work, the boy mashing boiled potatoes, the bonny girl sifting flour. In the dim reaches of her memory, Inez recalled helping her mother in much the same manner, starting at small tasks even as a young child.

She knew how to keep a house well enough, with a score of years for practice. Only when might she have a house of her *own?*

"True, I've no need for a cottage," she said around the clump of despair in her throat. "There's a room in the attics that will do well enough for me, with a window to catch the air come summer." She buttoned his coat, taking her sweet time about it, enjoying the hard stretch of his chest beneath her fingers.

"I won't ruin you by flaunting you as my mistress, and you are certainly not part of my *staff*." His temper was rising again. He yanked at the hem of his coat, straightening the seam across his shoulders.

"Then what, Joseph?" She froze, cold coursing through her. Slowly, fearing the truth, she lifted her eyes to meet his. A bronze fire burned in those chocolate depths. "You mean to send me back?"

He dropped his gaze. "It would be best for you," he muttered.

She wouldn't do it. He could set her outside, front door or back, and she would merely circle around and climb in the window. The need for him to hold her was so overwhelming it nearly blotted out her mind.

She took the edge of her apron and focused on polishing the brass buttons of his coat. Her chest ached as if it were a window and someone had thrown up the sash to let the wind blow through.

"I won't go back," she said. "There is nothing for me in London."

"Amaranthe will take you in."

"Perhaps I don't want to work in a great house." She moved to the buttons on his sleeve. "Perhaps I want to keep my own house for once."

"I could give you George Court. You could live there."

"And do what?" She couldn't meet his eyes.

"Read. Sew. Entertain callers." A long pause unspooled as she polished his buttons, slowly, taking every opportunity to touch him.

"As what? A merry spinster, all my life long?" The prospect didn't sound terrible, and once she might have relished such independence. Before she tasted Joseph Illingworth and realized he was hers.

"Unless you marry. But you said you did not want to marry again."

She knelt to polish the buckles of his shoes so he couldn't see her face. No, she didn't want to marry, not anyone else. But if were him— The thought brought a lump to her throat as if she were trying to swallow week-old bread. If *she* were his cherished bride, the lady of his home, his companion at table as they had been these days, the woman he shared his hearth and his bed with.

Tears blurred her vision. She wanted that so badly she could not speak the words.

He had this house now, was lord and master of his own estate. He had a title. He would have standing in the neighborhood. He was young and of sound mind and good health, full of vigor, sinfully beautiful to look upon. Every girl within leagues would want to marry him.

And he would choose one, because for as long as she had known Joseph Illingworth, all he had wanted from his life, after a respectable position and cakes with his tea and good books to read, was a house and a family of his own. So much had he wanted that, he threw himself again and again after a Susannah Pettigrew, a vain, silly girl who couldn't see past the end of her nose.

And he could not choose Inez, because every dictate of class and custom said she was not suitable for a man of his rank. When he married, he would cut all ties to her. And what future would she have, alone and without the man she loved?

Loved. It was too soon to tell him that. He hadn't brought himself to properly swive her yet, as if it spelled a commitment he wasn't prepared to make. She rose and took up the clothes brush, scrubbing the velvet of his coat to a smooth nap. Another excuse to touch him, to admire the fine shape of him beneath her hands. To leave her prints upon him, or press into him the knowledge that held her: *You are mine.*

Even if she wasn't his.

"I wish to have you with me," he said, his voice rattling like the wind through dry husks of maize after harvest. His chest beneath her hand was hard as forged iron. "I would keep you here, Inez, if I could."

"And dole out gifts and trinkets as my lover?" She attacked his coat with more vigor than was warranted, wishing she could beat sense into him. "I'm to dine at your table and loll on your couches, paying for my keep with your pleasure? I won't do it, Joseph."

Nor could she bear to be so idle. She'd never been idle a day in her life.

"You can't stay here as my servant."

This again. She smacked the brush on his shoulder, attacking one last crease. "I won't be a pretty thing to use at your whim, like a lapdog or toy. I want a wage from you, good and proper, so I can support myself when you're through with me."

He snaked an arm about her back and yanked her to him. His manhood pressed into her waist. She bit back a moan of satisfaction at the signs of his ardor. At least he felt *that* for her.

"I'll never be through with you," he muttered against her lips, and then he smothered her retort in a hot kiss.

She would never be through with him, either, even when he married and could no longer be hers. A low cry fluttered in her throat as she pressed herself against him, and she shifted her hips slightly so he could push between her legs, stirring that ever-present ache into instant need.

He plunged his tongue into her mouth, dominating, plundering, then hitched a hand behind her bare knee, lifting her leg so he could press against her all the more firmly. His fingers wandered up her thigh to the place between her legs, bare and open to him, and he slid a finger through her folds, already moist with wanting. She leaned her forehead against his shoulder, astonished at how quickly she responded to him, how his boldness and his claiming made her weak.

She pulled away. "You've to dinner."

"I'll be waiting for it to be over so I can have *this*." He yanked her back to him, bent his head, and licked his tongue between the breasts pushed up by her bodice. She groaned at how possessive he was with her, and how much she responded. An arc of heat flamed through her nipples and to her core.

He set her on her feet and headed to the doorway, then paused to look back at her, standing there trembling and inflamed by desire, one hand on the writing desk for support.

"You are more than a housekeeper, Inez," he growled before he left.

She nodded at the empty doorway. She was more than that. She *was*.

But when would the dratted man say what she meant to him, beyond this delicious passion that swept up and shook the both of them until all sense rattled free from her head?

And could she live with what he decided?

She faced the mirror and picked up one of his neckcloths, tucking it into her bodice to disguise the flush over her breasts. She patted her hair into place beneath her cap, retucked her skirts so her hems didn't drag, and took the servant's stair down to the kitchen.

She was the housekeeper for now, there was no other staff but Wenna, and there was a meal to serve.

And the man she loved to rescue from himself.

CHAPTER SIXTEEN

Penwellen was not the inheritance Joseph had anticipated.

He supposed he shouldn't be surprised. For when had Fate ever showered great things upon him? To others, perhaps, who had done something to earn their distinction.

Perhaps Creation kept some grand scheme of balance, Joseph thought as he paced the parlor of his new home. He was the get of a second son and a foreigner. A scholar with no real profession to speak of. And now a baronet by accident, a tradesman's grandson masquerading in a gentleman's coat, with no right of blood or ancient lineage to sit in the master's chair.

He had stepped into the shadow cast by Reuben, which hung over this house like poisoned air, seeping into every corner. If he wanted to make any good of his situation, he had to clean up that miasma first.

At least he wasn't the weak, useless man that he'd feared becoming. A week ago, he'd been an awkward virgin, rubbish when it came to women, but Inez had transformed him. She'd shown him how matters of desire were meant to work, at least for him. So that was one fine and beautiful thing—one astounding thing, really—that shone like a promise through the current gloom, hinting that better fortune might await down the road. Aye, even for him.

He couldn't think of Inez at this moment. He'd have a cock-stand through dinner, and he heard the front door open as Hoskyn, the solicitor, arrived. The visitor greeted Thaker, who was dressed in livery made for a smaller man and had sullenly submitted to his wife trimming his side whiskers in order to perform the roles of butler, porter, and footman this evening.

Joseph reviewed his standing like a man assessing the table where he had sat down to gamble everything. He held a title no older than the Civil War, an estate that, if he read the signs aright, had not been kept in good order, and a deaf-mute for a butler.

And the woman with whom he was engaging in coital relations pretending to be his housekeeper.

Yes, indeed, he would look a sorry sight to Mr. James Hoskyn of Liskeard.

"Sir Joseph. Good of you to receive me." The solicitor advanced into the parlor where Thaker had erected an oakwood folding table which his wife had cloaked with a swath of crisp linen. Joseph recognized the print on the creamware dinner service; Favella had chosen the pattern.

The silver was free of spots, and the room had been hastily aired and dusted. Some fragrant wood burned in the hearth. A fire on a mild night—that was an extravagance he'd seen in the duke's house, but never his own. Joseph wondered if he could afford the expense.

There was a friendly smile on Hoskyn's face as he stepped forward, offering a brief nod of his head, but his large, protuberant eyes roamed efficiently around the parlor, taking note of every detail.

The solicitor wore a coat of dark blue cloth with golden embroidery and a small bob wig, powdered gray. His necktie was plain, lacking any ruffles, and so was the watch chain hanging at his waist. Joseph, with the scratch wig he'd worn for travel and his best brown coat, was dressed no better than his solicitor. He would have to order a new wardrobe at once.

If his accounts could suffer the expense.

He must stop this habit of ever comparing himself to other men. He came out lesser in the comparison, every time. His father tried to teach him to be grateful for what God had seen fit to give him, yet Joseph had always thought his own portion mean and slight when he saw the vaster advantages some others possessed.

What a very small-minded way to exist. He would take the example of his father for once. Jonas Illingworth would have made an admirable baronet: courteous, benevolent, far-seeing.

Joseph gestured Hoskyn to a chair and then sat heavily, burdened by the weight of an unexpected grief. His parents' graves lay only ten miles away, in the quiet cemetery behind St. Cleer's church, and the knowledge pressed on his heart like a stone.

"My condolences on the loss of your cousin," Hoskyn began.

"I'm afraid it doesn't feel much of a loss. Speaking for myself and my sister," Joseph said, conscious he might come across as surly.

"Ah, the duchess. I hope she is in good health? Sir Reuben was very grateful for the way she supported the estate in the last year."

Joseph held back his surprise. Of course Anth would have sent money, if Reuben asked. The man himself didn't deserve it, but no one in his care deserved to suffer because of his greed or oversight.

"She is in very good health, and hoping to enlarge the Hunsdon nursery in the near future. Thank you for seeing me on short notice, and for acknowledging my claim. I fear my staff thought me an imposter at first. They said there have been several."

"Yes, oddly, there have been a number of strangers pretending to your inheritance." Hoskyn's brows rose, the dark hairs a contrast to his powdered wig. "Mrs. Thaker chased them away when she realized they were coming to steal from the house. I recognize you from your father's funeral, though it was some years ago. A sad event," he added politely.

"To be sure."

The memory was dulled by grief and Joseph's sense of bewilderment, at the time, over what he was to do next, and how he was supposed to look after his sister. Dimly he recalled Hoskyn, in a different wig, reading his father's will. The one that put his parents' tiny estate into a trust managed by Reuben, who, Joseph later learned, had conceded to fund Joseph's time at university but had directly transferred Amaranthe's allowance into luxuries for himself and Favella, before and after Anth had fled from his house.

Joseph scowled. He would not be anything like the former baronet. Nothing like.

Save that he was already swiving a woman under his roof, one under his protection. At his mercy, whether she thought so or no.

Hoskyn cleared his throat, perhaps concerned that Joseph's scowl was directed at him. "I suppose you do not wish to mix pleasure with business—"

"This is a business call, Mr. Hoskyn. Though I see fit to feed you for your trouble."

Jock, in the absence of any other messenger, had dispatched himself to Liskeard earlier, and taken the liberty, after contacting the solicitor, to add what he could find to Penwellen's kitchen stores from the shops. Joseph feared it was poor fare, and this dinner would set a bar in Hoskyn's mind that he would never be able to lift, later, to a more creditable standing.

But he needed to know how things stood with his new estate. With his life.

"Ah." Hoskyn withdrew a pair of spectacles on a chain, polished them with a colorful handkerchief, and put them back in his pocket. "Of course, I do not have the accounts before me, though I welcome you to visit me at my premises in Liskeard. Or I might bring them to you here," he added, and Joseph saw another of the new distinctions of being a baronet, aside from a grander reception in coaching inns. "But I believe, on the whole, I can give you a picture of where things stand."

"I hope it is a picture that will please me," Joseph said, rising as he heard footsteps in the hallway, someone bringing their dinner.

Hoskyn cleared his throat again. "I fear it will not," he said.

Thaker entered, carrying a platter that Joseph took little note of, because Inez entered the room behind him.

Inez. She had sat across the table from him at their dinners on the road. Or on his lap, last night, as he fed her in between kisses.

If she were the lady of his house, she could have received Hoskyn in the parlor and he would have offered her a bow in greeting, in place of Joseph's shabby reception. She would be garbed in a fine robe with jewels at her throat and hair, and she would sit down to a dinner service with a pattern she had chosen for her china, and she would fill in the gaps of conversation with clever remarks when Joseph ran out of things to say.

Hoskyn, too, regarded Inez with interest. "Oh, I say. You've brought your own staff. Where is your maid from, Sir Joseph?"

"London," Inez said, stepping forward with wine. She poured it into Joseph's glass first, meeting his eyes. Something fiery burned in those dark depths; she was angry with him. His gaze slid to her bosom and with great effort he hauled it back to her face. She waited, and he obediently swirled the wine to release the sediment, then sipped.

"My word." He sipped again. "This is quite good."

"Your cousin laid in an excellent cellar, Wenna says. One of his several indulgences for himself, while his people went about with less." Inez turned to Hoskyn with a cordial smile, and Joseph battled a stab of jealousy. "My mother was Portuguese, and my father from Goa. I grew up in Portugal, actually."

"Lisbon?" Hoskyn waited behind his chair, as if obeying the rule not to seat himself first in the presence of a lady. As if he sensed, from her proud and self-possessed demeanor, that Inez was meant to be the lady here.

She'd turned his rabble-scrabble request for provisions into something orderly and befitting a baronet's table. Standing at the sideboard, she handed the serving dishes to Thaker, his hands nearly bursting through the too-small silk gloves. He had never in his life of service been called upon to serve in the house, and he was doing his best.

"Sagres." Inez pointed discreetly where Thaker ought to arrange the dishes, then mimed serving up portions.

"Ah, that is where Prince Henry the Navigator had his school of map makers, is it not?" Hoskyn remarked. "Helping him map his conquests in the Age of Discovery."

Joseph would bet Hoskyn, with his easy conversation and genial smile, his sense of calm assurance, had never had a door slammed in his face in his life.

"We might serve ourselves," Joseph said to Inez, suddenly unable to bear the thought of her waiting on him. Calling himself his *housekeeper*, of all things, as if she were no more than a maid he was amusing himself with, and not the woman he wanted seated across the table from him in his lady's chair.

He wondered what Hoskyn would do if he invited Inez to join them.

"Sit," she said gently, and Joseph dropped into his folding chair as if the air had been let out of him. What was he to *do* with her?

She was correct: He couldn't masquerade her as his ward and trot her out for parlor conversations or strolls through the shops of Callington. He'd never be able to hide what he felt for her, and ten minutes of conversation would establish for the small but elect sliver of genteel Cornish society that she was not gently born.

And he could not keep her here as his mistress. One might take such liberties in London, where the sheer size and energy of the town overwhelmed decorum. But rural societies tended to adhere more closely to the niceties, at least the ones he'd experienced, for the very fact of their remoteness from fashionable centers. And if she were known to be a fallen woman, she'd be thoroughly shunned. It wouldn't be fair to her.

Yet to pretend to being his housekeeper. He glared at her across the small table, but she wouldn't meet his eyes, instead cutting the pudding of baked pillas, the Cornish grain that Joseph had never seen grown anywhere else. Once Hoskyn and everyone established that she was his servant, he couldn't elevate her beyond that.

He wouldn't be the first gentleman who had confused the roles of housekeeper and mistress, he knew that much. But gentlemen didn't marry their housekeepers.

He understood her reasoning. She wanted a wage from him, fair and honest, so she couldn't be caught whoring. But in so doing she'd erected a barrier thicker than the wall that had separated Pyramus and Thisbe.

Beautiful, proud, glorious, *aggravating* woman.

"You'll quite stand out in these parts, a woman of your good looks," Hoskyn said as Inez spooned pickles onto his plate. "Though there's many another like you here and about and along the coasts. Falmouth especially, but Plymouth too, I believe."

Inez looked up swiftly. "Like me?"

"Yes. Erm, that is to say." Hoskyn waved his hand before his face. "Less...fair of complexion?"

"Oh." Inez returned to the pudding, looking relieved; Hoskyn was referring to her skin color, not her erotic liaison.

Regret bit through Joseph's skin. In London, there were any number of people like her, Blacks, Indians, visitors native to the Americas, the Moor who ran the bookshop Amaranthe frequented. There was every shade of skin color on display. But he'd brought her to Cornwall, where she was bound to stand out.

She'd known that, and so insisted he give her a position of respect. Being the upper servant of a great house was no small standing in a neighborhood like theirs; servants and tradesmen and land owners alike would recognize and defer to her status.

His clever, soft-hearted, *beautiful* Inez. It was impossible not to love her.

"How bad is it?" Joseph couldn't wait until Thaker had finished spooning up the salad, buttered cabbage topped with roasted Cornish earlies, the new potatoes roasted in their skins and sticky with butter and parsley.

"Hmm. What's that?" Hoskyn was watching Inez with interest, but Joseph also recognized the wariness of the profession.

"You can speak in front of them. Thaker doesn't hear, and Inez is the soul of discretion."

Drat it. He'd called her Inez.

"You may call me Mrs. Da Costa," she said in her musical tone. Not chiding. Simply stating.

She did not wish to use her father's name? Interesting.

"She is fully informed of my circumstances," Joseph added, aware he was digging himself a hole. Was he trying to write a sign and place it around her neck, advertising to other men that she belonged to him?

Yes. Yes, he was.

Hoskyn sipped his wine and waited until Thaker and Inez had withdrawn before he turned to Joseph with a regretful air.

"I wish I had better news," he said.

MUCH LATER, sodden with wine and despair, Joseph climbed the narrow servant's stair to the second floor.

Inez was not on the ground floor, which held the kitchens and offices and a tiny room that doubled as a silver pantry and the housekeeper's parlor. The kitchen fire was banked for the night, the tables and counters cleaned and scrubbed, the scullery empty.

Wenna had promised she would start looking for staff on the morrow; she vowed there would be likely hands for the indoor and outdoor work to be found in Haye and Trevigro, Frogwell or Kelly Bray, or down to Newbridge, if need be.

How he was to pay them, Joseph didn't know, but he couldn't leave two women to run this house by themselves. Inez would know what they needed.

She hadn't taken a room on the first floor, with the family chambers, and his stomach turned and twisted like a stoat burrowing into a tree trunk. He wanted her nearby. He wanted her in his bed.

The rooms on the second floor were attics and servant quarters, tucked under the sloping roof, plain and small and tidy. Her chamber did, as she'd noted, boast a window, and through it shone the moon, bright enough to light Hoskyn on his way. Inez had offered the solicitor a room for the night, and Joseph knew she had spent their leisurely dinner readying a guest chamber for the man who was at the moment sealing Joseph's doom with black wax.

But the solicitor declined, saying he had a sister in St. Ive who would put him up for the night, not caring what hour he knocked on her door, and Joseph did not argue to keep him. Not when he knew Inez was waiting, though not like this, sitting in her chair mending something while the candle in its stick burned low on the small chest of drawers. The shadows it drew over her face were loving and mysterious, hinting at the depths of this woman he might never know.

She yawned and put her mending atop the drawers. It appeared she was darning a stocking—one of his. "You should be in bed," he reproved her.

"I meant to come help you undress."

"Very well, then. I could use your assistance. And company."

He swept her into his arms. She bit back a shriek as her feet left the floor, before she realized, like he did, there was no one to hear.

They were alone in the house. They were entirely, completely alone together, as they never had been before and might never be so again.

"I don't— You'll drop me," she reproached him, though she didn't struggle. Instead she linked her arms around his neck, trusting. He savored the warm weight of her, his lush, soft, woman.

"Bring the candle. I left mine in my room." He swerved his

arms so she could lift the stick and holder, holding it away from their bodies.

"Joseph. I can walk," she said as he navigated back down the stairs, angling his body so he didn't bump her head or feet on the walls.

"I want you in my arms. I want you in my arms at all times, as a matter of fact."

"Bad news?" she asked softly.

"The worst." He reached his room and paused beside a side table, where she set down the candlestick. "No, that's not quite true."

He set her on her feet but held her within his arms, resting his chin on the top of her head. She slipped her arms around his back, leaning against his chest, and everything stopped hurting.

"The worst would be to hear that my inheritance was a lie and the estate really belongs to someone else. Though that would save me a good deal of bother." He pulled the cap from her hair, then began hunting out hairpins, collecting them carefully in his palm. Her hair was soft as silk thread.

"In actual fact, Reuben has left me several debts and not much money. He hasn't done repairs to his buildings in quite some time. He owes his tenants several repairs, too.

"The land he lets has been planted for spring, but not the home farm, as there is no one but Thaker left. We have some animals, but the spring shearing hasn't been done, so there is no wool to market, and no one to oversee the lambing.

"The stables are a shambles. My cousin had ambitions to cultivate a racehorse and so spent a stupid amount on that. I can sell the animal back, Hoskyn tells me, though it will only pay off part of the debts. And I've no notion how I've to support this house. Or staff." He buried his face in her neck, inhaling her scent. "Or you."

"That is the way of it all over," she murmured. "You live on credit until you are back on your feet."

"All over, is it?" He rubbed his hands over her back, soothing himself with the quiet strength of her. Then he set to unpinning her bodice, freeing those lovely breasts.

She nodded, holding out her arms so he might undress her. "Aboard ships, certainly. Captains take on their cargo and sail for months, sometimes years, before they see a profit. Very often the crew have to wait to see their wages, too. We never knew, when my father returned home, if he would have coin in his pocket to support us.

"And the great houses run the same way. All on credit, until the harvest comes in, and one sees how much of it one may pay off for the year."

"You are far less worried about this than I am." He set her bodice aside and began unlacing her leather stays, a process much impeded by his need to pause and slide his hands over her bosom. So warm. So soft. So obliging she was, her dark eyes lifted to his in trust and innocence.

Mirroring back what he felt for her: lost, utterly lost, in desire.

"We will manage, Joseph," she whispered against his lips. Her stays opened and her breasts spilled into his hands, at long last, and he bent his face to kiss her.

"Hoskyn was kind but honest. I can keep the house if I am very, very frugal."

He lifted her again and carried her to the tester bed, draped with curtains of red and gold. Reuben's bedchamber carried a vaguely Eastern flavor, as if he imagined himself a Turkish pasha or Persian shah. Joseph felt the faintest bit like a king choosing a companion from his harem for the night.

Except his harem only held one girl, this one, and he would choose her over and over, every night from now through the rest of his days. She half-rose toward him, holding out on arm, and he crawled over her.

"Boots," she murmured, and he kicked off his shoes with a low laugh. "I know how to be frugal." She tugged him over her body and kissed him deeply.

"But how am I to pay you?"

"I'll work for room and board, and you can arrange a salary when funds permit." She slid her tongue into his mouth as she commenced undressing him, and Joseph felt the flame rising up to enfold him. This woman was a siren, a spellcaster.

All his awkwardness, all his fears had vanished. He knew how to please her. His mouth on her breasts brought pants and soft moans. She tugged off his coats and shoved her hands up his shirt, dragging her palms over his skin, taking as much pleasure in touching him as he did in touching her. When he lowered his weight to her body she shifted her hips to cradle him, fitting herself to the bulge in his breeches, and once again a great scissors came and snipped off the top of his head, letting thought tumble out.

All he needed was Inez. She was everything good and sweet and beautiful, and she made him feel powerful and whole.

"You'd be best to return to London with Jock," he muttered as he kissed his way down her body, pushing away the voluminous hem of her shift. "Let the Duchess take care of you."

"I've fended for myself this long." She fisted her hands in his hair, clutching at his shoulders as he kissed down her legs, then back up. Her chest heaved as desire shook her, and he marveled that it was this powerful for both of them. They were lost together in the storm and only the one could bring the other safely to the far shore.

"Don't make me leave you," she muttered, and the words punched inside his chest, bruising his heart, making it swell. No, he didn't want to part with her, not with *this* between them.

This passion. This craving. This sense that she saw what was good in him and brought those qualities to the light to show to the world in her tender, careful hands.

"I want you," he murmured, kissing the soft inside of her thigh, then curling his tongue around those parts of her that made her shake and cry out his name in a voice of desperation and amazement.

"Be with me." She pulled at his arm, panting for breath, tugging him toward her. "Be with me. Inside me."

He wanted nothing more. She fumbled with him to loosen the buttons of his breeches, then shoved them away. Her hand on his bare cock was ecstasy itself. He loved her sureness with him. He loved her want. Because it was for *him*.

"There cannot be a babe." He held himself poised at the entrance to utter bliss. Or what he'd been told was the portal to the only paradise this earth knew. Reuben and Eyde. Reuben and how many others. He couldn't leave her with a babe, because how could he support two when he couldn't support one?

"Don't spend inside me," she whispered. "Spill your speed outside."

"This is..."

He wanted to warn her. In case he fumbled. In case, at the last minute, all the old horrors and shames rose up before him, like they had with the others, and he curled into himself. He wasn't the kind of randy man who could rise for any willing woman, and he knew this about himself. It had been proven again and again, too many embarrassing times.

"This is new for me." He rested his forehead against hers, caught up in fear. What if he didn't please her? What if he was rubbish after all. What if—

"Then we can just have this," she whispered. She reached

between them, stroking him, cradling his tenderest parts. "I only want to be close to you, Joseph."

And that was the key, somehow, to his certainty. Everything was different with Inez, because her want matched his, and because it was Inez. He wasn't performing; he was connecting with her in the deepest way. He surged against her and she ushered him in, and the pleasure staggered, almost blinded him.

"Ye gods, Inez," he muttered through gritted teeth. "Ye gods."

"Yes," she whispered. "Joseph. Yes."

It was his name on her lips that nearly undid him. He didn't need to be taught the rhythm because it was there with instinct, and there was nothing wrong with him after all because when he moved within Inez, she clutched her arms and her legs about him and her eyes flew wide and her breath took on that halting pattern again.

"Good?" he managed, because he didn't know, this was his first time, but ye gods, if he'd known *this* was possible he would have risen from his chair in his study the first time Inez entered with the tea tray and he would have taken her into his arms and begun everything right then. Heat and need crashed through him, a torrent that shook him to his toes.

"Joseph," she whispered, her voice amazed and keen with need. "There—just that—oh, please, darling. *Please.*"

Then her breath caught and her eyes squeezed shut and her body seized and he understood she was there again, shaking with that culmination, coming apart like dandelion fluff. Her inner walls quivered around him with her pleasure and yes, *this* was paradise, because his entire mind was a white blaze and he gritted his teeth hard, clenching his entire body to catch that uprush of pleasure and hold it, hold it.

He slid out of her and almost spilled right then, the sweet glide of her body, but he managed to grab the nearest cloth and pull it between them and then he let it happen, let the need spill out of him, let the pleasure pump through him like the heavy effacing grind of a millstone. On the fringes of his consciousness he realized Inez was kissing him, kissing every part of his face, and when he could breathe again he kissed her back.

"That." He rolled off her body to flop beside her, staring at the underside of the canopy, trying to catch his breath.

The cloth was embroidered with naked gods and goddesses cavorting in a field of flowers. One, likely Zeus, reclined among a bed of crimson petals, his member fully erect. Of course Reuben would have such a portrait above his bed. Joseph felt the same way, still fully engorged, as though spilling his seed had only been the first vent of steam and his tool was ready for more, so much more, now that it understood its function.

Inez curled up beside him, hair spilling over his shoulder. He pressed a kiss to her forehead.

"Is it always like that?"

"No." Her smile was sleepy and sated and full of wonder. Her eyes held a light he almost couldn't bear to look at. "No, it is not. That was... I've never had it be like that."

"Will it be like that again?" he demanded.

She slung her knee over his thigh and nestled her body beside his, breasts pressing against his side. "Not if you send me back to London."

"No. Don't go." He pressed his fingers into her hip. "Stay."

"All right," she murmured.

He wiggled and shoved until he freed the bedclothes and pulled the covers over both of them, rising only to blow out the candle and discard the cloth he'd used—one less neckcloth for his wardrobe, he noted. Then he slid into bed beside her and she gave a warm sigh and he slid his arms around her and understood that he could never send her away, never.

And not only because of this, because he wanted this pleasure again with her, morning and night and perhaps sometimes in early afternoons. Because when he talked to her, she listened, and she was sensible and practical and knew more about the world than he did.

And because she was Inez, and she belonged to him. He knew that now, though he had no notion how he was to claim and hold her.

CHAPTER SEVENTEEN

"The Duchess," Inez said, because if they were going to talk about ways to refortify the estate, that was an obvious source of income.

"No," Joseph said at once, in that stubborn and immediate way of his.

He handed her the leather ribbons to hold the horse while he hopped down from the wooden plank that formed the driver's seat of the farm cart. His boots sank into the grassy field, and he shifted slightly to get his balance. He unrolled the parchment and looked about him, and a needle sank into her chest, as if someone were embroidering his name on her heart. He looked the lord of the manor, in a wide-brimmed hat that Thaker had loaned him and a sturdy frock coat with steel buttons, the skirts caught back for riding.

"She would help if you asked."

Inez wasn't certain how to hold the reins; she'd never handled a horse before. She imitated what Joseph had done, looped the straps of leather around her gloves and held her hands on her knees, gently. If Joseph were to be a farmer and she a farmer's lady, then she must learn things like how to handle animals and know the seasons and the weather and the rhythms of country life.

Not his lady in the sense of being a baronet's wife, of course. He couldn't marry her, foreign born, dark-skinned, the daughter of a lascar and a woman who had turned whore. A very great lord might be allowed to be so eccentric, but not a man of the gentry. Tradesmen might not extend him credit or merchants decline to work with him if they doubted his judgment. Laborers would try to cheat him and vagrants take advantage of his land. They would see it as justice to defraud a man who didn't uphold the time-honored decrees of class and nation and purity of blood.

She knew what it was like. It had been so in Portugal, and it was the same here. The prejudices were hard drawn, and they ran deep, like etchings in a copper plate.

"I won't ask," Joseph replied. "I spent six years, seven, being supported by my sister, when I ought to have been supporting her. I'm not coming to her with hat in hand when I ought to be able to look after myself."

"She would be happy to help you regain your feet, and you could pay her back when the estate is in heart," Inez said mildly.

The sun was shining and the day was warm, and the cranes-bill and clover were blooming. The hedges were twined with dog rose and elderflower, and carpets of bluebells and violets spread over the far prospects. She didn't want to quarrel, especially not with this beautiful land stretched out before them.

But if he wanted to keep this land and live upon it, they had to find some source of funds.

Inez thought of the heavy weight at the bottom of her stocking bag, still wrapped in cloth, undisturbed through her travels and now tucked in the cupboard in her room. The room in the attics that she called hers, which was not the same room where she slept. Spending the night in Joseph's room, Joseph's bed, was a wonderful luxury, and it would end as soon as the staff with which she had equipped the house began to suspect she was not adhering to her proper place in it, for thus would she lose all her authority.

"If nothing else will do, I'll go begging to my sister," Joseph said. "But I'd rather show her, and Hunsdon, I can solve my own problems."

Inez guessed that of the pair, the Duke of Hunsdon was the personage Joseph most strenuously did not want pitying him. But she said nothing.

"Besides which." He pushed hat back on his head, surveying the terrain. "If Hunsdon supplies funds to renew me, he'll think he might have a say in the governing of Penwellen. And I won't have him butting his nose in."

Inez didn't know the source of Joseph's grudge for the Duke. She'd met Malden Grey when he was a luckless would-be barrister, raised as the bastard son of a duke in a coaching inn in Bristol. He'd met Amaranthe Illingworth, fallen flat on his face for her, and had begged her to marry him well before anyone knew Grey's father had properly married his mother and it was the duke's second and third marriages that were bigamous and his later children illegitimate.

All three of the duke's half siblings lived at Hunsdon House, Amaranthe having taken them in hand with her usual brisk ease at telling people how to go on. If London society thought it odd that a peer of the realm should house his bastard siblings under the same roof with him, London society wasn't about to say so to a duke.

Inez thought again of her stocking bag, again steered her thoughts away. It would make her a thief in truth if she revealed her secret. And what would Joseph think of her?

He knew he found pleasure in her body, but he wasn't experienced enough to know that lust was not love, that passion was not a promise of enduring affection, that cravings could fade and surfeit could dull the appetite. And she didn't know what they had beside the wanting, at least for his part.

She knew what she felt. Hers was a craving that would not cease.

"Does Jock have ideas?" she asked.

The groom hadn't yet returned to London and, while not formally in Joseph's employ, had not quite the status of a guest, either. Wenna reported that he had taken lodgings in one of the cottages, he took his meals in the kitchen with her and Old Jupe, and he had awarded himself oversight of the stables and horses, a task he saw to quite aptly despite his twisted legs. This left Thaker to look after the other animals for the nonce, and Thaker was enjoying the respite.

"Jock went to Plymouth to see if he might find a buyer for the racehorse. I don't expect he'll get enough to pay off what Reuben still owes on the beast. I hope he can get a good price for the hounds."

"Have you considered keeping them?" Joseph loved dogs; she'd been able to ascertain that from his first meeting with the late baronet's pack.

"No," he said shortly. "Hounds eat a man out of house and home. The only service they supply is for hunting, and I do not intend to hunt."

The clipped tone of his voice said the matter was closed, but she also sensed the pain of a memory. She decided not to probe, not yet. She often saw a strange expression cross Joseph's features when he looked about him inside the house, as if he detected some unpleasant memory lingering atop the inoffensive furnishings and gracious design. As if, despite the genteel look of the home, shadows lingered in the corners with the dust.

Perhaps one day, he would see fit to confide in her.

Perhaps one day, she would mean more to him than a bedmate.

Joseph peered at the parchment unscrolled in his hands. "Haye Lane to the gravel pits," he read, then looked up. "Is this the gravel pit, do you suppose?"

"It would appear so." They were walking the boundaries of his estate, trying to ascertain from the rough survey Hoskyn had given him what land properly belonged to Joseph.

"Can I mine gravel and sell it?"

"Perhaps?" She didn't know.

Joseph looked about him, shoulders slumping. "The first baronet enclosed what common land he could to make sheep pasture, so there's not more land for further enclosure. The leaseholds are all in order and properly conveyed, so there's no more income to be got there. Hoskyn said I could farm the fields on the Norfolk system, and that might yield more, if I can keep the sheep from eating the turnips and clover."

He put a hand on the side of the wagon, levering himself back onto the plank beside her. Inez leaned into the comfortable weight of his leg against hers, as if she could offer support. The work horse, a glossy Suffolk Punch, snorted and stomped the ground as Inez handed over the reins. Joseph passed her the map and she studied it, matching the landmarks depicted on the rough sketch to what she could see in view.

"There's not a lot of waste that could be made arable," she noted. "The moors end here, though you've got a bit of river bottom over there, along the Lynher."

"Which my tenants use for fishing, and if I want to keep good relations, I'll give them access," Joseph said. "I've a mind to try fishing myself. I might like it."

"Then there's the forest at the back edge of the property. Your own piece of Lendra Wood, which Wenna says is quite ancient, so it seems a shame to cut it down to raise grain."

"We ought to explore Lendra Wood one day," Joseph said. "Pack a basket. Spend the afternoon. It feels like it could have been made a thousand years ago, or even earlier. It was trod by people who were here before the Romans came. Inside of it, one can believe in fairies and elves and hobgoblins."

Inez smiled to see him becoming fanciful. This was what she loved: when Joseph became speculative or erudite, talking to her of the things he imagined or read. "If we come across a friendly Puck who is a hand at the household chores, I won't mind help churning the butter."

"That is what that Treen was after the day before last," Joseph remarked. "Asking me if I had any notion of selling. He seemed particularly interested in the wood and the land around it."

Inez sorted through the visitors she'd shown inside in the several days since they'd arrived. Many were gentlemen of the neighborhood coming to call on the new Baronet, making certain to mention how welcoming their wives and daughters would be should Sir Joseph choose to call on or dine with them. Merchants offered their trade; tradesmen offered their services.

A card came from Lady Edgcumbe, wife of the Baron Edgcumbe, who invited them to call when the family summered at Cotehele, their manor in Calstock, which was only a few miles away. Swift inquiries on Inez's part confirmed that Lady Edgcumbe, though gracious and comely, had no children but a lively boy of thirteen, and her husband was a vice-admiral rising through the ranks of naval and political service. They would be valuable neighbors for Joseph to cultivate, and it seemed Reuben, and Favella, had done their best to be ingratiating.

"Treen." Inez recalled him now, a gentleman with large mother-of-pearl buttons on his coats, several chains tucked into his waistcoat, and a white-powdered physician's wig more suited to men of the professions. Inez would not swear to it, but she suspected the man wore face powder and rouge. When she opened the front door, he had surveyed her up and down like she was a trull showing off her wares, then gave her an openly appreciative leer.

She hated men like that—men who assumed the right to evaluate every woman for her sexual allure, and then thought it a favor to inform the woman where she fell in his ranking. "He's the one as runs the shop in Callington?"

"Along with several other interests, some which he shared with my cousin, according to the solicitor. I've yet to see that any of the speculations they engaged in together yielded a real profit. At any rate, he was keen to make an offer, and assured me he was the only interested buyer hereabouts who had the means to pay me a fair price."

"Would you sell?"

"Not unless I must. If I'm lucky, there will be roes and rabbits in those woods, to add occasionally to your table." He slid her a sidewise gaze. "If, that is, you insist on continuing as my housekeeper."

"I believe I will." Inez soothed her mittens over her linen apron, white and crisp and ironed just that morning, along with her cap and kerchief. "It suits me to have a say in the running of things. In George Court, you know, I always had to submit to the cook. But here, Wenna defers to me."

"And you've been very frugal about managing so far. Thank you."

"It is my pleasure," she said, glowing at his praise, and yet disconcerted by the compliment. It was true she had taken on less staff than a house like this perhaps required. Aside from her and Wenna, she had hired a kitchen maid, a scullery maid, a chambermaid, and a hall boy who could be put to work outside when the occasion warranted. She could hire a footman and make Joseph impressive to his friends and neighbors, but she feared a footman would be cheeky to a housekeeper who was young and foreign-born and, he would soon learn, sleeping in the master's bed.

Besides, a proper footman would want to report to a butler, and that was an extravagance the house could currently not support, given there was now to be an extra tax on indoor manservants. There was already the window tax to consider, the tax on any bricks they used to repair the outer buildings, and the taxes on the sheep, the carriage, and the silver plate.

"Though in truth," Joseph said aloud, "you could govern the household just as well were you the baronet's lady."

She went absolutely still. The sunshine, which had not seemed intense otherwise, not the way it could be in Portugal, now beat down on her plain straw bergère hat. Pinpricks of sweat filled her cotton gloves.

"It isn't done." Her voice came out a whisper, the low haunting whistle through a reed. "It isn't. A man of your stature marrying...a woman like me."

He watched for ruts and pocks in the lane that led along the stream, really no more than a ditch that was currently filled with water. It made a convenient boundary, and neither of them needed to consult the map. Her heart jumped about in her chest as if were a treehopper, one of the strange brown bugs Joseph had pointed out to her.

"A woman like you," he said slowly, turning the phrase over in his mouth. "Strong-willed, you mean. Beautiful. Clever, determined, passionate. A survivor. A woman who will not suffer a wrong to be done in her sight."

"I fear it." The words gusted from her. "I fear what your neighbors would say. Lady Edgcumbe, the mistress of Cotehele — She is the daughter of the Archbishop of York, remember. She may not at all approve of a baronet marrying his housekeeper."

And the rest of the neighborhood would follow the lead of their great ones; their tastes and opinions were the law of the land.

"You are not my housekeeper."

"But I am."

"You are..." He sputtered, pulling the reins as the gelding tossed his big head and tried to nip overhanging greenery from a passing tree.

She waited. What was she to him? Did he even know?

"You could be my lady," he settled for saying.

She studied him while she had him here, close at her side and with no other person to lay claim to his time and attention. She surveyed him as thoroughly and as greedily as Mr. Treen, not a gentleman, had surveyed her. Joseph was so much to look at, and every piece of him pierced her heart in so many ways, that sometimes she did not simply sit back to take in the whole of him. The way his limbs came together in that kind of powerful grace that made her think of a wild, territorial animal, a deer or a bear or a ram.

Some men affected ennui or disinterest, but never Joseph. That light of intelligence, of keen interest in the world around him, animated his eyes from the moment he opened them in the morning, his mind already working over some thought that had come to him in his sleep. He could not be diffident if he tried; he felt everything deeply. He was loyal and passionate and God above, so stubborn, and she wanted nothing more than to walk beside him her whole life and brush the wet from his collar because he would have forgotten his umbrella and be too preoccupied with his thoughts to care about stepping out of the rain.

But baronets did not marry the daughters of lascars and whores.

"I cannot," she said.

Whatever reply he might have made to that was lost in an enormous cracking sound. Then the horse bolted.

Inez fell out of the cart at once. She was no seasoned horse-woman or farm girl; she'd known to cling to the top of the stage-coach, but the sudden leap forward left her unprepared, and she simply toppled sideways off the bench. She hit the ground before she could draw breath to scream, and to her good fortune, she was thrown free of the wheel, which churned a clod of dirt that spattered her apron.

The next events happened more quickly than she could quite comprehend. Joseph shouted something, to her or the horse, she didn't know. The horse whinnied and fought as Joseph pulled back on the ribbons. Another sharp cracking sound, like a great falling branch; Joseph swore; and then he was tumbling off the side of the cart as well, and Inez cried out and did not catch her breath again until she saw him roll to his feet, unscathed, and start toward her.

"Inez. Are you hurt?"

She shook her head, not yet able to form words. Her chest was an empty cave. Her head felt like she'd stuck it inside a ringing bell. Before she could protest Joseph was on his knees beside her in the mud, his hands moving over every part of her.

"Wh-what happened?" Her teeth were chattering. Aston-ishing. She had never been afraid for her life before; it felt a bit like the ague, leaving her shaking and feverish and weak.

"Gunshot." His mouth was a grim slash. "Someone is shooting on my land, or close to my land. Spooked the horse."

"Sp-spooked me," Inez said, her teeth still chattering.

Joseph kissed her forehead, then her temple, as if relieved to find her unhurt. "Swivel gun," he said under his breath. "The first shot was the big barrel, which is meant for larger game. The second was the bird shot."

Joseph was a scholar. Aside from playing bowls now and

again, he didn't engage in sporting activities, not even drinking to excess. How did he know about the firing of guns?

"M-missed his shot, I s-spose."

"Kept me from gaining control of the horse," he growled. "I hope Arthur has the sense to head back to the stables, where Thaker will guess we've gone astray."

"Arthur." Her mind, still whirling in great loops, clutched on the small thing it could encompass and be sure of. "The horse's name is Arthur."

He grinned at her, but there was something feral in it. His hat had come off when he leapt out of the cart and lay some distance away down the lane. The birds that had scattered at the shot and the bellow of the horse slowly regathered in the tree-tops of willow and downy birch that lined the banks of the stream. She sat in a bed of soft grasses, the flowers of the bird cherry blooming above her. It was an enchanted bower, and if she were not recovering from a fright that had made her heart do somersaults and a fall that jarred her teeth, she would make something of it, being spilled into this woodland glade with her love.

"You could have been hurt," he muttered, pressing kisses to her cheeks, her temple, her chin. "You could have been hurt."

Inez snaked her arms about his neck and pulled his mouth to meet hers.

There was a wildness in his kiss that she answered immediately. The tender welcome and soft forays with which he met her in the evenings, when they stood in his chamber in a penumbra of candlelight, were gone. This was need, fierce and clawing. Want roared up within her like a bear at the baiting.

She wanted to show him she was not hurt, and she wanted to assure herself that he had not been harmed, and she wanted to assuage this keen buzzing that swarmed every nerve, like a hive of bees. She'd told him she could not be with him, when what she wanted with every fiber and granule of her being was to be with him.

She pulled him against her as she fell backward onto the grass and there was no finesse in her, no calculation, no cunning. She wanted him to cover her, she wanted him to fill her, and she wanted to possess him completely.

"Inez." He held one arm around her, supporting her against the earth, and the other he dragged down her breast and belly. "Darling."

"Joseph." She gave his name back to him, a promise on his lips. She was in the grip of a frenzy. Her blood pounded as it never had. There was one need driving her. She thought with the edges of her mind that it might be the fright urging her on, the response to that soul-cleaving moment of fear she might die and never be with him again. But she had him now, all the weight and strength and beauty of him here in her arms, and she wanted him fused to her so completely that he could never be taken away.

"Ye gods, Inez," he murmured against her lips as she tore at his breeches, yanking the flap free, and sliding her hand around his manhood, already erect and rearing.

"You want me," she said, and almost laughed with the heady promise of relief to come soon, soon. "You want me."

"Dear God, I do."

He stretched out over her and she rucked up her skirt with one hand while tugging him close with the other. His hot palm on her leg as he slid up the skirt of her petticoats, then her shirt, oh, it was glorious, glorious. She was wet and ready and full of want for him and he slid into her as clean as a cartridge sliding into a gun.

"Inez," he breathed.

"Please. Joseph. I need you."

She felt no shame in begging. She felt no shame in her legs

laid bare to the world and the rest of her still clothed—she was still wearing her *hat*, for pity's sake—while Joseph was inside her and she wanted this, him, and nothing else, ever, but the scent of his desire and his heavy breath in her ear and the hot weight of him pushing into her, and the pleasure, Lord in heaven, the pleasure that made white flashes dance behind her eyelids and made her feel her feet were in a fire.

He was fierce in his thrusts in a way he had not been before, as if he were seized with the same desperate need for their bodies to join, to find this solace and assurance in one another though the sun beat down on the treetops above their heads and the soft grass tickled the backs of her knees and the birds went on with their chatter not caring that the humans were coupling in a kind of frenzy.

His abandon elated her, his need ignited her, the twist of his lips in an agony of passion drove her to a primal ecstasy. She had no time to warn him, nothing but a gasp of "Oh, Joseph," before the climax felled her like a gunshot, slamming her down and pressing through her as if she'd been run over by the wagon.

"Inez—ah—" A strangled sound escaped him and he went stiff and still in her arms, his body arched like a bow, and she hummed with pleasure at the pulsing that was new and deeper and better than anything she'd ever known. She lifted her legs to wrap around his waist and hold him inside her so they could have this throbbing joy, this arc of completion together, and dimly she realized that this sense of fullness was because he had joined his pleasure to hers and they had reached the peak together, truly joined, truly one.

With a groan he withdrew and rolled to the side, a hot thread of liquid trailing over her leg. She could have sobbed and screamed because the pleasure was less now, it felt hollow, and what she wanted was to hold him forever and to know that she was with him and she was home.

She lay with her eyes closed, feeling the tide wash out of her slowly, leaving the salty taste of regret. She was apart and a single entity again, just Inez, not something more. The straw of the grass poked at the backs of her shoulders and rump, and something crawled over her neck. She slapped it away.

"Inez. God. I'm so sorry." She felt a cloth at her thigh, at her entrance, Joseph dabbing at the sticky trace of his need and his passion and his pleasure in her. Erasing the evidence as if it had never been.

"I'm so sorry," he said again. "I spilled inside of you. I didn't mean to. I couldn't—" He fell silent. "I should have— I should not have done that."

A tear squeezed out beneath her eyelid. She willed it away.

"It is all right."

"But a babe." His voice was ragged. He was not touching her any longer. She still felt him, felt her skirts move as he tugged them over her legs, as if he could not bear to look at the bare and tender parts of her that had craved and cradled him.

"I cannot leave you with a babe," he said.

As if a babe were an unwanted litter of kittens. Or a leaking roof. Something regrettable and to be avoided.

She thought of the ladies of Dark Lane, how they knew a child meant lost time at work and lost income, another mouth to feed. If the bearing of it didn't claim a woman's life, it was a claim on her time and her heart and her body ever after.

Then she thought of Derwa, the bright-eyed dervish who was the child of Eyde, the Duchess's dresser. Eyde, who had begun as a maid in Penwellen, this very house—and unless Inez presumed incorrectly, had been cozened by Joseph's cousin, the former baronet, who planted the babe and then turned her off.

Inez had heard Joseph tell the story of how his sister turned up on the doorstep of his lodgings in Oxford with fire in her eye, holes in the soles of her shoes, and a Cornish maid with a belly.

When he told it, it was a great lark, and only later had Inez understood the miles the two young women had come alone, seeking safety, because Reuben who had planted the babe would not claim paternity of it and Amaranthe, knowing what her cousin was, would no longer stay in his house.

Eyde, despite her babe, had found employment in Amaranthe's household, and now, with her daughter of Cornwall and her husband of Wales, she was in command of the wardrobe of a duchess and was the top of the heap at Hunsdon House, even commanding the butler, who was as green as a butler could be but a willing lad nonetheless. And Derwa was the companion to Hunsdon's half-sister, and the child had a mane of bright curls and an exhaustingly inquisitive nature and the energy of the sun at noontime but lasting all the day.

"Inez," he said quietly. "Speak."

Speak, and tell him she would be glad of a babe, to have evidence of his love and desire for her that she could hold to her heart? She would cherish a Derwa, an exasperatingly beautiful daughter with her father's relentless curiosity, or a son with his father's tousle of hair and animated expressions and ability to soothe the spirit of others with his calm, steady nature that ran as deep as a well, and as pure.

She would weep if she spoke what was on her heart.

She struggled up on one elbow, only now feeling how the fall from the cart, short as it was, had rattled her bones.

"I am taking a tea," she said to the ground. She fixed her gaze on the fallen log not far from her elbow and the tiny orange-red caps of mushrooms that clustered across it. The edges shed black strings that looked the eyelashes of a weeping maiden.

"I learned the recipe from one of the innkeepers along the road," she said. "It is meant to...keep my courses regular." Keep her from catching a babe, that was.

"I see." His voice was quiet. "So you are already...taking precautions."

"As have you." A thread of hurt laced his voice, and she lifted her gaze to meet his, surprised despite herself.

"Not enough." His mouth twisted, and he pushed himself to his feet. She saw again how powerful he was, strong and graceful and so robust. She had felt that power surging against her, and yet she had felt his tenderness, too.

"It is good," he said roughly, and held out his hand to help her up. "If you are being careful, too. Since I have not the self-control I thought I did."

"I wanted you," she said swiftly. "I wanted..." *That*, she nearly said, but *that* could mean nothing more than a tumble in the soft grass of the riverbank and not the melding of hearts and souls that she had felt.

It seemed she had been the only one who felt it.

He tossed out talk of her being his lady, but he never said the words *wife* or *beloved* or *mother of my child*. Perhaps that was not what he meant by *lady*. Perhaps what he meant by that status was being his housekeeper still and the companion of his nights, but now with the legitimacy of marriage lines on the record of the parish to show that the lust he felt for her was sanctioned by God.

She swallowed the bitter lump in her throat. Thank heavens for that innkeeper and her tea, because if there was a babe, Inez would not have the freedom to walk away if she wanted. To simply leave, taking the broken shards of her heart with her.

Joseph walked to retrieve his hat and slapped it against his legs to shake off the dirt. Then he looked over the field and put a hand above his eyes, shading out the sun.

"That looks like Thaker in the wagon already, out searching for us. Arthur must have run straight back to his stall and his oats. Whatever I'm paying that man, it isn't enough."

He turned to her and stilled as he caught the expression on her face. "Inez. I'll find the fool who did this and hold him accountable. I won't let anyone hurt you. All will be well."

They looked at one another, and she didn't answer, because she knew, despite the hand he extended and the warm sun of the day and the echo of pleasure that still ran through her like the hum of bees, he couldn't promise that he would not absolutely shatter her heart.

CHAPTER EIGHTEEN

Good enough to take his pleasure with, but not good enough to carry his babe.

Not good enough to plan a future around.

These were the thoughts that swirled and dipped like old crows, pecking into Inez's thoughts as Thaker drove her and Wenna in the cart to the market town of Callington.

At last, Joseph had declared what he felt for her.

Oh, he'd made that offhand remark about her running the house as his lady. But that had proven a fantasy, for the moment he realized what their passion could lead to, if it bore the conventional fruit, he'd been shaking with remorse and self-reproach.

To her, their joining had been beautiful, a culmination and confirmation of what she knew in her heart. A nearly religious ecstasy, if it wasn't sacrilegious to say so. To him, it had been a grave error.

She couldn't stay here. She couldn't endure wanting him and knowing he didn't yearn for her the same way. She hadn't been able to bear it before, all those times she'd fled George Court, and she *could not* bear it now. Not when her feelings ran so much deeper, twining and choking like many-fingered roots.

Wenna sat on the front board beside her husband as the cart jounced along the rutted road to Callington. Arthur, the carthorse, had shaken off his fright of the day before and stepped with a vigor meant to convey that pulling the nearly empty wagon with a few light humans was hardly a strain on his prodigious capabilities. Wenna kept sending back puzzled, inquiring glances, as if she sensed Inez's distress and was anxious to ease it.

Inez pressed her lips into a smile and motioned with her hand to indicate that she was contentedly admiring the passing countryside. Gentle hills swelled with green, soft as a mother's bosom. The dissolving morning fog lifted from the hollows to blur the etchings of occasional humps of trees. White lumps of shorn sheep browsed the pasture, waddling in their leisurely way.

It was all so very different from London, and from what she'd known in Portugal. Cornwall wasn't just the end of Britain; it was the end of the known world, an escape from the modern day into something far older. It was as if, passing the River Tamar and the rocky outcrops of Dartmoor, one left the Age of Enlightenment for an ancient world, one that straddled the border between human industry and magic.

But still not a place that would welcome her, different as she was. Not even its fantastic history could make this an enchanted wood where the woodcutter's daughter could win a prince's love and become the princess of a castle.

She'd been a fool to appoint herself his housekeeper, she saw that now. She would live always a step below his notice, a step below what he could acknowledge. How could she live with this snare around her foot, holding her in a place unworthy of him? How could she live in the grip of this passion, knowing that all of her, heart, body, and soul, was not enough for him to love and cherish, to claim as his own?

Thaker stopped the cart in Fore Street, the main road which led west on to Haye and east toward Tavistock, and far beyond it, London. That was where she would go. She would go today. She would find Jock and ask if he wanted to go with her.

No, she could not leave at once. The stocking bag and its heavy burden lay in the cupboard of her room.

Inez stood on the street, caught in the shadow of the great medieval tower of St. Mary's Church with its granite stones and battlements, which thrust its spires into the sky like the promise of justice. Or retribution.

That blasted bag. It was a shackle around her neck. A weight that would accuse her, always.

Unless she simply left it behind. Perhaps Joseph would find it. And perhaps there would be a reward if he returned the jewels.

Her moment of indecision cost her, for Wenna slipped a companionable arm around her elbow and pulled her along. Callington had earned its right to a market in the time of the great Elizabeth, and so the shambles were well developed, occupying what Wenna called Back Lane, which eventually stretched north and became the road to Launceston. The town could not be more than a thousand souls, with not above two hundred houses clustered around the triangle of its main roads, but here they could find all they needed.

"Molds for tallow candles." Wenna counted on her fingers, the way she remembered lists. "A length of linen for aprons and caps for the new maids. A side of beef for the master's table, and mutton for ours. I've my vegetable garden coming on, but we'll want more flour with the new mouths to feed."

Thaker signed something, and Wenna nodded. "Aye, and a rooster for the hens. We'll see ye round and about, me 'ansome."

She blew a kiss in his direction as Thaker moved the horse down the street, then stood looking fondly after him.

A small, cool dart tingled Inez's arms and shoulders. Envy. Wenna had a husband who adored her and two babes who, in the simple manner of children, thought the sun rose and set about their mother. Wenna went home at night to a snug stone cottage with a thatched roof to shelter her bed, and she sang as she went about her tasks in the kitchen, helped now by the extra hands to aid with the scullery and the laundry and dairy.

Wenna had found her place in the world, and joy in it.

"Yeast, should you want to brew your own beer." Wenna continued thinking aloud as they moved toward the first of the market stalls. Behind the wooden counter with its heaps of fresh courgettes and radishes, presided over by a matron who looked as if she'd been up since well before cock crow, a cloth was spread on the ground. On it sat a baby in an undyed linen gown, chewing on a wooden spoon, while on a small stool beside him sat a girl of six or seven, sewing a pair of gloves.

"Alright, Mistress White?" Wenna greeted the matron.

"We've no need of courgettes, with your garden," Inez noted. "But those are lovely gloves."

Mrs. White inspected Inez's forearms, covered in the knitted mitts she'd found in London. Fine ladies purchased gloves to cover their dainty hands; servants had no need of them during their work. Inez practically saw the woman's thoughts churning as the other tried to size up her status.

"Mr. Treen is the one as sells the gloves, miss," said Mrs. White. "His shop is one over, in Church Lane. My Jane's a proper hand, she is, kid or cotton. He likes her work particular."

"This pretty party is our new housekeeper at Penwellen," Wenna said. "Mrs. Da Costa."

"Ah." Mrs. White's face relaxed and warmed. "Penwellen,

then? Mr. Joseph—aye, but it's Sir Joseph now, ee's the brother to a duke?"

"Brother to a duchess," Inez answered. "Does Mr. Treen also sell pins?"

Wenna parted ways at Mrs. White's, for her work was done. Before Inez reached the next stall, word had gone down the shambles. Mrs. Da Costa was housekeeper to the new baronet! Former maid to the Illingworth lass as became a duchess! Mrs. White only let her move on to complete her marketing after promising to share recipes for ale and small beer, clotted cream, and vegetable seeds in the autumn.

Inez's heart cracked as she moved down the shambles and found eager welcome. She wouldn't be here in the autumn to share seeds for next summer's gardens. She would not be bringing the locally famous Penwellen cheese to the harvest festival. She would be gone, carried away like a cottongrass seed on the wind.

She had nowhere in the world she wanted to be, without Joseph Illingworth.

Yet she could not bear to remain near and know he felt so much less than she did. This had broken her again and again in London, and it was breaking her now. So she would do what she had always done.

But she ached to leave this. Finished marketing, arms laden down with every item on Wenna's list, she joined the couple as Thaker loaded meat in the cart. Wenna haggled for the flour that would last the summer until they had their own grain to take to Haye Mill, and Inez stood stroking the lengths of fabric that had come fresh from the looms of a place called Rosecraddoc, wanting to sob out her misery. The fabric would outfit the new maids at Penwellen, and she would never see them wear it.

"Ye've just pins to fetch, aye?" Wenna asked. "Me ansome

and self'll be at the Bull's Head for a pint and parwhobble when you wants us."

"I'm told I can find pins at Mr. Treen's."

Wenna shook her head. "Geddon, and doan let 'ee jowse you. Ee's a Devoner, that 'un."

Everyone Wenna didn't like was a Devoner—a foreigner. The little maid from the inn in Amesbury, too, had said something about Mr. Treen.

Joseph didn't like the man, either. But thoughts of Joseph were a spear in her heart, and Inez pushed them aside. She had nothing to drag back to London with her but heartbreak. She might as well leave with a full complement of pins.

Treen's millinery lay close by the church in an old timber building that had been refaced with stucco and painted to resemble the light gray local stone. Multi-paned windows set out into the street allowed glimpses of the many treasures inside. Two rows of windows looked from stories above, set close enough together to suggest the low, cramped floors of an earlier century. The window settings and cornice were very plain, as was the style of the doorway. Somehow Inez had expected a more extravagant presentation from Mr. Treen.

The extravagance waited inside in the form of the man himself, dressed in a glistening coat of orange silk with full skirts and an extra row of bronze buttons. He wore a powdered toupee with a long pigtail, a lace-trimmed neckcloth, and an unctuous smile. He bowed as if she were a lady of the gentry.

"My dear miss—what was your name, dear? I believe the baronet neglected to introduce us when I called at Penwellen the other day."

He affected a lisp, like a London dandy, and wore an enameled case for toothpicks and a silver snuffbox attached to the many chains across his heavily embroidered waistcoat. Mr.

Treen was a walking advertisement for his trade in fashionable accessories.

"Mrs. Da Costa," Inez said, and the name became easier each time she said it. As if there were a real woman named Mrs. Da Costa who was a capable administrator of the household of a titled man, a woman of skill and competence, a woman who merited respect from those around her.

"Oh, yes." Treen's gaze trailed over her figure, resting with an insolent length of time on her breasts and hips. "The housekeeper."

His sneer said he meant *housekeeper* to mean *whore*.

Inez stiffened her back. "I am in need of pins, Mr. Treen. Steel, if you have them. I won't trouble you long."

"Nay, you must not simply run away, Mrs. Da Costa. As if we were merely business acquaintances! When I wish us to be so much more."

Inez was accustomed to deciphering lecherous hints from men. There was the leer of invitation from the scoundrel who assumed she would be thrilled by the honor of his attentions. There was the shifty side-eye of the man straying from the course of faithfulness to another, the one who would blame Inez for leading his thoughts to wander.

Then there was the man who wanted to draw out the game, who wanted to stalk and survey, to stoke his own appetites while he teased his prey. Lord Wigsby had been such a one. Inez guessed Treen was another.

"I've friends waiting for me at the pub," she said. "Just a small packet of pins, and if you do not have them, it is no matter. I shall look for a peddler to come through."

Another lie, as she wouldn't be here.

"As if a woman like yourself should have any business with a peddler." Treen took her elbow without asking permission. "Mrs. Da Costa, everything about you suggests you are made for the gentlest of circumstances. I cannot think such a green baronet as the man I met at Penwellen has the sense to honor you as he ought. Begging your pardon if you feel any affection for your *master*," he added, in an emphasis on the word *master* that meant *protector* and not *employer*. "I hope in time your trust will not prove to have been misplaced. Do come meet my mother."

"I hardly think she will want acquaintance with a house-keeper, Mr. Treen."

"I am aware I do you an honor, but I cannot think that a woman of your qualities is destined long for the humble rank of *housekeeper*, Mrs. Da Costa."

He lowered his gaze to her bosom with frank appreciation. Inez was very glad she had worn her neckerchief crosswise over her bodice and tucked the ends into her waist. Treen lifted his eyes to hers and winked—winked!—as if they had reached a silent understanding.

"Oliver, watch the shop for a moment, will you? I'm showing Mrs. Da Costa upstairs."

Inez couldn't fathom what the man was about as he conducted her upstairs. As was the current custom in England, the receptions rooms were on the first floor, the piano nobile. Three women sat in the parlor, arrayed in the latest of fashion-able fripperies along with billows of silk and muslin, towers of powdered curls, and hats large enough to shelter a child's cradle.

"Heavens, you didn't say the housekeeper was a Blackamoor." The one introduced as Mrs. Treen lowered her chin and squinted at Inez in the manner of a woman growing near-sighted. "What striking looks you possess, child. You remind me of those Africans the Corytons have serving in their house. Brought from their estate in Barbados, I believe."

Inez held back her anger. Treen had brought her to parade

before his mother as a curiosity, and pretend he honored her by the introduction? "I am from Portugal, madame. Not Barbados."

"Is the baronet married? Affianced?" demanded the second woman, introduced as Mrs. Daw. She had been a mantua maker before retiring from trade to live in respectable leisure. Inez guessed Treen did not actually make hats; he saw himself more as a factor overseeing trades than a shopkeeper. The hats, like the gloves he sold, would be made by someone else, someone underpaid and undervalued for their work.

"Sir Joseph is not married, madame, nor promised," Inez said.

Mrs. Daw nodded. "All to the good. Perhaps my Ursula might have a crack at him."

Have a crack, Inez thought, as if the girl were trying out a carriage or a new style of hat.

"Will he entertain?" The third, introduced as Mrs. Abbott, was a hatchet-faced woman in widow's weeds, stabbing a needle into her embroidery as if it had provided offense. "Favella laid the most meager, miserly table and never had any dancing, and after she died, Sir Reuben entertained not at all. Most unaccommodating of him."

"I shall leave the entertainments to Sir Joseph's discretion, mum," Inez replied. "Though I hope he will prove an amiable neighbor."

Her heart pinched. Joseph would become a favorite in the neighborhood, she had no doubt. Another success she would not be here to witness.

"So hope we all," Mrs. Abbott said with a sniff. "Lord knows his father never made much of himself, content to be vicar of that tiny parish in St. Cleer. And marrying a woman from a foreign family to boot. But Melwin says the new baronet makes a fine figure, and I don't see why my Agnes shouldn't be able to stand next to your Ursula, Charity Daw." She glared at her neighbor, and Inez sensed the layers of a long rivalry twining about the room.

"Well, chances are his wife will want a housekeeper of her own choosing, so you'd best have your bag packed, Mistress Da Costa," Mrs. Treen advised. "Men are so fickle in their ways. Saving my dear Melwin, of course." She followed this with an indulgent look at her son. "How would you feel about a position in town? You would add a certain flair to our establishment, I will say."

"I agree, Mother, that Mrs. Da Costa is a delightful addition to our neighborhood," her son replied. "She adds a certain...*je ne sais quois*." Once more his gaze wandered down Inez's neck to the tiny patch of skin showing above her collarbone. "I do hope we will be seeing...much more of her."

"My dear Melwin," his mother simpered, "you are so quick to find the good in everyone. I do hope it will not prove your undoing one day."

"Never that, Mother." Treen's look turned shrewd. "Mrs. Da Costa, your Sir Joseph will have some doing to get his estate producing again, even with such loveliness at the helm of his household. Reuben was a careless landowner at best, and something of a fool. I did my best to help him. Offered to take some of the worthless land off his hands, put coin in his coffers." He gestured. "Perhaps we might discuss this downstairs, while you shop?"

The interview over, the ladies having gotten nothing useful out of Inez besides sticking their pins of disdain in her, Treen followed her back down the stairs. She felt his gaze on the back of her head, as if he were trying to plant a thought there.

"Just the furze and wastes on the south end of his property, near the spring," Treen continued as they stepped into the main room of the shop. "You might remember to him that my offer still stands, should he be reviewing his accounts for sources of funds. I do want to see our neighborhood's finest gentleman firm on his feet."

"Thank you for your concern, Mr. Treen. I am sure Joseph —Sir Joseph—is giving your offer due consideration."

"I hope he will. He's not likely to find another who will pay him for useless dirt. Oliver, pins for the lady." The lad delivered, and Treen placed the packet in Inez's hands with a small, unctuous bow.

"Should you ever have need of assistance, Mrs. Da Costa— of *any* kind—I hope you will put Melwin Treen at your service. You may find I am able to offer you advantages that Sir Joseph cannot."

This was the language a man used when he was trying to poach another man's mistress. Inez had witnessed enough of these transactions in Dark Lane to recognize the leer of a man who assumed she would be flattered by his offer. As if every woman was a whore in waiting, simply biding her time for the baited hook.

"Are you aspiring to court me, Mr. Treen? You seem so keen in your admiration. And it is true, no woman would wish to remain a mere *housekeeper* if there were a better position to hand." Inez couldn't resist fluttering her eyelashes at him and cocking one hip coyly to the side.

Such a look of horror fled over his face that she bit back a laugh, afraid it would become a sob of fury. He quelled it quickly, resuming the mask, but she saw the truth.

Exotic was not the same as *worthy of respect*. To such a man, she might ornament his bed, but not his house or his name. His prejudices were the same as his mother's—the same shared among all his class and kind.

Joseph was of that class and kind, now. The thought was an iron collar choking her neck.

"I admit I had not thought to aspire so high as marriage, Mrs. Da Costa."

Of course not. Because a *housekeeper* was a convenient woman. But not the lady of the house. Not the mother of a son and heir.

She turned for the door, but paused when he called after her, unheeding of the shop boy, Oliver, gaping after them.

"I am aware that your dear baronet is in straits, Mrs. Da Costa. I was more in Reuben's pockets than you know. I can put a significant down payment on a contract should he wish to sell me that land. And I can guarantee full payment in time."

A shopkeeper, buying up part of a local estate? Treen was indeed anxious to climb the ladder to gentility.

"Good day, Mr. Treen. Thank you for the great honor—" the words were ash in her mouth— "of introducing me to your friends."

He had paraded her before his mother and friend so they might shred her like a roomful of cats handed a plump mouse. He had meant to show her her place.

A woman who, in the market, could command the respect and best prices from the local tradeswomen and other servants.

But never, never a woman who would gain the respect of the genteel.

"I hope I might bring my mother to call at Penwellen soon, Mrs. Da Costa. I will live for the moment that I may again drink in your beauty."

"The beauty of a Blackamoor? You do indeed have exotic tastes, Mr. Treen." She was too well-mannered to slam the door, but she thought about it.

Fury gripped her in its claws as she hastily made the short walk to the Bull's Head. She saw the looks cast her way, curiosity about the newcomer. Her face would always make her stand out. She could never be accepted here. There would always be those who looked past the color of her face to the person behind it; Amaranthe had been one, Joseph with her, the ladies of Dark Lane, the staff at Penwellen.

But there would always be the Mrs. Treens of the world, ready to scratch at any interloper they deemed unworthy.

She had made herself unworthy by allowing herself to become a kept woman. And she had broken her sacred promise to her mother.

Jock sat at the counter of the pub, as usual surrounded by admirers. He beckoned to Inez, and she went, ready to beg her to take her from here at once.

Jock was in the same position she was. Some thought him less than a man because his body had been broken. Some admired him all the same. Men wanted to be him; women pursued him.

But Joseph had also hinted why Jock was absenting himself from London. He'd meddled with an earl's sister, and class was a line lovers did not cross without repercussions.

Her darling *mamãe* had loved across borders, falling in love with a foreign sailor. And following him to her ruin and death.

"Down from Plymouth, I see," Inez said by way of greeting.

Jock took the pint of ale the barkeep set before him, one likely supplied by an admirer. "Met a gentry mort and her cove with such a Canterbury story. Fresh home from a flight abroad, aren't they, a fortune hunter, he, and an honest woman, she. Wed a brace of years ago, quite a rumpus as he snaffled her out from the nose of her muckworm of a father. Now the mort wants to mend the fences she broke, with the pater and a few others she says she's done wrong."

He stared at Inez as if this intelligence should mean something to her. She had the creeping feeling, a damp cold snaking from her toes and working its way up her legs like a fog, that it did.

"This lady wouldn't be the daughter of a lord of my acquaintance," Inez said. The world was not that small. The peerage of Britain was not that small. Genteel daughters ran away from controlling parents all the time, didn't they?

"Depends," Jock answered. "The mort is on the lookout for her old abigail. Dark-skinned article, foreign born. Meant to part on amicable terms, but didn't make the last club, as the tide waits for no man. The mort says she would much desire—them's her words, they are—to ask the maid about something she might have in her possession."

Inez didn't ask how Jock had found out the connection. The admiration he received everywhere he went meant people confided in him all the time, sharing details of their lives as if they knew him, and he in return ought to know them. There were dark-skinned maids in service across Britain, true enough, but not so many that Jock could not come to some reasonable deductions, given a few hints. She had no doubt he had met Wigsby's errant, married daughter, now returned to England.

And the daughter would be searching out Inez for the same reasons as her father.

The reckoning had come. Inez felt a heavy chain clamping to the iron collar around her throat. They didn't indenture people to the colonies anymore, did they? Not after the upstart Americans had begun a rebellion.

No, what they would do is throw her into the hulks, the broken ships that floated in the Thames off Woolwich. London's prisons being severely overcrowded and a place needed for the excess, Parliament had decided to turn a ship captured from the French Navy into a floating penitentiary, and now there was a new way to store society's unwanted out of sight.

Did she go to Plymouth, it was likely Inez would go from town straight to prison. Or the gallows.

But if she went, she could lay rest, at last, to the ghosts of her past. Wigsby would leave off hunting her; he would have to quarrel with his daughter to get his jewels back.

And Joseph would never learn what Inez had done.

She had known she was leaving. That her time here was done. Fitting that it would end with a final accounting for her crimes.

It was time to pay the devil his due.

She looked into Jock's steady eyes. "You will take me?"

He nodded, once. Excellent discretion, for a groom. No wonder a marquess had depended on him. No wonder an earl's daughter had thrown her heart after him.

"I don't wish to tell the others. Especially Joseph."

He drew a finger across his lips to indicate a seal.

She closed her eyes and drew in a breath. This could be the end of everything. She could be headed for absolution, or the hangman's noose.

"I need to collect something from the house."

Again he nodded.

She took his glass from his hand and tipped it down her throat. The ale was warm, the foam bitter.

"How soon do you think we should leave?"

CHAPTER NINETEEN

"We might find deposits of china clay," Joseph mused to his companions. "The Penhales found some on their land when I was a boy. They never made a fortune, but the pits produced a decent amount. I wonder if William Cookworthy still has his china factory in Plymouth?"

Thaker signed something, and Wenna translated. "Me luv says there's tin up near Gunnislake."

Joseph nodded. "And a tin works near Harrowbarrow, too, I've heard. I saw signs of beamworks when we crossed Dartmoor." In fact the great moor was criss crossed with gullies that marked centuries of stream mining and past digging, but all the accessible deposits had been taken up long ago.

"Have you seen any likely rocks on Penwellen lands?" he asked Thaker, struggling with the signs but managing to convey his meaning, with Wenna's help.

Here at the southern edge of Dartmoor there was still granite underlying the green fields, with the occasional rocky outcropping marking the eluvial deposits. Joseph had grown up around mining talk and knew that the cassiterite which held the valuable tin might be found alongside tourmaline or hematite, such useful elements as arsenic and antimony, or, if one were very lucky, lead or silver.

Thaker shook his head, and Joseph told himself he wasn't disappointed, because he hadn't expected anything. He had been trained his whole life to humility, not ambition. His parents had insisted on modesty and being content with what God consented to give, whether it was good fortune or bad. Joseph had been taught to accept that he came from the lesser son, not the greater, and so must harbor smaller goals. He was taught not to expect fair treatment from those above, not to gamble on any turn of fortune, to work hard to keep himself, and to be content nevertheless if his hard work yielded only a small return, or none.

Amaranthe had tumbled into a great stroke of good fortune, falling in love with a bastard who turned out to be a legitimate duke, but that only proved the family curse had passed over her. Good heavens, Joseph hadn't been able to find a proper post since Amaranthe married. How could he expect to make something of this down-at-heels estate he'd only stumbled into through Reuben's bad luck, and not his own merit? He was plain Joseph Illingworth, the boy whom his uncle had thought a weakling, trying on the baronet's boots.

"Perhaps I'll find some wolframite," he said aloud, for his own benefit. "Feldspar, I'm told, could be used in making ceramics. Or mayhap Penwellen holds a vein of quartz. Useful for clock-making, I understand. The Romans thought quartz had great protective properties."

Wenna nodded. "Mayhap," she said, her tone masking skepticism with politeness. She was not Inez, who enjoyed hearing his random bits of knowledge and would spur him with further questions.

He swung the stick he held at a thick cluster of broom, shaking the yellow flowers and releasing the scent of vanilla.

Penwellen was destined to yield sheep and, if the growing season proved accommodating, the native grain they called pillas. Any slim profits they made would have to pay off Reuben's debts and be invested in improvements to the land and buildings, if he was to continue to charge tenants for leasing the cottages and farmhouses. If he were very fortunate, he would be able to give Inez what she wanted to spruce up the house and set a fine table.

Inez. His housekeeper. Joseph scowled to himself as he stalked along, finishing this interrupted survey of his property. What was he to do with Inez?

It didn't feel right to treat her as a servant. And she refused to be a kept woman. Her logic was natural enough, given that currently he could barely keep himself.

A generous man would let her go, send her packing back to London where she could ask Amaranthe for help finding a secure position. Inez was comely and intelligent and warm in her nature, with a temper that could turn fiery when she was crossed. It was not out of bounds to think that she might find a deserving man to marry. A man who could provide for her properly, give her a secure future, and perhaps some little luxuries to please her. Give her a home of her own to order.

Perhaps give her children. His heart pounded at the thought of his error just a few days earlier, when he hadn't taken proper care of her and stood the risk he might have started a babe outside the bounds of marriage. His lack of self-control was one more sign of his weakness where was concerned. He'd not been blind to Eyde's situation, not with the child being born in his lodgings, not with Amaranthe so fiercely protecting her. A babe would force Inez to marry him, and he didn't want her forced. He wanted her glad and willing.

Yet it turned out she was taking precautions, too. She did not want his babe either, and he didn't know how to take that.

He didn't deserve her, and it wasn't fair to keep her. But sending her to London might deliver her straight back into the clutches of Wigsby, and that was the excuse Joseph clutched at to excuse his selfish want. Keeping her at Penwellen meant keeping her safe. He wasn't the worst thing for her.

He wanted to be the best thing for her. He, Joseph Illingworth, wanted at last to be enough. To be worthy of the love of this remarkable and unparalleled woman. His father had somehow contrived to be worthy of his mother, though he knew some would never see past her ancestry. Malden Grey, the great clodpate, wasn't the least bit deserving of Amaranthe, God knew, yet he'd won her heart anyway.

Could Joseph win Inez?

She'd been quiet and subdued yesterday when she and Wenna returned from market, tending to the stores in the kitchen while Joseph helped Thaker wrangle the new rooster into the pen where he would be contained until he could be introduced to the hens. She'd been quiet that evening, when he asked her to dine with him in the small parlor. It seemed she'd forgiven him, as she'd come to his bed the same as always, and he'd been more careful, knowing that she shook him beyond the bounds of restraint. Their touching was tender and playful, and she moved him to depths he hadn't known he had in him.

But something was missing. Something about their joining was yet incomplete. She held herself back from him in the deepest ways. He knew her body, but he didn't know her mind, nor the desires of her heart, and he yearned to be the man she would trust in those gifts.

What could he offer that could be equal to the transformation she'd made in him? How could she ever find him worthy of her, when he had so little to give?

Joseph felt like that rooster: everything depended on having his lady accept him. Of course, she might reject him, same as

Susannah Pettigrew. Susannah Pettigrew had wounded Joseph's pride, but if Inez did not want a future with him, Joseph would be crushed into dust.

There was a cowardly part of him that didn't want the reckoning to come yet. He wanted to go on a while longer inside the illusion that Inez wanted him, and that he alone could be enough, for the time being.

A dog barked in the distance, and Thaker cocked his head. Joseph had a brief, absurd thought that Thaker had heard the animal, but then he sensed what the other man had detected: hoofbeats pounding the earth. It was what they called in Cornwall a dummity day, the light low and the sky overcast, and Joseph squinted across the lumps and slopes of the fields. Some distance away, beyond the line of trees that marked a small rivulet crossing one of the lower fields, a lone horseman rode away from them, flushed out by the hound, who followed it a ways, barking, until the boy walking with the hound called it back.

"Why, thas Dashel," Wenna said in surprise.

The Southern Hound, winded from its short run, trotted toward them, the dappled spots on its coat changing as it passed beneath the fringe of trees. Joseph saw briefly the scene from over a decade ago, the hunting dog on the ground, Reuben standing above it with his gun and his contemptuous sneer.

Joseph was not Reuben, to be careless with another creature. He had to speak with Inez directly. He had to tell her what was in his heart. If she crushed him to powder, so be it. It was time to be the man his father had raised him to be.

"Areah, 'ee's all dappered, 'ee is!" Wenna cried as the muddy dog reared up in greeting. "Put yer cabby paws on the ground, ye great burster."

"I thought Jock was off to sell the whole pack," Joseph said. "Were there no buyers?"

Thaker looked abashed, and Wenna grinned at him as she signed. "Didna want to part with the buzgut, did ye, me ansome? Dashel's proper attached to me luv, 'ee is, and better fit ye let them go on together, I think."

"And Thaker is proper attached to the hound in return," Joseph guessed, conveying as much to the other man with his gestures. Thaker tousled the hound's ears as the beast leaned against his leg, panting happily.

"Where's Jock gone to?" Joseph asked as the lad approached, one of the new stable boys that Wenna had canvassed for his staff from a local family. "We need him to take Arthur and see if he can intercept that gent taking a stroll across my property. Warn him that someone was shooting here a day or so agone, without my permission, I might add."

Wenna looked at him, and Thaker looked at him, and Joseph made the same connection: the fleeing man might very well be the trespasser, and had declined to shoot at them this time because there were four of them to his one, plus a dog.

"The jockey?" the stable boy piped up. "'Ee's taken Miz Da Costa away south to see 'er people. Plymouth again, I think 'ee said."

"Inez—Mrs. Da Costa has left? To Plymouth? She doesn't have people there."

Inez was gone. She had left him. Joseph felt the same thrill of terror jolt through his body as when the gunshot spooked the horse and Inez had fallen off the cart.

He had no life without her in it. She could not leave him. He must do whatever he could to keep her, worthy or not.

He wheeled and headed for the house. He needed to confirm the boy's divulgence. He needed to see what she had taken, to know how long she planned to stay away.

"What's a rider doing on my land anyway?" Joseph asked as

the others turned to walk with him. "Hunting for leverets?" The baby hares were a delicacy, he would admit.

"Fossicking, most like," Wenna mused. At Joseph's puzzled look, she translated. "Prospecting, I think they say upcountry."

Joseph slowed and signed to Thaker. "I haven't looked on the other side of the stream. I thought it was just rocks."

'Tis, Thaker signed back. *But he might've left something.*

Something that might identify the interloper. Joseph agreed. While he was desperate to know where Inez went, he had a responsibility to the people who lived on his property to ensure they would not be attacked while simply doing their job.

These acres on the southeast corner had been a delight to play in when he was a lad, the granite bones of the earth showing through. To his boyhood imagination the rocky outcroppings, with their colorful striations and clusters of embedded minerals, had served as the deserts of Arabia, the Mongolian steppes, and the high peaks of the Alps.

Now there was a great crater blasted into the ground, creating a cliff that young Joseph would have turned into the Scottish peak of Ben Nevis and undertaken to scale. It would have taken considerable force to break apart the granite shelves, and Joseph's hunch was confirmed when he pressed a finger to a smudge of black dust and then sniffed. Gunpowder.

"What were they looking for?" he wondered aloud.

"Lodes of ore," Wenna answered, signing for her husband. "Thas as how they make the pits deeper when all of the surface veins have been mined."

"Veins of what?" Joseph picked up a nearby fragment, what looked like a packed piece of earth. The surface was mottled with gray and red-brown spots, like a vellum page in one of Amaranthe's old manuscripts that had been left to mold and rot for a hundred years. It was a thin shard, but much heavier than parchment, and the sheared border held an edge that pressed against his palm.

He looked up, a suspicion solidifying, just as Thaker signed back. *Copper*, the other man said.

AN UNFAMILIAR HORSE was being walked in the front drive before the house when they returned, Joseph carrying a sack of the rock fragments with their veins of reddish-brown and green. Clouds hunched low in the sky, boding rain, and the low light reminded Joseph that Inez was gone. He must find where she went and follow her. Wenna'd had no notice she meant to depart, and if it were an errand for the house, she would have spoken to Wenna if not to him.

"Tell me," he said to the stable boy, who started forward to talk to the lad holding the other horse, "does that look to you like one of the horses they keep at the White Hart in town?"

"It do, sir."

"And bearing a remarkable resemblance to the mount Dashel flushed. The trespasser's."

"It might, at that, sir," said the boy.

Joseph was only partly inclined to be civil when he saw the visitor was Treen, and that Treen was not in the formal parlor but inspecting the morning room, which had yet to be cleared of its extra trunks and furniture to make the study Joseph was planning.

"Sir Joseph. Thank you for receiving me." Treen tugged off his glove and advanced with his hand out. Joseph didn't see how he could disoblige by not shaking the man's hand, but Treen's palm was limp and damp. He eyed Joseph's glove, marked with green dust, and then the rest of his attire, his plain coat and leather breeches.

Clearly the neighborhood expected the new baronet to

make a better account of himself than showing up in his dirt in his drawing room. Well, until Joseph found a way to make something of his land, he would be out upon it, and the neighborhood would simply have to acknowledge that the new baronet was not the fop his predecessor had been.

"Mr. Treen. I would have make myself better available had I known you intended to call." Joseph's tone held a hint of frost. He didn't wish to alienate the man, someone his own age and near his own standing, but Treen's ability to mushroom everywhere was becoming damned inconvenient.

"I was in the area, so thought I'd look in. Talk a bit more about continuing the agreement I had with your cousin."

"Ah. The agreement." Joseph tugged off his other glove and slapped them together. Treen was becoming overbearing about pressing this alliance. He insisted he'd been in a business partnership with Reuben, though the solicitor could find no record of any agreement.

"I know, as a gentleman, you'll honor another gentleman's word," Treen said with an oily smile.

But Treen was not a gentleman, Joseph wanted to point out. His father had been a publican who had failed at public houses in Saltash, Liskeard, and Pensilva before finally making a go of the Half Moon in Stoke Climsland. Treen's mother had been a barmaid and gave herself more airs than Favella ever had. From what Joseph could tell, Treen's record as a businessman was at least as fraught as his father's; the millinery shop was the second if not the third venture he had undertaken in Callington.

"Remind me again what the agreement was," Joseph said. "Mr. Hoskyn has so far been able to produce no trace of it."

"We had not proceeded to the step of putting things in writing, I grant you. Your cousin was a man of honor, as am I. And I was offering to help him, as he knew. Buying a few acres of the more worthless property, the ones he couldn't farm. With the attendant rights, of course. Water, and so on." Treen grimaced. "We would have had all things signed and tidied if he hadn't taken ill, poor devil."

"Ah." Joseph looked around the room. He would be some time cleaning up Reuben's messes. "I would offer you refreshment, but I understand my housekeeper has been unexpectedly called away."

"The lovely Mrs. Da Costa," Treen said. "We should all be so fortunate to have a housekeeper so comely."

Joseph gave him a severe look. "She is a woman in my employ and therefore under my protection."

Treen wore a small, satisfied smile, as if he'd discovered something, or had a suspicion confirmed. Then he adopted a moue of concern.

"I suppose I should warn you, then. Mrs. Da Costa came to my shop just yesterday. I did her the honor of introducing her to my mother, as I supposed would be the kind thing to do— A woman of her, shall we say, complexion may not be welcomed by the better people of Callington without our example. I am gratified to say that my mother and I have always been very open-minded. We take seriously the biblical injunction to love all of God's creatures."

"There is not a single reason Inez should not be perfectly presentable to your mother," Joseph said icily, aware he lied.

Mrs. Treen would be unlikely to welcome the daughter of a lascar into her drawing room, and certainly not, given her own social aspirations and affectations, the daughter of a trull. A woman who had set foot in Dark Lane would not be accepted into the parlors of those aspiring to gentility. It was only someone very innocent or very eccentric or very tender-hearted, and Amaranthe was all of these things, who would overlook a person's past and see an opportunity to provide assistance.

Now that she was the Duchess of Hunsdon, Amaranthe

could be as eccentric as she wished, and be admired for it, if not imitated. A Mrs. Treen of Callington could not afford to be eccentric, at least, not if she wished to rise.

What was Treen playing at, introducing Inez into his mother's circle? Attempting to show her that Treen, as her protector, could offer her a parent and a lively social circle, which Joseph could not?

Treen's smile shifted to one side. "I ought to tell you, man to man. Mrs. Da Costa made certain...advances to me. Indications, if you take my meaning. Of course, I wouldn't take advantage of a woman in her circumstances."

Joseph's head went up and back as if he were a bridled horse and Treen had yanked on the ribbons. "What circumstances do you believe she is in?"

"Did I say circumstances?" Treen raised his brow. "I meant rather...profession." He withdrew a snuffbox from his coat and opened it. "My friends will tease me that I am too nice, but I confess I am not tempted by common women. One simply never knows what they might bring with them. And such a woman will never be moved by affection."

Treen took a pinch of snuff, deposited on the back of his hand, conveyed his knuckles to his nose, and sniffed deeply. Immediately his eyes began to water, and he held the box out to Joseph.

Joseph shook his head. His father had smoked pipe tobacco, but had never taken snuff, nor had his mother. Amaranthe said Reuben and Favella had taken so much when she lived with them that she could no longer bear the scent.

"Inez," he said instead, "made overtures to you." He'd never heard his own tone sound so deadly.

Treen, preoccupied with closing his snuffbox and returning the enameled case to his pocket, then withdrew his handkerchief, a heavily embroidered silk affair.

"It seems she is on the hunt for a new protector, my friend. The reason for her current absence, one might suppose?"

"You'll forgive me if I have another appointment," Joseph said. "It is pressing." He was betraying himself, and he did not care if he showed Treen that his barbs had landed. Keeping up appearances with this one would be a daunting and never-ending task.

"I beg your pardon if I have upset you. I shall take my leave." Treen gathered his gloves and walking stick. He carried his chapeau bras beneath his arm, the better, Joseph supposed, to show off his freshly curled and powdered wig.

"Those lands," Treen said again. "We can discuss them at another time? I'm willing to pay a fair price. I want to see our new baronet well-established in the neighborhood, and I have leave to know, sadly, the straits in which the former baronet left you."

The thought of this man knowing the state of his finances was nearly as enraging as his suggestion—false, of course—that Inez had thrown herself at his head. Inez didn't like the man and made fun of his cologne.

"Do be careful as you are riding about," Joseph said as he showed his guest to the door. "I heard someone shooting on my property the other day. Someone I hadn't given leave to hunt here."

"Shooting?" Treen's dark eyebrows were incongruent against his pale wig. "How dreadful. I do hope ruffians are not making free on your acres."

"Nor the acres you're hoping to buy," Joseph said. "Rest easy, I will identify and deal with the interfering ape. I don't think enough people know it, but Reuben bred his dogs to be quite vicious."

"Did he." Joseph couldn't be certain, as Treen wore powder,

but his face seemed to blanch momentarily. "I will be certain to warn my friends."

"Oh, don't," Joseph said with false pleasantry. He pulled open the front portal as Treen gripped his walking stick. "I'd quite like to see the hounds tear any trespassers apart."

"And I thought Londoners would be civilized," Treen remarked, stepping across the threshold into the cloudy day, which had somehow grown darker.

"Not when we're crossed," Joseph answered. "Have a care where you step, Treen, and rest easy—Inez won't trouble you again."

"A beautiful woman is always trouble," Treen said with another of his oily smiles, and then, at long last, he turned to his horse.

Joseph had no time to congratulate himself that his suspicions were true. Treen was the one he'd seen riding earlier, but was he also the one who had shot at him? If so, he had put Inez in danger, and for no other reason than that he was bloody interested in a certain pocket of Penwellen land.

Wenna appeared in the doorway, and, as if she shared the thought that suddenly struck Joseph, she carried his outer coat, hat, and riding gloves.

She also carried one more item that made Joseph's eyes widen to see it. It went against all the training he'd received to be conciliatory, but when had minding his manners ever gained him what he wanted?

"Plymouth," Wenna confirmed. "That Jock took 'er, and Arthur in the cart. She never said why, or who she was going to see, but me lover says they had a natter a day agone at the pub, and Mrs. Da Costa seemed proper wisht by the end of un."

"Wisht?" Joseph echoed, taking his items from her.

"Pale. Sad."

There was only one reason he could think of that Inez

would drop all and take off for a port town with nary a word to the rest of them. Something had happened to her father.

"Treen, I know you'll forgive me, but I need your horse. It's a hack from the White Hart, isn't it?" Joseph pulled on his riding gloves as he strode toward the mount, a Hackney with strong lines and a deep chest. He needn't waste the time strapping spurs to his boots; this horse could go fifteen miles at a brisk trot.

"It is, but you can't mean— You can't take my horse!" Treen spluttered.

Joseph made a few quick adjustments and swung himself into the saddle. He dug a coin from his pocket and flipped it to the other man, exactly as if he were a servant.

"I just did. One of my trotters can see you home, and my boy will stop in the White Hart to tell them of the trade. Fearful accommodating of you, old man, but then I believe you owe me a boon. If you're to make free hacking about on my land, then I'm at liberty to borrow your horse."

He saw from the man's dark expression that he had made a firm enemy, but he couldn't spare a moment to care. Inez was going to Plymouth, so he was, too. She might be accosted on the road by ruffians; she might meet all manner of menace at the docks. She might even now be taking in news that would pull her world down about her ears.

He had to be there for her if that happened. And somehow —and he had no notion how he might do so—he needed to persuade her to come back to him, and stay.

CHAPTER TWENTY

Inez was exhausted already.

The journey to Plymouth had taken all day, with stops in St. Mellion and Saltash to rest Arthur and herself. Jock seemed tireless, endlessly alert as he drove the trap along the increasingly well-traveled roads. She hadn't been able to eat a thing at the coaching inns. The bun from that morning was a hard rock in her belly that rolled back and forth with her worries.

Priscilla would greet her with a welcoming smile and forgive her everything. Priscilla would turn her straight over to constable. Inez would be tried in the Plymouth assizes and tumbled directly into prison without ever seeing the light of day, or Joseph, ever again. He wouldn't know what had happened to her. She would die an old woman without her teeth, friendless and despairing and alone.

No, she recalled as she clutched the stocking bag in her lap, she'd stolen from a lord. She wouldn't be sent to prison. By the Bloody Code, she'd be executed, probably hanged, and who knew what they did to the bodies of felons here. It wouldn't matter to the judge that she had stolen at the behest of the lord's daughter. Inez's hands had gathered up the jewels, and her hands had kept them all this time. She was riding to a sentence of doom.

They ferried the trap and horse across the River Tamar from Saltash, and Inez knew the sea was approaching by the way the land turned marshy and the air grew heavy with the smell of wet earth and salt. To think this same sea lapped her old home in Portugal, and yet the land was so different. The square tower of an enormous medieval church hulked in the distance for a long time, a beckoning finger, and then all of a sudden the town sprang up about it like nestlings seeking protection.

"That's the minster of St. Andrews," Jock told her as they joined the traffic wheeling into town. "They say Katherine of Aragon touched down in Plymouth when she came to marry the Prince as was Arthur. Said a prayer for safe travels at the church, though it didn't do 'er nor 'er 'usband a scratch of good. That's yer namesake, ye great plodder," Jock said to the horse, who flicked his ears at his name.

"Sir Francis Drake, the great admiral and favorite of Queen Elizabeth, he lighted 'ere after his voyage 'round the world," Jock went on. "The priest is holding a service, and all sudden his church empties and his flock's pourin' down to the quay to hail the returning hero."

"Carrying wealth he looted from the Spanish." Inez pressed a hand to her belly as if she could keep the stone there from rolling about. "Your English buccaneers were not heroic to those whose ships they plundered."

Jock shrugged. "Drake died of fever abroad, didnee, and Queen Katherine died of a cracked heart when her King Henry cast her aside. So have a care what prayers you say in St. Andrews, that's the lesson I'd be taking."

He pointed. "That other, Charles Church, that's un the citizens built to appease Charles II after they gave 'im back his crown. And that," he said, pointing toward the tall spires that thronged like the arrowed tips of great barren trees, "be the quay, and the ships from all lands a' coming."

"Some Portuguese vessels, I don't doubt," Inez murmured. She sent up a quick, silent prayer that her father was safe. And that he hadn't stayed in England to see what she had made of herself: a thief, and a kept woman.

Jock drove them past the church and the guild hall onto a broad street that led straight down to the quay and the inlet they called Sutton Pool. He slowed before a stretch of modern houses, only a few decades old, their stucco fronts and Palladian proportions a polished contrast to the rubble and plaster of the earlier merchant's houses and stores.

Jock stopped before a timbered door, slightly recessed, with a modest fan light above. The house boasted two more stories of tall windows, none boarded up to avoid taxing, and a delicately painted string course in contrast to the deep brown of the window casings and a thick cornice above. The house spoke of comfortable wealth, and in Inez's experience, those made comfortable by their wealth usually declined to share it.

Her nerves assailed her. She couldn't knock at the front door, not as the lady's former servant. She was about to tell Jock to pull around to the back when the door opened and Priscilla herself appeared on the threshold.

Priscilla had always dressed in the height of fashion, and Inez held no doubt that her entire ensemble had come straight from the latest plates she found in whatever French mantua-maker had the honor to dress her. A *robe à l'anglaise* of blue silk trimmed with yards of blonde lace belled over her beribboned petticoats, and a straw hat bearing enormous puffs of silk and feathers tipped forward at a jaunty angle.

"Inez!" she cried, her tone all delight. "You are an apparition I have longed to see! I vow, I thought that groom had a cunning look in his eye when I spoke of you to him." She wiggled her fingers at Jock in an airy gesture, a blend of invitation and reproach. "But how did he produce you so quickly? He could never have gone all the way to London and back, unless some magical portal has opened in England while we were away."

Inez found herself borne inside on the strength of Priscilla's warm enthusiasm, propelled through a pleasant hall and up an expensively carved wooden staircase, and delivered into a tall-ceilinged parlor of gracious proportions. She was bestowed upon an upholstered chair where Priscilla declared, "There, I can see you in this ghastly gloomy English light, but it won't harm that beautiful complexion."

Inez was briefly touched that the young woman would guard Inez's skin as jealously as she guarded her own skin, white as bone china.

Priscilla deposited herself on a striped silk-upholstered settee in a well-practiced move that appeared artless but which Inez knew took some doing given the hoops required to give her bottom that shape. She proceeded to unpin her hat, leaving the lace indoor cap beneath, and spoke the serving girl who poked her head around the door.

"I won't be going out after all, Sally, for I shall be entertaining my very good friend. Please send in tea and those delightful little cakes that Cook makes. Oh, and do tell my beloved Monsieur Dervieux that his presence is required *immediately* in the petite salon."

Sally nodded but gave Inez a narrow-eyed stare, as if she had assessed at a glance that her lady's visitor had no higher status than the maid herself. Inez nearly rose from her seat, recalled to the impropriety of sitting in the company of her former employer, of behaving as if she were calling on a woman she had formerly served.

Her rump had scarcely cleared the lovely butter-yellow damask of the cushion when a thought struck, as if a bell had rung in her head: If she were wed to Joseph, a baronet's lady, she could sit in all company save that of the Queen.

Slowly, Inez lowered herself to her chair.

She wanted to marry Joseph.

The remark he'd made so casually had stuck in her head like seed that planted itself with tiny spikes, and here was the blooming of it.

She *wanted* to marry Joseph Illingworth. She would in a moment, were she so allowed.

She would never be allowed.

"You've come over with a strange look all of a sudden, my dear Inez," Priscilla said with a laugh. "I suppose you are surprised to see me in England again, and happily married, too."

Inez recalled herself to the task at hand. She was weighted to this chair now like iron filings to a magnet.

"That you were happily married, I never doubted," she said politely. "But to see you in England, I could only hope."

The other woman regarded her with a considering look, and Inez recalled a suspicion she'd had before of Wigsby's daughter: she played at the light-headed coquette, but she was really quite shrewd at the core.

"I hear my father has been giving you a devil of a time about the...er, aid you gave me in getting free of him," Priscilla said. "I do hope he hasn't been too much of a bother."

Inez swallowed an agonized laugh. Not too much of a bother. When for the past two years, she had looked about her each time she set foot on the street in London, knowing if he'd found her so easily the first time, he could again. Without a character reference she could only get the lowest of stations, laundry maid, cook maid, scullery, when she had been lady's maid to this elegant creature.

And in the laundry and the kitchen and the scullery there were footmen with roaming hands and butlers who thought the maids were perquisites of their employment, or men of the house who thought that because they paid a meager salary, the women in their employ should attend to all manner of their needs. She'd been chased from house to house as if pursued by the hounds of hell, and the only safe place she'd found to land was the household of Amaranthe Illingworth.

Where, instead of having to fight the attentions of Joseph Illingworth, she had found a greater threat to her happiness: she'd fallen in love with the great sodden oaf, and now that she knew the happiness of being in his arms, she never wanted to be anywhere else.

Inez swallowed another lie—they seemed to rise so naturally —and instead said, "I understand why your father would be anxious to locate me." She reached for her bag, wondering if now was the appropriate moment.

"That is very good to hear, because— Oh, my love. How wonderful that you could join us." Priscilla held out her hand with a smile that transformed her face from merely pretty to truly beautiful.

At the time, Inez hadn't understood why Priscilla Wigsby would abandon her status as a lord's daughter, her comfortable homes and allowance, her abundance of suitors, and the chance for a secure future to throw away her heart and hand on a French gambler of dubious pedigree and even more dubious prospects. Yet when Pierre Dervieux strolled into the parlor, dressed to the excess of fashion that would make him a veritable macaroni in London, his gaze went straight to his little wife, and the look of indulgence he gave her, returned with the abject adoration in hers, explained to Inez what she had not previously understood.

Priscilla Wigsby had thrown away her pampered security on the chance that this man would made her happy, and thus far, she had been given no cause to regret her choice.

"My love, allow me to introduce you properly." Priscilla giggled. "After all, you have both heard so much about one another from me. Pierre, this is Inez, the maid in my father's house who arranged that I might elope with you. Inez, this is my darling Pierre Dervieux, of the Potevin Dervieuxes."

Pierre made as elegant a bow over Inez's hand as if she were one of Priscilla's peers, and not a former servant. She knew the man had no more claim to aristocracy than she did; Pierre Dervieux had been making his living, when Priscilla met him, by his luck at the gaming tables in clubs and fancy homes. The same sure charm that had allowed him to bluff at brag allowed him to promise a life of romantic delights to Lord Wigsby's daughter, and win her on the strength of them.

Yet sacrifice she had, for despite her happiness, Priscilla was occupying rented rooms in Plymouth, rather than enjoying herself as a guest of the Parkers at Saltram House in Plympton, or invited to join Lady Emma and George, Lord Mount Edgcumbe, whose baronial seat was just across the bay.

She had traded her place of acceptance in what passed for the Polite World, and she didn't appear to miss it in the least.

So. A woman could fall and not miss a nest that had been a prison. But a woman who climbed into a nest others judged out of her reach—she would find many a door shut to her. A man might trespass the social boundaries with impunity, but the women who had committed their lives to upholding those boundaries would never tolerate an interloper.

Amaranthe Illingworth was her example here. Amaranthe had become a duchess, and the only women in England who outranked her were the Queen and the royal princesses. Yet Inez had heard certain high sticklers among the London *ton* reminding themselves that Amaranthe was the daughter of a vicar, whose grandfather had been in trade and whose mother came of Portuguese stock, and whose husband had, for all but the past year of his life, been an acknowledged bastard. What would they say about a lascar's daughter taking on a title? Like a female Robin Hood, or the cinder girl who won the heart of a prince.

Pierre finished his elegant bow, and Inez dropped her hand. Robin Hood had been a lord's son after all, so the legend ran, and the cinder girl came from a genteel family. She'd never been the daughter of a brown man in the land of the fair, and the evil stepmother had never rounded out the household income by selling her body for coin.

"My dear, you'll join us for tea? Inez and I have so much to catch up on. I must tell her all about our honeymoon trip in Greece, and I am certain she has had adventures of her own since I last saw her. After all," and she sent Inez a coy look, "she has yet to tell me how she came to be housekeeper for a baronet in Cornwall."

Jock had indeed thoroughly acquainted Priscilla with Inez's situation, she saw. Heat moved across the back of her neck, prickling beneath the smart kerchief swathing her bodice. She curled her fingers around her bag, as if anticipating the request.

Joseph's brown eyes held a hint of red, like cognac melted into chocolate. Dervieux's eyes were so dark as to seem like black coals, yet bright in his face as he turned back to Inez. His accent was unnecessarily thick for someone who had made his livelihood in Britain for as long as was said of him.

"I believe I will remain for a little minute of time, *mon*

bijou." His gaze moved over each line of Inez's face, as if he were studying her for a sketch. "But speaking of jewels. Do I recall you believed the mademoiselle had some items of yours that she should most certainly wish to return, as she cannot wish your father to discover them in her keeping?"

Here it was at last, then. All out in the open. Inez picked up her bag, letting the regret squeeze her heart briefly. What this treasure might have done for Joseph, to help him refurbish Penwellen... But the Da Costas had never been thieves, not even in their darkest moments. They were too proud for that.

Besides, if she surrendered of her own will, that might bear some weight in her testimony if this man handed her over to the magistrate. She hoped.

"La, my old work bag." Priscilla gave a bright, tinkling laugh as Inez set the item on the table. The linen-lined cotton bag, embroidered with crewel wools, had been one of the childish Priscilla's first efforts to create a stocking bag, and discarded after her skills, and her need to be adorned prettily for good company, increased.

"You clever thing, Inez. It was good of her to collect these for us, wasn't it, my dear? They would certainly have eased our way in those first few months, if only we had had the luxury of meeting you as we planned." Priscilla watched Inez's hands, not her face. "And to think she has held them safe for us all this time. Such a clever, darling, devoted girl. You always were so loyal, Inez. It is your best quality."

"*Oui*, to hold them all this time." The black eyes of the gambler still watched Inez. The prickling about her neck spread to her shoulders and down her back. The man was too perceptive. Too eager for the riches she was laying out before him, unrolling first the silk cloth in which she had wrapped the precious pieces, to protect them. He looked hungry and sharp. Inez wondered what kind of trouble Pierre Dervieux was in, that their main goal, upon returning to England, would seem to be the recovery of these jewels.

"And to never sell them to ease her own way. Nor surrender them when your father approached her," Pierre remarked.

Out of reflex Inex raised a hand to her throat and the faded bruise. There was still a tenderness at times when she swallowed, thanks to Wigsby's *approach*.

"I considered them yours," Inez said. "After all, you, Miss Priscilla, asked me to collect them for you. And deliver them to you at the inn where you were waiting to depart London."

"Do not forget, she is Madame Dervieux now," Pierre said, and Inez saw that he considered the jewels his. The pendeloque earrings with their heavy diamond clusters set in repoussé silver. The choker with its thick strands of garnet and carnelian, dangling tiny briolette-cut rubies in cannetille rosettes. A heavy brooch made of pinchbeck with table cut emeralds and citrines in a glass overlay, and the aigrette of small diamonds and aquamarine, made to decorate a lady's hat.

Pierre took the gold ring with its sapphire set in pearls, the gem a rounded square with many facets, and pulled off his glove to slide the jewel onto his finger. He had the look of a buccaneer opening a chest of purloined treasure.

"Oh." Priscilla said, her tone hushed. "I had forgotten how many there were." She touched the earrings. "Those were Mama's."

"They are all yours, madame," Inex said, setting the work bag on the small tea table as if surrendering that item, too.

Priscilla's eyes filled with tears. "These were Mama's dowry. She brought them to her marriage, and they were always meant for me. Inez, I thank you for this gift. Words cannot describe how much it moves my heart to have this piece of my mother returned to me."

Inez swallowed and nodded, unable to speak for the

swelling in her throat. What she would give to have something to remember her own dear mother by, other than struggle and tears because she had fallen in love with and married a man whom her family did not approve for her. Mariana Da Costa, like Priscillia Wigsby, had thrown off the dictates of society to follow the man she loved, and the world had been harsh to her for it.

But her mother had loved to the depth of her heart. She had never regretted her choice of a husband—only the choices she was forced to make to preserve her life with him. To the day she died, Mariana Da Costa had come alive in the presence of Ramesh Shirodkar the way she had no one else. Not even the presence of her cherished daughter.

Mariana had looked at Ramesh the way Priscilla looked at Pierre Dervrieux. It was an expression Inez felt on her own face whenever Joseph Illingworth walked into a room and illuminated it.

Pierre turned the ring on his finger, his lips curving in a fascinated smile.

"This means a great deal more than a family heirloom, my treasured one. This means we need not go begging to any of our friends, and you need not crawl to your father asking for his good graces." He straightened his shoulders, a man burdened with new purpose. "Choose a special piece, *mon bijou*, to hold to your sentimental heart. With the rest of these, I will win you the fortune you deserve."

"Oh, Pierre, my dearest love." Priscilla's lip trembled as she tried to affix the choker. Her fingers trembled too, and Inez, out of long habit, rose to help her with the clasp, pushing a few powdered curls out of the way.

Priscilla's attire was as smart as ever, but Inez's trained eyes caught the details. The lace ruching at the bodice of her open gown had a tear that a skilled lady's maid ought to have fixed with invisible stitches. Her linen cap edged with lace had frayed ribbons that begged to be replaced. And while her gown was indeed cut to the latest fashion, the seam at the back showed a dark line along the stitching; the fabric had been reused from another gown, carefully taken apart and then remade to suit the style.

It was commonly done among the thrifty; Inez turned and turned her gowns until the fabric wore holes. But in her father's house, Priscilla had never had other than new gowns handmade for her, and when a cap needed new ribbons, it went to the housekeeper—or Inez—and she to the milliner's to purchase a new one.

"Pierre, my one joy." Priscilla's voice turned caressing. "Perhaps we might hold onto these few baubles, and I might wear them? Need they go to the tables, like the others? Like everything else?" she said softly.

"My love. My glorious angel." Pierre crossed to his wife and caught up her dainty, pale hands. Priscilla had pulled off her silk gloves to touch the jewels, and her fingers looked very small, clasped in his.

"You knew you married a working man, *oui?* And this is the work I do. This is how I will provide for us. To give you the things you deserve, the riches with which I promised to drape you, the luxuries that will set off your perfect beauty. I will give you the world, *ma cherie,* but it will be a little while yet. I did not expect this streak of bad luck to turn against me. You have always been my, how do you say, lucky charm."

He kissed her hands, the backs, then the palms, a lazy, lingering kiss. Priscilla shivered. Inez stood behind her chair, embarrassed by the ease with which the lovers forgot she was there, simply the maid, support and decoration to their self-absorbed lives.

The girl drew in a shuddering breath. "I know, my darling

Pierre, all that you do is for me. You have said before. But also, remember, my angel, you said there would be a time where... where we..." She faltered and resorted to sending a gaze around the room, pleading and remorseful.

Inez understood. The petite salon, as Priscilla had so gaily named it, was rented lodgings, not her own roof. Those oils on the walls were not Wigsby or Dervieux ancestors looking down with benevolence on their patrimony, nor were they portraits and landscapes she had commissioned from the painters of famous friends. The color scheme of the parlor, indeed the entire house was not what Priscilla would have chosen; the furniture was not hers; and the room lacked the little adornments that English travelers so loved to acquire and display as proof of their taste and leisure.

"Soon, my precious one. I promise you it will be soon. You will have a little nest of your own, filled with pretty things to surround your pretty self, and all your friends will come to admire and envy you. I have no aim in my life but to make you happy. You know that, *oui?*"

"Of course, Pierre. You have told me so many times."

"And, *mon bien-amiée.* I make you happy, do I not?" He pulled her from the chair into his arms, an easy strength in the gesture, but also a possessiveness that had Priscilla melting against him, turning up her face for his kiss.

"Oh, you do, my only one," she moaned. "You *do.*"

Inez stepped away, her face heating. A year ago, two, she would have scoffed at a woman melting so easily to pretty lies and a caress.

But that was before she had done the melting of her own. Before she had encountered the man whose touch was alchemy, whose very presence transported her, and whose desires she had no wish to deny.

"Oh, this is a pretty sight. My ungrateful daughter, being pawed like a common trull in her very own drawing room."

Inez froze. An icy wave coursed over her, as if she had been thrown into a current of cold water. For a moment, she could not breathe.

Wigsby. Only the devil himself could have found her so easily, or a man who had made a pact with Old Scratch.

CHAPTER TWENTY-ONE

Wigsby's eyes were red-rimmed, and one side of his mouth was swollen around a split lip, giving a slight slur to his words. The bruise spread up the side of his face, ill covered by powder, with a plaster over the place where Joseph's fist had cut open his cheek. He limped slightly as he advanced into the room, and Inez retreated without thinking. Joseph had not caused that limp, she was certain. Yet the narrow slit of Wigby's watery blue eyes as they turned to Inez contained all the fires of hell.

"Papa." Priscilla shrank against her husband, who put a protective arm around her. There was no one to put a protective arm around Inez.

"You vowed that if I could get the jewels from her, you would not press charges," Priscilla reminded her father. "You would have no call to report her as a thief."

"You'll take Spanish coin every time, won't you, my adorable little goosecap." Wigsby sneered on his daughter and son-in-law alike. "'Tis how this gamester won you so easily, I don't doubt, and how he cozens you to stay and turn over all you have so he may waste it on himself and his mistresses."

Priscilla lifted her chin, as rounded and dimpled as the rest of her, though Inez noticed that the last years had matured the lines of the other girl's face to a degree. "Pierre has given me the world, Papa. I am happy, which you said I would never be."

"How can you be happy, puss, when everything you have goes into this man's pockets, to be fribbled away at the gaming tables?" Wigsby's gaze lit on the ring Pierre wore, and his eyes narrowed further. "He'll squander every last one of your mother's jewels, unless someone takes care to keep them from his avaricious grasp."

Priscilla touched the choker at her throat, where it sat very prettily, showing off her pale neck and powdered hair. "Mama meant these jewels for me, Papa. They are my dowry."

"You get no dowry when you marry a thief," her father snapped. "I will take these." He swung his head to glare at Inez. "And I'll take this bit of muslin as well, and deal with her as I see fit."

Priscilla clutched her husband's arm. "Pierre, do something."

Dervieux cleared this throat. "The jewels will stay, sir. They belong to my wife by right, and our claim will hold up in court, should you force it."

Wigsby growled low in his throat. "You think any English judge will want to see these pieces in the pocket of a Frenchman? A foreigner? You mistake English justice. No surprise, since your people have no sense of it. I won't need the assizes or a grand jury to plead my case. Any magistrate here or in London will acknowledge my claim to these jewels. And put *her* in the bridewell for a thief."

"You cannot prove..." Inez trailed off her feeble defense. She knew well enough how justice worked all around the world; the lord would be believed, no matter what he claimed, and the maid would be borne off in chains. It would take no more than production of her pedigree—daughter of a lascar and a Portuguese whore—to be confirmation of her guilt, no matter the charge.

Also, her words were lost in a sudden storm of knocking that came from the front door. Priscilla murmured to Pierre, a question or plea, as footsteps pounded up the stairs. And then Joseph loomed in the doorway like a messenger from the heavens, the herald of an avenging god.

Inez choked back a wild cry of joy at the sight of him: his coat dusty from the road, his boots caked with grime, his hat brim bearing the smell of the marsh, and his eyes burning.

His gaze went to her first and swept up and down her as if ascertaining every piece of her was in place. He looked at Wigsby, then the jewels laid upon the table like treasures offered to a queen. Then at Pierre, and at Priscilla's hand on her husband's arm. His brows drew together, giving him a gloriously fierce aspect. It was so rare to see Joseph out of temper, and the signs of passion, she would admit only to herself, were thrilling.

"You will not take Inez," he said, and his voice held a note of command that warmed Inez to her toes. "She is not a thief. She followed the instructions of her mistress and held the jewels in trust. I will vouch for her to anyone who demands, be it the King himself."

"*You!*" Wigsby howled. "I'll have *you* hauled before the magistrate in irons. I'll have you hanged like the common riffraff you are."

"A gentleman's son, and the Baronet Illingworth of Penwellen." Joseph raised a supercilious brow. He laid a hand on the hilt of the small sword at his hip. "I think we rather ought to settle this between us."

Joseph didn't own a sword of his own, or if he did, Inez had never seen him wear it, scholar that he was. The sword he wore now must have belonged to his cousin, or perhaps the baronet before him, for it was a small sword of decent size, with silver studs glittering on the hilt. It was made for the days when a gentleman's sword was a weapon as well as a mark of his status.

Wigsby groped for his own sword, which was a flimsy blade made for decoration, little larger than a butter knife. His face flushed. "You wouldn't dare challenge me, you insolent pup."

"I believe he has grounds, if you are persecuting a woman. And your own daughter, too," Pierre said coldly. His hand flew to his hip in a practiced gesture, where a small French dueling sword hung from a sash.

"Do not forget Inez, my love," his wife whispered, tugging the sleeve of her husband's elegant coat. Dervieux's attire, Inez noted with a swift and professional glance, unlike his wife's, was entirely without flaw or sign of mending. "He is threatening Inez, too."

"I won't be intimidated by the likes of you," Wigsby blustered. "And I refuse to meet you on the field of honor when you have no claim to such. You attacked a lord! The Bloody Code demands death for that!"

"And what does it demand for attacking a woman?" Joseph returned. "You have a habit, sir, of preying on those weaker than you. I must say I detest that in a man."

Wigsby's eyes bulged. "What would *you* know about being a man?"

Joseph drew his sword and held it before him in a loose but practiced grip, his pose graceful and rippling with coiled strength. Prepared for attack, but not willing to initiate unless pressed to the point. Something moved over his face then that Inez had never seen but found astonishing.

"I have learned one or two things, just lately, about manhood," he said, and his voice was low and full of a sureness she had never heard from him.

She knew Joseph Illingworth in all his moods: abstraction

when he was transported by a book and his mind traveled through the airy upper realms of Idea. Joseph densely absorbed in his own muddle and blind to the struggles of those around him. Joseph frustrated when he went knocking on door after door interviewing for posts and was told he wasn't fit for any of them. Joseph with his spirits razed to the ground when a baggage like Susannah Pettigrew, a woman who clearly needed spectacles, declared Joseph was not good enough for the likes of her.

Inez had seen the new side of him, too, when he returned from his Grand Tour. The new polish and ease within himself. An added depth and weight to him, as if the last bit of the pup had been rubbed away and the wolf returned, regal, sure-footed, new-forged.

She had seen him passionate and tender in their time together, traveling with her to undiscovered lands. She had seen him punch Lord Wigsby in the face, not so long ago, when she wouldn't have thought he had a thread of aggression within him.

And now, she saw him settle something within himself. His shoulders broadened. His chin lifted. So did the sword as he pointed it in Wigsby's direction. Joseph's gaze moved briefly to Inez, and his stare lit her like a fuse for a festival firecracker. The very air in the room crackled.

He was a man, finally, who knew his own worth. Who knew what he would fight for to the bitter end. And Inez was among those things.

The top of the list, apparently. Her heart swelled like that air-going sailing vessel that had been legendarily demonstrated at the court of King John of Portugal and his Queen.

"Dervieux," Wigsby snapped, "take his sword away. This insolent pup is threatening me."

Instead, Pierre drew his own sword. It was long and slender, in the French style.

Between them, the two men looked prepared to participate in one of those sword dances her father had told Inez the sailors of Marin, in Spain, performed in honor of St. Michael. Joseph had never looked so lethal, so dangerous, and so beautiful.

A man through and through, one who would never display the cruel arrogance or greedy pride of a Wigsby, and who would check injustice wherever he did find it.

Wigsby's face mottled as his rage mounted. His jaw worked as he forced out the words. "Baseborn knaves, the lot of you. I'll see you both hanged! You," he pointed a fat finger at Pierre, "for stealing my daughter and the wealth of a man's house, and you —" He stabbed the air in Joseph's direction— "for harboring a fugitive, threatening your betters, and being in general a cur and an insult to the name of gentleman. Tossing up the skirts of a foreigner and a whore."

He retreated to the table where the jewels lay, and his avaricious eye fell upon them. "I'll let you all leave me without complaint if you return my things."

Priscilla stepped in front of the table, gripping its edges behind her. "No. These are Mama's. You mayn't have them. Not when you took everything else from me."

"Took!" His lordship's eyes bulged further. Between that and the convulsions of his throat above his neck stock, Inez feared apoplexy. "When you stole from me, you ungrateful hussy! And enjoined your filthy maid to abet you in the effort."

"I would do it over again if it helped her leave your house," Inez said. "You treated her like your property, not a person in her own right."

"She *is* my property!" Wigsby roared. "So is this." He lunged for the table, pushing his daughter aside, and grabbed the jewels up in their silken cloth. He looked every inch like the spoiled bully he was, and did not even spare a glance for

Priscilla, who was caught in the arms of her husband, and then pushed behind him for protection.

Wigsby's beady, bulging gaze fell on Inez. "And I won't charge you with thievery if you come with me quietly."

"You dare," Joseph said.

Inez shuddered. "I won't."

"Then I'll have you taken up by the watch like the—"

"I wonder," Joseph said, advancing with his sword before him, "that you berate me for my affections, your lordship—" He made the address sound like a slur— "when I, if I am not mistaken, found you lately in the environs of Dark Lane."

Wigsby froze like a hare that had been spotted by the hound.

Pierre's brows rose. "Dark Lane? *La vache!*"

"What Lane?" Priscilla questioned. "Where?"

"In fact—" Joseph continued his advance— "I have it on authority from one of the Vestals of the house that she makes regular accommodations for you. Rather irregular accommodations, truth be known."

Wigsby's labored breath became audible in the utter stillness of the room. Inez held back a laugh so she might not spoil Joseph's attack. He was so very magnificent.

"You...you slander me. That is a hanging offense also."

"Not if it's true," Joseph said, his voice smooth as butter. "And I am told many of the ladies of Dark Lane can attest to the...vigor and imagination of your attentions. I am sure they would not mind sharing such information in a public venue. In court, mayhap, or with a satirist for *The London Magazine?*"

Sweat rolled from the brow of his lordship's wig. His fingers curled like claws around the bag of jewels. He pawed at his waistcoat as if seeking air.

"I could kill you," he said hoarsely. "That would silence your vile mouth."

"I am not the vile one among us," Joseph said, still in that tone of deadly politeness. "And lords can still be punished for murder nowadays. We live in the Dark Ages no longer."

"Papa." Priscilla was sobbing. "Just go. You've ruined everything, as usual. I was a fool to think we could reconcile."

Wigsby wavered. Really, for all his cunning, the man had the worst instincts for self-preservation that Inez had ever seen. It came, she supposed, from being born to what he was taught was a position of superiority, and bred with an undeserved sense of his own importance alongside contempt for anyone beneath him.

Joseph had block-headed tendencies from time to time, but he would never be a tyrant. He was too sensitive, too aware. And he looked a conquering hero of old in his dusty coat and dirty boots, with the civilized ruffle of his neckcloth above his waistcoat and the deadly small sword in his steady hand.

He looked like a highwayman, and Inez discovered a heretofore interest in a fantasy of being kidnapped and carried away by a gentleman of the road.

"I-I won't stand for this," Wigsby stuttered. "All of you against me."

"I am not greatly informed on points of law," Joseph mused. "But my brother, the Duke of Hunsdon, has some training as a barrister. He might be disposed to advise me about actions available to a persecuted daughter, or a persecuted former maid, when her master brings false accusations to a court of law."

Wigsby, his hands shaking, set the silk bag of jewels on the table.

"Robbers and thieves," he swore. "You brought me here merely to steal from me again. I won't stand for it."

"You will have to stand for it elsewhere, but not here, unless you intend me to stain this Axminster rug with your blood."

Wigsby paled beneath his powder. "Threatening a lord! I have witnesses."

"I heard mention of Dark Lane." Jock spoke from the doorway. Leaning on his crutches, which he had somehow got up the stairs, he didn't appear a man disposed to physical combat. And yet Inez suspected that, did Jock intend to bar his lordship's egress, Wigsby wouldn't make it down the stairs.

"I heard mention of the Duke of Hunsdon," Jock added with a careless air. "Meself, I wouldn't want to get on that one's hard side. He's a devil if you poke 'im."

Joseph sheathed his sword. "Jock, is his lordship's conveyance below?"

"Ready and waitin'," Jock confirmed.

Priscilla's face fell as her father stormed from the room without looking at her, his stare of accusation—and, Inez feared, retribution—focused on Joseph. When he was gone, Inez groped for the back of a nearby embroidered chair and sank down upon it, too overcome to worry about the niceties of being seated when Priscilla wasn't.

Joseph moved instantly to her side. "Did he hurt you?"

"Only threatened." She reached out and he caught her hand, and the warmth and solidness of him made her melt. She wanted to curl herself inside his dusty coat, button herself against his heart, and stay there always.

"I suppose that means we won't get the Meissen figures you wanted," Pierre reflected. "Nor the last of your clothes, *ma belle*."

"Pierre!" Priscilla put her hands to her face. "How *can* you think of my property at a time like this?"

"It is our property, *ma cocotte*, and our fortune," Pierre protested, putting his arms around his wife.

Inez leaned her head against Joseph's chest. "How did you get here so quickly?"

"Treen very obligingly gave me a horse. A sound, strong hack from the Callington coaching inn."

"Didn't founder 'im, neither," Jock added. "He's in the mews behind, mendin' is bellows."

"Proper done, me ansome," Inez said with a smile. "As Wenna would say. I assume she told you?"

He stared into her eyes. "Why didn't you tell *me*?"

Inez glanced at the table with the jewels spilling from the silk cloth. It was all out of the bag, so to speak. He would see what she had done. Every argument for her lack of worth, laid before him as evidence.

She'd wanted to mend things. She'd wanted to come to him clean and free and ask him to say, clearly and finally, what she meant to him. But now, surely, she was tainted.

"I didn't want you to see," she managed past the knot in her throat. "I wanted it all to be at an end. Over and behind me."

"Inez. My darling." Joseph went to one knee beside her, clasping her hand between both of his. She could barely feel his grip through the heavy leather riding gloves. He stripped them off, threw them on the table, and repossessed himself of her hands.

"Don't you know there is nothing you could do that would alter my esteem for you?"

"Esteem," she echoed. It seemed a soft word. A word that daintily skirted the fringes of the roaring blaze that grew in her simply at his nearness, at his touch. At the earnest, steadfast way he stared at her, the cognac gleaming in his eyes. His eyes went that color when he was in the grip of passion. Inez tightened her hold on his hands.

"That is a weak word," he admitted. "Call it adoration. Call it—rapture. I am completely borne away by you, Inez. I do not exist when you are not with me."

"Do not exist?" she murmured. Her heart fancied itself a balloon again, rising, swelling, dancing on air. Her ribs ached with the effort to constrain it. She gripped his fingers all the more firmly. "That is perhaps coming it too strong—"

"Jock would say I am rushing my fences," Joseph admitted. "After only a week together, in truth. But in that week, Inez, I have discovered myself. I finally feel I know who I am." He pulled their clasped hands to his chest, above his heart, which she could not feel beating through all the layers of fabric, but wanted to fancy she could.

"I am not ashamed of the man I am, when I am with you. It's a change I welcome. I feel stronger. Better. Bolder. And more..." He groped for the word.

He was going to say something about lust. No, she begged silently, let lust not be what drew and bound him. Let desire not be the sum total of his regard for her. Lust was what her mother's patrons came to relieve themselves of in that tiny, cramped room. Lust was what earned the ladies of Dark Lane their keep.

She wanted the force that had made Amaranthe Illingworth take the leap from being a vicar's daughter to a duchess. She wanted what had drawn her father back to them, every time, and what had pulled her mother across land and sea to be with her beloved.

"I have been searching for a companion," Joseph said, looking into her eyes, and she saw his heart there. "God knows it was above all what I wanted. I looked in all the wrong places, of course."

Inez nodded. He had. And all the while she was right beneath his nose—

"And all while you were right there," he said. "In my house. I knew the first time you entered the room where I sat..."

He leaned back on his heels. She leaned forward. She

remembered that moment when she had first beheld Joseph Illingworth in his study, bent over his books, that lock of unruly hair falling across his brow, his coat hung over the chair and his shirtsleeves rolled up and his fingers stained with ink as he scrambled to take notes at the speed with which his mind moved. She had fallen under his spell in that moment, and she had never even tried to escape.

"I remember I was reading Priestley," Joseph said. "I babbled something at you about it. And you simply nodded and listened and did not tell you to be off with myself."

"You'd discovered something," she murmured. "You were delighted."

He nodded. "And then you appeared. And I looked at you, with your kerchief about you and you holding that tray with tea and biscuits and listening to me natter about Priestley's theories of mind, and I thought—insofar I was thinking of anything—I thought, 'This is the kind of woman the Stoics admire.'"

"A servant?" she cried. "A maid who will bring you tea while you labor? When you never—" She punctuated this speech with small blows of their clasped hands against his chest, giving vent to her feelings— "paid—any—*attention* to me—"

"Inez! I could not approach a woman under the roof of my household. In the employ of my sister?" He looked incredulous. Shocked, the dear, besotted, supremely aggravating man. "That is what Reuben did. I vowed never to be like him."

"You tell me this *now*?" she cried, and communicated her spleen by punching him again with their clasped fists. She wanted to kiss him, but her mind stumbled over his words. "You approached me that night after Wigsby—that night in your home. And on the road, when we were traveling. I was under your protection then, too. You said it many a time, to every innkeep and publican."

"That first night, I knew I was leaving, so you could not be forced to oblige me. You invited me of your free will, I recall." His gaze on her heated, and Inez blushed. She recalled, only too well.

"And the next day. I told you to return to London. You didn't. You returned just in time to stage a rescue, and after that —" He shrugged. "After that, I knew marriage would be the end of it, if you would relent on your feelings about the matrimonial state and have me."

"You oaf!" Inez cried and clobbered him again. "You never told *me* that!"

"I thought I did!" he exclaimed. "With my words, and with my body. I cannot—I do not—I would not have responded to you as I have, did I not love you already," he said, and though he didn't look at Pierre and Priscilla, who were watching them avidly, the blush on his cheeks said he was aware of their riveted spectatorship. "I am—it is the way I am built, I'm afraid."

He'd never touched a woman before her. Never found his pleasure with a woman before her. Inez held that piece of him, all hers. All of him was hers, in whole.

She was the one he chose, the one he gave himself to in the most intimate of exchanges. The only one in the world with the privilege of being this close to him, and knowing his private ways. All the Susannah Pettigrews of the world could go trip themselves with their own garters.

"What a great deal of trouble you would have saved me," she said softly, "if you had told me any of this a good while ago."

"I thought it was obvious." He had the grace to look abashed. "I sought you out for counsel. For company. I confided in you as I confided in no one but my sister. I thought surely you knew my heart."

Inez sniffled, feeling emotion perilously close to breaking

through her composure. That Stoical self-control that he so admired, being of that school of philosophy himself.

"I didn't," she said. "You must spell it out for me, scholar that you are."

They stared into one another's eyes. Inez squeezed his fingers to urge him on, and he returned a rueful smile.

"I see now why fellows write these speeches out before-hand, and study them," he said. "I look at you and all but a handful of words fly out of my head."

"Which ones remain?" she whispered, keeping on her eyes on his face as if he might disappear if she blinked.

He opened his mouth, then paused, as if groping for words.

"Go back to the bit where you said you loved her," Priscilla put in encouragingly. "There's a fair start, I'd say."

Pierre shook his head. "Too many words. What he must do is kiss her."

"That is how you wooed me, is it not, my—" Priscilla's speech was ended as her husband demonstrated exactly what he believed was the fit response for the occasion.

Inez stared into Joseph's beloved face, hoping what she saw written across his features was true, and not merely what she hoped to see.

"You love me," she whispered.

"Yes." He kissed her knuckles.

"And you wish to marry me?"

"Emphatically," he said. "Above all else."

She faltered. "It will not look well on you," she said. "Marrying the woman who was your housekeeper. The daughter of a lascar and a—"

"Inez!" Priscilla cried. "Do you love him?"

Inez blinked. "Yes. Of course I do."

"Then why would you break both of your hearts?" Priscilla demanded. "This is love! Rare and precious! Seize it with both hands. I left my father's house under dark of night, ran away from all my friends and acquaintance, went to a far and foreign land to be with my love—"

"Paris is not so different from London, *monoiseau*," Pierre murmured. "At least, not the Paris you know."

"Yes, but they all speak French there," said his impatient wife. "Inez! *Écoute-moi! Carpe diem!*"

Inez sniffled again, not certain whether she wanted to laugh or weep. "Car-pay what?"

"It is a Latin phrase," Joseph explained. "An injunction by Horace to enjoy the day, for little may be expected from the next. Epicurus has something of the same sentiment, and the prophet of Ecclesiastes, who writes—"

Inez, to prevent him from quoting any Greek or Latin at her, took the expedient of following Pierre's advice and kissed him.

His mouth opened on hers, and he slipped a hand to the back of her neck, squeezing slightly. His kiss was ardent, a firm declaration, a taking possession, and she needed no other answer than this.

"Very well," she whispered against his lips. "We might marry."

"As soon as possible, I hope," Joseph said, and continued kissing her.

Priscilla wiped her eyes and applauded. "A wedding! I shall be the first to bestow a gift." She opened the silk cloth and hunted through the tumbled pieces. "This. I am told it is in the Iberian style."

The setting was foil-backed silver and the stones gleamed pink and red, coral and red topaz alternating along the necklace just large enough to draw attention, but small enough to appear dignified. Differently sized gems of faceted topaz shone from the main setting, shaped in a slight curve, and three pendants dangled girandole-style from it, the largest the size of a robin's egg. Priscilla held the necklace before her like one of Cleopatra's attendants robing the famous queen.

Pierre coughed. "Are you certain that is appropriate, *mon amour?* He is only a baronet, and his wife should not wish to appear vulgar. Perhaps a smaller piece—"

"Pierre, my other half, do be silent. Inez risked her life, and my father, to gather and keep my mother's jewels for me. And when she knew where to find me, she came at once to return them. We owe her our thanks."

"She has our gratitude, certainly, but a necklace worth several thousand pounds?"

"Thousands?" Inez said, the words strangled.

"This will suit your coloring, and beautiful jewels are never out of place. I shall play the lady's maid this time, my dear, and fasten it upon you, but look here—you may detach the girandole pendant to make a brooch, or you may wear the whole across a stomacher. It is a very versatile piece. My mother wore it at her presentation to the Queen."

"All the more reason to keep the piece, if it has sentimental value, *mon chat,*" Pierre said, but his wife would not be deterred.

"Allow me." Joseph held out his hand, and Inez watched, entranced, as Priscilla poured the gems into his palm. He fastened the clasp at her throat, and Inez shivered from the brush of his fingers on her skin as much as at the heavy fall of the stones, the gold cold against her breastbone. She felt cherished, and beautiful, and worthy, finally, of a man like Joseph Illingworth.

Priscilla clapped her hands. "*C'est bon!* If you are married here, Pierre and I might be witnesses."

Joseph rose and threaded his fingers through Inez's. "We will be married in Callington," he decided, "for that is our new home."

Tears of joy or the relief at coming home at last to a shore she never thought she would find, a safe haven at the end of the storm; Inez didn't know the precise source, but she let them fall. "Home," she echoed, marveling over the word. What she had wanted for so long, he was offering.

If his love indeed was true.

CHAPTER TWENTY-TWO

"Callington," Joseph said as he sat beside Inez in the cart on the road north to that city. A fair morning shone over their heads, all the world bright and new for the pair in love. Chiffchaff and willow warblers sprinkled song through the air. Campion and early gentian daubed the grasslands with white and purple. The earth smelled different, out here where she could smell the earth, away from the constant coal fires of London.

"We'll have the banns read for three weeks and be wed in St. Mary's," Joseph proposed. "I'd love to lead you to the church door of St. Clarus, where I grew up, but that is my parish no longer. If you wish for the distinction, I can apply to the bishop for a common license, and then we only need wait seven days."

"I will wed you wherever you like, *coração*, but if we wish to please our neighbors we must host a wedding breakfast, so you had better give me three weeks to prepare."

He turned his warm, frank gaze upon her, and Inez felt, as ever, the melting impact of his dark brown eyes. This man was hers. He had declared himself so at last. She had pinched herself when she woke in the small chamber Priscilla gave her to sleep in the previous night, not sure she hadn't been dreaming. But at breakfast, when Joseph rose eagerly from his chair and stepped toward her to drop a kiss on her hand and lead her to the table beside him, the look of delight on his face, and the way he tempted her with coddled eggs and toast, assured her she was adored and cherished. They rode side by side home, with Jock riding Arthur and steering their way, and she sat beside Joseph, as she had at breakfast that morning with a lord's daughter and her husband, as an equal.

She wasn't an equal. It was a masquerade. And yet she was still going to place her hand in his and trust where he led her, and hope quicksand did not of a sudden open under her feet and swallow her whole.

"*Coração*," he repeated, being careful to get the pronunciation correct. "That means?"

Her cheeks tightened with heat. "My heart."

Would he wish for doting from her? Would he accept it? He was not a man to abide fawning. Courtesy, he demanded and gave, elegance of manner, he had cultivated on his Grand Tour, but he was not a man to scatter flattery or compliments unless extremely well-deserved.

"I suppose it would mortify Jock if I kissed you right now, in the open air," Joseph said.

"True, though his back is to us, and—"

She had not finished the thought before Joseph leaned forward and kissed her. Tender and delighted, with a taste of the passion held in restraint for when they were finally alone.

She felt giddy. Yesterday she had traveled south feeling she went to her doom. Today she rode back to Haye with Joseph, and in a few weeks, she would be Penwellen's mistress and his lady.

A baronet's lady. Lady Illingworth.

Her father would burst with pride and weary his shipmates with boasting. Her mother had wished for nothing more but that Inez find a position that would afford her respect and security. With Joseph, she could add to that love. Her mother would be weeping with the angels, could she see this.

If she could see her daughter, Inez reflected, grasping greedy and unashamed at a boon she didn't deserve, because to be without Joseph Illingworth in her life was a future she didn't want to imagine.

"I should wish to take you on a grand honeymoon excursion," Joseph said. "To Italy, or Greece, or France—"

"Or Portugal. I could show you Sagres."

"And I would love to see it." He squeezed her hand. "But I think our ambitions at this time should be modest, given the demands I must address on the property."

"I shall be content if we went no further than St. Cleer and you showed me the places of your childhood," she said. "But also, I have not seen Kit's Hill, or Dunpath Well, or King Doniert's stone. And we might visit some of the places your father wrote about in his manuscript."

"Yes, I want to find that manuscript, so I might revisit it. He had such an interest in antiquarian things, and I think some of his findings were quite unique and worth further consideration. Castlewitch, for instance, which we will pass in a moment, once we are through Viverdown Down. There is a hill and an old stone wall there, and my father had a notion it was a henge from the days of the earliest Britons. He also said..."

He was off, and Inez listened, fascinated as always by the turns of his mind and the lore he had accumulated, and content to simply be near him and enjoy his animated state. But eventually he drifted into silence, staring into the middle distance, and she saw her opening.

"That necklace," she said quietly. "That Priscilla gave me. One stone from it would do much for Penwellen. A handful of them would allow you to make all the improvements you like, and do much more besides, I should think."

"No," he said at once. "It is your wedding gift from Mrs. Dervieux, and all the dowry you are likely to have. I won't touch it."

"The purpose of a dowry is to contribute to the marital income," Inez pointed out.

"You have other jewels or baubles you prefer to wear? Other items in your jewel box you like better?"

"You know I have none, nor a jewel box to put them in," she answered, a little stung.

"Then keep the necklace, my darling, for not taking your possessions is the only gift I can give you for the duration." A pause elapsed, and then he said what he was thinking. "I will not be another Pierre Dervieux."

"She married beneath her, and is happy," Inez murmured.

Joseph met her eyes. "But you fear I will be marrying beneath me, and not be as happy?"

She looked away.

"Inez—"

"Oh, my goodness, that rise over there. Is that the henge you spoke of? Shall we go examine it? We can compare it to what your father wrote."

"I don't know what my father wrote, since he gave his friend all his papers," Joseph grumbled. But he did not press her, and she wondered if it was because he was aware as she of the resistance he would meet when he tried to introduce his former housekeeper and a foreign-born woman as the new Lady Illingworth.

"Jock," Joseph said suddenly, "turn here. We will examine the henge. And then cut above Coombe and come at Penwellen from the south. I want to show Inez—and you also—what I have discovered."

She knew he must see it too, the great yawning gulf that stretched between them. And she wondered if marriage truly could bridge such a gap, or if they would both tumble into the abyss.

JOSEPH BROODED as Jock drove them across the fields.

He'd claimed his woman. He'd followed her to Plymouth, he'd wrested her from the grasp of Wigsby—again—though it seemed less of a heroic gesture given he'd had Dervieux and Wigsby's own daughter to second him on this occasion. Inez might feel that swords were somehow not as sturdy a fighting means as fisticuffs. Yet here she was beside him—had agreed to marry him, at that!—but he hadn't won her yet, not entirely.

There was still some final barrier he hadn't breached, and until he knew was that wall was, he couldn't bring it down.

They passed the cottages of Doublepools, then the lone, crooked stone that marked the east boundary of his property. The land was at last under cultivation, thanks to Thaker's help, but he would have to pray to all the powers for a good growing season, and a long one, for his own farm and the ones he leased.

He didn't want to worry Inez with those concerns. He wanted her to believe he could provide for her. That he had something to offer her in return for the gift of her hand and her faith and her fealty.

She turned to him suddenly, her face partly hidden beneath the brim of her broad straw hat so all he saw was part of her cheek and the firm line of her jaw. Her beauty was a blow to him, always. When he'd come into the parlor at Plymouth and saw her standing there, so proud, so alone, he'd wanted to fall to his knees in homage then and there.

"Joseph," she said.

"Yes?"

"Whose horse is that?"

He followed the direction of her pointing finger. A horse in saddle, with his reins trailing, trotted across the field toward them. The Hackney put in harness with Arthur, the one Joseph had ridden south, neighed a greeting, and Joseph wondered if the trotter were a fellow from the White Hart's stables.

"I hope the rider hasn't been thrown and is injured somewhere," Inez remarked after Joseph had secured the horse to the back of the cart, where it ambled along behind them in an agreeable way.

"I hope someone isn't on my property that should not be," Joseph said grimly, thinking of Treen.

She watched his face carefully. "Are you regretting your offer of marriage to me?"

Had he been driving, he would have fumbled the ribbons.

"To you? No. Not in the least. I am only..."

Here it was, the chance to see the last barrier before him. To know how large, and how high, it truly loomed. He was not a man who would shrink from a challenge, and never would be again. Not when she was the prize.

"I fear you will think me too hasty," he said quietly. "I can only offer you an estate in need of repair, and my hopes. And whatever virtues you might see in my humble self, though I am not aware there could be many."

She laid her hand upon his. As always, her touch stirred the fire that lay banked within him, that hunger, that need for her.

"I do not wish to wait, unless you do," she said.

"I do not. I wanted to carry you to Penwellen as my bride on our very first night together."

"At Amesbury?"

"At George Court. The first day I kissed you, and knew for certain you were the companion I had searched for."

Her gaze searched his. He saw her longing, and he saw her question. "I—"

The impact came a half-second before he heard the sound, the thunder of a gunshot. His hat flew off his head, and he would swear later, with the precise attention that came from extreme peril, that he heard the quiet *thunk* as the round hit the thick felted wool.

He recognized from his hunting days the bellow of a double barrel shotgun. The second barrel would be loaded and primed, ready to fire. He recognized, with the same speed of thought, that they were fortunate the shooter was using cartridges, for if he had fired lead shot, all of them would have been hit already.

"Down," he shouted to Inez, pulling her shoulder. "Down!"

The second shot would have hit Jock, save the man did something extraordinary. He leaned low over his second horse, caught the harness, and swung himself onto the back of the Hackney in what seemed one long, fluid move. An instant later a knife appeared in his hand, and he cut the traces holding the horse to the cart. A moment after that he was away at a thundering gallop, bent low over the back of the animal, moving not away from the source of the danger, but toward it.

Crouched on the bottom of the cart with her, his heart beating out of his chest, Joseph moved his hands over every inch of Inez he could reach. "Did he hit you? Are you hurt?"

Her eyes were wide, dark pools, full of fright and anger. Her fingers curled into the wool of his coat. "He could have hit you. He *wanted* to hit you."

"He might have hit *you*." He couldn't follow that train of thought any further. "I have to find him. I have to end this."

She peeked out from above the front rail of the cart. "It appears Jock has already found him."

Another rider flew across the fields far ahead of them, mounting a slight rise in the distance. The hard line of a shotgun crossed the man's back, the metal catching the light. Joseph didn't recognize the figure, or the horse he rode, but he wouldn't escape, not with a professional jockey closing the distance between them.

Jock had been born in a saddle, to hear him tell it, and while he won plate enough at Newmarket to earn him the title of King, his real skill had been overland racing. He would run the shooter to ground, and Joseph wanted to be there to look into the villain's face and demand an accounting.

He scrabbled for the ribbons and handed them to Inez. The second harness hung awkwardly, but Arthur was, as most intelligent horses, keen about his own comfort. He would seek the stables with his stall and hay, and Inez would be safe.

"Aim for the oak," Joseph told her. "Beneath it is a spring. At the spring turn due north and you will run straight into the house. Tell Thaker we need assistance. Tell him to bring all the lads."

Her lip trembled slightly, but she nodded and took the ribbons. "Don't let him shoot you."

"I won't give him time to reload." He gave her a quick, hard kiss, then pulled himself onto the back of the trotter hooked to the back of the cart. The shooter had been on horseback; there was another one of them about, who had been the rider of this horse. And he was potentially in possession of a gun.

He had to end this now. Joseph didn't ride as fast as Jock, or as efficiently, but he caught up with them when Jock had the man on the ground, hands in the air, and his gun with the action broken open over Jock's knee.

"It were accident, gor. An accident. Didden mean to hit a body, did nus?" The man's Cornish accent was so thick it took Joseph a moment to tease out his words.

Joseph recalled how close that first blast had come to missing Inez. How close to missing *him*, and his hat, somewhere in a newly sown field of soybeans, was the proof of it.

How fragile their life together was, and how much he feared that it would not stand up to hard use. In a moment of illumination, Joseph wondered if this were Inez's fear also, that last reservation that held her apart from him. She had watched her parents struggle for being mismatched in the eyes of their families and their separate cultures. Did she expect the same end of them?

"Who hired you?" Joseph demanded to know.

The man's eyes widened at the fury in Joseph's voice. He submitted to Jock binding his hands behind him, though he winced at the indignity.

"No one, sir. Wouldn't shoot at the lord o' Penwellen, sir. Rotten bad luck is all it is."

"You may say your piece to the magistrate," Joseph said. "Jock, bring him to the house. I must see if Inez is—"

A scream rent the air then. Inez. Screaming his name, or the beginning of it. She sounded as much outraged as afraid, at least before the short syllable cut away to abrupt silence.

His blood was cold and he didn't feel a thing as he urged the horse to a gallop, as fast as it could go.

Inez had made it to the enormous oak. She sat in the cart. She wasn't alone.

Treen sat beside her on the bench, and as Joseph neared, he saw the pistol Treen held, the barrel shoved against her side, digging into her bodice.

Joseph's first, ludicrous reaction was outrage. Treen was no gentleman. He had no business owning a set of dueling pistols, nor even one of them.

Joseph crashed to a halt, sawing at the reins the way he'd never treat an animal under other circumstances. Inez was unhurt, but she looked furious and frightened. Her eyes were wide and haunted.

"Joseph," she said in a low voice, "I am sorry."

"He is the one who shall be sorry." Joseph confronted the other man. "Treen, we will settle this now."

Treen offered a smile that was more like the grinning teeth of a skull. "Yes," he said. "We will settle this."

CHAPTER TWENTY-THREE

"If this is about the copper, allow me to tell you that you've been pitched gammon," Joseph said. "It's a lie."

He stood in the gravel drive before his own home, as helpless as a prisoner at the gallows. Treen sat in the cart, Inez as his hostage. The gun barrel no longer sprouted from her side like some horrific appendage but lay in Treen's lap underneath the leather bag he wore across his body. Yet Joseph knew the gun was there, and Inez knew the gun was there, and both of them were submitting to Treen's demands for the moment because of it. As much as he wanted to leap at the man and sink his teeth into him, Joseph couldn't take the risk that he would harm Inez.

"As to that," Treen replied. "I believe Mr. Hoskyn has some information that, sadly, can be of little use to you now, since you will be signing over your property to me, as we agreed. Hoskyn, you might as well tell him."

The solicitor stood within the open double doors, blinking out at them from the gloom of the house. Joseph supposed Treen had invited him to the house to give his signature to the contract Treen meant to force Joseph to sign.

"Er," Hoskyn said. "Won't you come inside to discuss this matter, Mr. Treen? Sir Joseph," he added respectfully.

"We are all very comfortable here. The report, Hoskyn, if you please," Treen commanded.

Joseph faced the solicitor, wondering how he might communicate the danger they all were in. "That copper vein will have been mined out years ago," he said. "There's been no workings on Penwellen in the century since my great-grandfathers were granted this land. Any ore here was exhausted by the time of the first Charles."

Hoskyn cleared his throat. "Begging your pardon, sir, but the man I brought out to assay the area, at your suggestion, came to a quite different conclusion. He believes there are rich deposits here yet underground. The rock formations and his samples are similar to what has been found elsewhere in the area, where the mines are yielding well."

"An open cast mine, then," Joseph said. "We can construct one with relative ease. But the available ore will be taken up quickly, I would bet on that, and I don't have the capital to construct an engine that can drill deep and drain the water to do it all properly."

"You don't deserve those acres," Treen said shortly. "Reuben intended to sign it over to me. The contract was as good as made, and fool that he was, he had no idea what could be made of that piece of land. I did and do, and so I should be the one to carry the prize away. He made me a promise, and you need to make good on it, Illingworth."

"You will address him as Sir Joseph," Inez muttered.

"I owe you nothing, Treen. You have trespassed on my property, you have threatened my person, you have threatened the person of my intended wife—"

"Wife!" Treen recoiled. "You would make a common trull your bride? How your cousin must be spinning in his grave."

"I hope if Reuben has an unquiet rest, it is due to his own trespasses, and not mine," Joseph snapped.

"Ahem." The solicitor turned the brim of his hat in his hands, unsure whether he ought to clap it upon his head to shield him from the elements or keep his head bare out of deference. "Unless there is explicit direction in the last will and testament of the previous baronet leaving direction as to the disposal of his property or alienation of his assets, there is no encumbrance on the property that can direct the current baronet's use of it."

"There was a verbal contract!" Treen snapped. "We made a gentleman's agreement."

"You would have to be a gentleman, Treen, to make such an agreement." Joseph glared at the man.

"And you prove yourself less than a gentleman by not honoring it." Treen glared back.

In the standoff that followed, Inez stifled a moan and shifted on the bench of the cart. Arthur stamped his feet, ears flicking in all directions as he picked up the tension in the air.

And the sound of another horse approaching. Iron wheels crunched on gravel, accompanied by the clop of shod hooves, and an open carriage came into view, carrying three ladies within it.

"Mother!" Treen barked as the conveyance rolled to a stop. "What in Hades are you doing here?"

"You said you meant to call on the baronet to discuss that matter of his land." His mother flipped up the lace veil hanging from her bonnet, protecting her face from the dirt and sun, and surveyed her son with some astonishment. "Melwin, what are you doing with the housekeeper?"

Inez made another inarticulate, angry sound. Joseph curled his hands into fists. "He is kidnapping her, madame. The future Lady Illingworth."

"Melwin, what can he be saying?" Mrs. Treen cried. "You are not one of those fast rogues of London to carry off women." Here she sent a glare toward Joseph. "Sir Joseph, surely you cannot mean to marry such a woman? A man of taste and breeding like yourself? It is one thing to appreciate the beautiful and exotic, as does my Melwin, but to make such a woman your lady— It simply isn't done."

"And yet I will be doing exactly that, madame, as soon as your husband releases my bride."

Mrs. Treen stood in outrage, wobbling in the coach. Her companions, the two other biddies with her, promptly pulled her back into her seat. Inez had told Joseph about these three, Mrs. Treen, Mrs. Abbott, and Mrs. Daw. The Three Furies, she had called them after her interview, and they were the tradesmen's wives and widows who arbitrated what passed for Polite Society in Callington.

They would not easily share the mantle with a new baronet's lady, Joseph guessed, knowing what he did about old biddies who dictated social circles. If they excluded Inez now, she would never be accepted by them.

A glance at his beloved's face informed him that social acceptance by the Three Furies was currently last on Inez's list of concerns. She edged slowly away from Treen, gathering the ribbons. Whatever she communicated to Arthur, the horse was growing restless. If he bolted, Inez might fall, or Treen might fire his pistol.

"I am very curious about the grounds upon which you find me unacceptable," Inez said to Mrs. Treen. "Is it because I am employed as his housekeeper, or because I grew up in Portugal?"

"You know very well it is your lack of morals I object to, young woman, and I would ask you not to be impudent to *me*. You should consider it a sign of distinction if my son *did* wish to kidnap you. He has such exquisite taste."

"I would consider it a relief if he released me," Inez retorted.

"Treen," Joseph commanded, starting forward, "let her go."

The bag on Treen's lap moved, and Inez went ramrod-straight, her eyes flaring wide. Joseph had no doubt she felt the barrel of the pistol against her stays. Rage shook him.

"Mother, you have, as usual, imposed yourself at the least convenient time," Treen said. "I am negotiating an exchange of property with Mr. Hoskyn and Mr. Illingworth. This is no place for a lady."

"Then let Inez go," Joseph said. At the same time, Inez turned a scathing stare on her captor and emphasized, "*Sir* Joseph."

"Mr. Treen, this is all very irregular," Hoskyn said. "I cannot accept nor put my signature to an agreement that is made under any conditions of compulsion or duress, against the full consent of all involved parties. It would appear— I say, you're Henry Jock."

Hoskyn's expression turned to surprise, then admiration as Jock approached, a shotgun broken open over his knees, herding a rough-looking character on a Dartmoor pony before him.

"Thas 'een," the villain said sullenly. "Thas the gent as hired me to shoot at ye."

"Oh, I say," Hoskyn said again. "This is a most distressing revelation."

"Mark it, Hoskyn," Joseph said. "I may need you to bear witness."

Inez turned to face the mounted man, a day laborer by the looks of him, and one who had not seen good wages in some while. His hands were currently bound to the saddle before him, the ribbons to the bridle between his fingers. "Why?"

"Why'd I put me own head in the noose? Ain't doin' me any good where it is now, 'tain't."

"But why kill Joseph?" Inez's worried eyes went to him.

Joseph shrugged. "A better chance of negotiating with the next owner, or buying pieces if the estate has no heirs. And in the meantime, Treen would be porting off as much copper as he can carry." He sized up the man who had shot at him. "You ruined my hat."

The other's eyes went wide. "Aye, proper job, that! Didna mean to come as close as yer whiskers, beggin' yer pardon, sir. Meant to spook himself and the lady. Doan want murder on me soul, I doan."

"It was Treen's goal to finish me." Joseph nodded.

"These are vile accusations, and I won't stand for them," Mrs. Treen yelped. "Melwin, how can you stand for this? Do something."

"Your precious son," Joseph snapped in irritation, "is at this moment holding my bride at gunpoint. I'll thank you not to intervene on his behalf."

Mrs. Treen's eyes widened, and her companions gasped and tittered in the register of disapproving old hens. "My Melwin would never—"

"Give over," Jock said, nudging his horse toward the cart. The shotgun was empty, yet the weapon on his lap bore a menace of its own. He laid a hand on Arthur's bridle, and the horse immediately stilled, ears flicking forward. "Better yet," Jock said to Treen, "give the pistol to the lady."

Treen looked around the group, his eyes round as a hare's on a hunt. "You're all against me," he said. "Not a one of you is going to do what is right and give me what I am owed."

"Melwin!" Mrs. Treen yelped as the barrel of the gun emerged. "Your father's travelling pistol?"

He handed it, butt first, to Inez. She slid her hand around the grip and inspected the flintlock mechanism as if she knew what to look for. Then she clicked off the safety and pointed the pistol at Treen.

"You shot at me and Joseph, before," she said. "You tried to kill him."

Treen's eyes bulged from his head, his gaze locked on the bore of the barrel. At this range, if Inez fired, she would not miss.

"Not kill," he gurgled. Then he attempted a laugh that sounded much like a chicken being relieved of its head. "I wouldn't stoop to *murder*."

"I might," Inez said.

And that was the tableau they were making when the travelling carriage arrived.

"WHAT AN HONOR," Mrs. Treen simpered for the round dozenth time. "The Earl and Countess Tremarron. Your estate is near Camborne, I believe?"

"Tremarron is and has been there these few hundred years," the Earl rumbled in assent.

"La, a real Earl, and in Cornwall! And his lovely Countess, too. Can you say, my friends, that we have seen anything so grand in these days? This is Mrs. Daw, ladyship, my old and faithful friend, and this is Mrs. Abbott."

"How lovely to meet you," the Countess condescended to say. "I do hope we have not surprised you too much by coming upon you so suddenly."

"Won't stay long," the Earl promised. "Only meant to stop for a look-in. On our way to London, you know." He bestowed a fond look upon his wife. "Mean to arrange some doctoring for my lady, best we can find. In an interesting situation, the Countess is."

Her ladyship, who was gorgeous in an open robe of quilted blue brocade, with an embroidered stomacher pinned to her front, laid a hand over her midsection to delicately communicate that her interesting situation involved being *enceinte*.

"And Pierre Dervieux thought you might wish to invest in my mines," Joseph said for not quite the dozenth time, as if repeating the information might make sense of it.

The ladies were seated in the larger drawing room of Penwellen, which had, during Inez's short tenure, become a brighter, warmer place. The dust was gone from the furniture and hangings, the chairs and chaises had been arranged into cordial groupings, and the paintings beamed benignly from the walls, without their previous glower.

Inez herself, once freed from her captivity, had led their visitors into the room as if they were her valued guests, seating the Countess first and with graceful solicitation, and then seeing to the comfort of Mrs. Treen and her biddies, who didn't dare look her in the eye. Jock leaned by the door, his crutches detracting not a bit from his authority as guard over Treen, who stood beside him looking as if the most painful dyspepsia was making its way through his body.

"Know it's sudden," the Earl said gruffly. He was a large man with the rounded, well-fed look of one who had been born a peer and because of it had never encountered opposition in his life. "Was only playing cards with the man last night. Quite the blade, that Dervieux. At any rate, he mentioned you were developing a copper mine, and I'm in search of an investment. Druther have a few business interests to round out the estate, you know. Support my new heir and all." Once again he directed a doting look at his wife, who returned it.

"Such a wise notion, m'dear," she said fondly.

Wenna brought in a large silver tray with the tea things and gave Inez a questioning look. Inez, as if she were their hostess and not the housekeeper, reposed herself on a comfortable striped chaise and suffered Wenna to set a small folding table before her, whereupon she set to the preparations for pouring.

For Joseph, that small, elegant act focused and settled him. Inez, preparing tea, the lady of his house. Everything would come right.

"I am not certain how much the land can be expected to yield," Joseph said.

Hoskyn cleared his throat and made a small movement to put himself forward. "I believe you will find the report very promising, once you have had opportunity to review it, Sir Joseph. Particularly if you might set up a mine with a steam engine that can dig deep and remove the water that is likely to fill it. For which it seems the Earl might be so obliging as to provide the capital. Your lordship." He bowed deeply, holding a hand to his small periwig to keep that article from slipping forward on his head.

Treen groaned. "Thousands of pounds," he said. "Likely to yield over years."

The Earl sent him a look of curiosity. "I say, who is the magistrate for these parts, then? Acland's MP but in America fighting the rebels. With Burgoyne somewhere in New York, I hear. And Skrine—he's the one in Walpole's pocket. Played cards with him a few times as well. Won a fair bit of blunt, I recall."

"You are so clever, milord," his lady murmured, accepting the cup of tea Wenna delivered with a gracious smile. "I have no doubt a joint venture will prosper with you to fund the machinery, my love, and Sir Joseph to provide the land." She studied Inez. "And you are to become the new Lady Illingworth, Priscilla tells me."

Inez carefully poured tea into the saucer with its milk. "I have that honor, your ladyship."

"Oh, no," Mrs. Treen said. It was she for whom the tea was

meant. "Sir Joseph is, or will be, our leading gentleman. He intends to make the proper marriage. An heiress, I am sure. Perhaps a Coryton from Pentillie, or one of the Robings from Rosecraddoc—"

"Were you born in England, then?" the Countess asked curiously, addressing Inez.

"No, mum. In Portugal, where my mother's family is from. My father was a sailor from Goa. That is—"

"Part of the Portuguese State of India, I know." Her ladyship smiled. "The Earl has had dealings with the Viceroy. He is a very clever businessman, is my love. He will be a good partner for Sir Joseph."

"But Portugal," Mrs. Treen tittered. "The Earl quite condescends to befriend foreigners, though one would only expect such gentility of his breeding."

"Portugal and England have long maintained friendly relations, Mrs. Treen," Inez said. "Our countries have never been at war."

"My mother's family was from Portugal," Joseph said.

"And Queen Charlotte has Portuguese blood." The Countess sipped her tea. "In fact they say her branch of the Portuguese royal house comes from Africa."

Mrs. Treen gulped her tea and spluttered. Mrs. Daw and Mrs. Abbott looked with great interest into their own cups, as if reading their fortunes in the tea leaves.

"We must be along, my love, if we wish to join the Courtenays at Powderham as we promised." Her ladyship set down her cup and smiled at Inez. "Fanny has just been delivered of her tenth—can you imagine?"

"I cannot," Inez said, "but I wish her very well."

The three matrons made polite murmurs, their eyes wide with reverence as they looked upon intimates of the Earl of

Devon and his family, who resided at the ancient and imposing Powderham Castle.

The Earl levered himself to his feet. "As you say, my love. Sir Joseph, I'll leave your man the direction for my man, and they can draw up the papers we require." He held out his hand to his lady, still addressing Joseph. "Shall we wish you to make us known to the new Duke of Hunsdon and his lady? I hear the Duke was a hey-go-mad rakehell back in the days of being plain Malden Grey, but he seems to have sobered up now." He winked at his helpmeet. "Expecting an heir settles a man, I believe."

"My sister the Duchess would be a proper acquaintance for the Countess, I hope," Joseph said. "Since her ladyship seems to have no quarrel with Portuguese blood."

He felt a vile satisfaction at sliding "the Duchess" into his speech and watching the three matrons titter again. The new baronet consorting with earls and laying claim to kinship with a duchess was quite acceptable to them. And the Countess had swept all before her with that pointed reminder about the heritage of the beloved Queen. Joseph was in quite good charity with the lord of Tremarron as he walked the earl and countess to his door.

"I look forward to a long and profitable enterprise," he said, and the Earl, to Joseph's great delight, shook his hand.

"As do I. S'pose that's your man with the constable?" the Earl said as Thaker pulled the Illingworth gig into the yard. "Well, what can you expect from a man whose mother was a barmaid?"

"Almost anything, I should say," Joseph replied. "Same as any man."

The Earl pondered this as he handed his lady into their coach.

"The land," Treen moaned as Jock herded him into the hall. "Thousands. It all should have been mine."

"Now, Melwin." His mother smoothed her mittens, showing her nerves had been much fortified by her tea. "We shall sort this all out in a trice. Sir Joseph is clearly a man of judgment. He'll understand that you might have gotten ambitious, particularly as you are so anxious about the care of your Mama, but we shall all be friends in the end. And Lady Illingworth as is to be." She simpered at Inez, ready to quite forgive her for the error of being born a foreigner. "I hope you will call on me in Church Street, and that Melwin and I shall have the honor of toasting your health at your wedding breakfast."

"Oh, do call upon me as well, Lady Illingworth as is to be," Mrs. Daw was quick to add.

Mrs. Abbott did Inez the justice of looking her up and down. "Not as handsome as my Ursula," she pronounced, "but quite a fetching way about you. Does the baronet have any eligible brothers? Nephews? Cousins or good friends?"

At last, they were alone. Joseph shut the door on the Earl and his lady, on the gig with the constable and his new charge, on the matrons collecting themselves to follow. Wenna whisked the tea tray back to the kitchen, and Joseph regarded the woman who was to be his bride.

Who had, in a matter of weeks, become his all-in-all.

With a swoop, he lifted her into his arms. She gave a small shout of surprise.

"Mrs. Da Costa. Lady Illingworth as is to be. I have something I would like to discuss with you upstairs."

She slid her arms around his neck, her eyes full of laughter. "We cannot have a proper conversation over tea?"

"Wenna has already taken away the tea tray, and it must be upstairs." He headed toward the open staircase, bumping her shoes against the railing. "Careful—your skirts—your feet—"

Inez giggled. "You might put me down, and I walk of my own accord. I've done so many times."

"A moment. I think if I change the angle—turn us sideways—"

"Joseph, we're not going to fit through the hallway. There is no need to carry me abovestairs."

"It's an ancient Roman custom, meant to prevent bad luck or mischievous spirits from attaching themselves to the bride and following her to her new home. May as well begin as we mean to go on."

He put her on her feet only when he'd achieved his bedchamber. Then he pulled her into his arms for a rousing kiss, and Inez melted against him.

"Welcome home," he murmured against her lips.

Home. That word pushed that strange lump into her throat, like a chunk of roast beef. Penwellen was her home now. Joseph was her home.

"You won't run away again?" He began the process of removing her bodice, divesting her of pins.

"No further than you can catch me," she promised, assisting at her disrobing. "I had to settle with Priscilla. I couldn't come to you a thief."

"And Wigsby will not threaten you again," Joseph said. "Or, if he does, I'll do something that will require Mal to argue eloquently in my defense."

She thrilled as he ran his hands over the places her outer garments exposed. "I think we might make friends of the Dervieuxes, if they remain in England. So long as you do not let Pierre lure you to the gaming table."

"I should hope not. But if he has made me a connection with the Earl of Tremarron, I shall be grateful. It's a young title, but the man is held in regard in these parts."

"If he supplies the capital to build the engines, and the

mines yield as Mr. Hoskyn thinks they will, you shall not have to worry about Penwellen's fortunes." She applied herself to the task of undressing him in turn.

"And I shall be able to keep my Lady Illingworth in the style in which she deserves." He paused, his hands stilling at her stays, and his gaze met hers with a smolder that made her belly shift and give way. "If we are to be married, there need be no more caution in bed."

"None at all," she agreed. She raised on tiptoe to kiss him, then stopped. "But Joseph—before. You were so upset." She drew in a shaky breath. "Do you fear having a child with me? Because I am—"

"No," he said against her lips, and kissed her thoroughly between his declaration. "No. I only feared to plant a babe on you and thus force your hand to marry me. Once married, I will plow your luscious fields as often as you will permit me, and plant whate'er I can. Let us see if we can rival the Earl of Devon in progeny."

"Plow me!" she said, pretending indignation, but thrilled at the idea of bearing a child with him. A little Joseph, or a tiny inquisitive Amaranthe. Perhaps a wee daughter who resembled Inez's mother, whom she could name Mariana, or a roustabout boy in whom Joseph would see his own ancestors.

Children for their home, warmth for their future, and a legacy for Penwellen. A beautiful dream, one she had thought meant for other people, placed fragile and eloquent into her hands.

"The children may be dark, like me," she warned him as he tugged at her shift and bend his head to her breasts. Desire lifted her instantly, like a great soaring wind.

"They will be beautiful, and if anyone here has a problem with lineage, we will bring down the Duke and Duchess of Hunsdon and trot them out to roll over any objections."

"Finally," Inez murmured, "you mean to use your connections to your advantage."

"I want every advantage I might offer you, my love."

"Joseph." She grasped his arms as he laid her upon the coverlet and rose over her. She met his eyes. "All I want is you. That is all I ever wanted."

"And I am enough for you," he said, wonder in his voice. "Imagine that."

"More than enough, my love." He slid inside her, and she wrapped herself around him. Her eyes popped open. "And if *you* ever run away—go off to Dark Lane again, or something like it—"

"Never," he vowed, moving inside of her, his eyes hazy with passion and love. "This is my place. This is my home. You are all I have longed for, my love."

"We are home to each other," she murmured, and joyed in the promise of the future together as they last barriers dissolved and they walked, hand in hand, toward it and the beautiful land they could claim as theirs alone.

She had found her place in the world, and it was him.

ABOUT THE AUTHOR

Misty Urban fell in love with stories at an early age and has spent her life among books as a teacher, scholar, editor, writer, and bookseller. Her favorite stories take you new places, teach you new things, and end with a win. She especially likes romances about unconventional heroines who defy the odds and the unexpected heroes who woo them, so that's mostly what she writes. When she puts down the book she likes to take long walks, drag her family to new places, or hang out around water, dreaming up new stories.

Visit her at mistyurban.com
Join author's newsletter

ALSO BY MISTY URBAN

Ladies Least Likely

Viscount Overboard

The Forger and the Duke

The Painter Takes an Earl

The Mad Baron's Bride

Marry Me, Marquess

My Lady Melisende

The Knight Falls First

Lady Daring

Tell Me Sweet

The Baronet's Bartered Bride

Contemporary Novels

My Day As Regan Forrester

My Thing with Timothy Kay

OLIVERHEBERBOOKS

A small press bound by the belief that every voice matters.

Sign up for our newsletter to learn about new releases and more.
https://oliver-heberbooks.com/subscribe/

Follow us on social media:

facebook.com/oliverheberbooks

instagram.com/oliverheberbooks

amazon.com/oliverheberbooks

youtube.com/@OliverHeberBooksPublisher